Dear Reader,

Welcome to Harlequin's 50th anniversary celebration! This year also marks the 15th anniversary of Harlequin Temptation, so we editors are especially thrilled to recognize Jayne Ann Krentz and her contribution to the phenomenal success of the line. From 1984 to 1992 Jayne wrote twenty-four books for this steamy new series—each one of them a masterpiece of romance writing. *The Private Eye* was published in 1992.

Though Jayne went on to write longer books and appears regularly on the *New York Times* bestseller list, those of us who "remember when" will always think of her as a Temptation author. Luckily, when one star moves on, another usually takes her place, and we've been extremely fortunate, over the years, to have attracted so many talented authors.

Among the brightest of Harlequin's new stars is Lori Foster, who richly deserves the honor of being paired with Jayne Ann Krentz. Following in Jayne's footsteps, Lori consistently creates vibrant characters, page-turning plots and sizzling romance. *Beguiled* is no exception.

To all of you readers, thank you for your loyalty and enthusiasm—without you, there would be no celebration. Happy 50th anniversary!

The Temptation Editors

HARLEQUIN CELEBRATES
FIVE DECADES OF ROMANCE

LIMITED COLLECTOR'S EDITION 2 IN 1

JAYNE ANN KRENTZ
THE PRIVATE EYE

LORI FOSTER
BEGUILED

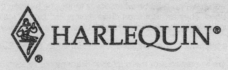

HARLEQUIN®

TORONTO • NEW YORK • LONDON
AMSTERDAM • PARIS • SYDNEY • HAMBURG
STOCKHOLM • ATHENS • TOKYO • MILAN • MADRID
PRAGUE • WARSAW • BUDAPEST • AUCKLAND

ISBN 0-373-83412-8

HARLEQUIN 50th ANNIVERSARY LIMITED COLLECTOR'S EDITION VOLUME 4

Copyright © 1999 by Harlequin Books S.A.

The publisher acknowledges the copyright holders of the individual works as follows:

THE PRIVATE EYE
Copyright © 1992 by Jayne Ann Krentz

BEGUILED
Copyright © 1999 by Lori Foster

Visit us at www.romance.net

Printed in U.S.A.

Table of Contents

The Private Eye
Jayne Ann Krentz

Prologue

IT NEVER PAYS TO PLAY HERO.

One of these days, he'd finally learn that lesson once and for all, Josh reflected. He sat on the edge of the emergency-room examination table and scowled at the closed door. He was not in a good mood. He didn't like hospitals and he didn't like realizing he'd been unlucky enough or stupid enough or slow enough to end up in one tonight.

Could have been worse, he reminded himself. If Eddy Hodder's knife had struck a few inches lower, he would have been spending the night in the morgue.

Josh took a cautious breath and winced. The doctor had just told him his ribs were bruised, not broken, but it was hard to tell the difference. The big question now was whether or not the ankle was fractured or just badly sprained. The X rays would be back any minute.

Everything else had been patched up fairly easily. The raw scrape on his shoulder had been bandaged quite neatly and the gash on his forehead where Hodder's knife had caught him had been closed with sutures. Unfortunately the local anesthetic was already wearing off. He deserved everything he got, Josh told himself grimly. He was in the wrong business. Or maybe he'd just been in it too damn long.

He was about to continue with the self-recriminations when the door of the emergency room swung open. A young man in a white coat sauntered in looking far more authoritative than any young man had a right to look. Josh wondered why doctors, cops and other such professionals were all starting to look so incredibly young to him. Maybe it was only private investigators like himself who aged rapidly.

"Good news, Mr. January. It's only a sprain. We'll tape it up for you and have you out of here in no time."

"Terrific." Josh eyed his swollen left ankle, feeling a sense of dark betrayal. *Stupid foot.* "How long?"

"How long for what?" The doctor opened a white drawer on the other side of the room.

"How long until I can walk on it?"

"Could be quite a while," the doctor said, sounding cheerful at the prospect. "You'll want to rest it for at least a week and it will probably bother you a bit from time to time, after that. We'll send you out of here on crutches."

"Crutches?" Josh swore with great depth of feeling.

The doctor turned around, holding an elastic bandage in his hand. His smile lit up the room. "Could have been worse. Heard you nearly got yourself killed when you went into that building after that Eddy Hodder character. The cops are in a room down the hall with him right now. If it's any consolation to you, Hodder's in worse shape than you are."

"Yeah, that really makes me feel a whole lot better," Josh growled.

"Thought it would. But you're going to be hurting for a while, yourself. No getting around it. I'll give you some pills for the pain when you leave. My advice is to take some time off from your job, Mr. January. You need a few weeks of R and R. That means rest and relaxation."

"I know what it means." Josh set his teeth as the doctor went to work on his ankle. "Take it easy, damn it. That hurts!"

"Sorry. Every jarring movement is going to annoy you for a while," the doctor announced happily.

Josh glowered at him. "You enjoy your work?"

"Love it."

Josh winced again as the doctor tugged on the elastic bandage. "It shows."

McCRAY WAS WAITING for him out in the hall. Short, balding and comfortably rounded at the waistline, McCray was the closest thing to a friend Josh had. He was also Josh's partner in Business Intelligence and Security, Inc., one of the biggest private security agencies in the Pacific Northwest.

McCray shook his head ruefully as Josh swung forward on the crutches. "Well, well, well. Aren't you a sight. How do you feel?"

"Like hell."

"Yeah, that's kind of how you look, to tell you the truth. I've signed the paperwork for you and I've already talked to the cops. Gave them a full report. We're free to go."

Josh shifted his shoulders, trying to get more comfortable on the crutches. All he succeeded in doing was sending shock waves through his bruised body. "The girl okay?"

"The girl's fine. Mad as hell at you for ruining her life, she says, but fine. Her boyfriend, Hodder, was on parole when he pulled this kidnapping stunt. He's headed straight back to prison and will probably stay there awhile. The young lady's father, our client, is everlastingly grateful, of course."

"Send him his bill first thing in the morning. Might as well take advantage of the gratitude."

"My, you are feeling nasty tonight, aren't you?"

McCray pushed open the glass doors of the emergency room and Josh hobbled out into the cold Seattle night. "You know what, pal?"

"What?"

"You need some time off. Maybe a month or so."

"Now listen, McCray—"

McCray held up his palm. "I'm serious, January. You're burned-out, you're beat-up and you've got a real bad attitude. What you need is a month of easy living. You need someone to wait on you hand and foot. You need home-cooked meals, tea and scones in the afternoon, and a stress-free environment. In short, you need a complete change of scene."

"You got any special place in mind?" Josh asked, irritated.

"As a matter of fact, I do." McCray opened the passenger door of his faded blue Oldsmobile. "Get in. I've got a letter I want you to read."

"Who's it from? *Ouch!* Damn it to hell."

"Here, let me have those crutches. I'll put them in the back seat. The letter's on the dash."

Josh lowered himself gingerly onto the car seat, grimacing as he eased his left leg inside. He saw the envelope sitting directly in front of him on the dash. He picked it up and glanced at the letterhead. The bright lights outside the emergency room provided enough light to read the words "Peregine Manor."

Josh opened the envelope. A colorful brochure depicting a fanciful Victorian mansion fell out, along with a neatly typed letter. A glance at the brochure showed that Peregine Manor promised the ultimate in cozy luxury and gourmet dining on the spectacular Washington coast.

The letter promised a job.

"I think you should take the case," McCray told him as he got behind the wheel.

Josh scanned the contents of the letter. "This isn't a case. It's a joke. This Ms. Margaret Gladstone obviously has a vivid imagination."

"That's the whole point," McCray said patiently as he pulled out of the hospital parking lot. "A cushy setup. A piece of cake. A snap. You get all the perks of a fancy luxury inn for a month and in exchange all you have to do is a little sleuthing for the sweet little old lady who wrote that letter."

"Piece of cake, huh? What makes you think this Miss Gladstone is a sweet little old lady?"

"Who else would write a letter like that except some old-fashioned little spinster lady? What have you got to lose? You need to get away for a while, Josh. We both know it. You aren't going to be any good to us at BIS until you get out of this lousy mood you've been in for the past few months. Like I said, you're burned-out, pal. You've been in the business too long."

"You've been in it just as long," Josh muttered.

"Yeah, but it hasn't been nearly as hard on me. I don't get personally involved the way you do. I'm a deskman."

It never pays to play hero, Josh thought again. He glanced down at the letter lying on his knee. Something told him Miss Margaret Gladstone was not a little old lady, sweet or otherwise. And his hunches were almost always reliable.

Josh wondered why he was suddenly consumed with curiosity to know more about the woman who had written the crazy letter promising an even crazier job.

Maybe he did need to get away for a while.

1

A BLACK CAR TURNED into the driveway and drove straight up to the front door of Peregrine Manor. It was five o'clock and already dark. A driving November rain drummed against the windows of the parlor so that the people gathered there could not see who was driving the vehicle. But there was little doubt as to the identity of the new arrival.

"I reckon that'll be our man," the Colonel said with satisfaction. He pulled a gold pocket watch out of his well-worn dinner jacket and peered at it. His white mustache twitched. "Right on time. Good sign. I admire a man who knows the importance of being punctual."

"I do hope we've done the right thing," Odessa Hawkins murmured in a worried tone. She was seated next to the Colonel, a glass of sherry in her be-ringed hand. She, too, was dressed for dinner. Her faded blue gown was almost as old as the Colonel's jacket, but she wore it with the poise and elegance that had been bred into her over sixty-five years.

"We've been over this a hundred times, Odessa. It wasn't like we had a lotta choice, you know. Maggie's right. Sometimes you gotta get yourself a hired gun to handle this kinda thing." Shirley Smith took a swallow of her martini and shot Odessa an irritated glance through the lenses of her rhinestone-studded glasses.

Shirley was about the same age as the other woman but her background was considerably different. No one had taught Shirley Smith the social niceties at a tender age. To her, dressing for dinner meant slipping into a pair of stiletto heels and an extremely tight, strapless dress of shocking-pink satin that ended well above her bony knees. She was wearing her entire collection of rhinestones this evening. She even had a tiara perched on her heavily teased, brassy blond hair.

The Colonel nodded solemnly and patted Odessa's hand with deep affection. "Shirley's absolutely right, my dear. You mustn't fret. We had no choice in the matter. It was time to take decisive action."

Maggie Gladstone scanned the faces of the three permanent tenants of Peregrine Manor and mentally crossed her fingers. She sincerely hoped she had done the right thing. Hiring a private investigator was an entirely new experience for her. Nevertheless, she'd read enough mystery novels to be fairly certain what to expect from the man in the black car. Excitement bubbled up in her. She was about to meet a real live private eye!

"I'll go introduce myself and get him checked into his room. He's had a long drive from Seattle. I'm sure he'll want to change before dinner." Maggie put down her glass of sherry and leaped to her feet.

"Yes, of course," Odessa said regally. "Remind him that we dress for dinner here at Peregrine Manor." She pursed her lips. "I do hope he is a *proper* sort of detective. One of the old-school types that one always finds in those lovely British mysteries—not one of those brash young men who are always dashing about waving their guns on television."

"Strikes me we might need a man who knows how to handle a pistol," the Colonel declared ominously.

"Dang right," Shirley agreed. "The last thing we need is some snobbish little wimp. This is a job for a guy with guts, as my Ricky always used to say."

Maggie paused in the doorway of the parlor. "He's from Business Intelligence and Security, Inc. It's one of the most exclusive security firms on the West Coast. We were very lucky to get him. I'm sure he's no wimp. Now, please hush, all of you. We don't want him to hear us discussing him."

"Run along and greet him, my dear," Odessa said.

"Yeah," added Shirley with a grin. "We'll behave."

Maggie hurried out into the hall and caught a glimpse of herself in the huge, gilded mirror that hung near the front desk. She had chosen to wear a black silk jumpsuit that she thought complemented her slender frame. Her mass of tawny brown curls had been swept up on top of her head, caught with a gold clip and allowed to cascade down her neck to her shoulders.

Maggie frowned critically at her own image and hoped she was projecting a savvy, with-it attitude. She wanted the fancy private investigator to consider her sophisticated and businesslike. High-powered city people sometimes thought they could bamboozle folks who lived in small towns such as Peregrine Point. She didn't want this expensive security expert to get the idea he could stay here at the manor for a month rent-free, write up a short report and then leave. Maggie wanted action.

Something thumped against the door. It didn't sound like a polite knock. Maggie grabbed the knob and yanked open the door.

She stared in amazement at the man who was standing on the front porch. Her heart sank in disappointment. He was clearly not the private investigator they'd all been anticipating, after all.

The poor man had obviously just been released from the nearest hospital emergency room. He was balanced on crutches and his left foot was heavily taped around the ankle. There was a large white bandage on his forehead. Both of his eyes were outlined with dark, purple bruises.

"Oh, dear," Maggie said. "I was expecting someone else."

The man scowled down at her. The glowering frown only served to make an already hard-looking face appear downright ferocious. The shadow of what looked like a day's growth of beard emphasized the effect. His black hair was wet from the rain, as was the denim of his work shirt and jeans. Could her first impression have been erroneous? He was certainly tall enough to suit her image of a professional man of action, and he was built along the lean, solid lines she had envisioned. Furthermore, there was something extremely dangerous about the expression in his cold, gray eyes.

But it was a safe bet that no real private investigator would show up for a case looking like the walking wounded.

"Do you mind if I come in?" the stranger growled in a low, raspy voice. He sounded as if he'd endured a number of hardships recently and was getting fed up with practicing the virtues of tolerance and patience. "It's damn wet out here."

"Yes, of course. Come on inside and dry off." Maggie stepped back quickly. "But I'm afraid you can't stay. We aren't taking visitors until after the first of the year. Maybe not until spring. We're, uh, refurbishing. You didn't have a reservation, by any chance, did you? I thought I notified all the confirmed reservations. Who are you?"

"January."

"Yes, that's what I said. We hope to be open again in January. It all depends, you see. Now, if you do have a reservation and you weren't notified that Peregrine Manor has had to close for a while, I'm very sorry. I can probably get you a room for the night at one of the other bed-and-breakfast places in town. No one is full at this time of year except on the weekends."

The man moved into the hall, managing the crutches skillfully but with obvious annoyance. "I said, I'm January. Joshua January." He quirked one black brow. "I believe you sent for me."

Maggie's mouth fell open in shock. "You're January? The private investigator from Business Intelligence and Security, Inc.?"

"Right." He transferred both crutches into his left hand and ran his right hand through his dark hair. Raindrops splattered the worn Oriental rug on the floor. "Now, if I could have some help with my luggage, I'd appreciate it. It's a little tough to manage suitcases when you're on these things." He indicated the crutches.

"But, Mr. January—"

"Call me Josh." He shot an impatient glance around the small lobby. "Where's your bellboy?"

"We don't have one anymore. Look, Mr. January, there must be some mistake."

"No mistake." Balancing precariously on the crutches, he fished a familiar-looking sheet of paper out of his front pocket. "This is Peregrine Manor, isn't it?"

"Well, yes, but—"

He opened the sheet of paper and started to read aloud in a grim monotone. "'In exchange for professional investigative services, I am prepared to offer a month's lodging at one of the most charming bed-and-breakfast inns in the Northwest. Peregrine Manor is a truly fine example of delightful Victorian architecture, offering unique and distinctive rooms furnished in period style.'"

"Yes, but—"

"'At the manor,'" Josh continued in a relentless tone, "'you'll be able to relax and enjoy the splendors of the Washington coast in winter, a very special time of year here. You'll awaken each morning to a hearty, home-cooked breakfast and in the afternoons you'll be served tea and scones.'"

"Please, Mr. January—"

"'In the evenings we encourage you to enjoy conversation and sherry with the other residents of the manor before proceeding on to dinner in our gourmet restaurant. After dinner you'll be treated to cozy evenings by the fireside. Come join us at Peregrine Manor and indulge yourself in the tranquil environment of this lovely, unspoiled—'"

"*All right*, Mr. January. That is quite enough, thank you. I recognize my own words."

He looked up and for the first time Maggie realized how cold his eyes really were. They were a chilling, icy shade of gray that reflected no warmth and even less patience. Joshua January had been well named.

"Good. So much for that." Josh refolded the letter and stuck it back into his front pocket. "You, I take it, are Ms. Margaret Gladstone?"

"Well, yes."

"Fine. I'm the licensed investigator you hired. I think that settles the matter. Right place, right people, so let's get on with it. I'd like the key to my room, if you don't mind."

Maggie stared at him. "But you…you're…" She waved a hand in a small, embarrassed gesture that indicated his crutches and bandages. "You're not quite what we had in mind, Mr. January. I'm very sorry about your obvious difficulties, and I mean no offense, but we feel we need a man of action—if you know what I mean. We have a problem here at Peregrine Manor and we need an investigator who is in good physical condition."

His mouth curved briefly in a humorless smile. "Good physical condition? On top of everything else? That's expecting rather a lot, considering what you're paying, isn't it?"

Maggie was incensed. "Now, see here, Mr. January, I am providing room and board at one of the choicest inns on the coast for an entire month. That is hardly a pittance."

"Do you have any idea what the usual hourly billing rate is for round-the-clock BIS services, Ms. Gladstone?" Josh asked very softly.

"Well, no." Of course, she hadn't bothered to inquire. Maggie had known full well she didn't have the kind of cash it would take to pay for full-time security service. She could barely pay the electricity bill these days. "I didn't inquire as to your usual rates because I assumed that what I was prepared to offer in exchange for services rendered was adequate compensation."

"Not even close, Ms. Gladstone."

"Then why did you accept the case?" she shot back.

"Let's just say I happened to be feeling in a real charitable mood when your letter arrived. You're my good deed for the year, lady. Now, if you don't mind, I'd like to get my room key. I would also like to have my luggage brought upstairs as I am in no condition to handle it myself. I am supposed to be waited on hand and foot, according to my partner."

"Why do I have the distinct impression that you are rarely given to acts of charity, Mr. January?"

He grinned without any warning and there was something extremely predatory looking about his excellent teeth. "Perhaps because you are a very perceptive female, Ms. Gladstone. Shall we get moving, here? It has not been a good day. In fact, it hasn't been a good week or even a good month. I am more than ready to indulge myself in a little tranquillity."

Maggie considered throwing him out and decided that was an impossible task, even if she could get the Colonel to assist. Josh January might be hobbling around on crutches and appear somewhat the worse for wear, but he still looked awfully solid. "I suppose that since you're here now, you may as well spend the night."

"Ah, a touch of the gracious charm I was told to

expect." Josh inclined his head in a mocking bow. "Thank you, Ms. Gladstone."

"I'll get your key." She stalked past him and went behind the desk to take a key out of one of the little boxes on the wall. "Number 312."

"The third floor?" He gave her a disgusted look. "Forget it. I'm not climbing up and down two flights of stairs every time I leave the room. You said most of the guest rooms were empty. There must be something available on a lower floor."

He had a point, but Maggie was too annoyed by his tone of voice to admit it. She snatched another key out of a box. "Number 210 in the east turret." That was the room right next door to her own, she realized with a start. Not that it mattered, she decided. She automatically fell into the standard sales pitch. "Quite a nice room, if I do say so, myself. Excellent view of the sea. Canopied bed. Your own fireplace with wood supplied. Now, then, if you go on up, I'll see to your luggage."

Josh frowned and glanced through the open door to where the black car was parked in the rain. "Have you got someone around who can give you a hand?"

"Certainly," Maggie said, lying through her teeth. "Your luggage will be no problem. It will be brought up shortly."

"Suit yourself." He shrugged and then adjusted the crutches under his arms. "I smell something cooking. I'm starving. What's the deal on dinner around here?"

"We, uh, were expecting you to join us here at the inn," Maggie replied uneasily. "But perhaps you'd rather drive into town," she added a touch eagerly. "There are a couple of nice seafood places."

"Too much trouble. I'll eat here. I'm supposed to eat home-cooked meals. I'll be down as soon as I've showered and changed. Lord, I could use a drink. It's been a hell of a drive." The crutches thunked on the bottom step.

Maggie bit her lip, watching him progress heavily up the staircase. "I don't believe I mentioned it in my letter, but we—that is, the other residents of the manor—have established a little tradition of dressing for dinner. I go along with it." She eyed his jeans and work shirt. "I rather assumed you might do the same."

"Don't worry," Josh said from halfway up the stairs. "I'll dress. I rarely go out to dinner buck naked."

Maggie closed her eyes in momentary despair and then opened them again when she felt a cold blast of rain sweep into the hall through the open door. She grabbed an umbrella from the old-fashioned stand, gritted her teeth and went out into the downpour to fetch Joshua January's luggage.

She was beginning to wonder if she had made an enormous mistake in hiring a private investigator, sight unseen. Furthermore, she had a hunch it would be extraordinarily difficult to undo the error. Mr. January did not appear to be someone who would take kindly to being fired.

In fact, Maggie decided as she opened the rear door of the black car, Joshua January didn't look like the kind of man who did anything he didn't want to do. Rain thundered on the umbrella as she peered into the dark interior of the vehicle. She groaned aloud when she saw the luggage looming there. Apparently Mr. January didn't believe in traveling light.

She reached inside and lifted out one of the smaller cases. It was surprisingly heavy and was constructed of metal. She scurried back to the front door of the inn and set the case down in the hall. The Colonel appeared in the parlor doorway. His eyes brightened when he saw the metal suitcase.

"Oh-ho, a computer, I see." The Colonel nodded to himself, looking eminently pleased. "Our man is a high-tech sort of investigator. Excellent. Excellent."

Maggie glanced at the case and felt a wave of relief. The computer was a very positive sign, she told herself. Perhaps Joshua January *did* know what he was doing, after all. "I've heard that most modern investigations are done with computers."

"I'm sure the old methods are still employed," the Colonel said. "No substitute for fieldwork, I expect. But there's no doubt computers are the key to all the records that are maintained on people in this day and age. Yes, sir. Our man appears to know what he's doing."

Maggie wondered if the Colonel would still feel that way once he got a look at the crutches and bandages "our man" was currently sporting. She turned and dashed out into the rain for another suitcase.

Five minutes later she had two suitcases, a garment bag and the computer all safely in the hall. She eyed the stairs with a silent sigh.

"Need a hand with those, my dear?" the Colonel inquired gallantly.

"No, thanks. They're light as a feather." Maggie managed a bright, reassuring little smile. The Colonel, being the gentleman he was, was more or less obliged to make the offer, but they both knew his doctor had sternly forbidden him to put his bad back at risk. "I'll whisk them upstairs and be back down in a few minutes. Mr. January said he would be delighted to join us for dinner."

"Excellent." The Colonel turned and sauntered back into the parlor.

Maggie waited until he was out of sight and then she bent down to hoist the two suitcases. She staggered toward the stairs, wondering if the weight of one of the bags was caused by a very large gun of some sort.

At the second-floor landing she paused to catch her breath and then took a fresh grip on the suitcases before plodding down the hall to 210. January had been right, she reflected. The third floor would have been a bit much.

A moment later she set the suitcases down a second time and rapped sharply on the turret-room door.

"Hang on. I'll be there in a minute," January growled back.

Maggie used the short wait to catch her breath. By the time the door was open a crack, she was no longer panting. But the sight of Joshua January wearing only a towel around his lean waist and the remains of some shaving cream on his face was enough to take her breath away all over again.

"Oh, it's you." Josh glanced at his luggage, reached down and hauled first one and then the other suitcase into the room.

"I could have done that." Maggie's mouth was suddenly dry and her pulse seemed to be pounding as hard as it had when she'd climbed the stairs with the suitcases. Then she noticed the huge dark, blotchy bruises on his ribs and shoulder. "Good heavens! It must have been a really miserable drive for you."

He followed her gaze, glancing down at his chest. "Bruises always look the worst a couple of days after the accident."

"Can I get you something?"

"A shot of whiskey and a decent meal when I get downstairs will take care of everything. Where's my computer?"

"In the hall. I'll bring it and the garment bag right up," Maggie whirled and fled back down the corridor. The sight of January's broad, muscled shoulders gleaming in the soft light of his room was having an odd effect on her nerves.

Perhaps it had been the glimpse of the canopied four-poster bed behind him that had created the disturbing sensation. The whole scene had been far too *intimate*.

When she got the computer upstairs she knocked quickly. "I'll leave it outside the door, Mr. January," she shouted through the wood. "See you downstairs."

BACK IN THE BATHROOM, Josh scraped the rest of the shaving cream off his jaw and listened to the sound of Maggie Gladstone's footsteps scurrying down the hall. *Nice going, January. Apply the chill factor, why don't you, and send the only interesting female you've encountered in God knows how long running in the opposite direction.*

His hunch had been correct. Maggie Gladstone might be a spinster, but she sure as hell wasn't elderly. In fact, she was extremely attractive in a rather unusual way. There was a sweet, wide-eyed innocence about her, even though she had to be close to thirty. He was willing to bet she'd been a small-town girl all her life. Maybe a schoolteacher or a librarian. She probably read a lot of mystery novels and thought private eyes were the last of the paladin kings—lone crusaders who fought for truth and justice on the side of the little guy.

Definitely not his type.

Nevertheless, Josh could not deny he had felt an almost-irresistible urge to thread his fingers through the mass of tawny curls that had cascaded down Maggie's neck. She had looked sleek and lithe, yet rounded in all the right places in that black jumpsuit she'd been wearing.

He was thinking about sex. He must be feeling better.

He gazed broodingly at his dark, forbidding reflection in the mirror and wondered what the hell he had gotten himself into by accepting this bizarre job in Peregrine Point.

He'd been crazy to let McCray talk him into it. Half out of his mind from the painkillers they had given him at the hospital. That was the only explanation.

He surveyed his bruised and battered body. None of the damage was permanent. *This time.* But there was no getting around the fact that a man who was about to turn the big four-oh didn't bounce back the way he would have five, ten or fifteen years ago.

He was definitely getting too old to be dashing into dark buildings after people who had no strong inhibitions about smashing other people with tire irons, knives and assorted other implements of destruction. *Too old to play hero.* When in hell was he going to learn? Josh wondered grimly.

He stifled a groan as he leaned over the sink to rinse the shaving cream from his face. Maybe this time he *would* need a month to recuperate, just as McCray and the doctor had suggested.

And there was always the book, Josh reminded himself. He needed to bite the bullet and take a crack at writing that mystery novel he'd been contemplating for the past couple of years. Peregrine Manor was just the kind of place where a man could settle in and find out whether he was meant to be a writer.

Josh bit back a savage oath as he limped heavily out of the tiny bathroom. The ankle was only sprained, not broken, but when he accidentally jarred it, the damn thing seemed to ache a lot more than a fracture would have. At least the bruises would fade in a few more days.

He gave the frivolous room a single, disparaging glance and shook his head. The place looked like something out of a fairy tale with its rounded tower walls, heavy velvet drapes and the gingerbread trim on the furniture. The bed itself was an ornate monstrosity. Josh knew he was going to feel like an idiot when he levered himself up into the thing via the little wooden steps on the side. He wondered if the management would supply an old-fashioned bed warmer at night.

For some reason that thought brought Maggie Gladstone to mind again.

Josh jerked a suitcase up onto the silly-looking bed and opened it. Inside he found a clean white shirt and a silk tie. There was a fairly decent Italian jacket and a pair of slacks in the garment bag. It was beyond him why anyone would bother to dress for din-

ner in a place like this, but he was willing to go along
with the program. Up to a point.

He grinned fleetingly at the thought of what Maggie Gladstone's expression would be when she saw
him wearing a pair of unlaced running shoes with
his Italian jacket and silk tie. There was no way he
was going to get a pair of dress shoes onto his still-
swollen left foot.

Twenty minutes later, Josh made his way slowly
and carefully down the carpeted stairs. There was a
tantalizing aroma in the hall that indicated dinner
was a real possibility. Things were looking up. He almost regretted the way he'd snapped and growled at
poor little Ms. Maggie Gladstone.

Then he reached the inn's front parlor, saw the rest
of his clients waiting for him and changed his mind
again.

Maggie turned toward him at the sound of the
crutches on the hardwood floor. She gave him a polite but extremely wary smile. "Oh, there you are,
Mr. January. Allow me to introduce you. Mrs.
Odessa Hawkins and Miss Shirley Smith."

"Ladies." Josh inclined his head as he lowered
himself cautiously into a chair. "Call me Josh." The
two bright-eyed women on the sofa twinkled at him.

"We are ever so grateful you were able to accept
our offer, Josh," Odessa said with a gracious smile.

"You can say that again," Shirley declared. The
rhinestones in her glasses flashed in the light as she
examined the crutches and bandages. "What the
heck happened to you, anyway? Have a shoot-out
with some bad guys?"

"I had an accident," Josh answered smoothly.

"Oh. Sorry about that." Shirley looked disappointed. "Thought maybe it was bad guys."

Maggie took charge again, nodding at a patrician-looking gentleman with a magnificent white mustache and ramrod posture. "And this is Colonel Amos Boone."

"Retired," murmured the old soldier as he strode forward to shake Josh's hand. "U.S. Army. Everyone calls me the Colonel."

"I see."

"What sort of hand weapon do you favor, sir?" the Colonel asked with professional interest. "Automatic pistol or revolver? Always carried a Colt single action, myself. Back when I was on active duty, that is."

"I'm not particularly interested in guns," Josh replied.

Maggie frowned. "You mean you don't carry one?"

"Not if I can avoid it. Which is most of the time, believe me."

The Colonel nodded wisely. "Martial-arts man, eh? Not surprised. You've got the look. Always could tell those martial-arts types."

Maggie's attractive mouth tightened as she gave the crutches a pointed glance. She smiled a little too sweetly. "Let's hope that's not his forte, Colonel. If it is, we're in trouble, aren't we? A martial-arts expert on crutches does not inspire confidence."

"Don't worry, Maggie," Josh said very gently. "My crutches have been licensed as lethal weapons."

The Colonel cleared his throat and hastened to interrupt before Maggie could respond to the goad. "I say, sir, what can I get you to drink?"

"Whiskey, if you've got it." Josh glanced doubtfully at the liquor cabinet.

"Certainly, we've got it." The Colonel opened one of the doors on the cabinet and removed a bottle. "Good Tennessee sippin' whiskey. Just the thing on a night like this." He splashed a modest amount into a glass and handed it to Josh with a flourish.

"Thanks." Josh took a swallow and enjoyed the heat all the way down. He caught Maggie studying him covertly. It was easy to read her thoughts. He smiled blandly at her. "The answer is no."

She blinked and Josh took some small satisfaction from the flash of surprise in her eyes.

"I beg your pardon?" Maggie said.

"I said the answer is no, I am not a lush. Hard-drinking private eyes exist only in novels. Heavy drinking isn't conducive to clever sleuthing, and we real-life types have a living to make. I hope you're not too disappointed?"

"Relieved is the word," she answered dryly. "Discovering you had a drinking problem in addition to being accident-prone would have been somewhat discouraging under the circumstances."

"Yeah. I can see that." Josh leaned his head back against the cushion and deliberately narrowed his eyes with lazy menace as he watched her. He realized he was beginning to enjoy himself. He swirled the whiskey in his glass and said absolutely nothing until Maggie began to fidget uneasily. It didn't take long. The lady was out of her league when it came to wars of nerve. "Now, then, suppose you all tell me just what it is you want done in exchange for a month's free room and board?"

Maggie straightened her shoulders and fixed him

with a determined glare. "Now, see here, Mr. January. I have contracted for first-class professional investigative services. We expect an investigator who is fully capable of taking on the responsibilities of this job. Do you really believe you can handle this assignment in your present condition?"

Josh smiled slowly. "You get what you pay for, lady. And believe me, for what you're paying, I'm the best that's available."

2

MAGGIE DID NOT LIKE Josh's smile. It made her more uneasy than ever. It also made her angry. It occurred to her that her emotions had been all over the place in the short time January had been at Peregrine Manor. In the past forty minutes she had experienced everything from hopeful expectation to extreme irritation. Somewhere in the middle, she was forced to admit, there had also been a powerful element of pure, physical attraction.

Physical attraction was all it could be, she assured herself firmly. The man was certainly not going out of his way to endear himself to her. In fact, it would take very little at this point to make her dislike him intensely.

It was time to take charge of the situation. She had set this whole thing up so she would have to see it through. Maggie returned Josh's taunting smile with a stiff, mockingly polite one of her own.

"Mr. January—"

"I thought I told everyone to call me Josh."

It wasn't worth an argument, Maggie reflected. "Very well, Josh. I'll be blunt and tell you straight out that you are not what I expected when I set out to hire a private investigator."

"I rarely am. What people expect, that is. For some reason I always seem to come as a surprise."

"I can understand that," Maggie said. "Now, then. As we appear to be stuck with you—"

"Really, Maggie," Odessa interjected reproachfully. "There's no need to be rude to Josh."

"Yeah, he ain't really done nothin' yet," Shirley added. "Give the guy a chance."

The Colonel cocked a disapproving brow at Maggie. "Quite right, my dear. We must give our man an opportunity to do his job. Personalities should not enter into the equation."

Maggie flushed under the gentle rebukes. She could see the laughter in Josh's eyes. "I fully intend to give our—I mean—Josh a chance. As he himself has just told us, we appear to be getting what we paid for."

Josh held up a hand. "I have an idea. Why doesn't one of you tell me why you all think you need a private investigator? I believe Maggie's letter said something about 'disturbing occurrences' here at Peregrine Manor. What disturbing occurrences?"

Predictably, everyone started to talk at once.

"The most unsettling incidents..." Odessa began in a worried tone.

"Felt we should get a professional to look into them," the Colonel confided. "A lot at stake, you know. Potentially millions."

"Warnings," Shirley said eagerly. "That's what they are. Warnings. And I don't mind tellin' you I'm scared."

Josh held up his hand again. "I said one of you should give me the details. Not all of you at once." He looked straight at Maggie. "You wrote the letter and you're apparently paying my fee, such as it is. Tell me what, exactly, is going on around here."

The Colonel cleared his throat in an attention-getting manner. "He's quite right, Maggie. If we all talk at once we'll only cloud the issue. Lay out the facts for our man."

"All right." Maggie crossed her legs and absently started to swing her foot as she gathered her thoughts. Josh January was the kind of man who dealt in hard facts. He wouldn't be interested in hunches and intuition. "A series of incidents have occurred here at the manor which have alarmed all of us to some degree. In fact, the real reason we're closed for the off-season this year is because of those incidents."

"Give me some specifics," Josh urged, his gaze on her swinging foot.

"First, there are all the mechanical and structural problems that we've been experiencing." Maggie realized he was watching her foot, which was half out of her patent-leather pump. She carefully uncrossed her legs and slid her stocking-clad foot back into the shoe. "At the height of the season the large freezer and the refrigerator we use in the kitchen went on the fritz. We lost several hundred dollars' worth of food. But worse than that, we had to close the dining room on the biggest weekend of the year. A lot of people with reservations for dinner were very upset. The inn was full and everyone was irritated at the inconvenience."

"Go on," Josh prompted.

He seemed to have lost interest in her foot since she'd put it back inside her shoe. Now, Maggie realized, for some reason he was watching her hands.

"We've had continual problems with the furnace, although it was installed less than two years ago."

Maggie finally realized that her fingers were fluttering as she talked. She folded her hands in her lap. "Then one day I happened to do a routine test on the smoke detector in the basement and discovered that the batteries had been disconnected. That really worried me. The Colonel keeps all his equipment and files in the basement, you see. A fire that started down there would be disastrous."

"Equipment and files?"

The Colonel shrugged modestly. "I do a bit of experimenting. We'll get into that later, if you like."

"I see." Josh switched his gaze back to Maggie. "Anything else strange going on?"

She bit her lip. She was afraid Josh wasn't very impressed so far. "As I said, there have been a variety of little, annoying breakdowns. The new hot-water tank went out. The guests were very irate over that, I can tell you."

"Some of them shouted at Maggie in the rudest possible terms. Very upsetting," Odessa confided. "The Colonel was forced to speak to one man who was exceptionally ill-mannered."

"'Conduct unbecoming,' as we used to say in the military." The Colonel shook his head with a frown. "I sent the fellow packing, of course."

Maggie smiled wryly. "Unfortunately you sent him packing before he had paid for his room."

"Maintaining standards is considerably more important than money," Odessa declared.

"Right," Shirley agreed. "Gotta have standards."

"Very true," the Colonel murmured. "Can't tolerate just any sort of behavior, you know."

Maggie stifled a small sigh. It was much easier to take the high road on that subject when one wasn't trying to keep the books balanced. She realized Josh was watching her intently again. She hurried on with the rest of the tale. "In addition to the trouble with the hot-water tank, we had trouble with the toilets. Then the rooms with fireplaces, such as yours, all developed problems in the chimneys. The rooms filled up with smoke whenever the guests lit their fires. The fire trucks were here every night for a week before we had to make a rule that no one could use the fireplaces."

Shirley shook her head grimly. "We finally got 'em cleaned out and working, but it was one thing after another and first thing you know, word started getting around."

Josh glanced at her. "What word?"

"You know. Like the manor was not a nice place to stay anymore. Too many problems. Old-fashioned wiring. Inconvenient. In need of repairs. Folks said the new management was letting the place go down the tubes. Maggie started losing bookings."

Josh gave Maggie a thoughtful look. "Is that right?"

She nodded unhappily. "After the trouble with the fireplaces, I decided it would be better to say we were closing for the off-season this year. I told everyone repairs were going to be made over the winter and that things would be back in tip-top shape by spring. But the truth is, the place is already in good shape. Great-Aunt Agatha saw to that."

"Who's Agatha? Besides being your great-aunt, that is," Josh inquired.

The Colonel answered that one. "Agatha Gladstone was one of the finest ladies you'd ever want to know. She owned this place for forty years. Died last year and left the manor to Maggie, here."

Josh absorbed that. Maggie could see questions in his eyes but he didn't ask them. Instead, he focused on his original line of inquiry. "Okay, let me get this straight. There have been a series of small but annoying mechanical and electrical problems here at the manor. The inn started getting a bad reputation and you decided to close the place down except for your three regular guests, here."

Maggie blinked at him in surprise. "Odessa, Shirley and the Colonel are not guests. They are permanent residents. The manor is their home, too. Aunt Agatha made that very clear."

The Colonel nodded. "Had an understanding, don't you see? We're a family. Agatha's gone, rest her soul, but now we've got Maggie."

Josh eyed Maggie. "Uh-huh. Just one big happy family."

Maggie frowned. "The point is, we don't believe all the incidents over the past few months have been due to sheer bad luck. We want you to find out who or what is behind them, and what his motive is. Before you begin, you should know that we all have different theories you really ought to check out."

Josh sipped his whiskey. "Would anyone mind if we ate dinner before we explored these theories? I'm hungry. I was promised home-cooked meals, if you'll recall."

Maggie stood abruptly and managed a tight smile. "Not at all. If you'll excuse me for a minute, I'll go check on the casserole."

"I'll come with you," Odessa said.

The Colonel rose gallantly as the two women

headed for the door. "Maggie and Odessa do the cooking around here these days," he explained to Josh. "Had to let the chef and kitchen help go when we closed down for the winter. Shirley and I clean up."

"Just one big happy family," Josh murmured again.

"Don't knock it," Shirley remarked. "It works."

Maggie glanced back over her shoulder as a thought occurred to her. She paused in the doorway, wondering how a man could simply take off for an entire month. "Do you have a family, Josh?"

"No," said Josh. "The only one I have to worry about is myself. I like it that way."

Maggie shivered under the wintry chill of his words and hurried down the hall after Odessa.

"What do you think of him?" Maggie hissed under her breath when she caught up with the older woman.

"Seems quite a capable young man," Odessa answered cheerfully as they entered the kitchen. "I feel we're in good hands, dear."

"Capable? The man's on crutches, for heaven's sake. And he doesn't seem all that professional to me. His attitude seems wrong. And he doesn't even carry a gun. I thought all private eyes carried guns."

"Perhaps that's only true in those novels you're always reading, dear. Have you ever actually met any private investigators?" Odessa opened the refrigerator door and removed the tossed green salad she had prepared earlier.

"Well, no. But I've read enough mysteries to have a good idea of what to expect in an investigator." Maggie grabbed a set of hot pads and opened the oven door. Fragrant steam wafted upward. "It occurs to me that maybe Josh January accepted this job because he thought the manor might be a nice place to recuperate from his accident. He probably thinks our problems will make for a real cushy assignment."

"I wonder what happened to him?" Odessa tossed the salad greens with the dressing that had been made from her own secret recipe. "Do you suppose it was an automobile accident?"

"More likely someone got really annoyed with him and pushed him down a flight of stairs," Maggie muttered darkly as she hoisted the casserole out of the oven.

"You're not far off," Josh said from the doorway. He leaned with one shoulder propped against the wall, both crutches in one hand. Somehow he managed to look casually arrogant and mildly predatory, even though he was precariously balanced. "Someone did get really annoyed with me."

Maggie set the casserole down very quickly. It was the heat of the oven that was causing a flush to rise up her neck, she assured herself. She glanced pointedly at his crutches. "I didn't hear you coming down the hall."

Josh grinned evilly. "I know. Moving stealthily is child's play for us professional private eyes. We take special courses in it." He tapped the crutches soundlessly on the Oriental rug in the hall. "The carpeting makes it easy, you see. Even with crutches. You might want to remember that."

"I will," Maggie snapped.

"Pay no attention to Maggie," Odessa said lightly. "She was just being clever. Maggie has quite a sense of humor." She smiled serenely as she carried the salad past him out of the kitchen. "Do have a seat at the big round table in the dining room, Josh. We'll have dinner ready in a moment."

"Thanks." Josh waited until Odessa had disappeared into the dining room before turning back to Maggie. "Anything I can do to help?" he asked blandly.

"I doubt it," Maggie replied. "Not in your present condition." She swept grandly past him, casserole in hand.

"Remind me not to be standing at the top of any staircases when you're around," Josh murmured to her back.

MAGGIE HAD BEEN DEAD-ON, Josh reflected midway through dinner. He had taken on this ludicrous excuse for a case primarily because it had seemed like a cushy job and because he needed some time to recover from his "accident." Very clever lady, that Maggie Gladstone. He would have to keep an eye on her. It would be one of the perks of the job.

The case itself was going to be a cinch, of course—just as McCray had predicted. The situation here at Peregrine Manor was a clear-cut case of some unfortunate luck coupled with some vivid imaginations. Things were constantly going wrong in big old houses. His client had obviously panicked over a few minor incidents that were actually nothing more than perfectly normal problems.

The trick would be to stretch out this so-called case for an entire month. If he did stay the four weeks, as planned, he could get some good solid writing done on the book. He would do it, he decided promptly.

When he was feeling fit again and had decided whether or not he was cut out to be a mystery writer, he would prepare an imposing report to present to his client. She and her "family" would be suitably impressed and probably relieved to be told no one was behind the incidents. *Piece of cake.* In the meantime, he could sit back and get himself waited on, hand and foot. Maggie's cooking was excellent, if this first meal was any indication.

Josh polished off his second helping of the very tasty vegetable-and-cheese casserole. He was considering a third serving when Odessa, with the unfailing graciousness of the born hostess, offered it to him.

"Do have another helping, Josh. A gentleman recovering from a serious accident needs to build up his strength." Odessa smiled warmly.

"You talked me into it." Josh scooped out some more of the casserole. "I'm ready to listen to your theories now. Why don't you start, Odessa?"

"Certainly." Odessa put down her fork and pursed her lips in a disapproving fashion. "I am convinced that one of my nephews is behind the effort to close down Peregrine Manor. I have three, you know. Nephews, that is."

"Why would any of your nephews want to close down the manor?"

"Retaliation for my having recently written all three of them out of my will, of course," Odessa stated. "A nasty, ungrateful, selfish lot, those nephews. I have finally decided not to leave any of them a single share of my gold-mining stock. I hold a considerable interest in a company called Lucky, Inc. I fear my nephews have learned about my intentions to disown them. They think they can terrorize me into changing my mind."

Josh managed not to smile at that. It was highly unlikely that any lady who held a "considerable amount" of valuable stock would be wearing a gown as faded and worn as the one Odessa Hawkins had on tonight. Odessa may have been wealthy at one time, but the air of faded elegance about her now was unmistakable. He was certain someone had hocked the diamonds in her massive dinner ring years ago. That was glass glittering on her finger. He would bet on it.

"I, however, have a different theory," the Colonel intoned portentously from the head of the table. "I believe I mentioned earlier that I am conducting some experiments down in the basement. I don't mention the fact to just anyone, but the truth is, I am something of an inventor. I have been making tremendous progress on a potentially valuable alternative fuel that would make oil-based fuels obsolete. I venture to say it will revolutionize the automobile industry, as well as the manufacturing sector of our economy."

"Interesting." Josh abruptly swallowed an oversize bite of casserole and remembered the disconnected smoke-detector batteries down in the basement. *Just what I need,* he thought ruefully. *A month spent in a mansion with a crazy inventor who likes to play with flammable substances.*

"Naturally, I've suspended all experimentation until you get this matter sorted out for us," the Colonel went on. "Can't risk the results of my experiments falling into the hands of the wrong parties."

"No," Josh agreed quickly. "Can't take the risk.

Suspending your experiments for the time being is very wise." *Wait until I'm out of town before you go back to playing inventor.*

"Well, I don't happen to think these incidents have anything to do with Odessa's terrible nephews or the Colonel's experiments," Shirley announced. She peered shrewdly at Josh through her rhinestone-studded glasses. "It's *him*. He's sending me a warning."

Out of the corner of his eye Josh saw Maggie nibble anxiously on her lower lip. A sure sign that she was uneasy. Josh wondered what it would be like to nibble on Maggie's lip, himself. The idea was very appealing. He forced his attention back to Shirley. "Who's sending you a warning, Shirley?" he asked patiently.

"Ricky." Shirley's eyes suddenly filled with tears. "Excuse me. Didn't mean to make a scene." She yanked off her glasses and dabbed at her eyes with her napkin. "It's just that every time I think about him, I get scared."

Josh sighed and turned to Maggie. "Do you know who this Ricky is?"

"He's a gangster," Maggie muttered, looking embarrassed. "Shirley says she used to be his, uh, girlfriend."

"That's right," Shirley sniffed. "Ricky 'The Wrecker' Ring. Twenty years ago they didn't call him 'The Wrecker' for nothin', you know. But he was a gentleman, through and through. Always treated me like I was a queen. Until the day they hauled him off to prison, that is. I know he probably thinks I betrayed him, and now he's going to get revenge."

Maggie coughed discreetly. "Shirley says she

changed her last name fifteen years ago when she moved out here to the coast. She's been worried ever since that Ricky would find her when he got out of prison."

Josh lifted his brows. "When was he due for release?"

"He was supposed to get out a few years ago," Shirley replied, wiping her eyes again. "I expect it's taken him this long to find me. But now he has and he's lettin' me know he's going to get even for what he thinks I did. I'd run if I could, but I can't afford to go anywhere. Peregrine Manor is my home."

Josh wondered whether he should mention to this little group that if a powerful mob figure wanted to kill someone like Shirley Smith, the job would probably have been done by now. Then he reminded himself that he had a whole month ahead of him here at the manor. He didn't want to start punching holes in his clients' theories too quickly. They might fire him if they thought they didn't need him. He had a hunch it wouldn't take much to convince Maggie she could dispense with his services.

"All right," Josh declared in an authoritative tone that clients generally responded to quite readily. "That takes care of three of your theories." Privately he had begun to reflect on the possibility of dessert, but forced his attention back to the matter at hand. "What's your explanation for the incidents, Maggie?"

"Perhaps I should go over it with you later, Josh," she said hastily. "You've been given enough to analyze for the moment. Dessert, anyone?" She jumped to her feet and began clearing the table with quick, anxious movements.

Josh watched her with amusement. Her gaze slid away from his as she loudly stacked dishes. It was clear she realized that the pet theories of her fellow residents at Peregrine manor were ridiculous. She wasn't anxious to give him another explanation to mock.

"Dessert sounds great." Josh was surprised to discover he actually felt quite content sitting in Peregrine Manor's dining room surrounded by the engaging bunch of eccentric lunatics.

Things were looking up. Either that or he was losing it fast.

"Always did like a man with a healthy appetite," Shirley remarked as she got to her feet. "Now, never mind those dishes, Maggie. You know the Colonel and me are the ones who do the clearing up around here. You know, my Ricky would eat like a horse. 'Course, he needed a lot of energy in his line of work. Expect you do too, eh, Josh?"

"Yes, ma'am," Josh agreed. "I lost my appetite for a while after my accident, but I seem to be getting it back." He deliberately caught Maggie's eye. "For a lot of things."

"I'll get the apple pie," Maggie said. She vanished into the kitchen as if pursued by small demons.

Odessa smiled knowingly at Josh. "You're having quite an effect on our Maggie."

The Colonel gave Josh a man-to-man look. "You go easy with her, sir. Don't tease her unless you're serious. Our Maggie is a small-town girl. She isn't used to dealing with men of your stamp."

"Men of my stamp?" Josh arched an eyebrow.

"Now, you know what I mean," the Colonel continued calmly. "You've got the look of a man who's accustomed to going after what he wants. All I'm saying is, don't go after our Maggie unless you're real sure you want her. We're right fond of our Maggie. Wouldn't want to see her get hurt, if you take my meaning."

"I take your meaning." Josh leaned back in his chair and eased his injured foot carefully out in front of himself under the table. He tried to recall the last time he had been warned off a woman but could not. "You all know Maggie well?" he asked casually.

"Oh, my, yes," Odessa offered. "We all saw a lot of her when she was growing up. Her parents lived in Washington. Maggie spent most of her summer vacations here at Peregrine Manor. Haven't seen as much of her in recent years, of course. Not until Aggie died and left her the manor. But we've all kept in touch. Her folks have retired to Arizona but they get up here at least once every summer."

Josh fiddled idly with his coffee cup as he delicately probed for information. The technique was second nature to him after all these years in the business. "What's she been doing with herself in the past few years?"

"After she got out of high school she went off to college and became a librarian," Odessa explained. "She's been working at it ever since in a couple of different towns around the state. She gave up her last position when she inherited this place. Her folks were against the notion, but Maggie insisted."

"Her boyfriend must have had a few thoughts about Maggie changing careers and moving here to Peregrine Point," Josh observed. He realized he was suddenly tense, waiting for the response that would tell him if Maggie was involved with someone.

"Boyfriend? Maggie doesn't have any boyfriends." Shirley gave a snort. "Not unless you count that Clay O'Connor fella."

"O'Connor?" Josh repeated gently.

"New in town as of last year," the Colonel said, looking concerned. "Opened up a real-estate office. Seems to be doing fairly well. He and Maggie have started going out to dinner together lately. Took in a movie last week."

Josh listened to the nuances in the Colonel's tone. "You don't approve of O'Connor?"

The Colonel shrugged. "Nothing wrong with the boy, I guess. Polite. Successful. Just seems a bit soft around the edges, if you know what I mean. The kind who should have done a stint in the military to toughen him up."

"'Soft around the edges' is right. Not the kind of man my Ricky would have wanted behind him in a fight," Shirley declared forcefully. "Maggie can do a lot better than Clay."

"I'm not so sure about that," Odessa countered with a small sigh. "Clay is really a very nice man, as Maggie says. No different than most men these days and better than a lot of them. At least he's got a steady job and he knows his manners, which is more than I can say about some."

"That don't say much for men in general these days," Shirley muttered. "A good job and slick manners don't necessarily make for a good man. Like I said, Maggie can do better."

"Maybe you're all a bit overprotective of Maggie," Josh suggested thoughtfully.

The Colonel smiled with just enough steel to remind Josh that the man had once trained other men for war. "Maybe we are. Like I said, we're a family."

3

SEVERAL HOURS LATER Josh lay propped against the overstuffed bed pillows and stared sleeplessly up at the chintz canopy overhead. It cut off his view of the high ceiling, but he probably could not have seen much there, anyway. He had opened the heavy velvet drapes earlier but a dense cloud-cover was obscuring the moon tonight. There was almost no light coming in through the window.

His thoughts shifted restlessly back and forth between three subjects: Maggie in the room next door, the book, and the idiotic case he had accepted here at Peregrine Manor. Of the three, it was his awareness that Maggie was sleeping in the room next door that was having the strongest effect on him. Inwardly, he sighed. He was too old to be reacting to a woman with this kind of sudden, intensely erotic need.

But the truth was, Josh admitted, he had been strangely fascinated by her from the moment he had opened her crazy letter. Perhaps it had been the incredible audacity of her appeal for help in exchange for a month's free rent that had intrigued him. And most people would never have approached a major security firm for this ridiculous little situation here at Peregrine Point.

No doubt about it, it had taken nerve to write that letter. Josh admired nerve.

He turned on his side, wincing as his bruised ribs protested. He listened for sounds from the room next door. All was silent. Earlier he had heard the water running in the tiny bathroom and his imagination had fed him tantalizing images of Maggie getting ready for bed.

He tried to decide what it was about her that appealed to him. She wasn't stunningly beautiful. She had a surprisingly sharp tongue for a sweet little small-town girl. And Josh just knew that she was going to be one of those demanding clients who wanted a lot more than they were willing to pay for in the way of service.

But something in her had struck a responding chord within him and the more he thought about it, the more he was afraid he knew just what that chord was.

He recognized in Maggie the same naive, misplaced desire to ride to the rescue of the weak and innocent that had once driven him into his present line of work. That explained what she was doing here trying to keep this white elephant of an inn going, of course. She was going to do her best to protect the home of those three aging eccentrics down the hall.

Maggie Gladstone clearly hadn't yet learned that playing knight in shining armor was a thankless task and generally a waste of time.

The clock on the bedside table ticked softly, recording the passage of what was apparently going to be an endless night.

The hell with it, Josh decided. If he wasn't going to get to sleep, he might as well get some work done. He would get started on the book tonight. Sooner or later he was going to have to find out whether he could pull off the task of getting the characters in his head down on paper. *Make that computer disk,* he told himself as he pushed aside the heavy quilt.

Josh levered himself to an upright position and rolled off the edge of the high bed with a sudden surge of enthusiasm. It was not until he was halfway off that he belatedly remembered the small set of steps on the side. By then, of course, his right foot had missed them entirely and he was off balance.

He grabbed for the ornately carved bedpost. The damn thing was apparently broken. It turned beneath his hand, providing no support at all. His fingers slipped off it. In a reflexive movement that he regretted an instant later, Josh put his injured left foot down to catch his full weight. His heel hit the floor and waves of pain shot through him.

"Damn it to hell." Josh gritted his teeth against the agony in his leg and grabbed desperately again for support. His fist closed around a handful of the chintz bed hangings.

Unfortunately the bed hangings had not been designed to bear weight. They tore free of the canopy frame. There was no time to clutch at anything more substantial. Josh toppled awkwardly back onto the edge of the bed, promptly slid off it, and landed heavily on the floor. His bruised shoulder and ribs, which had been healing rather nicely up to that point, took the brunt of the fall.

Josh closed his eyes, clenched his teeth and waited for the agony to recede. While he waited, the torn bed hangings drifted lightly down to settle on top of him.

Josh remained on the floor, tangled up in chintz, and gathered his strength to fight off the pain. He was amusing himself by running through a list of four-letter words that seemed suitable to describe quaint, charming Victorian inns furnished with period pieces when he heard anxious pounding on the door. He knew at once who it was.

"Josh? Josh, are you okay?" Maggie's voice was filled with concern.

Hell. Just what he needed, he thought, disgusted. It wasn't enough that he already felt like a damn fool. No, now he had to face the ignominy of having his client race to the rescue. Somehow his restful, relaxing month on the coast was not getting off to a good start.

"I'm fine, Maggie," he managed. "Go back to bed."

"You don't sound fine. You'd better open the door. I thought I heard something heavy fall in there."

"A little accident," Josh gasped, spitting out a mouthful of chintz drapery.

"Another accident?" she asked in obvious dismay.

"Don't worry about it," he got out through teeth that were still set against the roaring protest of his battered body. The woman was clearly forming the opinion that he was a clumsy idiot. He could hardly blame her.

"Josh, you sound terrible. I'm coming in."

"No." That threat galvanized him into immediate action. Josh lurched to a sitting position beneath the shroud of bed hangings and had to suck in his breath as a new wave of pain surged from his ankle and bruised ribs. "Damn."

The door opened on the far side of the bed. A narrow shaft of light cut a swath across the floor as Maggie stuck her head inside the room. "Josh? Where are you?"

He realized she couldn't see him because he was lying on the other side of the huge bed. "Over here. Look, Maggie, there's no need to get excited, okay? I'm all right."

"What on earth happened?" She flipped the light switch beside the door. "Good grief, what have you done to the bed?"

"It's more a question of what your bed has done to me. Did you know one of the posts is loose?" Josh inhaled deeply as he tried to free himself of the enveloping fabric. He promptly sneezed. "And when was the last time you washed these things? They're full of dust."

"Oh, dear. I'm sorry about that. It's been a while. This was my aunt's room. I didn't see any reason to keep up the regular housekeeping in the unused rooms. Here, let me help you."

He heard her bare feet padding across the carpet and resigned himself to the inevitable humiliation of being found on the floor. "As long as you're here, you might as well give me a hand. Just get this stupid drapery off me."

"Of course. Josh, I really am sorry about this. Did you miss the step when you tried to get out of bed? Sometimes people get disoriented and forget how high these old beds are. You're not going to sue or anything, are you?"

"That's a thought," he muttered darkly.

"It wouldn't do you any good, you know. The only major asset I've got is this inn and you probably wouldn't want it." She started to lift the chintz fabric away from him and then paused abruptly just as she got it free of his face and shoulders. "Good grief."

"Now what?" He looked up and saw that she was staring straight down at him. She was blushing furiously.

He also saw that her hair was down, forming a delightfully sleep-tousled cloud around her face. She had put on a quilted robe but hadn't taken the time to tie the sash. Tiny flowers and bits of lace trim adorning an old-fashioned, high-necked flannel nightgown peeped out through the opening of the robe.

Maggie looked warm and cozy and ready for bed. In spite of the pain, Josh felt his body responding in an unmistakable fashion. He wondered idly why nature had made it possible for the male of the species to feel desire and pain simultaneously.

"I'll get you a robe," Maggie said in a small voice and promptly started to drop the draperies back down on top of him.

"*Wait*. Damn it, don't bury me under that stuff again." Realizing belatedly what the problem was, Josh managed a rueful smile. "Guess I should have warned you I sleep in my shorts, huh? Look, if this is too much for your maidenly modesty, just get out of here. I can take care of myself."

"Don't be ridiculous. I'll help you back into bed." She swept the remainder of the fabric away from him and turned quickly to deposit it on the nearest chair. A small cloud of dust wafted upward. "I suppose I really should get these washed as long as they're down."

"Good idea." Josh grabbed on to the edge of the bed and started to hoist himself up off the floor. The movement brought more protest from his ankle and ribs. He bit back another groan.

Maggie whirled around at his small sound of stifled pain. The embarrassment in her gaze was immediately replaced by concern. She reached out to grasp his arm. "Here, lean on me. When we get you back on the bed, I'll run downstairs and get you some ice for that ankle. Would you like some for the shoulder, too?"

Anger at the embarrassing situation in which he found himself swept through Josh, mitigating some small portion of the pain. "I don't need any ice and I don't need a nurse. Just leave me alone, okay? I'm not dying. Not even close." It was only his masculine pride that was on the critical list, he decided.

"No, but you are obviously hurting." She released his arm as he heaved himself into a sitting position on the bed. "Just stay there. I'll be right back with the ice. Is there a robe in your closet?"

"No. Don't own one."

"Oh. Well, I'll be right back."

Before he could stop her, Maggie was out the door. Josh swore under his breath and sat very still, waiting for her to return. As long as she was going for ice, he would be a fool not to use it. Hell of a way to impress a client, he reflected. *Hell of a way to impress a woman.*

By the time he heard Maggie's returning footsteps on the stairs a few minutes later, the pain had receded to a dull throb in both ankle and ribs. He was going to live, after all, Josh told himself grimly as the door to his room opened. Furthermore, he had his raging hormones back under control.

"Luckily we keep some ice bags around for emergencies," Maggie said cheerfully as she came back into the room. "Just lie down and I'll put one on your ankle. I brought one for your shoulder, as well."

There was no point protesting. Josh propped himself in a sitting position against the pillows and winced as Maggie carefully positioned the ice bags. "Thanks." He knew he didn't sound particularly gracious.

Maggie straightened and regarded him with a worried expression. "Do you have any pain pills?"

"Yeah, but I don't need any. I'll be all right in a few minutes. The ice will do the trick." He slanted her a hooded look. "I'm really doing my best to shatter your romantic notions about dashing private investigators, aren't I?"

She smiled at that. "Well, yes, as a matter of fact. You certainly aren't anything like the ones in the novels I've read. I've never heard of one falling out of bed, for instance. But I guess I can cope with reality. Do you still think you can handle this case?"

"With one hand tied behind my back."

She swept an assessing gaze down his bruised and battered frame. "How about with one hand and one foot tied behind your back?"

"I'll manage."

"How?" She gave him a frankly inquiring look.

"What do you mean, how? The usual way."

"I'm serious." She sat down in the chair near the bed and carefully folded her robe around her knees. "How do you intend to approach this case?"

Josh shrugged and tried to compose his words so that he sounded halfway professional. "Well, I think in this particular case, my initial approach will be to eliminate everyone's pet theories. I don't think any of your permanent residents is going to be satisfied with the results unless I've definitely proven them wrong first."

"Hmm." Maggie was quiet for a moment. "You could be right. I take it you don't believe that any of the theories you heard explains what's been going on around here?"

Josh cautioned himself not to say too much too soon. He didn't want to talk himself out of the job. "I didn't say that. I said I think they should each be checked out thoroughly. You know the old saying, 'When you have eliminated the impossible, whatever remains, however improbable, must be the truth.'"

Maggie's expression brightened. "Sherlock Holmes. *The Sign of the Four*, I think. I'm so glad you've studied the classic detectives."

"Uh, yeah. The classics." Josh decided not to tell her that it had been nearly thirty years since he had read Sir Arthur Conan Doyle, and that he had long since forgotten the origin of the quote. The only reason he had remembered it at all was because it so frequently fit his cases.

"I suppose you'll be using your computer to eliminate the impossibles in this case?"

"Huh? Oh, yeah. The computer." Josh mentally crossed his fingers. He hadn't planned on using his computer for anything except working on the book. "We do a lot of investigative work on computers these days."

"Yes, I know."

There was nothing like having a mystery enthusiast for a client. He was going to have to watch his step. Josh sought for a way to change the subject.

"You never told me *your* pet theory, Maggie. You implied you had one."

She gave him an uncertain glance. "Well, yes, I do. But you'll probably think it's pure fantasy."

"Try me."

"Well…" She hesitated. "To be perfectly frank, I've begun to wonder if someone is after Aunt Agatha's emerald brooch. I haven't been able to find it since she died, you see."

Lord, Josh thought in amusement. *Now we've got emeralds involved in this thing.* "Why would anyone go to the trouble of creating a lot of trouble here at Peregrine manor because of a brooch?"

Maggie leaned forward intently. "It's my theory that whoever is causing the trouble is actually trying to force the manor to close down entirely so that he or she can search the premises for the brooch."

Josh tried to look suitably impressed. "You think it's hidden somewhere here in the house?"

"It's possible. You see, my aunt died very suddenly from a heart attack. She had no time to give last-minute instructions. She had been in excellent health and had no reason to worry about her future. She always loved that brooch and she kept it in her jewelry box rather than in a safety deposit box. But when I went through her things after the funeral, the brooch was missing."

"Who was supposed to get the brooch after her death? Was it mentioned in her will?"

"Yes. It was to come to me, along with the manor. She left very specific instructions that it was to be treated as a sort of long-term investment."

"An investment?" Josh frowned.

"Yes. For the manor. Aunt Agatha told me privately that I was to sell the brooch if it ever became necessary in order to keep Peregrine Manor running."

"But why? What's so important about keeping the manor open?"

Maggie gave him a startled glance. "It's their home."

"Whose home? You mean Shirley's, Odessa's, and the Colonel's?"

"Right. If the day ever came when the inn could no longer pay its own way as a hotel, Aunt Agatha wanted to be sure it could still shelter her friends."

Josh whistled softly. "Are you telling me your aunt left that kind of responsibility on your shoulders?"

Maggie frowned. "She didn't exactly force it on me. She talked it over with me many times before we made the decision. I didn't mind, really. You see, I've always thought running Peregrine Manor would be fun. And it is. To me, it's the ideal job. I learned a lot about innkeeping while working here during the summers. And I must say, the manor was doing very well before the trouble started a few months ago."

"But now you're not doing so well," Josh suggested. "And the brooch is gone. Probably stolen long ago by some thief who posed as a guest in order to get access to it."

"I don't think so," Maggie said slowly.

"Did you aunt wear the brooch in public?"

"Certainly. Once in a while."

Josh nodded grimly. "Then a lot of people knew she owned it and that she didn't keep it in a safe-deposit box. Believe me, Maggie, it's probably long gone."

"Even if you're right, that doesn't mean my theory about the reason behind the trouble around here is wrong," she pointed out, looking stubborn all of a sudden. "Someone might have decided the brooch is lost somewhere in this house, which is very likely, and has decided to look for it. In order to do that, he has to get the rest of us out. At least for a while."

Josh drummed his fingers on the bed, trying to be patient. "Tell me something, Maggie. What are you going to do if you can't save the manor for your aunt's friends?"

She sighed unhappily. "I don't really know. None of them have much in the way of financial resources. I know Odessa talks about her stock holdings, but Aunt Agatha once told me Odessa had purchased that mining stock years ago and never seemed to get any dividends."

Josh smiled briefly. "Which pretty much eliminates one theory, doesn't it?"

Maggie returned his smile with a wry one of her own. "You mean the one about the three nephews who are furious about being left out of the will? Yes, I'm afraid so. But I haven't had the courage to tell Odessa that. She's so proud. Being a possessor of stock is very important to her."

"Well, I'll check it out—just to be thorough. If I discover that the stock really is worthless, maybe I can find a tactful way of telling Odessa her nephews aren't trying to terrorize her without having to inform her that the stock is no good," Josh suggested.

"That would be very nice of you."

"So, what will you do if you can't find a way to keep the manor open for those three, Maggie?" he asked again.

"I don't know," she admitted. "All I can do is try."

He had been right, Josh thought. A naive little lady Don Quixote, tilting at windmills on behalf of the weak and the innocent. "It's a waste of time, you know."

"What is?"

"Playing hero. Never pays."

She gave him a searching look. "How would you know?"

"Experience," he said, and was amazed at the sudden harshness in his own voice. "How the hell do you think I got started in this business in the first place?"

"Because you wanted to rescue people?"

His jaw tightened. "When I first started, the last thing I planned to do was create a corporation like Business Intelligence and Security. I was just a one-man operation in the beginning. I had some damn fool idea that I could help balance the scales of justice for those who couldn't do it on their own. Like I said, I wanted to play Sir Galahad. I wanted to charge off to protect those who couldn't protect themselves."

"What happened?" she asked gently.

Josh wished he had never started this conversation. But for some reason he couldn't seem to stop it now. "What happened was that I eventually learned that it's damn tough to play hero because it's often impossible to tell the bad guys from the good guys. That's what happened."

"I don't understand."

"Hell, Maggie, during my first five years as an investigator I took on every sob-story case that walked through my front door. And none of them were what they seemed."

"Tell me," she whispered, her eyes wide and searching.

"You want to know what being a private eye is really like?" he asked roughly. "I'll tell you what it's like. Parents came in with tears streaming down their faces and asked me to find their little lost girl. I'd track down the kid and discover that she had run away from home because she was more afraid of being abused by her father than she was of life on the streets."

"Oh, Josh."

"I'd find missing wives for distraught husbands, and the wives would tell me they had gone into hiding because their husbands routinely beat them and threatened to kill them. They'd beg me not to tell my clients where they were."

"How awful…"

"And then there were the child-custody cases," he continued, feeling savage. "Parents wage war with each other and the poor kids get caught in the firing line. The children serve as the battle prizes. Spoils of war. A way for the parents to hurt each other. I was supposed to take the side of whichever parent had legal custody. No one gave a damn about the kids themselves."

Maggie was silent. "I think I see what you mean. It's not quite like it is in mystery novels, is it?"

"It damn sure isn't. At least, not most of the time. I finally got smart and decided that since I wasn't going to be able to save the weak and the innocent from the bad guys and since I seemed to have a talent for the business, I might as well get into the end of it that paid well. A friend of mine and I created Business Intelligence and Security, Inc. We got some plush offices in downtown Seattle, hired a staff and went after corporate business. The nice thing about white-collar crime is that there isn't so much emotion involved. And hardly anyone gets killed."

"I suppose there is a big demand for corporate security consultants these days," Maggie ventured.

"Yeah, and although I never thought I'd say it in the old days, it's cleaner work than the kind of thing I used to do. Give me a nice computer-fraud situation or a loading-dock security problem anytime." Josh stopped abruptly, shocked at how much he had told her.

He knew what had gotten him started. It was seeing in her some of the same useless, naive nobility that he himself had once had. It had goaded him into trying to tear the rose-colored glasses from her eyes.

"You know," Maggie said quietly, "I didn't want to say anything, but I have been wondering exactly why you took this case. Frankly, I was surprised when your office called and said you were on your way."

Josh eased his shoulder into a more comfortable position and studied his throbbing ankle. "You weren't the only one."

"BIS was the last company I expected to get a response from. But I had tried every small agency in the Seattle phone book. No one was willing to come out here to Peregrine manor in exchange for a month's free room and board. I was getting desperate, and I figured I had nothing to lose by approaching some of the big firms."

"I'll bet most of them laughed in your face," Josh responded glumly.

"Not exactly. But all I got from the rest of them

were form letters telling me they didn't handle my sort of case."

"Your situation here is a little unusual," Josh allowed.

Maggie nibbled on her lower lip. "So why *did* you take this case, Josh?"

"Felt like a change of pace," he said simply, shifting again on the pillows. "Like I said. The case is unusual."

Maggie studied him for a moment longer and then got to her feet. "I think there was more to it than that." She smiled tremulously as she came over to the bed. "You know what I think?"

He slanted her a speculative glance, wondering if she had figured out that he was using Peregrine Manor as a place to convalesce. "Why do you think I took this case?"

"I think that, in spite of what you say, you're still playing hero." Her eyes were soft as she bent over the bed to adjust the ice pack on his ankle. "I think something in my letter appealed to your old desire to rush to the defense of the weak and the innocent. You don't want to admit it because you're much too macho. You're too used to hiding your real motives behind the facade of the tough, cynical private eye who's seen it all."

Josh shot out a hand and caught her wrist. Maggie made a small, startled sound. Her gaze flew to his and he took some satisfaction in seeing the dawning awareness in her bright sea-green eyes. "If you really believe that, lady, you're setting yourself up for a major fall. Take some advice. Don't waste your time attributing any fancy do-gooder motives to me. I'm a businessman. Period. You'll get what you paid for."

"You've already told me I'm not paying the going rate. So what, exactly, will I get?" Maggie made no attempt to withdraw her hand from his but Josh could feel the tension radiating through her.

"I'm not sure yet." His voice slipped into a husky growl as he realized just how soft her skin was. The scent of her filled his head. A new surge of arousal shot through him. Without even thinking about it, he used his grip on her wrist to tug her closer.

Alarm and sensual awareness flared simultaneously in her eyes. "Josh? Josh, stop it. For heaven's sake, I don't even know you."

He smiled slightly. "But I know you."

"No, that's not true." But she still made no effort to pull free. Instead, she was watching him with a fascinated look. "You don't know anything about me."

"I know you're small-town born and raised. You were a librarian until recently. I know you spent your summer vacations here at Peregrine Manor when you were growing up. I know your parents live in Arizona. I know you've been dating a real-estate broker named O'Connor." Josh smiled dangerously. "Want me to continue?"

Her lips parted in astonishment. "How did you...? Wait a minute. You grilled the Colonel and the others, didn't you?"

"I'm a private eye, remember? Digging up information is my business."

"You mean prying into other people's lives is your business."

He shrugged. "Same thing. You get used to it after a while. There is no such thing as real privacy in the modern world. In any case, I figured I was entitled to do a little digging where you're concerned. Your friends were warning me off, you see. It annoyed me."

She frowned in confusion. "Warning you off what? *Me?*" She was clearly shocked.

"Right. The Colonel as good as told me not to try to seduce you unless my intentions were honorable."

"How embarrassing." For the first time she started to struggle. Her hand twisted in his grasp. "You can bet I'll have something to say to all three of them. They mean well, but I don't appreciate people interfering in my private life."

Josh tightened his grip on her wrist for an instant, not wanting to let her go. But when she struggled again, he released her. "Does that mean you're interested in being seduced, regardless of whether or not my intentions are honorable?"

"Don't be ridiculous." She stepped back quickly from the bed. "I don't know the first thing about you. Why on earth would I want anything more than a business relationship with you?"

"Who knows? Maybe because I understand you better than you know. I told you, I used to have a few things in common with you."

"Well, it certainly doesn't sound like we have anything in common now," she snapped.

"You never know. We might be kindred souls in search of each other."

"That's crazy."

"Life is crazy. Who would have guessed a week ago that I'd be lying in this bed having a midnight conversation with a prim little ex-librarian who reads too many mysteries?" Josh leaned over and opened the drawer in the bedside table. He pulled out the notepad and pen he had stuck inside earlier in the event that he awoke with a brilliant idea for the book.

Maggie watched him with deep suspicion. "What are you doing?"

"Evening the score. Only fair that we go into this on an equal basis." Josh scrawled McCray's private phone number at the offices of Business Intelligence and Security—the one that bypassed the secretary. When he was finished, he tore off the page and handed it to Maggie. It was amazing how many people automatically took anything that was handed to them, even if they didn't want it. "Here."

"What's this?" Maggie reluctantly took the page and glanced at the phone number.

"You said you didn't know anything about me. Okay, I can fix that. The man who answers that number is named McCray. He's my partner. When you call him, tell him I said he was to tell you anything you want to know about me. He can provide proof of the excellent status of my health—sprained ankle and assorted bruises, aside. He can also give you my credit rating and verify that I have no criminal record or children. He'll even tell you my shoe size and the color of my favorite tie, if you want to know."

"But I don't have any questions about you." Maggie angrily crumpled the paper in her hand. "At least not any *personal* questions."

"You never know." Josh folded his arms behind his head and watched the bright flags of indignation flying in her cheeks. "If you decide you're interested in something more than a business relationship with me, you might suddenly have a lot of questions. Very sensible, these days. A woman can't be too careful, can she?"

"Apparently not. Look what I got when I tried to do something simple like hire a private investigator. Of all the nerve."

"I said the same thing when I read your letter offering me a month's free room and board here at Peregrine Manor. Nerve is something else we have in common, too, although I suspect I've got more of it than you do. Nature of the business I'm in, you know."

"I don't doubt that you are an extremely nervy individual, Mr. January." Maggie turned and stalked toward the door.

"Maggie?"

"Yes?" She paused, her hand on the knob.

"I'll be waiting for you to make that call. I want you to know exactly what you're getting into."

"Don't hold your breath."

Josh smiled. "But I will be holding my breath, Maggie. Because if you do make that call, I'll know you're personally taking down the Keep Off signs the Colonel posted around you."

She stared at him. "You're not really interested in me. Not as a person. You're feeling challenged. That's what it is. Your masculine ego is just acting up because my friends warned you to stay away from me."

"They warned me to stay away unless my intentions were honorable," he corrected softly.

She sniffed in disdain. "They could hardly be *honorable*."

"You won't know that or anything else about me for certain unless you make the call to McCray. This is the modern age, Maggie. A smart woman checks a man out before she gets involved with him."

"I do not intend to get *involved* with you. Good night, Mr. January. You are, if you don't mind my saying so, very well named. I have never met anyone quite so cold-blooded."

"Then you have lived a very sheltered life, Maggie Gladstone."

Josh watched with satisfaction as she started to slam the door on her way out of the room. At the last minute she apparently changed her mind, no doubt afraid the noise would be heard down the hall. She closed it very softly with a self-control that spoke volumes.

She was at least fully aware of him now, Josh decided. As aware of him as he was of her. The month at Peregrine Manor was going to prove interesting.

After a few minutes he removed the ice from his leg and levered himself carefully up and off the bed. This time he found the steps. Balancing on his good leg, he studied the ornately carved bedpost that had turned so easily beneath his wildly clutching fingers.

He recalled what Maggie had said about this room having once belonged to her Aunt Agatha.

Josh took a good grip on the post and slowly turned it counterclockwise. The post squeaked softly in protest and then the entire upper portion came loose.

Josh lifted that section of post off the joining portion and realized he was looking into a small, hidden "safe." There was a little jewelry box resting inside the hollowed-out bedpost. He plucked it out and opened it.

An old-fashioned emerald brooch winked in the light of the bedside lamp.

Was he a hotshot private eye or what? Just give him a clue and he was a regular Sherlock Holmes.

Grinning to himself, Josh replaced the lid and dropped the box back into the hidden chamber. Then he carefully repositioned the upper section of the bedpost and screwed it back into place.

There was no point in solving the mysteries of Peregrine Manor too soon, he reminded himself as he got back into bed. He had a month to kill here. A month in which to delve deeply into the mysteries of one Maggie Gladstone, spinster, amateur sleuth and reader of detective novels. He realized he was looking forward to the next four weeks with more enthusiasm than he'd felt about anything in a long, long while.

Josh went to sleep feeling as if some great weight had begun to be lifted from his shoulders.

4

MAGGIE AWOKE the next morning feeling surprisingly rested and refreshed. She realized that she hadn't been sleeping very well lately. The nightly stress of listening for strange noises, the concern about whether she had double-checked every lock on every window, the growing worry about the future of Peregrine Manor—all had taken their toll on her during the past few weeks.

Apparently there was much to be said for having a man like Josh January in the house. In spite of the crutches and bruises, there was something oddly reassuring about his presence. It was unfortunate he had made that pass last night. Now she was going to have to make a point of keeping him in his place. *No more going to his rescue in the middle of the night,* she told herself.

Maggie showered and quickly selected a pair of jeans and an orange sweatshirt from her closet. When she had put them on, she went to stand in front of the dressing table and picked up a brush.

She had just finished tying her thick hair back into a ponytail when her eyes fell on the crumpled sheet of yellow paper lying on the table. Maggie went very still as vivid details of the night before returned to her.

There had been a disconcerting and thoroughly

devastating masculine arrogance about the way Josh had sprawled on the big bed in the turret room. His dark hair had been disturbingly tousled. The crisp, curling thicket on his broad chest had fascinated her. It had been all she could do to keep from staring. She had wanted to run her fingers through that black mat in the worst way. And she had ached with a desire to soothe the massive bruise on his rib cage.

The brooding speculation in his eyes had ruffled her senses as nothing else had ever done. When he had talked of his bitter disillusionment with his chosen work, she had sensed the fundamental integrity of the man. Only a man who had a strong sense of integrity would have become disillusioned. Obviously, Josh hadn't gotten into the business for the money.

Maggie acknowledged with an uneasy little shock that she would never forget that scene in the room next door. It would haunt her for the rest of her life.

And even though she knew there must be no repetitions, a part of her would always wonder what it would have been like to go to bed with Josh January. She had never in her life experienced such a powerful, deeply feminine curiosity, and she felt ill-equipped to deal with it. Her quiet, uneventful past had not prepared her for even a casual approach from a man like Joshua January.

And casual was all it had been. Maggie's mouth tightened as she finished surveying herself in the dressing-table mirror. She would have been shaken to the core to discover that Josh was even mildly interested in her, but it was a certainty that he hadn't been half as affected by her presence as she had been by his. She'd been well aware of his half-aroused body, of course, but that meant very little. Men were very physical creatures, very easily aroused. She was old enough to know that. Josh must consider her an amusing challenge—no doubt because he had been warned off her by the Colonel. But that was all there was to it.

She certainly was not going to call the number on that sheet of yellow paper, Maggie told herself firmly. She wondered if he started all his relationships with a mutual background check. Very likely. The man clearly had no romance in his soul. Maybe his profession had destroyed his sense of passion and discovery even as it had destroyed his faith in human nature.

Nevertheless, Maggie couldn't bring herself to throw away the piece of paper. She picked it up and scanned the boldly scrawled figures. There was a lot of male bravado in those numbers. Josh must have been sure she would make the call.

Disgusted, she opened a drawer in the dresser and shoved the crumpled sheet inside. She slammed the drawer shut and left the room.

Halfway down the stairs the aroma of freshly brewed coffee floated up to greet her. Odessa had apparently risen early. Maggie inhaled deeply and smiled with pleasure. The smile was still on her face when she swung the kitchen door open.

"Good morning, Odessa," Maggie said before she realized who was inside. "That coffee smells wonderful."

"Thanks," Josh drawled from the far side of the large room. "I make good coffee, even if I do say so, myself. Here, have a cup."

Maggie stopped short at the sight of him. He was leaning against the tiled counter, sipping coffee from a mug. His crutches were propped beside him. He looked very sexy in a denim shirt that was open at the throat. And there was no getting around the fact that the man looked good in a pair of jeans. His dark hair gleamed in the wintry sunlight that streamed in through the window.

Maggie forced herself to take a deep, steadying breath as she stepped forward. She was going to be dealing with Josh for the rest of the month, so she had to get used to seeing him in the mornings.

The thing to do this morning, she decided, was to establish the ground rules. It was clear that Rule Number One was to act as if nothing at all had happened last night. After all, she thought with an odd sense of regret, nothing *had* happened. He hadn't even attempted to kiss her. He'd just invited her to do a background check on him.

"Thank you." Maggie took the cup he held out. "I take it you're an early riser?"

"Looks like you are, too." Josh grinned fleetingly, his gaze holding hers over the rim of his cup. "One more thing we have in common, I guess, huh?"

She shrugged, choosing to ignore the taunting gleam in his eyes. "I'm one of the cooks around here, if you'll recall. I have to get up early, whether I like it or not."

"Ah, yes. I'm looking forward to the home-cooked breakfast that was promised in your letter. And the tea and scones mentioned in the brochure, too. Haven't had a scone in years. Do you put raisins in yours?"

Maggie nearly choked on her coffee. "The tea and scones are only served when the manor is open for guests. I would have thought that was obvious."

"Nope. Tea and scones are part of the deal." Josh's expression was unreadable. "As far as I'm concerned, I signed on for this job based on what was promised in that letter and the brochure that accompanied it. It's a binding contract."

"Oh, for heaven's sake, Josh. I was merely listing the amenities of the manor. Surely you understood that. I didn't mean to imply that you were going to be served as if you were a paying guest."

"That's exactly what was implied. And I'm holding you to what was promised." He ticked the items off on his fingers. "A home-cooked breakfast, tea and scones in the afternoons, and a gourmet dinner."

"Is that so? Well, when do I start getting some investigation services in return?"

"Relax. I've been on the job since the minute I walked through your front door. You're in good hands, lady."

"Wonderful. So reassuring to know the future of the manor is in the hands of an investigator who has problems just getting out of bed," Maggie grumbled. She caught her breath as she realized she had just broken her own rule about not mentioning the previous night. Her gaze flew to Josh's and she knew it was too much to hope that he would ignore the comment.

"I may have a little trouble getting out of bed, Maggie, but I can guarantee you I know how to get into one."

Maggie lifted her chin proudly. "I think I should tell you I do not appreciate that kind of humor. Furthermore, as I am your employer, it is within my rights to set the standards of behavior I shall expect from you in the future. I wish to make it very clear that I expect that behavior to be entirely businesslike and professional in nature. Do you understand?"

"Got it." He took a swallow of coffee and smiled again. "Going to make that phone call to McCray today?"

"No, I am not. I have no reason to make it."

"I'll give you a reason," Josh said softly.

Before Maggie realized his intentions, he set down his coffee mug on the counter and reached for her.

"*Josh.*" Maggie looked up at him as tension suddenly rippled through her. She felt herself being tugged gently, inevitably, forward, and for the life of her she couldn't summon up the will to resist. Curiosity was swamping her good sense.

"I wanted to do this last night," Josh muttered.

He bent his head and his mouth brushed lightly across hers. The kiss was full of masculine invitation and tantalizing promise. Maggie tasted coffee and an intimate warmth that made her shiver.

Josh lifted his head almost at once, breaking the contact before she even had time to decide how to react. He watched her with lazy, glittering eyes as she instinctively touched her lips with wondering fingertips.

The brief embrace had been a hint of possibilities, not a full-blown kiss, she reflected. Still, she had felt it to the soles of her feet. Just as she had known she would. Just as *he* must have known she would.

"I didn't do it last night because I figured it would be a little too much for you. And a little too soon." Josh slid his hands slowly up her arms to her shoulders and then wrapped them gently around the nape of her neck. "You're not accustomed to making quick decisions about people the way I am. You don't know how to look into a person's eyes and see if you're being lied to. But me, I'm an old hand at it. I've been sorting out the lies from the truth for so long that it's second nature."

"You're right," Maggie replied breathlessly. "I don't have that skill. So, how will I know if you're telling me the truth about yourself?"

"For starters, you can make the call to McCray," he said gently.

That brought Maggie down to reality with a thud. She stepped back quickly and Josh let her go. "No, thanks. Then I'd have the added problem of not knowing if I could trust McCray, wouldn't I?"

"Like I said, he can supply proof to back up anything he tells you."

Maggie smiled nervously. "Excuse me, I'd better get started on your home-cooked breakfast. Wouldn't want you to say I'd stiffed you out of your fee."

He chuckled. "Right. Word of mouth travels in my business, same as it does in yours. You might have trouble hiring another investigator in the future if you don't pay me."

Odessa appeared in the doorway. "Squabbling again, are we, children? My, my. Never saw two people strike sparks off each other the way you two do."

"She started it," Josh said cheerfully.

Maggie groaned. "And here I was just beginning to think you were man enough to take responsibility for your own actions."

Josh sipped his coffee. "Depends on the actions."

"Now, now, my dears, that's enough of that sort of thing." Odessa bustled about the kitchen, selecting grapefruits from the tray on the counter and a knife from a drawer. "Stop teasing her, Josh."

"Yeah, Josh." Maggie arched her brows. "Stop teasing me. Your threat is meaningless, anyway. You know darn well I'm hardly likely to ever need a private investigator again in my entire life. What do I care if I get blacklisted by your union for nonpayment of your fee?"

"You never know," Josh murmured. "A lot of women are using investigators these days."

Odessa gave him a surprised glance. "Why on earth would young women be going to private investigators?"

"To have background checks run on the men they're dating," Josh explained. "BIS gets requests all the time, but since we focus on corporate security, we generally refer the potential clients to smaller agencies."

Maggie was startled. "You're serious, aren't you?"

"I'm always serious when it comes to business," he assured her.

Odessa looked thoughtful. "What kind of women go to investigators to have their boyfriends checked out?"

"Smart women." Josh shrugged. "One major group of female clients are women who have established careers and are financially independent. They're at risk of being married for their money, same as men are. They want to make certain they're not marrying con artists who will clean out their bank accounts and then split. Another growing group of clients are women who want to be sure they're not dating men who are secretly bisexual or using drugs."

"Makes sense to me," the Colonel remarked from the doorway. "In the old days a young woman's parents and neighbors knew a lot about the man she wanted to marry. They did the background checks, you might say. But these days there's no one to protect the ladies."

"Or they won't listen if you do try to protect them." Josh slid Maggie a meaningful glance. "Give a lady a little friendly advice these days and she takes the bit in her teeth and runs in the opposite direction."

"Speaking of running." Maggie set her cup down on the counter with a loud thud. "We'd better get breakfast on the table, hadn't we, Odessa? I'm sure Josh is eager to get started on his inquiries. Colonel, would you like to show him around Peregrine Manor this morning? You could point out all the places where we've had problems. He might be able to find a clue or something."

"Certainly," the Colonel agreed. "Be delighted."

"A clue." Josh looked politely enthusiastic. "What a good idea. Clues are very helpful in my line of work."

"We'll just have to hope you can recognize one when you see it, won't we?" Maggie murmured as she pulled a frying pan out of the cupboard.

"Not to worry," Josh retorted. "I brought along my handy-dandy official private investigators' manual. I believe there's an entire chapter devoted to finding and recognizing clues."

"A manual, you say? How reassuring." Maggie measured flour for pancakes. "Did you see it advertised on the back of a cereal box and send away for it with a coupon?"

"Probably," Josh said. "I eat a lot of cereal. I almost never get real home-cooked breakfasts, you see."

"Well, well, well. Fireworks already." The Colonel winked at Odessa. "Sounds like things are going to be lively around here for the next month."

Shirley walked into the kitchen, yawning. "You know what my Ricky always used to say about two people who went at it right off the bat like Josh and Maggie here?"

"No. What did Ricky 'The Wrecker' used to say?" Josh asked.

"He'd say they were either meant for each other or else they would wind up throttling each other. One of the two."

"An interesting choice," Josh observed blandly.

MAGGIE WAS RATHER surprised to discover that during the next few days Josh fitted himself very comfortably into the routine at Peregrine Manor. As his injured ribs and ankle improved, he even turned out to be surprisingly useful around the place. He was always up first and had the coffee going by the time Maggie came downstairs. Furthermore, he seemed to be quite handy in the home-repair department. He gave her a hand painting three of the guest bathrooms, fixed a broken toilet seat and rehung the canopy over his bed.

And he did not make any more passes.

"I still don't know if you're much of an investigator, but you're certainly saving me a bundle of money that I would normally have spent on Dwight," Maggie told him at one point.

"Who's Dwight?"

"Dwight Wilcox is a handyman in town. He usually takes care of the minor repairs around here for me," she explained.

By the end of the week Maggie realized she had already grown accustomed to Josh's presence. The intimacy of sharing the kitchen with him in the early-morning hours had become something she unconsciously looked forward to each day.

As far as she could tell, he was dutifully making inquiries into the incidents at Peregrine Manor. Josh spent a lot of time with the Colonel examining the basement where many of the problems had occurred, and he talked to Odessa and Shirley at length. He asked questions about the nephews and about Ricky "The Wrecker" Ring. Furthermore, he disappeared into his room for hours on end to work on his computer. It all seemed very professional to Maggie.

The only really annoying aspect of the situation was that she was getting very tired of making tea and scones at three in the afternoon.

"I wonder what he does on that thing?" Shirley asked on Friday. She was sitting at the kitchen table along with the others. They were all watching Maggie mix up the scone dough.

Josh had been up in his room for the past three hours and Maggie knew he would be down any minute demanding his afternoon rations.

"Checking out the information he's collecting." The Colonel looked knowledgeable. "Our man is a modern sort of investigator, just as I've suspected. Does most of his research on a computer, he told me. Quite bright, too. Shows a good grasp of technical matters, in general. Understood most of the details I gave him about my experiments, for example."

Odessa nodded, not looking up from her knitting.

"Very easy to talk to, I'll say that much for him. I told him all about my three atrocious nephews. He certainly seemed to understood how nasty family can get. Said a lot of his early work in the investigation business involved unfortunate family situations."

Josh appeared in the doorway, minus his crutches. "Those scones ready yet?"

Maggie glanced at him as she bent over to shove the pan of scones into the oven. "No. Not for another fifteen minutes. Where are the crutches?"

"I don't need them anymore. See?" Josh walked carefully into the room. He still limped but it was obvious he was again mobile. "I'll be all right as long as I don't try to run up and down the stairs. Boy, am I hungry."

"Yes, it has been a whole three hours since lunch, hasn't it?" Maggie muttered.

Josh glanced at his wristwatch and frowned. "More than three hours. What's happening around here? Says in the brochure that teatime is at three o'clock every afternoon. It's now 3:05."

Maggie shot him a narrow-eyed look. "Speaking of stairs, what would happen if you took an unfortunate tumble down a flight?"

"I'd sue," Josh assured her. "Tea ready?"

The wall phone rang before Maggie could tell him to fix it himself if he was in that big a hurry. She picked up the receiver.

"Peregrine Manor," she snapped.

"Maggie?" The familiar male voice on the other end of the line held a faint, inquiring note.

Maggie relaxed and leaned back against the wall. "Hello, Clay. Sorry, I was busy. How are you?"

"Just fine," Clay O'Connor said in his easy, pleasant tones. "Thought I'd check and make sure we're still on for this evening."

"Of course. Six o'clock, right?" Automatically Maggie glanced at the calendar beside the phone and saw where she had written "Clay -dinner -six" on that day's date.

"Right." There was a slight pause. "Listen, I hear you've got a guest staying at the manor. Thought you'd decided to close for the winter. Change your mind?"

Maggie realized with a start that she hadn't invented a solid cover story to explain Josh's presence to outsiders. Her gaze swung toward Josh who was watching her intently from where he was sitting at the table.

"It was kind of unexpected, Clay." She sought frantically for an explanation. Clay O'Connor was a very nice man, but she didn't want anyone outside the small household at the manor to know that she had hired an investigator. "I'll tell you all about it this evening. See you at six."

"Maggie—"

"Got to run, Clay. I've got scones in the oven. Bye." Maggie hurriedly hung up the phone and scowled at Josh.

"Problems?" Josh inquired softly.

"We've got to think up a good reason for your being here at the manor, Josh. I don't want the people in Peregrine Point to know I've hired a private investigator. It might get back to whoever is causing the trouble around here."

"That's right," the Colonel chimed in. "When we made the decision to hire you, we agreed to keep your real purpose here a secret."

Josh eyed Maggie. He looked very thoughtful. "You don't think your friend O'Connor could keep his mouth shut?"

Maggie winced. "I'm not worried about him keeping quiet. I'm afraid he'll laugh at me. He thinks I'm getting paranoid about the incidents."

"Got it." Josh nodded. "Don't worry, I'll come up with a good cover story by the time he arrives to pick you up this evening. Six o'clock, wasn't it?"

"Yes." Maggie removed the kettle from the stove and poured boiling water into a teapot. For some reason she felt vaguely uneasy. She realized she didn't know how to read the expression in Josh's eyes.

Josh flashed a wicked grin. "Leave everything to me. I keep telling you you're in good hands, Maggie."

Maggie shot him a suspicious glance. She didn't like the sound of that. "Perhaps we'd better work on the cover story together, Josh."

"Forget it. This is my area of expertise."

"But, Josh—"

The Colonel interrupted. "Now, Maggie, he's right. Leave all that sort of thing to our man, here. He's a professional."

"I think the scones are done," Josh said helpfully. "By the way, we're almost out of jam. You'd better put it on your shopping list, Maggie."

"Thank you for reminding me," Maggie answered through set teeth.

"That's what I'm here for, ma'am. To check out the details."

Odessa smiled happily. "Such a relief to know you're on the job, Josh."

"Sure is," Shirley agreed. "Like my Ricky always

used to say, when you want something done right, hire a professional."

Josh smiled. "I'm sure Ricky knew all about hiring professionals, Shirley."

MAGGIE DRESSED FOR DINNER with some trepidation that evening. She had been worrying all afternoon about the "cover story" Josh was supposedly inventing. The closer six o'clock got, the more she fretted about it.

She slipped into a long-sleeved black dinner dress that hugged her small waist and flared out around her calves in a rich swirl of fabric. She brushed her hair out so that it hung freely around her shoulders, and was pondering the question of earrings when a knock sounded on the door.

"Clay's here," Shirley called. "Let's see how you look, honey."

Maggie opened her bedroom door. "Tell him I'll be right down, will you?"

"Sure. Hey, you know what? I've got a necklace that would be perfect with that dress. Hang on, I'll get it."

"That's all right, Shirley, really...." Maggie's voice trailed off as Shirley disappeared down the hall.

The older woman reappeared a few minutes later with a long rhinestone-studded necklace of ancient vintage. "Here you go, honey. This'll be perfect."

Maggie smiled weakly, unwilling to hurt Shirley's feelings by refusing the gaudy necklace. "Thanks, Shirley." She put the long string of rhinestones over her head. It hung to her waist. The rhinestones twinkled cheerfully as they fell across her breasts. Maggie glanced in the mirror and smiled. The tacky, glitzy look was rather appealing in its own way.

"Have a good time, honey." Shirley waved from the top of the stairs. "Seeing you off like this always makes me think of the days when Ricky took me to all the best places."

"Thanks for the loan of the necklace, Shirley."

Maggie heard voices in the parlor as she went down the stairs. When she caught Josh's soft, deep tones, she hurried quickly down the last few steps. She had wanted to be present to monitor things when he gave his cover story. She was learning that, left unsupervised, Josh was somewhat unpredictable. She moved into the parlor just as Josh and Clay were shaking hands.

"Pleased to meet you, January," Clay said. "I heard Maggie had someone staying here. Thought she'd closed the place for the winter season."

"A mutual friend prevailed on her to make an exception for me," Josh explained easily. "I'm writing a book and I needed a quiet place to work. The friend suggested Peregine Manor and talked Maggie into letting me come here for a month." He turned his head as Maggie walked through the door. "Isn't that right, Maggie?"

A writer. Of course. It was perfect. Why hadn't she thought of that? Maggie wondered. She smiled in relief and immediately felt more cheerful. Josh might be a pain in a certain part of the anatomy from time to time, but he really could be clever on occasion. Posing as a writer seeking solitude and inspiration was a wonderful explanation for his presence at the manor.

"Yes, that's right," Maggie added brightly. "A

mutual friend of ours talked me into it. And since Josh doesn't care that we're doing some refurbishing around the manor, I decided to make the exception. Ready to go, Clay?"

"You bet. You look lovely tonight, Maggie." Clay smiled warmly at her and the smile was reflected in his pale blue eyes. He was an attractive man with an engaging, friendly air that stood him well in the real-estate business.

Tonight Clay was dressed for dinner in an expensive wool jacket and slacks. There was a chunky gold ring set with a diamond on his hand and a thin gold watch on his wrist. His sandy brown hair had been moussed and blown-dry into a smooth style that made him look very sophisticated and urbane next to Josh.

Somehow the contrast between the two men had the effect of making Josh look decidedly tough and dangerous. That was primarily because Josh hadn't yet changed for dinner, Maggie decided, feeling charitable.

He was still wearing jeans, running shoes and a work shirt. His dark hair had probably never known the touch of mousse. Maggie wondered if he had deliberately come downstairs in his jeans and work shirt in order to make his cover story more realistic. He actually *looked* like a writer, she thought. Not that she had ever actually met one in person.

"We really should be on our way." Maggie smiled at Clay.

"Don't worry, honey," Clay said with a charming laugh. "This is Peregrine Point, not Seattle. We don't have to worry about losing our table at the Surf and Sand Restaurant."

"Yes, I know, but I'm really very hungry." Maggie took his arm and urged him toward the door. She didn't want him hanging around asking questions. Josh's cover story might not hold up if Clay got inquisitive.

"Have a good time," Josh murmured from the doorway. The words were polite, but Maggie thought there was something strange about his tone—something she couldn't put her finger on.

"Thanks." Maggie glanced back over her shoulder and was jolted by the laconic gleam in Josh's eyes. She frowned.

"What time should we expect you home?" Josh asked. He propped one shoulder against the door frame and folded his arms.

"Don't worry about it," Maggie retorted with a cool smile. "I've got my own key. I own the place, remember?"

"Oh, yeah. That's right."

Maggie was relieved when the door closed firmly behind her and Clay.

"How long has he been here?" Clay asked as he helped her into the front seat of his silver Mercedes.

"Not long. A week."

"Seems to have made himself right at home." Clay closed the car door and went around to the driver's side. "Who's your mutual friend? The one who suggested he stay here?"

Maggie experienced a moment of panic. It was a perfectly natural question under the circumstances and she ought to have been prepared for it. Darn it, she *would* have been prepared if Josh had taken the trouble to tell her his cover story before Clay's arrival. But, no, he had to try to impress her with his cleverness. She would speak to him about that later, Maggie decided.

"Oh, just someone we both know in Seattle," she said airily. "To tell you the truth, as long as Josh doesn't mind staying at the manor while we're refurbishing, I don't mind having him there. Things are going to be a little lean this winter without any paying guests. Usually our weekends are booked solid, even in November and December."

Clay nodded with obvious concern. "I know. It's going to be rough for the next few months, honey. Sure it's worth it?"

Maggie sighed. "I have to try to save the place, Clay. I've told you that."

"Honey, I admire your kind heart, but take it from an expert—that old mansion is a white elephant. You'll wind up pouring all your income back into it and in the end, you'll probably have to sell, anyway. You'd be better off dumping the place now and clearing some profit."

Maggie's mouth tightened. This was not the first time Clay had suggested she sell the manor. She had to admit that from his point of view, it made perfect sense. Clay was in the real-estate business, after all. He knew about this kind of thing. "I know you're probably right, Clay. But the thing is, I've made a commitment to the Colonel, Odessa and Shirley. I have to try."

Clay took one hand off the wheel to reach over and pat her hand. "I understand. Just remember that if you change your mind, I'll be glad to help you find a buyer. And I won't even charge you my usual commission. How's that for a deal you can't refuse?"

Maggie smiled ruefully. "Thanks. I'll keep it in mind."

AT ELEVEN O'CLOCK that evening, Maggie was back on her doorstep, saying good-night to Clay. Unfortunately, it was getting harder and harder to find polite ways of getting rid of him.

Maggie knew in her heart that all she had ever wanted with Clay was a casual friendship, and she was starting to feel a little guilty about that. Clay was beginning to push for a much more intimate relationship. She wondered how much longer she should go on accepting his invitations when she knew she was never going to fall in love with him. Perhaps it was time to gently end it.

"Clay," she began as she fished her key out of her purse. "I've been thinking."

His mouth curved in amusement as he hovered close. "So have I. I see the lights are off in the parlor, which means the Colonel and the others have gone to bed. Why don't you invite me in for a nightcap and we'll do our thinking together?"

Maggie bit her lip. "The thing is—"

Before Maggie could get her key into the lock, the door opened. Josh loomed in the shadows.

"Thought I heard someone out here," he said as he reached out to flip on the hall light. "I was watching television in the study. Come on in. We can all have coffee or something. You play cards, O'Connor?"

Clay's eyes narrowed with obvious annoyance. "Sorry, I don't care for cards. Maggie says she has to get to bed early. I'd better be on my way." He nodded stiffly to Maggie. "Good night, honey."

Maggie smiled anxiously, aware that Clay was upset by finding Josh at the door. "It was a lovely evening, Clay."

"I'll call you." Clay stalked back down the steps and out to where his Mercedes was parked.

Josh shook his head sadly. "They all say that."

Maggie glowered at him as she stepped into the hall. "In Clay's case, it happens to be true. He *will* call me."

"Yeah, he probably will." Josh helped her out of her coat. "Come on into the parlor. I've fixed you a nice cup of hot chocolate."

"*Chocolate.* Josh, were you by any chance waiting up for me? The answer had better be no. Because if I thought for one moment that you deliberately staged that little scene at the door in order to make Clay go home early, I'd be furious."

He gave her an injured look as he limped into the parlor and turned on one of the lamps. "I thought you might want to discuss the progress I've made so far on your case."

Maggie stared at his broad-shouldered back. "You've actually made some progress?"

"You don't have to sound so surprised. It is my job, you know. How many times do I have to remind you that I am a trained investigator?"

"I don't know why that fact keeps slipping my mind," Maggie responded grimly.

5

JOSH POURED the hot chocolate he had carefully prepared earlier. As he did so, he felt the tension that had been eating at him all evening dissolve at last. It made him realize that he had been waiting for Maggie to return from the moment she had walked out the door on another man's arm five hours earlier. It was only sheer willpower that had kept him from actually pacing the floor for the past hour.

The Colonel, Odessa and Shirley had assured him that Maggie never stayed out late with Clay O'Connor, but that hadn't relieved Josh's mind. He knew in his gut that it was just a matter of time before O'Connor tried to talk Maggie into staying out very late. Maybe even all night. Josh had seen the determination in O'Connor's eyes when Maggie had swept into the parlor to greet him at six. O'Connor was on the make. There was no doubt about it.

During the evening Josh had come to the decision that Maggie Gladstone was not going to fall into Clay O'Connor's bed while he, Josh, was anywhere in the vicinity. If she was going to fall into any man's bed, it was going to be his own, Josh told himself.

He'd known he was attracted to her from the instant he had seen her. He'd known he wanted her that first night when she had hovered over his bed, adjusting ice packs. But he'd learned just how severely he was hooked during the past few hours as he had tortured himself with thoughts of another man touching her.

The interminable wait for Maggie to come home tonight had taught Josh that in some subtle way during the past few days, he had come to think of Maggie as *his*. The surge of possessiveness he experienced at that thought made his hand tremble slightly. The pot he was holding rattled against the rim of Maggie's cup.

Maggie frowned in horror. "Don't drop that, whatever you do. Aunt Agatha once told me that pot has been in the family for generations."

"In spite of your obvious opinion to the contrary, I am not a complete klutz." Josh set the pot firmly on the end table. He wondered dourly what McCray and the rest of the staff at BIS would say if they knew his new client thought him clumsy and accident-prone. Hell of an image he had going for himself here, Josh reflected.

Maggie smiled with a hint of relieved apology when she saw that the pot was safe. "It's just that that particular pot is rather valuable. If I ever do have to sell this place, I'll be counting on making enough profit from the furnishings to provide the Colonel and the others with some financial security."

Josh lowered himself cautiously onto the sofa beside Maggie. "What brought that up?"

"What?"

"Selling the manor. Every time I've talked to you, you've always made it clear you're not even considering that alternative."

Maggie sighed and leaned back against the sofa cushion. She toyed absently with the long rhinestone necklace she was wearing. The stones sparkled like diamonds in the soft light.

"Clay and I were discussing it earlier in the evening," Maggie explained. "I told you he's a real-estate agent. A very good one, apparently."

"I know. I saw the Mercedes and the gold ring on his pinkie." Josh had also pumped the Colonel, Odessa and Shirley for every scrap of information they had on Clay O'Connor. He hadn't learned much more than he had already guessed.

"He really thinks I should dump the manor," Maggie continued. "Says I'm pouring money down a hole trying to keep it open. He's been after me to cut my losses for several weeks now."

"When did you start dating him?"

"Two months ago." Maggie fiddled with her teacup. "He's really very nice, you know."

"No. How would I know?"

"Well, he is," she muttered. Then she gave him a reproachful glance. "That reminds me. I had to fast-talk my way around the subject of our 'mutual friend' when Clay asked me about her. Or him. You really should have briefed me on your cover story, Josh."

"What did you tell him?" Josh asked, unconcerned.

"Not much. Just that the friend lived in Seattle. Then I changed the subject."

"Sounds like you handled it well."

"Nevertheless, I expect to be kept better informed in the future. And speaking of being informed, let's have your report."

Josh shrugged. "I think we can safely discard Shirley's theory of who's behind the trouble here at the manor. I made some inquiries about Ricky 'The Wrecker' Ring and the answer came back today."

"Oh, yes. Your computer inquiries." Maggie smiled eagerly. "What did you learn?"

Josh decided there was no point in telling her he'd learned everything through a simple phone call to the home office where one of his staff had run a quick check. "Ricky Ring got out of prison five years ago. From all accounts he was a model prisoner—spent most of his time inside teaching other inmates how to read. Since getting out, he's routinely devoted twenty hours a week to a local literacy project. He's living a quiet life down in Portland and shows absolutely no signs of going back to his erring ways. His present income appears to be derived entirely from T-bills and government securities that he bought years ago before he went to jail. In short, Ricky is a reformed man."

"No indication that he's out for vengeance?"

"None."

Maggie gazed thoughtfully into her chocolate. "Well, I never did think Shirley's explanation was sound. What about Odessa's nephews?"

"I did some checking on them, too. All three nephews live on the East Coast. Not one of them has ever made a trip to Washington, and apparently not one of them has any intention of doing so. Furthermore, they are all doing quite well financially. Two of them are lawyers and one of them is in banking. I'm still checking on the mining stock Odessa owns."

"That leaves the Colonel and his fuel experiments, doesn't it?"

Josh was about to tell her that from what he'd seen of the Colonel's work, they could safely discard that theory, too. There was no way anyone was going to turn water into a combustible substance. At least, not going at it the way the Colonel was. But Josh thought he would save that revelation for later. He had to make his work last for the next three weeks.

"I'm still working on the Colonel's theory and your idea that someone is after your aunt's emerald brooch," Josh said smoothly.

"I suppose you think my theory is as nutty as all the others that are floating around here."

"What makes you say that?" He slanted her a surprised, assessing glance. Her tone of voice alarmed him. This was not the upbeat, gung-ho Maggie he had come to know during the past week. "You're kind of down tonight, aren't you?"

"A little," she admitted. She set her hot chocolate on the table, leaned her head back and gazed forlornly out the window into the darkness. "Clay talked all evening about how smart it would be to sell the manor. He meant well, I know. But still, it was depressing hearing him lay out all the practical reasons why I should get rid of the place. He says I'm not doing the Colonel, Odessa and Shirley any favors trying to save it."

"Yeah?"

Maggie nodded wearily. "He says they'd all be better off financially if I sold the manor and gave them a share of the profits. I don't know, Josh. Maybe I am being foolish, trying to save it. What if there really isn't something mysterious going on around here for you to find? What if it's just a big old house slowly fading away?"

"Hey, let's not jump to the worst possible conclusions so soon." Josh realized with a start that he didn't want Maggie to have to face reality quite so quickly.

To his chagrin, he was suddenly stricken with a wild, impulsive desire to help her salvage her dream. *Bad move*, he reminded himself. *It never pays to play hero.*

But it was too late. Josh knew he was already looking for ways to ride to the rescue.

"Maybe Clay's right, Josh. Maybe it would be doing Odessa and Shirley and the Colonel a favor if I sold the place now. I know they love it and think of it as their home, but—"

"Give me the rest of the month," Josh said quickly. "Just give me the amount of time you contracted for in the beginning. That's all I ask. Okay?"

She turned her head on the cushion and looked up at him with damp eyes. "But what can you do besides prove our theories wrong? What if there isn't anything odd happening?"

He framed her face gently with one hand and leaned close. "Maggie, you hired me to fix things. Let me do my job for the rest of the month and we'll see what happens." He grinned briefly and brushed his mouth lightly against hers. "What have you got to lose? I work cheap, remember?"

"Oh, Josh, I just don't know. I was so sure in the beginning, but Clay says—"

"Forget O'Connor, okay?" Josh stroked his thumb along her lower lip. "You haven't made that call to McCray, have you?"

"Well, no." She went very still as she looked up at him. Her mouth trembled slightly. "I really don't see why I should."

"Maggie, sweetheart, you are very kind, but a little

naive." He brought his mouth down on hers and this time he didn't pull away.

Maggie held herself tensely as he slowly deepened the kiss. And then, to his incredible delight, she began to respond. Josh felt his whole body react instantaneously to the promise of her stirring softness. His blood sang with the thrill of a desire that went all the way to his core.

When she moved again it was to put her arms tentatively around his waist. She was careful of his ribs. Josh probed gently and her mouth opened for him.

With a rush of passion he could barely restrain, he realized that he was already fighting for his self-control. The effect Maggie had on him was electrifying. He was suddenly insatiably hungry for her. But it was too soon to take her to bed. If he tried, he would no doubt scare her off entirely. He had to go slowly, he told himself. But he was no longer sure he could wait. It had never been like this. At least not for more years than he could recall.

"Josh?"

"Maggie, sweetheart. Just let me touch you. Please, love." He eased her down carefully onto the cushions of the old Victorian sofa and sprawled heavily on top of her. She was soft and sleek beneath him, the gentle contours of her body accepting all the hard, rough-edged places of his. He was overwhelmingly conscious of wanting to be careful with her, of wanting to let her respond to him in her own time.

Josh groaned; the husky sound of need chained by willpower emanated from somewhere deep inside him. He kissed the curve of Maggie's cheek and then her throat. When he raised his head to look down at her he saw the wonder and uncertainty in her beautiful eyes. And then he saw the sweet passion that was flickering to life within her.

Josh reached out to switch off the lamp and the shadows enveloped them.

"Josh. *Josh.*"

His name on Maggie's lips was a breathless whisper in the darkness. It sent a shudder of desire flaring through him.

"I'm right here, sweetheart." He stroked a finger inside the V-neck of her dress, tracing its outline down to the lowest point just above her breasts. Then he slowly drew his finger back up to her throat where her pulse beat warmly in the soft hollow.

"You are a very strange man," Maggie said seriously.

That made him hesitate. "Why do you say that?"

"I don't know. There's just something different about you."

"Different from what?" he demanded.

"Different from any other man I've ever met."

Josh relaxed slightly. He smiled in the shadows. "Okay, I can live with that, I guess. It's not the most inspiring compliment you could give a man under these conditions, but I suppose I can put my own interpretation on it."

She touched the side of his face with gentle, questing fingertips. Her shadowed eyes were still very serious. "What would be a more inspirational remark?"

He slowly started to undo the large black buttons that closed the front of the dress. "You could tell me I'm incredibly sexy."

"You are," she said with a simple, touching honesty. "But I figured you already knew that."

The words struck him like lightning. His hand stilled on a button as he paused to gaze down at her. "*Maggie.*"

"Hmm?" She was fingering the buttons on his shirt.

"Maggie, sweetheart, do you mean that? You really think I'm sexy?"

"Yes. The sexiest man I've ever met."

"Oh, Maggie." He choked back an exultant laugh and hugged her fiercely. "I forgive you for all the nasty cracks you've made about me during the past few days. I'll even forget you called me accident-prone."

She relaxed in his arms and giggled softly against his chest. "You like hearing you're sexy?"

"I like hearing it from you. I like it very, very much." Josh went back to work on the buttons of her dress. "Mostly because *I* think *you* are incredibly, astoundingly, amazingly sexy."

The laughter went out of her again. She clung to him with sudden urgency. "Josh, there has to be more."

Josh sucked in his breath as his ribs protested her abruptly fierce hug. "There *is* more, sweetheart." He took a cautious breath as she released him. "A lot more. Give me a chance to show you."

He had the front of the dress open now. Rhinestones spilled across the upper curves of her breasts. He eased his hand inside and found the softness of a warm globe cupped in lace. When he brushed his thumb over its sweetly shaped curve he felt the velvety nipple stir and begin to harden. He realized she was holding her breath.

"Relax, Maggie. Trust me tonight."

"I do trust you. It's crazy. But I do." She put her arms around his neck and kissed the taut line of his jaw. Her leg shifted alongside his on the cushions.

Josh could feel the promise of surrender in her and he was awed. The soft, giving warmth of her made him powerfully aware of his own maleness. He sensed that he was being given a rare and wonderful gift and that he dared not ruin the experience by demanding more than Maggie was prepared to give at this point.

Josh reached down and found the hem of her dress. He eased it upward to her thighs and sighed when he felt the warmth between her legs. He lowered his mouth to one breast, dampening the nipple beneath the lace with his tongue. When she moaned softly, he began to explore her more thoroughly.

Slowly he eased the silky panty hose down her legs to her ankles. Then he peeled them off her delicately arched feet. He slid his hands back up her legs and gently pushed her thighs more widely apart. She resisted slightly and then surrendered to his gentle, insistent pressure.

His fingers brushed against the soft nest that sheltered her secrets.

"*Josh.*"

There was a throaty passion in her voice. And uncertainty, as well. Josh couldn't tell if he had gone too far or if she wanted him to go further. He brushed his fingers against her again and felt the wet heat. He kissed her deeply. "Do you like that, Maggie?"

"*Yes.* Oh, *yes.* Please, Josh." She was starting to clutch at him, moving her head restlessly.

Josh took a deep breath to control his own skyrocketing need. He cupped her intimately with the palm of his hand. "You're burning up, sweetheart, aren't you? You're on fire for me."

Her answer was to arch herself against his hand. Josh stroked one finger slowly inside her and felt her shiver in response. "You're so tight," he said in wonder. "Tight and hot and wet. All passion and fire." He stroked again—a little harder—and she gasped.

"I don't…I can't… Josh, I feel so strange. What are you doing to me?"

He heard the confusion and excitement in her voice and realized with amazement that Maggie didn't recognize her own impending climax. It dawned on him that Maggie was going to learn the passionate power of her own body at his hands—and a glorious exultation roared through him. He felt simultaneously humble and magnificently proud. He could give her something almost as wonderful as what she was giving him; something no other man had ever given her.

"Don't fight it, sweetheart. It's going to be so good. You're going to go up in flames. Tighten yourself, Maggie. Yes, that's it, harder, harder. Yes." He stroked her gently, finding the small, engorged nub of feminine sensation with his thumb.

He knew it was happening even before she did. It was unmistakable. Her whole body suddenly clenched and tiny, shivering ripples quivered around his invading finger. Josh almost lost his own self-control at that moment.

"*Josh.*"

She was going to cry out. Josh sensed it and as much as he yearned to hear the sweet sound of her release, he knew he had to protect her privacy. The parlor was directly under the Colonel's bedroom.

Josh captured Maggie's mouth with his own, swallowing the soft, joyous sounds. He held her while she convulsed beneath him and took as much pleasure in the release as Maggie herself did. It was an odd sensation to be so enthralled by a woman's passion that he could forgo his own without resentment. All Josh wanted in that moment was for Maggie to be happy and to know that he was the one who had made her so.

Maggie eventually collapsed into a soft, warm heap beneath Josh and for a long time he was content to just lie there on top of her, savoring the scent and feel of her. The minutes slipped past.

Maggie shifted slightly at last. "Josh?" she whispered.

"Mmm?"

"Josh, that was…quite wonderful."

He grinned to himself in the darkness. "Yeah, it was. Never seen anything like it."

She laughed softly. "You're teasing me."

"No, I'm deadly serious. It was wonderful." He finally raised his head and kissed the tip of her nose.

"Oh, dear. I didn't realize. I wasn't thinking. I mean, you didn't—" She broke off as he silenced her by kissing her mouth.

"No, I didn't. But that's okay, too," he assured her. "When it happens for me, I want to be deep inside you, Maggie. And it's a little too soon for that. You need time to get to know me better. I want you to be sure of me, sweetheart."

She shook her head in wonder. "You're playing the noble hero again, aren't you?"

He frowned. "I've told you, I gave that role up a long time ago."

"I don't believe you." She traced the line of his nose with a soft fingertip.

Josh opened his mouth to tell her not to get the wrong idea about him, but something stopped him. A tiny sound from somewhere in the house. A sound that was not quite normal.

"Josh? What is it?" Maggie looked up at him. "Is something wrong?"

"Hush." He touched her mouth with his fingers, silently warning her. When he knew she had gotten the message, he sat up slowly on the sofa.

The sound came softly down the front hall—a small, muted click that could have been metal on metal. Maggie sat up beside Josh, fumbling with the buttons of her dress. He could feel her watching him and knew she wanted to ask questions. But she obviously knew when to follow instructions. She kept silent.

Josh touched her shoulder and put his mouth to her ear. "Stay here. Don't move."

She nodded and then put her lips next to his ear. "Call police?"

"No. Not yet. But be ready." He stood and moved to the door of the parlor. He listened intently, straining to hear the soft clinking sound before he stepped out into the hall. He caught it echoing faintly and knew for certain, now, that it was coming from the basement.

Josh limped forward and silently cursed the weakness of his still-healing left foot. He went quietly down the darkened hall, his bare feet making no sound on the carpet. When he reached the door that opened on the basement stairs he hesitated once more.

Silence.

Josh unlocked the door and opened it. The hinges made only the faintest whisper of sound. The stairs to the basement descended into an inky darkness. If there was anyone down there, Josh thought, he had the eyes of a cat.

But his instincts told him the basement was empty. Josh waited another moment and then decided to chance the light. He flattened himself against the wall and crouched low. There was no need to make a target out of himself, just in case someone was hiding among the wine bins and filing cabinets. He reached up over his head to flip the light switch.

The lights came on and Josh swept the large room below in a single glance. The basement was empty. He straightened slowly. "Maggie?" he called softly over his shoulder.

"Right here." She hurried barefoot down the hall. "Is everything all right?"

"Yeah, I think so. I was sure I heard something, though. I'm going to go on down and take a closer look." He started down the stairs, using the handrail to take the weight off his bad foot. Maggie floated along behind him like a nervous little ghost.

The cold draft that swept the room caught Josh's attention first. He glanced toward the two narrow, ground-level windows near the basement ceiling. One of them was open.

"Hell." He reached the bottom step and crossed the concrete floor. He sensed Maggie following him with her gaze.

"Josh, that window should be locked. We always keep it locked."

"It was locked," Josh told her quietly. "I checked it

earlier, myself. But the latch is not much more than a toy. Easy to pry open from the outside. Hell, maybe it fell open on its own. It's old."

He contemplated the window for a moment longer and then studied the arrangement of filing cabinets and boxes stacked beneath it. An ancient blanket had been placed on top of the metal cabinets. There were some bits of dirt scattered on it. Josh touched them with his fingers.

"What have you found?" Maggie came close. "Dirt?"

Josh nodded slowly. "If there was someone in here, he came and went through that window. Could have used these boxes and cabinets to climb down and back up again."

Maggie considered that. "It's a very narrow window, Josh."

"It's big enough for a slender man to crawl through."

"Or a woman." Maggie looked around the cold basement. She crossed her arms and hugged herself. A shadow flitted across her face, giving her a vulnerable look. "Josh, do you think someone was actually in here?"

"I think it's a real strong possibility," he said quietly.

"But what would he want? There's nothing of any great value here, except for the manor's wine supply. But it's safely locked up in that wire cage over there." Maggie nodded toward the wine-storage area on the other side of the room.

"The wine might be enough of a temptation to draw a prowler," Josh remarked thoughtfully. "Teenagers, maybe."

But Maggie's eyes were narrowing as a more sinister thought apparently struck her. "You know what I think?"

"Uh, no, Maggie. What do you think?"

"I think someone climbed in here to search for Aunt Agatha's emerald brooch."

Josh let that pass. The last thing he wanted to do tonight was shoot holes in Maggie's theory. He'd already shot holes in everyone else's. "What do you say we take a look around and see if any of the cabinets look like they've been jimmied open."

"Right." Maggie started determinedly toward the bank of file cabinets the Colonel used to house his research data and the reports on his experiments.

She stopped short with a soft shriek. "Oh, my God, Josh! Look! There's water pouring out of that pipe. If it gets into the cabinets it will ruin the Colonel's papers."

Josh looked up from a stack of boxes he was studying and frowned. Sure enough, a steady stream of water was leaking from a joint in the pipes that ran overhead. The volume of water increased even as he watched.

"Hand me that wrench hanging on the wall," he ordered as he lunged across the room, cursing his awkward, broken stride. "Damn it, not that one, the other one. The big one. Yeah, that's it."

Josh reached the file cabinets, planted his hands on top of two of them and hoisted himself up until he was standing amid the clutter on the metal surface. His shoulder twinged painfully but he ignored it.

Water was starting to pool and flow over the side of the filing cabinets. The cabinets, which were already groaning under the weight of the Colonel's accumulation of paperwork, trembled at this additional punishment. Josh could only pray they wouldn't collapse beneath him.

"Here, Josh." Maggie thrust the wrench up at him. "Hurry. The Colonel will be brokenhearted if all of his papers are destroyed."

"You think I don't know that?" Josh fitted the wrench to the pipe joint and applied steady pressure. The flow of water diminished quickly. Josh gave the joint a few more turns, tightening it securely until the leak stopped.

When he had finished, he handed the wrench back to Maggie and slowly eased himself down to the floor. Maggie picked up some old cloths and began mopping up the water on top of the cabinets.

For a moment neither of them spoke. Hands on his hips, Josh stared up at the pipe and thought about the faint sound of metal on metal that had brought him down here.

"Someone was definitely in here, Josh." Maggie tossed the wet rags onto the floor. "Someone climbed into this basement and deliberately loosened the pipe joint."

"Looks like it," Josh agreed, still contemplating the pipe.

"If we hadn't discovered the water coming out of that pipe tonight, the entire basement would have been flooded by morning. It would have been a disaster."

"Yeah. It would have been a mess, all right." Tonight's incident put a whole new perspective on this cushy, piece-of-cake case. It was now clear to Josh that the things that had been happening at Peregrine

Manor could no longer be written off as due to over-active imaginations.

"What are you thinking?" Maggie asked uneasily.

"That the problems you've had might be the work of a vandal. Maybe some local sicko who gets his kicks causing this kind of trouble. Or a kid who's bent on doing mischief just for the hell of it."

Maggie chewed on her lower lip. "The sheriff did suggest that possibility when I called him after the first couple of incidents," she admitted. "He said to be sure I locked everything up securely at night. I haven't bothered calling him again. But, Josh, it's not just wanton vandalism. I know it isn't."

Josh glanced at her and saw the anxiety in her eyes. He sighed. "You still think this has something to do with your Aunt Agatha's emerald brooch? Maggie, I don't want to quash your theory, but it doesn't make sense that a prowler would try to flood the basement while he searched for a valuable piece of jewelry."

Maggie frowned. "It does look like he was trying to destroy the Colonel's papers, doesn't it? Do you suppose there might be something to his theory, after all?"

"No," Josh said flatly. "I don't."

Maggie drummed her fingers on a file cabinet. "It's possible someone *thinks* he can create it and is after the formula."

"Damn it, Maggie…"

"Okay, okay. It's highly unlikely."

"Highly unlikely."

"But not impossible," she said coaxingly.

He gave her a wry glance and realized for the first time that in her haste to rebutton her dress, she had put the top button through the wrong hole. The dress was skewed across her breasts. The edge of her lacy bra peeped out at him. He found the sight incredibly endearing.

"All right," Josh replied gently. "I'll concede it is not completely beyond the realm of possibility that some other screwy inventor thinks the Colonel is on to something and wants to see how the experiments are progressing or wants to destroy them. But, to be brutally frank, I'm still ranking that theory very low on my list."

She nodded. "Fair enough. In exchange, I'll agree to consider your vandalism theory."

"It's a deal," he murmured. There was a short, suddenly charged silence as the conversation on possibilities and theories came to an end. The expression in Maggie's eyes started to change.

Josh recognized the exact instant when it occurred to her that they were still alone together and the night wasn't over. Uneasiness and a deep, feminine shyness shimmered in her sea-green eyes.

The moment was lost and Josh knew it. He reminded himself that he had never intended to take things any further tonight, anyway, no matter how tempted. He smiled with what he hoped was reassurance. "Why don't you go on upstairs to bed, Maggie? I'll relock the window. Tomorrow I'll rig up something to keep it from being opened from the outside. We can talk about this in the morning."

Maggie hesitated and then nodded quickly. "Good night, Josh."

"Good night, Maggie."

He watched her dash back up the stairs and felt as

though she were taking a part of him with her. It was all he could do not to call her back.

But Josh knew he had to let her go tonight. She needed time. Besides, he told himself, the memory of Maggie shivering in his arms as she found her first real, exquisite release would be more than enough to warm his bed and his dreams tonight.

6

THE BEACH WAS shrouded in fog. On the horizon, the gray sea met the gray sky in such a seamless fashion that it was impossible to tell where one began and the other ended. Bundled up in a hooded down jacket, Maggie stood at the water's edge and tried to come to terms with the unsettling emotions that were churning inside her.

There was no getting around it. She was falling fast and hard for Joshua January. The realization simultaneously thrilled and terrified her. He was so different from every other man she had ever known. A part of her recognized something deep within him that mirrored a fundamental part of herself. She knew in her heart that Josh January was one of the good guys in a rough world.

And yet, for all her instinctive certainty about him, Maggie was forced to admit that there was a great deal she didn't know about Josh. She had always assumed the man she would someday love would be safe and comfortable. Josh was neither.

She should never have allowed him to kiss her and touch her the way she had last night. She was his employer, for heaven's sake. He was working for her. Where was her common sense? She ought to be keeping a strict, arm's-length distance between them. Things were complicated enough around Peregrine

Manor. She didn't need to add a potentially explosive affair with Josh to the brew.

But last night had been extraordinarily special, Maggie thought with a rush of joy. She had felt incredibly beautiful and passionate and free in Josh's arms. The exhilaration of the experience still hadn't faded entirely. If she closed her eyes, she could relive the glorious moment. Her body even began to respond to the memory.

"Hello, Maggie." Josh's deep, dark voice broke into the delicious spell that bound her. "I had a hunch I'd find you down here this morning."

She turned, with a tremulous smile on her lips, and watched as he emerged from the fog. He was wearing a shearling jacket over a pair of jeans. He had his hands buried in the warm pockets of the jacket and the fleece collar was turned up to protect his neck. He looked potently, vitally *male.* In some strange fashion his recent injuries only seemed to underscore the sensual danger the man projected.

"Hello, Josh." Maggie tried for the light, sparring tone that had characterized so much of their conversation till now. "I suppose you tracked me down to see about your home-cooked breakfast?"

He smiled. "Breakfast can wait. I wanted to talk to you, but you didn't come downstairs to the kitchen the way you usually do."

"I felt like a walk on the beach this morning."

Josh nodded. "Yeah. Me, too." He took his right hand out of the pocket of his jacket and held it out for her.

Maggie hesitated and then slipped her hand into his. His fingers curled warmly around her own. She couldn't think of anything to say as they started along the beach. It was one of the few times in her life that she had actually felt tongue-tied.

"It's okay, you know," Josh said after a bit.

She looked up quickly. "What is?"

"You don't have to be nervous, Maggie. I'm not going to pounce on you."

"I didn't think you were," she retorted.

"Yes, you did. But I told you last night I'll give you time, and I meant it."

She drew a deep breath. "I think it's only fair to tell you that I don't really want a brief affair with you or anyone else, Josh. I've never gone in for that sort of thing. I don't intend to start now. Not even with you."

"I know." He squeezed her hand gently. "I'm not into brief affairs or one-night stands, either. Messy and unsatisfying."

"So, what does that leave?" she asked carefully.

His mouth curved almost whimsically. "It leaves you and me and something else."

"Josh," she began in a little rush before she lost her nerve, "this probably isn't a good idea. You and me, that is. I mean, I am a client and you do work for me and I live out here on the coast and you live in Seattle and we're really very different people when you think about it—"

"Are we?"

"Well, yes," she said helplessly.

"I don't think so. I think we've got a lot in common. I knew it that first night. You just need time to realize it."

"Josh, please—"

"Have dinner with me tonight, Maggie."

"What?"

"Have dinner with me. In town. A real date."

"Oh."

He grinned fleetingly. "Is that an answer?"

"No."

"Is *that* an answer? Come on, Maggie. Take a chance."

She scowled. "All right, Josh. I'll have dinner with you. But you probably shouldn't read too much into it."

"You can't hold it against me if I look for a few clues. It's instinctive, you know? I'm a trained investigator."

She smiled unwillingly. "You're impossible, that's what you are."

"I'll be on my best behavior. After all, I am fully aware of the fact that I can be replaced at any moment by Clay O'Connor."

Maggie started to laugh. She couldn't help it.

"What's so damn funny?" Josh demanded.

"The thought of you selling real estate. It boggles the mind."

AT MIDMORNING A KNOCK on the kitchen door caused Maggie to put down the vegetables she had been peeling for soup. She peeked through the curtains and saw a familiar beat-up old pickup parked in the driveway behind the manor. She smiled as she opened the door for Dwight Wilcox, her faithful handyman.

"Hi, Dwight. How are you this morning?" Maggie wiped her hands on her apron.

Dwight ducked his head by way of greeting and gave her his customary morose expression. Maggie had never seen Dwight display any other emotion.

Today he appeared completely oblivious to the cold, driving rain that was pounding down around him.

He wasn't very old—perhaps twenty-five or twenty-six—but it was clear that Dwight had already found the world sadly wanting. Maggie sometimes wondered if he had ever, in his entire life, been happy.

Dwight was garbed in his handyman's uniform, which consisted of a peaked cap over his unkempt brown hair, a pair of twill pants and a shirt in a dull shade of green. He also had on his thick-soled boots and, as usual, he was chewing gum.

"Mornin'." Dwight was a no-nonsense speaker. Every word was clipped short and there were no extras. "On my way into town. Figured I'd see if you wanted that furnace checked. You said something about it the other day. I brung my tools." He hoisted the toolbox he was holding in his right hand.

"Great." Maggie stepped back to let him enter the kitchen. "I'm glad to see you. I don't want to take any chances on the heating system going down again. Not at this time of year."

Dwight nodded and tromped across the kitchen toward the door in the hall that opened to the basement steps. Maggie followed. She was unlocking the door when Josh appeared on the second-floor landing. He braced himself by putting both hands on the railing and looked over.

"What's going on down there?" he called easily.

Maggie looked up. "This is Dwight Wilcox, Josh. I told you about him. He takes care of things around here for us. He's going to service the furnace just to make certain it's running smoothly. Dwight, this is

Josh January. He's staying here at the manor for a few weeks."

Dwight squinted up at Josh from beneath the peak of his cap. "'Lo."

Josh nodded and started down the steps, limping only slightly. "I'll come down there with you, Wilcox. I know a thing or two about electric furnaces."

"That right?" Dwight looked skeptical.

"Enough to figure out where to put the lubrication oil in," Josh assured him blandly. "Besides, I need the break. I've been writing all morning."

"Josh is a writer," Maggie said quickly, just in case Dwight had not gotten the point. Dwight was very helpful when it came to mechanical matters, but it was difficult to tell how much he was taking in when one spoke to him. His eyes always reflected a sort of wary bafflement, as if everything going on around him was almost too complicated to comprehend. The only things Dwight Wilcox seemed to feel really comfortable with were his tools.

"Suit yourself." Dwight went down the steps to the basement.

Josh followed. "How's lunch coming?" he inquired as he went past Maggie.

"Don't worry about it. You aren't in any danger of immediate starvation."

"Just making sure I get everything that's coming to me."

"You were only promised breakfast, tea and dinner," she reminded him.

"Yeah, but I figure the little extra work I'm doing on the side around here should be properly rewarded."

"What extra work?" Then a suspicion took hold.

"Josh January," Maggie hissed, "if you're implying I should reimburse you for your talents as a...a..." Words failed her.

"Lover?" he supplied helpfully.

"I can think of more descriptive words."

"Such as?"

"Go on down those stairs before I decide to assist you," Maggie growled.

"Sure thing. By the way, I made reservations for us this evening at a place the Colonel recommended." Josh grinned and went on down the steps. He held on to the handrail, taking the weight off his left foot as much as possible.

Maggie stood in the doorway and watched both men for a while. Then she went back into the kitchen to finish the soup. She wondered why Josh had accompanied Dwight into the basement.

AT SEVEN O'CLOCK that evening Josh and Maggie were shown to their seats in a cozy little restaurant perched on the cliffs above the sea. Maggie glanced around expectantly. It was Saturday night and the place was crowded. The pleasant hum of dinner conversation mingled with the clink of dishes and glassware. The delightful smell of freshly broiled salmon drifted over from a nearby table.

As soon as their orders had been given to the waitress Josh leaned back with a satisfied look in his eyes. "It's a relief to get you out of that house, sweetheart. I hadn't realized until now what a dampening effect the Colonel and the others were having on our relationship. I have the feeling that if one of them catches me stepping over the line with you, I'm going to find myself facing a shotgun and a preacher."

Maggie knew she was blushing, but she tried to keep her tone light. "The Colonel and Odessa are a little old-fashioned. Shirley would be more tolerant, I imagine. Being a gangster's moll probably gives one a less rigid outlook on certain matters."

"Don't count on it. Shirley would be as tough on me as the other two." Josh sipped his wine. His eyes gleamed.

Maggie felt herself growing more flushed. She started fiddling with her salad fork. "Look, don't worry about it, okay? You're in no danger of a shotgun wedding just because of a little fooling around on a sofa last night."

"I wasn't fooling around, Maggie. I was very serious."

She frowned, not sure how to take that. It seemed safest to try another topic. "Josh, why did you go down into the basement to watch Dwight work this morning?"

He grinned wickedly. "Do I make you nervous, Maggie? Is that why you're changing the subject?"

"Yes. Now answer my question."

"Okay. You're the client." He sat forward and folded his arms on the white tablecloth. The humor vanished from his gaze. "I wanted to see if Wilcox showed any surprise when he discovered that your basement wasn't flooded."

Maggie's eyes widened. "You suspected Dwight might have been the one who crawled through the basement window last night?"

"It was a possibility. He's slender enough to fit through that window and he knows his way around tools. Furthermore, as your handyman, he's had plenty of access to the manor. He could have sabotaged things like the chimneys and the refrigerator."

"Yes, but *Dwight?*" Maggie started to laugh. "I'll bet he showed absolutely no reaction whatsoever down in that basement. Am I right?"

"Right. The guy never missed a beat. Didn't even blink."

"That's our Dwight. Sorry to screw up your theory, but you really can't tell anything from Dwight's face. He's worn that same expression—or rather, lack of it—since the day I met him. I don't think Dwight would have shown any emotion if he'd walked down those basement steps and found an alligator that had crawled up from the sewer."

"Is that so?" Josh looked thoughtful.

Maggie smiled. "Look, forget Dwight. There's no way he could be behind the kinds of things that have been happening at the manor. He has his talents, but, to be honest, I don't think he's capable of the sort of devious cleverness that it would take to plot an entire series of harassing incidents. And what possible motive could he have, even if he were smart enough to dream up such a scheme? What made you suspect him?"

"Maggie, let me explain something here. You're my client. By definition, that makes everyone else a suspect. That's how I work."

She stared at him in amazement. "*Everyone* else?"

"Everyone else," he confirmed.

"Come on, Josh. Even the Colonel and Odessa and Shirley?"

"Yeah. Even them." Josh took another sip of wine and turned his head to look out into the darkness.

"You can't be serious? What possible motive would my three tenants have?"

Josh swung his gaze back to hers, his eyes cold and intent. "You want some possibilities? I'll give you possibilities. We'll start with the Colonel. He's told everyone that he's a genius and that he's on the brink of perfecting a new and unlimited fuel for the world. What if, deep down, he knows his experiments are a joke and he's begun to fear he'll be found out?"

Maggie frowned. "You think he might be trying to destroy his own files before someone exposes him as a fraud?"

"A lot of the incidents you've described to me have originated in the basement of the manor where the Colonel keeps his papers. If he staged the destruction of his own files and made it look like the work of fuel-industry spies or malicious vandals, he could tell everyone that his experiments had been seriously set back, perhaps for years."

"You think the Colonel would risk destroying the manor just to protect his own illusions? I don't believe it," Maggie stated.

Josh smiled wryly. "That only goes to show how naive you are, Maggie."

"I am not naive. It's just that I've known the Colonel for years and I don't believe he would do anything potentially violent or harmful."

"He was a career military man," Josh reminded her gently. "He spent years studying and learning violent ways. For all we know, he was trained in sabotage. But if you don't like him for the bad guy, try Shirley."

"Shirley?"

"Uh-huh. She's been living with an illusion for

years. She thinks the great love of her life, Ricky 'The Wrecker' Ring, abandoned her because he thought she ratted on him. Believing that he left her because of that and not just because he found another girlfriend might be comforting for her. She might have gone over the edge mentally and decided to stage the incidents at the manor to convince her friends that Ricky still cares enough to seek vengeance."

"I see what you're saying. But I'm sorry, Josh. I don't buy that one, either."

He nodded obligingly. "Okay, try this one on for size. Odessa wants you to sell the manor but she knows that everyone else, including her lover, the Colonel wants to hang on to it."

"Her *lover?* The colonel?" Maggie was stunned. "But they're just good friends."

"You think people their age don't enjoy sex as much as everyone else? Trust me, Maggie, they're more than just good friends."

"But they have different bedrooms. They don't sleep together." Maggie was flustered.

"That generation still tends to be discreet. Especially in front of the younger generation."

"Yes, but—"

"Never mind. My point is that it's possible, because of her feelings for the Colonel, that Odessa doesn't want to openly encourage you to sell. But maybe because she realizes they'd be financially better off if you did, she's staging the incidents, hoping you'll eventually decide the manor's more trouble than it's worth."

Maggie groaned. "Now you're really clutching at straws, Mr. Private Investigator."

"I've got news for you, sweetheart. I've seen cases

where people have killed other people for far less cause than any of the three motives I've just given you."

Maggie studied him for a moment. "I can understand how the business you're in would have a tendency to turn a person extremely cynical," she said gently. "No wonder your eyes look so cold sometimes. You *are* well named, aren't you?"

His eyes narrowed. "The business I'm in hasn't made me cynical, Maggie. It's made me realistic. I've seen enough of human nature to know that it's unreliable, untrustworthy and capable of incredible cruelty and greed."

"So you formed your motto based on experience, is that it?"

He scowled at her. "What motto?"

"It Never Pays To Play Hero." Her mouth curved faintly. "Poor Josh. It must be a constant battle for you."

"What's a constant battle?"

"Trying not to play hero. Unfortunately for you, I have a hunch the role is a natural one."

"The hell it is," he shot back. "I abandoned it long ago."

"I'm not so sure about that." She leaned forward. "You gave motives for everyone else at the manor, but what about me?"

"I told you, you're the client," he growled.

"That doesn't make me innocent."

"I don't think you're behind the incidents, Maggie," Josh told her, sounding annoyed. "Let's change the subject."

"All right. If that's what you want. There's a little

something I've been wondering about all day," she said. "A professional question."

He gave her a hooded glance. "What's that?"

"Do you make love to all your female clients?"

"No, damn it. As a matter of fact, I have a strict policy against it. Extremely unprofessional. Getting emotionally involved with a client is about the stupidest thing a PI can do."

"I see." Maggie suddenly felt immensely more cheerful. Josh wasn't the kind of man who would break his own rules easily. The fact that he was breaking one of them with her warmed Maggie to her soul.

A MUTED MURMUR of voices from the study greeted Maggie and Josh when they walked back in the front door of the manor a few hours later. Josh swore softly but without any real heat.

"Hell. The television's on. Sounds like our three chaperons have waited up for us." He slipped Maggie's coat from her shoulders and hung it in the hall closet.

Laughter twinkled in her eyes. "How sweet. Just like you did the night Clay took me out to dinner. I don't know what I'd do without so many people looking out for my moral welfare."

Josh grinned ruefully. "We're just trying to keep you out of trouble, Maggie."

"I may have to sell the manor just to gain some privacy," she retorted as she started down the hall toward the study.

Josh followed, wondering exactly what she meant by that. Perhaps Maggie was telling him in her own obscure fashion that she wouldn't have minded coming home tonight and finding that her chaperons had all retired for the evening. That thought brightened his mood.

He watched Maggie come to a halt in the doorway of the study. She smiled at whatever she saw inside and turned to glance back over her shoulder. "The TV is on, but will you look at my three faithful guardians?"

Josh looked over her shoulder and saw that the Colonel, Odessa and Shirley were all sound asleep in front of the blaring television set. "So much for worrying about a shotgun wedding tonight."

"I told you not to panic about that."

"Yeah. You did." Josh went past Maggie into the study and switched off the television. Then he turned on the light. "All right, everyone, rise and shine."

"What's that? What's that?" The Colonel blinked and sat up. "Oh, it's you, January. Gave me a start."

Odessa stirred and opened her eyes. "Oh, dear. What time is it?" She smiled brightly at Maggie. "You're back. Did you have a good time, dear?"

"We had a lovely evening," Maggie assured her.

Shirley yawned and reached for her rhinestone-studded glasses. She put them on and peered closely at Josh. "'Bout time you two got home. Enjoy yourselves?"

"Had a great time right up until we walked in the front door a few minutes ago and realized you three had waited up for us." Josh lifted an eyebrow at Shirley. "It wasn't necessary. We're not exactly kids, you know."

Shirley harrumphed. "It was the Colonel's idea."

"I don't see what he was concerned about," Josh

said smoothly. "I'm being paid to look after Maggie, remember?"

"Yeah, well the Colonel said that was a bit like paying the fox to watch the henhouse." Shirley yawned again. "But I guess we've done our duty. I say we all go to bed."

"Good idea." Odessa got to her feet and pulled her sweater more tightly around her. "Seems a bit chilly in here, doesn't it?"

"I'll check the thermostat," the Colonel offered. "Come along, my dear." He nodded at Josh. "You two will be right up, I imagine, won't you?"

"I'm not sure," Josh said. "Haven't quite decided what I'm going to do for the rest of the evening. I was considering the possibility of staying down here and ravishing Maggie in front of the television."

Odessa smiled fondly. "No, do stop teasing everyone, Josh. It's time we were all in bed." She started toward the door, making it quite clear that she expected everyone else to follow.

Josh watched her lead the small parade toward the stairs. Then he glanced at Maggie. He saw the laughter in her gaze; and beneath the laughter, he was sure he saw the promise. He stifled a groan. It was tempting, but he really was getting too old to engage in a lot of hot-and-heavy petting on a downstairs sofa.

He reached out a hand, caught hold of Maggie's and tugged her close. Then he steered her after the others, who were already halfway up the stairs. He held her back a few steps. When she turned her head to look at him with a question in her eyes, he smiled faintly and leaned down to whisper in her ear.

"The next time we get close, it's going to be in a bed," he whispered. He had the satisfaction of seeing her blush very nicely. Unfortunately, her response only served to make him hungrier for her.

A moment later Josh said a painfully gallant goodnight to Maggie at her door under the discreetly watchful eyes of the Colonel, Odessa and Shirley. He saw her safely inside and then reluctantly went next door to his own room.

He closed the door behind himself, loosened his tie and eyed the computer sitting on the desk. It was clear he wasn't going to be able to sleep for a while. He would only succeed in thoroughly frustrating himself if he went to bed in his present, half-aroused condition.

The book was waiting.

So were a few questions that needed answering. And he was supposed to be doing a job around here. Josh glanced at his watch. It was nearly midnight, but McCray was something of a night owl.

Josh walked over to the phone and dialed his partner's home number. He sat down on the bed and propped his shoulders against the headboard.

The phone was answered on the other end at the first ring. "Yeah?" McCray sounded preoccupied.

"It's January."

"Not quite," McCray said. "My calendar says early December."

"McCray, when are you going to get tired of weather jokes?"

"Probably not as long as I've got a partner named January. Working a little late, aren't you?" McCray chuckled. "The doctor told you to take it easy. You're supposed to be getting lots of rest and relaxation. How are the ribs and the ankle?"

"Almost back to normal. How are things going at

the office?" Josh cradled the phone between his shoulder and his ear while he unfastened the cuffs of his white dress shirt.

"That's right. First things first. Ask about the office. You know, January, you don't lead a balanced life. That's your problem. It's time you had a wife and kids, like me. Something to bring you home at night."

"Just answer the question, okay? I'm not in the mood for one of your lectures."

"No sweat, pal. Fact is—and I know it will come as something of a shock to you—but we're managing to scrape along here without you quite nicely. Finished the analysis for Coswell, and we've got a new client who wants us to set up a security system for his electronics firm. What can I say? Business is booming."

"Glad to hear it. Listen, I've got a couple more questions for you."

"Want me to check out a few more aging gangsters?"

"Forget the gangsters." Josh stripped off his tie and tossed it over the back of the nearest chair. "Try a guy named Dwight Wilcox. He's apparently lived in Peregrine Point for a couple of years. He's the regular handyman here at the manor. I doubt you'll find anything, but it's worth a shot."

"Should be easy. I'll have Carol get on the computer for you tomorrow morning."

"Right. Phone me as soon as you've got the report."

"This case turning into something?" McCray sounded interested.

Josh thought of the water-pipe incident. "Looks

like it. Probably just a malicious-mischief situation. Any word on that Lucky, Inc. stock?"

"Company went bankrupt years ago. Looks like it was a scam from the beginning. The mine's a worthless pit."

"So much for any possibility that someone's after Mrs. Hawkins's stock," Josh mused. "I was fairly certain that was a dead end. Just wanted to check it out. By the way, McCray?"

"Yeah?"

"There are a couple of things I want you to put into the mail for me tomorrow morning."

McCray listened as Josh told him what he wanted. Then McCray howled with laughter. "You're kidding. You want me to put together a file on you? What the hell for?"

"Just do it, okay?"

"You got it. I'll have it in the mail tomorrow morning. Should reach you in a day or two. Mind telling me why you want to know your own credit rating, blood type and marital status?"

"None of your damn business, McCray."

"Wait a second. Let me guess. You've fallen for the client, haven't you? Ever since you told me she wasn't exactly elderly, I've been suspicious. Well, I'll be damned. You want some advice, January?"

"No."

McCray ignored him. "If I were you, I'd give her flowers rather than a file on yourself. Much more romantic, you know? I've been meaning to talk to you about the way you deal with women. I hate to hurt your feelings, pal, but the bottom line is that you're not all that good with them. You don't understand how they think. As evidence, I submit the fact that you spend far too much time working."

"McCray, I urge you to keep in mind that I am the senior partner at BIS."

"Yes, *sir*." McCray was still chortling as he hung up the phone.

Josh replaced the receiver and sat quietly for a long moment. Then he got up and shrugged out of his dress shirt. He took off his shoes and trousers and padded barefoot across the room to the closet. He found his jeans, stepped into them, then went over to his portable computer. He opened the case and locked the screen into the upright position. Then he sat down and went to work.

As had been happening more and more frequently of late, Josh was soon lost in the story he was creating. The mystery flowed for him in a way that real life never did. He was in the process of having his lead character, Adam Carlisle, walk into a trap while checking out a suspect, when the knock came on the door.

"Josh?"

The sound of Maggie's voice, soft and tentative, brought Josh back to the real world as nothing else could have done at that moment. *Something was wrong.*

He got to his feet and crossed the room in two long strides that sent only a few twinges through his left ankle. He yanked open the door and found Maggie on the other side. She was dressed for bed and wearing the quilted robe she had worn that first night. She looked nervous but determined.

"What's wrong?" Josh demanded, automatically glancing down the hall behind her. All was quiet.

"Nothing's wrong. I just, well, I was wondering if you'd like to kiss me good-night. That's all." She smiled tremulously and clasped the lapels of her robe more tightly together.

Relief poured through him and with it a shot of anger for the moment of alarm she had obliged him to endure.

"*Kiss you good-night?* Hell, lady, I thought something had happened. Don't ever do that to me again."

She winced and took a step back. "Look, if it's too much trouble, forget it. Damn, this is embarrassing. I was afraid it would be. I should have talked myself out of it." She gave him a bright, brittle little smile as she took another step back. "Sorry about this. I'll see you in the morning."

Josh scowled as Maggie turned and fairly leaped toward the door of her own room.

7

MAGGIE HAD HER HAND on the doorknob when Josh's fingers closed forcefully around her wrist.

"Hold it. Where do you think you're going?" His voice was very soft as he pulled her around to face him.

Her face aflame, Maggie turned reluctantly and saw that he was smiling now—a slow, sensually menacing smile that did wild and wicked things to Maggie's insides. The sight of him bare to the waist filled her with a pervasive longing. She wondered if she were actually melting somewhere deep in the pit of her stomach. The warmth was amazing.

"I didn't mean to scare you," she muttered, thoroughly embarrassed now, and wishing she hadn't given in to the impulse of a moment earlier.

"I was working." Josh tugged her closer. "When you knocked on the door my mind was on something else entirely and I overreacted. Ask me again."

She was very close to him now. The heat of his skin flooded her senses. She put her hands on his shoulders and luxuriated in the muscled strength she found there. "I can't ask you again. I used up all my nerve the first time."

His mouth curved as he tipped up her chin with his forefinger. "How about if I ask you?"

She smiled. "Okay."

"Will you kiss me good-night?"

"You really want me to?"

"I really want you to," he assured her.

She frowned worriedly. "You're not just saying that?"

"No."

"You're not just trying to make me feel less embarrassed?" she persisted.

"No."

"Because I wouldn't want you to do me any favors, you know. I mean, if you're not as interested in this as I am, just say so up front," she said firmly.

Josh swore softly. "At this rate we're going to waken the chaperons."

Obviously he just wanted her to get on with it, Maggie told herself. She took a deep breath, closed her eyes and stood on tiptoe. Then she raised her face to his.

Nothing happened.

"Josh?" She opened her eyes and found him studying her with laughter in his eyes.

"I'm waiting," he explained.

Annoyed, she braced herself with her hands on his shoulders and brushed her mouth quickly and rather awkwardly across his.

"You call that a kiss?" he asked with interest.

"It doesn't work if you don't cooperate," she muttered.

"Ah. So cooperation is what you want. Damn. You should have mentioned that earlier."

Before Maggie could think of resisting, he caught hold of her wrist and pulled her into his room. Then he shut the door and crowded her back against it. He loomed over her, his hands placed on either side of her head.

"Now, then, let's try this again." Josh brought his mouth very close to hers. "Kiss me."

Maggie swallowed a small, choked laugh that was part relief and part anxiety and put her arms around his neck. She gave herself up to the heat of his kiss with blissful enthusiasm. She could get addicted to Josh January's kisses, she thought. There was certainly nothing the least bit cold about the man in this department.

Josh moved in closer, sliding his bare foot between her slippered feet. She could feel the hard thrust of his leg all the way up the insides of her thighs. When he slipped his hand down her back and cupped her buttocks through the fabric of the robe, she sighed against his lips.

Her robe had parted and the movement of his leg caused her nightgown to ride up. With a thrilling shock, Maggie realized that she could feel the heat of his body burning hers. She clutched at him, feeling deliciously pagan.

"Maggie," Josh whispered thickly. "Maggie, sweetheart, you really want me, don't you?" He sounded dazed. "It took a lot of nerve for you to come here like this."

She turned her face into his shoulder. "Yes."

"It's okay, love. It's okay. Why are you shivering? It's all right. Everything's going to be all right. I want you, too. Very, very badly."

He swept her up into his arms and started toward the bed.

"*Josh.*" Maggie was horrified. "Your ribs. Your ankle. Put me down. You'll hurt yourself."

"We're not going far, Maggie. I think I can make it. Just remember to be gentle with me when we get there." There was sensual laughter in his voice as he carried her the few steps to the massive, canopied bed.

She studied him anxiously as he set her down on her feet and pulled back the covers. "You really shouldn't be lifting anything heavy in your condition. Are you sure you're all right?"

"You'll find out shortly, won't you?" Josh deftly loosened her fingers, which were clutching the edges of her robe again.

"Josh?"

He paused and looked into her eyes. "It's your choice, Maggie. If you'd rather wait, we'll wait. I'll understand. It's the way I had planned things in the first place. I don't want to rush you."

She took a breath and shook her head. "No. I don't want to wait."

"I'm glad," he said simply and slid the robe from her shoulders.

Maggie trembled when Josh started to lift the nightgown over her head.

"Relax, sweetheart. This is going to be very good. For both of us." Josh dropped the nightgown onto the floor and stood looking down at her. He plucked tenderly at first one budding nipple and then the other. "Don't be nervous."

"It's not that." She hugged herself, shielding her breasts from his inspection. "I'm cold. That's all."

"Then why don't you get under the covers?" Josh lifted the quilt, inviting her into the cozy warmth of the big bed. "I'll build a fire."

She tingled under the heat of his gaze as he

watched her scramble into bed. She pulled the sheet up to her chin. Maggie wanted to be nonchalant about it but she knew her swift dive for cover only betrayed her tension. She wasn't accustomed to having a man warm her naked body with his eyes alone, the way Josh had done.

Safely ensconced under the covers at last, she watched as Josh went over to the stone fireplace, knelt down on one knee and expertly lit the kindling beneath the logs. Flames crackled to life.

Josh stared into the fire as it began to burn. "You're beautiful, Maggie," he said at last without turning his head. "Did I tell you that?"

"No." She was curiously touched. The sincerity in his voice was bone-deep. Josh was not one to hand out compliments lightly. "Thank you."

Josh got to his feet. "I just wanted you to know. Someone told me once that I wasn't very good with women. I'm not romantic enough, or something."

Maggie swallowed heavily. "I think you're the most romantic thing that's ever happened to me."

Josh studied her for a moment and then he smiled slowly. "You mean that?"

"Yes."

"I'm glad." He flipped off the wall switch, plunging the room into intimate shadow. The light from the fire bathed the bed in a soft, golden glow.

Silhouetted in the firelight, Josh unfastened his jeans and peeled them off. His gaze never left Maggie as he kicked off the briefs he wore underneath and walked to the bed.

Maggie looked up at him, transfixed by the evidence of his arousal. *He wants me,* she thought. The knowledge filled her with sensual assurance and a glorious feeling of her own power as a woman. She stopped clutching the sheet and held the covers back.

"I only came here for a good-night kiss." Maggie smiled at Josh as he slid in beside her.

"It's going to be one hell of a kiss." He put his hand on her bare shoulder and stroked slowly down her side to her hip.

Everywhere he touched her, Josh's fingers burned her skin. The fire pulsed through her, sending her senses spinning with a restless, excited energy.

But then Maggie relaxed completely as Josh pulled her close. The last of her tension and lingering uncertainty vanished, to be replaced by a growing passion.

This was right, she thought as her head fell back across his arm. This was what she had been waiting for all her life. Josh was the hero of her dreams.

She gazed up at him from beneath her lashes as he leaned over her. With questing fingertips she explored the muscular curve of his shoulder and the strong planes of his chest. She loved the feel of him, loved the power and the strength of him.

Maggie kissed Josh's throat and heard him groan in response. Then his leg was sliding between her thighs again and this time there was no denim to get in the way.

"So beautiful," Josh muttered, his lips on Maggie's breast. "So full of heat. I need your fire to warm me. Sometimes I think I've been cold forever." His hand slid down over her stomach and then lower still. His fingers threaded through the tight curls. "Open for me, sweetheart. Take me into your warmth."

A knock on the door came just as Maggie started to part her legs for Josh's touch.

"January? You in there, man?" the Colonel called softly.

"Hell." Josh groaned and rested his forehead on the hollow of Maggie's shoulder. "I don't believe this. Say it isn't so."

Still disoriented from the riot of excitement and passion that was singing through her, Maggie cradled Josh's head in her hands and stared up at the canopy. She tried to figure out what was happening.

The Colonel rapped softly once more. "January? Still awake?"

"Josh?" Maggie threaded her fingers urgently through his dark hair. "It's the Colonel. He's at the door."

"No one could be this unlucky," Josh growled as he reluctantly raised his head. "Not even me." He rolled to the side of the bed, got out and grabbed his jeans. He raised his voice to call out softly. "Hang on, Colonel. I'll be right there."

Maggie felt the laughter well up in her at the sight of Josh's grim face. She struggled to conceal her amusement but Josh saw it. He glowered down at her and then leaned over the bed, trapping her between his arms.

"You," he ordered very, very quietly, "are not to move. And don't you dare make a single sound. Not one peep. Got that?"

"Yes, sir." She grinned up at him from the pillow and reached out to tug playfully on his chest hair. She was feeling very bold.

Josh stifled another groan and straightened. Then he caught hold of a fistful of quilt and yanked it up over Maggie, covering her from head to toe.

Maggie lay curled in the pleasant warmth and listened intently as Josh crossed the room and opened the door.

"What's wrong, Colonel?"

"Believe the furnace is down," the Colonel announced briskly. "It's been getting colder and colder. When I got up to reset the thermostat a second time, I realized it wasn't functioning. Thought we'd better have a look. Could be a malfunction, but the last time this happened, we suspected sabotage, if you'll recall. Couldn't prove it, but we all knew someone had monkeyed with the damn thing."

"It was working fine after Wilcox serviced it. I watched him myself."

"Well, something's gone haywire. I'm going downstairs to have a look. Thought you might want to come with me. No need to awaken the ladies. They'd only worry."

"Right. I'll come with you," Josh replied.

Maggie waited until the door had closed and she could hear the sound of footsteps on the stairs. Then she pushed back the covers and sat up in bed. Her amusement faded rapidly as she contemplated the possibility that another "incident" had occurred.

She slid to the edge of the big bed and got to her feet; she found her quilted robe on the floor and pulled it on quickly. She would follow the men downstairs and see what was happening. The Colonel would think she had been in her own room all along and had simply been awakened by the cold.

Maggie walked over to pull the fire screen in front of the blaze Josh had built and saw the glow of the computer monitor. It was facing the far wall, which was why she hadn't noticed it when she'd entered earlier.

Josh had obviously been working late on the case, she thought. She was touched by his dedication to the job. She was certainly getting her money's worth.

Curious, Maggie stepped closer to read the text on the screen. She had always wondered how real-life private investigators worked....

I went down the darkened corridor, pausing briefly at each door to read the sign outside. The office building had been closed for hours. The guard was a creature of habit and would be doing his rounds on the third floor now. I figured I had maybe thirty minutes before he got to the twelfth floor.

I found Stallings's suite at the end of the hall. A quick check of the lock revealed that getting inside would be easy. Maybe dead easy. A man like Stallings, who was getting ready to steal millions and was prepared to cover up his theft with murder, didn't use cheap hardware-store stuff like this. I stroked the little lock as carefully as if it were a woman.

It was simple. Nothing to it. All in the wrist, you know. No doubt about it, I could be inside in fifteen seconds, max. The damn thing was practically an open invitation.

The last time I'd accepted this kind of invitation, though, I'd almost gotten killed. But what the hell. I was born to be socially flexible.

I went to work on the lock. I was wrong. It only took twelve seconds to open it. I spent the time wondering why Stallings was making it so easy for me to get into his private office.

Maggie sat down and stared at the screen, stunned by what she was reading. It looked as if Josh was writing a book!

Her work as a librarian had made her very familiar with computers. She frowned down at the keyboard and found the key that enable her to scroll through the text on the screen. She made her way back through the story until she found a chapter heading. It *was* a book. A mystery novel, from the looks of it.

She had been cheated! She hadn't gotten herself a private investigator—she had gotten a writer. No wonder Josh spent so much time up here in his room. His *free* room. And no wonder he was so insistent on having his home-cooked meals and his tea and scones. Unpublished writers were notorious mooches—always down-and-out and looking for a handout. Josh probably thought he'd landed in clover when he'd talked his way into this cushy job.

Maggie jumped to her feet, outraged by the way she'd been taken in. Josh wasn't even a published mystery writer, she reminded herself grimly. If he were, she would have heard of him. She'd read hundreds of mysteries.

She glanced around the room, her eyes narrowing. It was time she found out just what sort of man she was dealing with, she decided. She stalked over to the dressing table and started jerking open the drawers.

A collection of socks and briefs had been neatly arranged in the top drawer. There was nothing in the other two. Maggie stomped into the bathroom and surveyed the array of shaving gear on the counter.

She headed for the wardrobe next and flung open the doors to reveal several shirts, his one good-quality jacket, and a tie. The two suitcases she had laboriously brought up the stairs that first night were stacked on the floor. Maggie knelt down and pulled them out. They were both unlocked and empty.

Disgusted with the lack of clues as to Josh's true identity, Maggie closed the closet doors and considered the rest of the small room. Her gaze fell on the nightstand beside the bed.

She walked over and jerked open the drawer of the little table. A blush rose furiously in her cheeks when she saw a little foil packet lying inside next to a pen and notepad. The man obviously believed in being prepared. He'd probably been a Boy Scout. She slammed the drawer hurriedly and went back to the computer.

Slowly she sat down in front of the screen again and began to read.

"DAMN." Josh crouched in front of the furnace's guts, which had been revealed when he'd removed the access panel. He teased one wire out from the nest of control wiring and examined the neatly severed end. "Look at that sucker. Someone sliced right through it."

"Sabotage," the Colonel muttered. "I knew it."

Josh nodded. "Sure looks that way. No telling when it was cut, but it must have been done recently. Probably while Maggie and I were at dinner."

"You think someone got in while Odessa and Shirley and I were watching television?"

"It's possible." Josh remembered how he and Maggie had found all three asleep in front of the droning television set.

"Our hearing isn't what it used to be," the Colonel

admitted. "And we had the television on loud. Someone could have gotten in here and cut that wire without us hearing him, I suppose."

Josh put his left hand on the furnace housing and levered himself to his feet. He wished he'd thrown on a shirt before leaving the bedroom. The basement was cold. "The windows are both closed," he observed as he crossed the room to look up at them. "Closed and locked."

"What do you think is going on here, January? You're the expert."

"I think," said Josh, "that I'd better splice that cut wire so we can get some heat going in this place. The whole house will be freezing in another hour or so. Tomorrow morning I'll take a look around outside and see if I can find the point of entry."

The Colonel nodded, looking suitably impressed. "Right. What about the ladies?"

Josh shot him a sidelong glance, wondering if the Colonel had any notion of where Maggie was at that moment. He didn't want her embarrassed in front of her three old-fashioned tenants. "We'll tell them everything in the morning. Like you said, there's no sense worrying them tonight."

"Fine. I'll go on back to bed, then. Unless you need any help with that wiring."

"No, it's just a simple splicing job. I can handle it. I've had a fair amount of experience with this kind of thing." Josh hunkered down in front of the exposed wiring.

"I suppose you use a lot of electronic equipment in your line of work, don't you?" the Colonel remarked, apparently pleased at the notion.

"Yeah, and you can't go calling in a service technician every time something goes wrong on the job. You learn to make do." Josh used his pocketknife to strip the insulation back on the severed wire.

"Thought so. Well, then, see you at breakfast."

"Right." Josh relaxed as he realized the Colonel was oblivious to Maggie's present location. He concentrated on the task of splicing the control wire as the older man went back up the stairs.

A few minutes later Josh replaced the access panel, dusted his hands and took a last look around the basement. The ground-level windows were definitely locked and they could not have been relocked from the outside—not after the way he had rigged them this morning. That meant whoever had sabotaged the furnace must have entered the basement through the doorway at the top of the stairs.

Which meant that the intruder had let himself into the main part of the manor through a door or window upstairs while three of the residents were at home. It was the first time, as far as Josh could tell, that the vandal had taken such a daring risk. The bastard had walked straight down the front hall, as if he owned the place.

Josh frowned as he climbed the stairs to the first floor. He didn't like the idea that whoever was staging the "incidents" was apparently getting bolder. It was a sign that the sabotage and vandalism might soon grow more menacing. At the rate things were going, someone would eventually get hurt.

He had to put a stop to this now, before it got out of hand, Josh decided. He had hoped his presence in the house would discourage whoever was behind the incidents, but clearly that was not the case. And now the guy was getting desperate. Desperate men did dangerous things.

Josh walked through every room on the first floor, checking locks. Every window and door was securely fastened. *An inside job?* Josh wondered as he went up the stairs to his room. He thought of the list of suspects and motives he had given Maggie over dinner.

He doubted that Odessa or Shirley would have known how to disable the furnace. On the other hand, it didn't take a lot of mechanical aptitude to figure out that cutting a wire would cause trouble. But then, there was the water-pipe incident. Someone had definitely entered the house from outside to pull that one off. Or had someone inside merely wanted it to look that way?

Possibilities and motives clicked rapidly through Josh's brain as he reached the top of the stairs and opened the door of his room. The first thing he saw was Maggie sitting in front of the computer. The eerie blue glow of the screen bathed her face in a cold light. She looked up as he entered the room.

Josh saw the suspicion and anger in her gaze and his stomach clenched with despair. What a fool he had been! He'd forgotten all about the computer and the book when Maggie had come knocking on his door asking him to kiss her good-night. And now he was going to pay the price of his stupidity.

"Maggie, honey." Josh closed the door very softly and stood there, trying to think clearly. His brain, which had been in overdrive a minute earlier, suddenly seemed to have turned to cobwebs. He had to explain this, he told himself desperately. He had to make her understand. He took a deep breath and tried again. "I know you must be wondering about what you're seeing there on that screen."

She leaned back in the chair, crossed her legs under her robe and folded her arms. She gave him a disdainful look. "I suppose you're going to tell me that since you're posing as a writer, you wanted to have some props around in case anyone came snooping. I suppose you think I'll believe that you just selected some mystery novel at random and typed up a few chapters so anyone who came in here would believe you really are a writer."

Josh watched her carefully, aware that he wasn't quite certain of her mood. He felt as if he were walking on eggs. "I wrote that myself," he admitted.

"I know." She shot to her feet and strode over to the window. Her arms were still folded across her chest and her chin was tilted at a proud, defiant angle. "As soon as I'd read a few pages, I was sure of it."

"Maggie, I know what you're thinking."

"Do you?"

"Yes. You think you've been ripped off. That you ordered up a private investigator and got a con artist, instead."

"And did I?"

"No, damn it." Josh hooked his thumbs in the waistband of his jeans and braced his feet. He felt as if he were getting ready for battle—one of the most important of his life. The stakes, he suddenly realized, were higher than he had ever dreamed they could be. But then, he'd never wanted a woman the way he wanted Maggie Gladstone. "Give me a chance to explain, Maggie. You owe me that much."

She stood with her back to him and stared out the window. "Are you really Josh January?"

"Hell, yes. I told you to call that number I gave

you, remember? I told you that if you had any questions, my partner would answer them. And send you the proof."

"You're a genuine private investigator? Owner of Business Intelligence and Security?"

"Yes, damn it. I can show you my license. Listen, Maggie, this isn't what it seems. I'm doing what you hired me to do. I swear it." Josh felt desperate. He, of all people, knew you couldn't trust a man's word or any piece of paper he showed you unless you knew him very well. He could hardly expect Maggie to believe him. She had only known him a few days.

"Are you quite certain you aren't some aspiring writer, a friend of the real Josh January, perhaps? Maybe the real January had no more intention of taking me on as a client than any of the other investigators I contacted."

"I am the real Josh January."

Maggie ignored him. "Maybe not. Maybe you're just his friend. Maybe, because of that and because you're trying to write a mystery, he figured you could fake it out here for a month. After all, how hard can it be to pull the wool over the eyes of three aging retirees and one naive innkeeper?"

"Maggie, I'm telling you—"

She nodded thoughtfully. "I can see where it would have sounded like a neat arrangement. You're recovering from an accident. You've got some time on your hands and you want to write a book. What a deal! You get a free vacation and an opportunity to work on your manuscript. In addition, you even get to play private eye for real, for a few weeks. What fun."

"Damn it, Maggie."

"And, just to top things off in the fun-and-games department, you decide to seduce the client. Is this how you big-city guys amuse yourselves?"

That did it. Josh stormed across the room, moving so quickly that he got a sharp warning twinge from his left foot. It was painful enough to make him wince, but he paid no attention to it. He had more important things on his mind.

When he reached Maggie, he put his hands on her shoulders and spun her around to face him. "I *am* the real Josh January," he said through clenched teeth. "I am the senior partner in BIS. I am investigating this case for you. *And I also happen to be trying to write a book.* I give you my personal guarantee that you are not getting stiffed. I'll find out whoever is behind these incidents. And I will find him real soon."

"I'm getting what I'm paying for, is that it?"

"Yes, damn it. That's it. I'll admit I accepted this job initially because I was recovering from an accident. My doctor and partner talked me into getting away for a while. To be honest, this case looked like a cinch. I figured I could solve it for you within a month and at the same time do some work on my book."

"What about the big seduction scenes?"

He groaned. "Sweetheart, you're the first client I've ever tried to seduce. And so far, I haven't had much success, I might add. Maggie, our relationship has nothing to do with the case. I give you my word of honor."

"You really do like me a little?"

He was shocked to see that she was smiling now. He could hardly believe his eyes. "Maggie, it's a lot more than 'like.' I promise. I want you very much.

I've never met anyone I've wanted as much as I want you. Please believe me."

"Hmm."

He flexed his hands on her shoulders, willing her to give him a chance. "Look, honey, I can't give you any proof tonight. I don't expect you to take my word for everything. All I ask is that you wait until you can verify what I'm saying before you make any decisions."

"I suppose we could do it that way," she agreed slowly.

Hope rose in him. "Tomorrow morning you can call that number I gave you or you can wait a day or two and I'll have something to show you. Something that will prove I am who I say I am."

"Proof. That's all you can think about." Maggie wrinkled her nose in exasperation. "Oh, never mind, Josh. I believe you."

"You do?" He stared at her, dumbfounded. "Without proof?"

"Forget the proof. Nobody would make up a ridiculous story like the one you just gave me." Maggie ducked out from under his hands and took two steps to the bed. She hopped up on the step and sat down on the edge of the thick mattress. "So, are you coming to bed or not?"

"*Maggie.*" He couldn't believe it. She was smiling at him in feminine welcome. She was willing to take his word for everything he had just said. Josh took a hesitant step closer to the bed. "Do you mean it? You want to spend the night here in my bed?"

She laughed softly. "The thing about you, Josh, is that you're exactly like that Adam Carlisle person in your book: You're one of the good guys."

8

THE INSTANT Josh entered her he felt as if he had found a part of himself that he hadn't even realized was missing. Maggie's welcoming feminine heat consumed him and made him feel complete. For a split second of startling clarity, Josh recognized what was happening. *She's mine now*, he thought as her body tightened around him. *She was meant for me.*

In the next instant the crystal-clear understanding vanished amid the excitement that was sweeping over him. Sheer, glorious physical sensation took over. She felt so good...better than anything he had ever known. His thoughts were scattered as the intense, primal reality of their lovemaking swamped his senses. But the feeling of need and possessiveness remained lodged deep in his mind, even as Josh gave himself up to the sweet pleasure of the moment.

He was fiercely aware of Maggie's arms wrapped tightly around him as he surged deeply into her. He felt the tiny bite of her nails as they sank into his shoulders. He drank the small, soft cries from her lips as she surrendered to the passion they were sharing.

"Put your legs around me, sweetheart," he managed as he sensed her body begin to tense.

She did as he said, locking her legs around his hips, offering the very core of herself to him. Josh groaned as he felt himself slide a little farther into her.

"So deep," he muttered against her mouth. "I'm so far inside you, I feel as if I'm a part of you."

"You are," she said simply. Then her head moved restlessly against the pillow. "Oh, *Josh*."

"Yes, love. Now. That's it. Let it happen *now*. I can't hold it any longer. *Yes!*" He drove into her one last time as he felt the first delicate ripples of her release.

The sensation was unbelievably erotic. She was literally caressing him in the most intimate manner possible. Josh's body threatened to explode and then it did explode. He captured Maggie's mouth with his own to drown his own hoarse shout of satisfaction as she breathed her exquisite cry of completion.

When it was over, Josh pulled her close and curled her body into his own. She fell asleep beside him, her relaxed body evidence of her trust.

Josh lay quietly for a long time. He stared up at the shadowed canopy and tried to comprehend what was happening to him. He felt different somehow. Something important in his world had changed. Maggie was at the heart of that change. She was very precious.

He would protect her, Josh told himself. At all costs, he would shield her and care for her.

He finally fell asleep himself on that thought.

MAGGIE AWAKENED feeling vaguely disoriented. She stretched languidly, wondering why the bed felt different. When her toe came in contact with a masculine leg, she froze in shock. And then memory came flooding back.

Josh had made love to her last night.

And it had been wonderful. The most wonderful experience of her life.

Maggie snuggled into the unfamiliar masculine warmth. Josh's arm curled around her, his hand coming to rest on her breast.

"Josh?"

"Yeah?" He sounded half asleep.

"Josh, are you awake?"

"No." He tightened his hold on her and his thumb began to glide slowly across her nipple. "Don't bother me. I'm dreaming."

"Well, in that case..." Smiling to herself, Maggie let her hand drift down across his broad chest. Her fingertips reached the tangled thatch of dark hair below his flat belly and she tugged gently.

"You're playing with fire, lady." Josh nibbled on her shoulder.

"Promises, promises. I— Oh, my goodness." Her fingers were suddenly filled with the heavy, thrusting warmth of him. "I *am* playing with fire, aren't I?"

"Told you so."

"I think I could get to like this game."

"You obviously have an aptitude for it. Maybe it's time I demonstrate a few of the finer nuances." Lazily, Josh stirred and started to inch his way down her body. His mouth was on her breast and he had one leg between her thighs when he abruptly stilled.

"Josh? What's wrong?"

"Damn." Josh raised his head and sat up, shoving aside the covers. He glanced at the clock beside the bed. "It's six-thirty."

"So what? We were up late last night." She reached for him, urging him back to bed.

His eyes narrowed as he looked down at her. "So the Colonel, Odessa and Shirley will all be getting up soon. The last thing I want is for you to run into one of them out in the hall on your way back to your own room."

"Don't worry about it, Josh." She smiled coaxingly up at him. "I'll be careful."

"Darn right, you're going to be careful. You're going to hop straight out of that bed, put on your robe and get your little tush back to your own room."

Maggie sat up slowly, a little surprised by his tone. She wrapped her arms around updrawn knees and tilted her head to one side to study him. "Are you really that concerned about the Colonel and the others finding out we spent the night together?"

"It would be embarrassing for you and for them." Josh got out of bed. He reached down to tug back the covers.

When he did so, Maggie was left sitting stark naked in the center of the white sheet. She smiled brilliantly up at him. "I think I can handle any embarrassment that I might experience."

Josh stared down at her, his eyes warm as he took in the sexy, inviting picture she made. "Well, you're not going to handle it as long as I have anything to say about it. It's my job to protect you, remember? Let's go, Maggie."

"I'm not a kid, Josh."

"Yeah. Well, you're not exactly an experienced woman of the world, either." He jerked on his jeans.

"I think I resent that remark. May I remind you that I was the one who took the initiative last night?" She fixed him with a proud grin. "If we'd waited for you to make a move I'd still be alone in my own room."

"We'll argue about who takes the initiative in this relationship some other time." He reached down to catch hold of her wrist and yanked her gently up off the bed. Maggie sighed and gave up the battle. She stood meekly while Josh tossed her nightgown over her head and fastened her robe.

"Are you always this grouchy in the mornings?" she asked as he tugged her toward the door.

"It varies." He turned, his hand on the doorknob, and kissed her soundly. "Sometimes I'm in a really terrific mood. Unfortunately, this morning isn't one of those days."

"Just my bad luck, I suppose."

"Right." He opened the door and gave her a little shove that sent her out into the hall.

The first person Maggie saw there was Odessa. The older woman was poised at the top of the stairs, preparing to descend. She was gazing straight at Josh's door as it opened.

"Good morning, dear," Odessa called in a cheery tone. She looked totally unfazed by the sight of Maggie emerging from Josh's room. "Sleep well?"

Maggie heard Josh groan on the other side of the door. In spite of her bold words to him a moment earlier, she felt herself blushing. She tried to plaster a nonchalant smile on her face.

"Good morning, Odessa. I slept quite well, thank you." The thing to do, Maggie decided, was to act as if nothing out of the ordinary was occurring. "How about you?"

"I got quite chilled in the middle of the night. The Colonel must have set the thermostat too low. But it's warm and cozy this morning, isn't it? And how is Josh today?"

"Josh," said Josh, emerging from the bedroom with a grimly determined expression, "is just fine this morning."

Odessa started to say something else but before she could speak, Shirley's door opened.

"Hi, everyone." Shirley pushed her rhinestone-studded glasses firmly onto her nose. She beamed at Maggie and Josh. "So you two have decided to take the big step, eh? Congratulations. Knew it was just a matter of time. We'll have to have an engagement party, won't we, Odessa?"

"*Engagement party?*" Maggie felt her stomach turn over. Behind her she was aware of Josh lounging in the doorway.

"Of course," Odessa responded. "I'm sure we have some champagne left down in the basement." She turned as the Colonel appeared from his bedroom. "Don't we have some champagne left, Colonel?"

"I expect we do. What are we celebrating?" The Colonel looked down the length of the hall and saw Maggie silhouetted in Josh's bedroom doorway. He gave a great start of surprise. "Ah. I think I get the picture now. I take it we have something important to announce here?"

"Don't they make a darling couple?" Shirley asked with a fond look. "Reminds me of my early days with Ricky."

"You know, dear," Odessa said lightly to Maggie, "I hate to say I told you so, but I did tell you that I thought you and Josh were made for each other. Didn't I say that, Colonel?"

The Colonel nodded, his eyes on Josh. "I believe you did say that, my dear."

Odessa smiled again. "And here they are engaged already. I think it's just lovely."

Maggie's initial embarrassment was giving way to a sense of panic. She realized she'd been waiting for Josh to take control of the situation, but he was making no move to do so. A quick sidelong glance out of the corner of her eye revealed that he was just hanging out there in the doorway, one shoulder propped against the wall, his arms folded across his chest. She wanted to yell at him, order him to stop the teasing before it got out of hand. But evidently he wasn't going to do a darn thing.

"All right," Maggie said, trying for an indulgent little laugh. "You've all had your fun. I think this has gone far enough. No more jokes, all right? It's too early in the morning for this kind of humor."

"Who's joking?" Shirley asked with perfect innocence. "We're all happy for you, honey. It's time you found yourself a real man. Nothing against that nice Clay O'Connor, mind you, but anyone could tell he wasn't for you."

The Colonel gave Josh a steely look. "Set a date yet?"

"No," replied Josh in an astonishingly calm voice. "But we'll get around to it one of these days."

The Colonel nodded again, looking satisfied. "Well, then, congratulations to you both. We'll see you at breakfast. Take your time. We can get things going without you for one morning. I used to make a fair cup of coffee in my military days. My fellow officers told me you could float horseshoes in it." He held out his arms to Shirley and Odessa. "Shall we go, ladies?"

"Yes, indeed." Odessa took his right arm. "I'm famished."

"So am I." Shirley took the Colonel's other arm with a flourish. Then she gave Maggie a teasing grin. "And I expect you two have worked up quite an appetite yourselves. See you in a few minutes."

Maggie stood rooted to the floor until her three tenants had vanished from sight. Then she whirled around to confront Josh. He cocked a brow when she pinned him with a frosty glare.

"Just what in the world do you think you're doing?" Maggie hissed. "They think we're engaged!"

"Yeah, I got that impression."

"Well, why did you let them *get* that impression?" she retorted. "Why didn't you say something? Why didn't you try to explain?"

"And just how the hell was I supposed to explain the fact that you were coming out of my room at six-thirty in the morning wearing your nightgown?"

"You didn't have to go along with the notion that we're engaged," Maggie wailed softly. She was feeling trapped. "Why are you standing there like a bump on a log? Doesn't this bother you just a teensy bit? Aren't you the least bit concerned by the fact that those three believe we're halfway to the altar?"

"What should I have said?" Josh asked softly. "Should I have told them I spent the night with you but my intentions weren't honorable? That would have been a little hard for them to handle, Maggie. They're from a different generation, remember."

"Since when do you worry about other people's approval?" Maggie's eyes widened as a thought struck her. "Josh, you're not really afraid of a shotgun wedding, are you? I know you joked about it, but you can't possibly think the Colonel would try anything like that. Not in this day and age."

Josh glanced down at his folded arms and then back up to meet her anxious gaze. His own gray eyes had gone cold and unreadable. "Maybe I didn't feel like upsetting everyone, Maggie. I'm supposed to be doing a job here, remember? There's a little matter of professionalism involved. Lord knows my behavior has already crossed the line. I should never have let you into my room last night. But what's done is done, and I'd just as soon be able to complete this job without getting everyone hostile. It would complicate matters a whole lot. I need cooperation to solve this case."

Maggie felt as though he had struck her. She instinctively retreated a step as she realized just what he was saying. "You're allowing them to think we're engaged just so you can complete this case?"

He frowned. "It's the best way. Maggie, I think I can wrap things up here in a few more days. I've got a couple of hunches I want to check out, and then I'm going to see about setting a trap for whoever is behind the incidents here at the manor."

"I see." Maggie swallowed heavily. Josh would be leaving in a few days.

"In the meantime, I don't want to muddy the waters any more than I already have. I can't afford to send out any alarm signals to the person who's causing the trouble here. We've got to make everything look as normal as possible around the manor. Frankly, this isn't the worst thing that could have happened."

"It's not?"

Josh thought. "No. In fact, the more I think about it, the more I believe this just might be the right move."

"I don't understand." Maggie's mouth felt dry now. She wondered with horror if she were about to burst into tears.

"Yeah, I think this unfortunate little misunderstanding is going to work to our benefit," Josh stated. "Don't you see, Maggie? It's the perfect cover for the trap I'm going to set."

Maggie gazed at him, feeling sick. "I don't understand."

Josh straightened in the doorway and started back into his own room. "Don't worry about it, sweetheart. I'll explain the details later. In the meantime, just go alone with the engagement story, okay? I want everyone to believe it, including the Colonel, Odessa and Shirley."

"But, Josh—" Maggie broke off when Josh gently closed the door in her face.

She stood staring blankly at the door for a full minute before whirling around and dashing into her own bedroom. She would not cry, she vowed as she stripped off her robe and jerked off her nightgown. She hurled the nightclothes onto the bed as she strode toward the small bathroom. *She would not cry.*

But Josh's words about the "unfortunate misunderstanding" being a useful cover story proved too much for Maggie's bruised feelings. What had she expected? she asked herself forlornly. Of course, the man wasn't going to allow himself to be pushed into a real engagement. Nobody was *that* honorable, these days. In any case, the last thing she wanted to do was try to force him into doing "the right thing."

When she stepped under the shower, Maggie's tears mingled with the spray of the water. It wasn't until she'd actually started to cry that she admitted to herself what had really happened to her during the past few days.

She had fallen in love with Josh January.

THE KITCHEN PHONE RANG just as Josh and the Colonel were telling everyone about the mysterious severed wire inside the furnace. Maggie jumped up to answer it. She plucked the receiver off the wall.

"Hello?"

"Josh January, please," said a crisp, male voice on the other end of the line.

"Just a moment." Maggie put her hand over the receiver and looked at Josh. "It's for you."

"Right." He got to his feet and took the phone out of her hand. "Yeah? Oh, it's you, McCray. No, you didn't interrupt anything except breakfast. Just give me what you've got and stop trying to get cute." There was a short pause. Josh's expression turned into a scowl. "McCray, that is not funny. None of your cold jokes are funny. When are you going to get that through your thick head? Just tell me what you've got on Wilcox."

Maggie and the others stopped talking at the mention of Dwight Wilcox's name. The Colonel assumed his pondering expression and Odessa looked disapproving. Shirley's eyes widened in fascination.

"He's investigating Dwight?" Odessa asked Maggie.

"I guess so." Maggie went back to her grapefruit. She was not in a chatty mood.

"Wilcox does know his way around our basement," the Colonel observed softly. "And he also knows how to handle tools."

"I don't know," Shirley murmured. "Somehow I can't picture that Dwight planning all those crazy incidents. My Ricky always used to say that it took real brains to be a successful criminal. The dumb ones got caught early."

Josh ignored the commentary going on around the breakfast table. He had taken a notepad out of a nearby kitchen drawer and was busily scribbling down information.

"Okay, McCray. It's not much, but it's information. Check something else for me this afternoon, will you? See if Johnny has the time to do some background work on the manor itself, will you? No, I don't know what I'm looking for at this point." Josh slid a glance across the four rapt faces around the table. "Old legends involving money or treasure… anything of interest. Yeah, right. That kind of thing. Call me back when you've got something. Take it easy."

"Well?" Maggie gave Josh a challenging look as he came back to the table and sat down. "What did that McCray person find out about Dwight?"

"Not much." Josh glanced down at the page on which he had written his notes. "Wilcox was in some trouble with the law a few years ago."

Shirley stared at him. "Our Dwight is a crook?"

"Not much of one, by all accounts." Josh tore out the sheet of paper, folded it in half and stuck it into his pocket. "He got picked up on a robbery charge. Did eighteen months. He's been clean ever since."

"Robbery?" Maggie put down her grapefruit spoon. "Are you sure?"

Josh nodded. "At this point it doesn't mean much. He was just a kid at the time and he didn't get away with it."

"Not surprising," Shirley muttered. "Told you he wasn't all that bright."

"Still, it may mean the young man has criminal tendencies," Odessa observed. She frowned at Maggie. "Perhaps we shouldn't have him do any more work around here, dear."

"Who else are we going to get?" Maggie picked up a piece of toast. "It's not like Peregrine Point is full of handymen."

"Nevertheless, perhaps we should start advertising for someone else," Odessa stated.

Maggie put down her toast. "Aunt Agatha hired him, didn't she?"

The Colonel nodded solemnly. "That's right. About two years ago. Shortly after he moved to town. She was always quite satisfied with his work."

Josh held up a hand. "Look, there's no point discussing what you're going to do about Dwight Wilcox right now. I don't want Maggie making any changes in the way things are run around here yet. It would alert whoever is behind the incidents that we suspect they are more than just incidents."

The Colonel nodded again. "Quite right, January. We must all continue to give the impression that we think we've suffered from nothing more than bad luck around here."

"Bad luck is right." Maggie got to her feet and

started toward the sink. She thought about the horrendous dose of bad luck she had experienced earlier that morning when she'd walked out of Josh's room and ran straight into Odessa. "There certainly has been a lot of it around here lately, hasn't there?"

"Nothing we can't handle," Josh responded dryly.

THAT AFTERNOON Maggie found herself sitting beside Josh in his black Toyota. She hadn't asked for an escort into town. Indeed, she had done her level best to try to talk Josh out of accompanying her. But he had been in one of his insistent moods. Maggie was learning that when Josh decided to do something, it was extremely difficult to deflect him from his chosen course.

"I don't need help picking up the groceries, Josh. I could have handled the shopping on my own." Maggie stared out the window at the gray ocean. A new storm was coming in fast. She could see the rain sweeping over the sea. It would hit land in another half hour.

"No problem." Josh's hands were relaxed and competent on the wheel of the Toyota. "I need to pick up a few personal items myself."

"I could have bought shaving cream or blades for you," she muttered.

"Yeah, but I felt like the outing." Josh slanted her a glance. "How come you're sulking today?"

"I am not sulking."

"Bull. You've been in this mood since you ran into Odessa and the others outside my room this morning. Hey, you're not still worried about our phony engagement, are you?"

"What if I am?"

"Maggie, I've told you, everything's going to work out just fine. Leave it to me, okay?"

"I left it to you and look what happened." Maggie turned her head to glower at him. "This is all your fault, Josh. Some private investigator, you are. You could have at least checked to see that the coast was clear this morning before you shoved me out the door. But, oh, no. You couldn't wait to get me out of your bedroom."

"You really are mad, aren't you?" Josh threw her a surprised look.

"Yes, I am. I do not like this, Josh. I do not like any of it."

"Take it easy, Maggie. In a few days, I'll have this thing sorted out."

"Oh, that's just ducky. Then what happens? What am I supposed to tell the Colonel and Odessa and Shirley when you leave town?" Maggie wailed. "They'll think I've been abandoned. They'll feel sorry for me."

Josh studied the road ahead. "Tell them you changed your mind and decided to call off the engagement. They'll understand."

"They will not understand. They'll think that what happened between you and me was nothing more than a one-night stand, and they'll be right."

"So don't call off the engagement."

She stared at him in disbelief. "Are you crazy? What am I supposed to do after you leave? Pretend we're still engaged? How do you expect me to carry that off?"

"I'd be willing to help," Josh said quietly. "We can string our engagement out for a few months and then say we've changed our minds."

"Oh, sure. And just how are we going to string out our engagement when you're in Seattle and I'm here in Peregrine Point?"

"I could come out for a while on the weekends. You could come into the city. Let's be honest here, Maggie. We're attracted to each other. Last night was very good. You know that as well as I do. Why shouldn't we go on seeing each other?"

Maggie closed her eyes. "I wish you would stop being so damn reasonable about the whole thing. You're missing the point here. Don't you understand what I'm trying to say? I don't want a fake engagement."

"Not even for the sake of solving this case?" Josh asked.

Maggie groaned and turned her attention back to the heavy gray rain that was moving in from the sea. "I feel trapped," she whispered.

"Don't worry about it," Josh said lightly. "You've got me around to rescue you, remember? I'll figure something out."

"You're the one who's always saying that it never pays to play hero."

"I'm not playing hero this time. I got you into the engagement. I'll find a way to get you out of it without embarrassing you any more than you already are."

"I'm not embarrassed," Maggie retorted fiercely. "It's just awkward, that's all. The Colonel and the others are all so old-fashioned and protective."

"Tell me the truth, Maggie. You were embarrassed as hell when you walked out that door this morning and saw Odessa, weren't you?"

She sighed. "Yes."

"The engagement was the only way to handle the thing," Josh continued relentlessly.

"And so convenient," Maggie shot back under her breath. "You'd worked it into your cover story before I could count to three."

Josh was silent for a long moment. "Is that what's really bothering you?" he asked at last. "You're angry because I'm using our phony engagement as part of my cover?"

"I don't want to talk about it anymore," Maggie declared. They were in town now and Josh was slowing to turn into the small supermarket parking lot. "The damage is done, so we'll just have to hope some good comes out of it."

"Trust me, Maggie. You did last night."

"Well, I learned my lesson this morning, didn't I?"

9

MAGGIE WAS LOADING grocery sacks into the back of Josh's car when Clay O'Connor hailed her from across the street.

"Maggie," he called out as he emerged from his office. "I thought that was you."

Maggie straightened and turned to wave. Downtown Peregrine Point consisted of a mere two blocks of shops. O'Connor Real Estate was located directly across from the grocery store. Clay had obviously spotted her from his office window.

Maggie watched as Clay checked for oncoming cars and then quickly crossed the street without bothering to go to the corner. He was dressed for the crisp cold day in a handsome, chunky-knit sweater and a pair of wool trousers. His hair was styled in a full, curving line that could only have been achieved with the aid of mousse. The diamond in his heavy gold ring flashed briefly when he moved his hand. He looked as if he had stepped right out of a men's fashion magazine.

The sight of Clay, with his cheerful, open face and dazzling smile made Maggie vividly aware of the contrast between him and Josh. It was like the contrast between day and night. With Clay, one got what one saw. But instead of the reassurance that fact should have provided, it only made him seem bland and shallow to Maggie. Josh, on the other hand, brought to mind the old adage about still waters running deep. He made her think of hidden depths and disturbing passions. Deep water was frequently dangerous, Maggie reminded herself.

"I almost didn't see you," Clay complained lightly as he reached her. "Didn't recognize the car. Who does it belong to? That writer fellow?"

Maggie felt herself blushing. It dawned on her how monumentally awkward the phony engagement was going to get. She had to try to keep it contained, she told herself. She didn't want it spread all over Peregrine Point. But even as she frantically tried to figure out a way to control something as uncontrollable as gossip in a small town, she knew her efforts were futile.

"Hello, Clay. Yes, the car belongs to Josh. He had to come into town for some things so he gave me a lift." Maggie hoisted another sack into the vehicle. Mentally she toyed with the notion of telling Clay the truth.

"You know, Maggie, I've been thinking about that guy." Clay's handsome features shaped themselves into serious lines. "I don't want to alarm you or anything, but does it strike you as a little strange that he showed up when he did?"

Startled, Maggie straightened quickly. She frowned as she turned to face Clay. "Strange?"

Clay shrugged and braced one hand against the roof of the Toyota. "Well, here you are, closed for the winter and all, and then he lands on your doorstep for a month. I bring you home from a date and he's waiting at the front door. The next thing I know the two of you are seen having dinner in town. And now he's shopping with you. Seems to me he's really made himself a part of the family in a hurry."

Maggie chewed on her lower lip. "You know how it is, Clay. He's the only guest at the manor these days, so we've just sort of made him a part of our household for the month. Most of the time we don't see all that much of him. He's always upstairs working on that book of his." That statement certainly had the ring of truth about it now, Maggie reflected grimly.

Clay eyed her thoughtfully. "Have you ever actually seen any evidence of that book?"

"Yes, as a matter of fact, I have." Maggie was relieved to be able to tell the full truth for once. Lately there had been far too many half-truths and downright fabrications. "It's a mystery novel. Very exciting, from what I saw of it."

"Hmm."

"What is it, Clay?"

He gave her his charming, crooked little smile. "Hell, don't pay any attention to me, Maggie. Sheer jealousy motivating me, that's all."

Maggie felt wretched. And slightly guilty. "Clay, I'm sorry if you feel I, well, if you think I implied that my feelings were stronger toward you than they actually are. I mean, I've enjoyed your company very much but I wouldn't want you to think that I…"

Clay's charming smile turned wistful. He touched her mouth with his fingertips, gently silencing her. "Hey, don't worry about it, Maggie. I'm a big boy. I know that for you our relationship has been casual so far, but I plan to change all that. In the meantime, I can handle a little competition."

Maggie began to seethe with annoyance. This was so awkward. "Clay, it isn't exactly competition. I wouldn't want you to think I'm trying to play games. Josh and I, well, we've become quite friendly since he moved into the manor. That's all."

Clay's smile widened into a grin. "I'm not worried. I figure I've got the edge. After all, January will be gone in a couple of weeks and I'll still be here, won't I?"

"Clay, that's very sweet of you—really, it is."

"Remember that I'm a sweet guy by nature," he advised ruefully. Then his expression sobered. "Maggie, I meant what I said earlier. You really don't know all that much about January. If he says or does anything that makes you nervous, promise you'll call me immediately."

"But, Clay—"

"Just promise, honey. I want to know you'll feel free to call me if anything happens at the manor."

"Like what?" Josh asked in an icy drawl as he materialized from between two parked cars.

Maggie jumped at the unexpected sound of his voice. She turned her head and saw that he was carrying a small, white paper sack in his hand. It bore the logo of the Peregrine Point Pharmacy. "Oh, Josh, there you are," she said weakly. "I was wondering what had happened to you." She made a show of glancing at her watch. "Good heavens, just look at the time. We'd better hurry. It's starting to rain."

Josh ignored her. He absently dangled the little white bag while he smiled at Clay with faint challenge. "Did I hear you say you were worried about something going on at the manor?"

Clay took his hand off the Toyota's roof and shoved it deep into his pocket. "Maggie and I were just having a friendly little chat. We've been friends for several months now, haven't we, Maggie?"

"Uh, yes. Yes, we have, Clay." Maggie wanted to crawl into a hole and hide. Never in her life had she been the subject of conflict between two grown men. It was terribly embarrassing. "Listen, we have really got to be on our way. I'll see you later, Clay. Josh, will you please hurry? I've got things to do back at the manor."

"Sure thing, sweetheart." Josh turned his back on Clay and sauntered over to the passenger door of the Toyota. He opened it with a cool possessiveness and ushered Maggie inside. Then he went around to the driver's side and got in behind the wheel. "See you, O'Connor."

Maggie waved at Clay as Josh swung the Toyota out of the parking lot. "Honestly, Josh, that was extremely rude."

"What was rude?"

"The way you behaved toward Clay. And don't you dare act as if nothing happened back there. You were very uncivil and you know it."

"The guy was trying to warn you off me, wasn't he?"

Maggie tilted her chin. "He was merely pointing out that I know very little about you and that it was rather odd the way you turned up at the manor when you did."

"I turned up at the manor because you hired me," Josh growled. "And don't you forget it."

"I could hardly tell Clay that, could I?"

"Not as long as you want me to do my job," Josh agreed coolly. "So what did you tell him?"

Maggie sighed. "Not much. Just that you'd sort of become a part of the household lately."

Josh gave a roar of laughter. "Just an old friend of the family, huh? O'Connor will have to be a hell of a lot dumber than he looks to believe that."

"There's no need to talk about Clay like that. He is not dumb. He's a very nice man—which is more than I can say about some people around here."

"Is that right?" Josh abruptly slowed the Toyota. He turned off the road and pulled into a secluded parking area. A thick stand of fir shielded the car from the view of passing drivers.

"What are you doing?" Maggie glowered across the seat at him.

"I want to talk to you and it's hard to do it at the manor. Too many people around." Josh switched off the ignition and sat for a long moment, his brooding gaze on the rain-spangled sea.

Maggie sensed that their conversation was about to change significantly. "Josh? Is something wrong?"

"What did you think of it, Maggie?"

"What did I think of the way you talked to Clay? I told you what I thought of it. I thought it was rude. It was pure *machismo* in action. And it didn't make me feel especially valuable, either. I know for a fact I'm one of the few single women under the age of fifty here in Peregrine Point. It's not as if the two of you chose me out of a crowd and decided I was worth squabbling over."

"Forget the scene with O'Connor." Josh rested his hands on the steering wheel. "What did you think of the book?"

Maggie studied his harsh profile. "The book?"

"You're the only one who's read any of it, so far. Last night while I was downstairs messing around with that furnace you had time to read quite a bit of it. How far did you get?"

"Josh, I'm sorry I read what you had written. It was very wrong of me to pry like that. But you have to realize that I was afraid I'd been conned."

"How far did you get?" Josh repeated, spacing each word out carefully for emphasis.

"A couple of chapters," she admitted.

"So what did you think?"

Maggie smiled slightly. "I thought it was terrific, Josh."

His head came around quickly, his eyes intense. "I want the truth."

"The truth is that I have read an enormous number of mysteries and I can assure you that what I saw of yours is as good as the best," she said quietly.

He exhaled deeply. "You really think so?"

"I really think so. Your main character, Adam Carlisle, is wonderful. He tries to go through life with a protective coat of cynicism, but underneath he's a born hero. That's very appealing. He's the good guy. The one who will fight for the weak and the innocent, even while he's grumbling about how being a hero doesn't pay. He's a lot like you, isn't he, Josh?"

"Hell, no. He's just a figment of my imagination."

"I think he's more than that," Maggie replied. "He's your alter ego. He gets to solve the kind of clear-cut cases you got into the business to handle— the kind where there's an innocent victim and a real villain. The kind where there's no question about right and wrong. He gets to do battle against genuine evil and win."

"It's always so simple with Adam Carlisle's cases," Josh agreed softly. "And he gets to step over the line occasionally to make certain justice gets done."

"He gets to play hero. Deep down, readers love real heroes and they love it when justice is done. More than that, I think readers *need* those kinds of stories. They satisfy something deep inside. You're writing straight to the heart of that market, Josh. You're going to be a success."

"You're not just saying that?"

"Josh, I can't believe you've actually got any doubts. You're always so sure of yourself."

His hand moved in a small gesture of dismissal. "Like I said, so far, yours is the only opinion I've had—besides my own, of course."

"Tell me something. Is Adam Carlisle going to have a girlfriend who gets to help him solve the cases? I love mysteries that feature a strong relationship between the main character and someone else. I hate it when there's only a single male protagonist who goes around sleeping with all his female clients. I mean, that just really bugs me."

Josh turned to her, a gleam of amusement in his eyes. He unbuckled her seat belt and wrapped a hand around the nape of her neck. He pulled her close. "You said I was a lot like Adam Carlisle. In some ways you may be right. He does not sleep around with his female clients any more than I do." He brushed his mouth tantalizingly across hers.

"Glad to hear it," Maggie breathed tremulously.

"I believe I will think seriously about giving him a permanent female companion." Josh tugged her closer. The white paper sack from the pharmacy crackled beneath his weight.

"What was that?" Maggie asked, glancing down.

"Nothing." Josh urged her back into his arms.

"Hang on. We're liable to crush whatever you've got in there." Maggie picked up the paper bag and started to set it on the floor. It slipped from her hand. "Oops."

"I'll get it." Josh moved swiftly to scoop up the contents of the sack—but not swiftly enough.

Maggie saw the brightly colored box of condoms that had fallen out. "Josh. You *didn't*. Tell me you didn't just buy those in the Peregrine Point Pharmacy. How could you?"

"It was easy. I just opened my wallet and took out some cash. Next thing you know, the entire box was mine." Josh shoved the offending box into the sack and tossed it into the back seat. "What's the big deal? We *are* sleeping together, remember?"

"One time." Maggie's head came up sharply. "We slept together one time, Josh."

"So?"

"So now everyone in Peregrine Point will know," she shouted. "How many times do I have to tell you this is a very small town? How could you do this to me?"

"I thought it added credence to the cover story," Josh said innocently.

"*Cover story?*" Maggie's mouth fell open. Fury welled up inside her. She reached for his throat with both hands.

Josh caught her wrists and chuckled softly. "Maggie, Maggie, take it easy. I was just teasing you."

"This is my reputation you're playing with. I don't consider it a fit subject for teasing," she snapped.

He smiled soothingly. "Sweetheart, in a day or two everyone will hear we're engaged, and that should take care of the gossip."

"But we're not engaged. Not really." She squeezed her hands into small fists. Frustration burned within her. "Damn, this is getting so complicated."

"Maggie, will you stop worrying? I've told you I'll take care of everything."

"Oh, sure. I've got news for you, Josh. Your big plan to pretend we're actually engaged for a while and then just fade off into the sunset isn't going to work." Maggie grabbed her purse, opened it and jerked out a tissue. She blew her nose, furious at the tears that were threatening to fall. She wouldn't cry a second time, she vowed silently.

Without a word Josh pulled her close against his chest. He said nothing as she began to cry in earnest.

"This is so humiliating." Maggie sniffed and wiped her eyes on Josh's shirt. "I don't know why I'm acting like this. I think I've been under too much stress lately."

"Probably." Josh continued to hold her close. He didn't seem to mind the fact that she was dampening his shirt. "Maggie, it doesn't have to be a fake engagement."

"What?" She stirred against him, finding comfort in the warmth and strength of his arms.

"I said, it doesn't have to be a fake engagement. We could make it a real one."

Maggie went still. Then she slowly lifted her head to stare at him. "A real one?"

He smiled slightly and caught her chin in his hand. His thumb slid over her lower lip. "Why not? It seems to me we've got a lot going for us. We're attracted to each other. Why don't we try? I think we could make it work."

She drew back slowly, struggling to comprehend what he was saying. "My God. You're playing hero again, aren't you?"

He frowned. "What the hell does this have to do with playing hero?"

"You *are*." Maggie scrambled back to her side of the car. "You're playing hero. You're offering to make the engagement a real one because you're beginning to realize how much the fake one is upsetting me. You feel responsible. Well, I won't have it, Josh."

"You won't?"

Maggie straightened her shoulders and rebuckled her seat belt. "Absolutely not. I've got my pride, you know." She finished drying her eyes and dropped the crumpled tissue into her purse. "I don't need rescuing that badly. I am not some weak, innocent, helpless victim, you know. I can take care of myself. I've been doing it just fine, so far."

Josh leaned back into his corner and studied her

from beneath half-lowered lashes. "You think I'm made of such sturdy stuff that I'd actually commit myself to marriage just to play hero? Better think again, Maggie. I've told you before, my days of playing hero were over long ago."

She heard the cold anger in his voice and shuddered. Warily, she glanced at him and saw that he was not in a good mood. In fact, he looked extremely dangerous. "Then why did you suggest we make the engagement something more than a cover story for this case?"

"I told you why. I think we've got enough going for us to make a marriage work. Hell, I'm nearly forty. It's time I settled down. You're almost thirty, and so far, you haven't encountered any real-life hero who's going to sweep you off your feet and put a ring on your finger."

"I do have some possibilities," she flared. "I'm not a lost cause. There's Clay, for example."

"Come on, Maggie. You can't be serious. You were already getting bored with O'Connor when I arrived on the scene."

"How do you know that?" she demanded, furious.

"It was pretty damn obvious when you came back from that date with him," Josh retorted. "You were grateful to me for getting rid of him."

"I never said that."

"You didn't have to say it. I'm a private investigator, remember? I pick up clues real good when they're right in front of my eyes."

"Is that so? Well, here's a clue for you, Mr. Private Investigator. When I finally decide to get engaged for real, it will be because I'm in love and because the man involved loves me. It will not be because the romance happens to be a useful cover story. Nor will it be because the guy has an overdeveloped sense of responsibility or because he thinks he should settle down and he's not going to do any better. Do you hear me?''

''I hear you.'' Josh tapped one finger against the steering wheel.

A long, heavy silence fell inside the vehicle. The rain had reached the shore now and was drumming relentlessly on the roof of the Toyota.

Maggie began to fidget nervously. She wished she hadn't gotten so emotional about the whole thing. She wished she were a more devil-may-care sort of person. She wished she could simply enjoy the romance and passion and adventure that had so unexpectedly come her way. She wished last night had not seemed so monumentally significant.

She wished for a lot of things; but most of all Maggie wished she hadn't fallen in love with Josh January.

''So,'' Josh went on after several minutes of apparent contemplation of the problem, ''do you think you might be able to fall in love with me one of these days?''

Maggie considered the two alternative responses to that question. She could either scream and sob hysterically at the injustice of a universe that had created such an insensitive species as the human male, or she could compose herself and react in a mature, sophisticated manner. With a great effort of will, she chose the latter.

''Who knows? I've got so many other things on my

mind at the moment, I haven't had time to consider it." Maggie managed a bright little saccharine smile and glanced at her watch. "Don't you think we'd better be on our way? It really is getting rather late."

Josh regarded her in acute silence for another long moment and then, without a word, he switched on the Toyota's ignition with a decidedly savage twist of the wrist.

MUCH LATER THAT NIGHT Josh sat alone in his room and put the finishing touches on his plan to trap the Peregrine Manor intruder. His scheme was simple, as was the case with most such schemes. If his suspicions were correct, he wasn't dealing with a criminal genius. No point in getting fancy.

Another consideration was Josh's own gut-level feeling that he had to move quickly to put an end to the harassment. He had sensed the escalating level of danger after the incident with the furnace. Whoever was coming and going in the basement was either getting bolder or more desperate. He had to be stopped.

When he was eventually satisfied with his plan, Josh made the decision to put it into effect the following day.

That left him with nothing of particular interest to do tonight. Maggie had already gone to bed and showed no signs of sneaking across the hall to his room a second time. And he didn't feel like working on the book.

But it was a cinch he wasn't going to get to sleep easily—not after that conversation with Maggie in the Toyota this afternoon. Not after the way Clay

O'Connor had tried to warn Maggie about getting chummy with strangers. Not after the way Maggie had blithely refused to admit she was falling in love.

Josh chewed on all three annoying occurrences for a while and then got to his feet. He went over to the window and stood looking out at the night-shrouded sea.

Why was Maggie fighting her feelings for him? Josh wondered. He'd been asking himself that same question since early that morning. He'd been so sure of her last night. She had given herself to him in wholehearted, loving surrender. A woman like Maggie couldn't fake that kind of sweet passion. Besides, she respected herself too much to get involved in short-term affairs, Josh was certain.

But when he had calmly agreed to the engagement under the watchful eye of the Colonel, Maggie had been furious. Josh had been forced to fall back on the excuse that an engagement would be useful cover for him while on this case. That gambit had apparently only enraged her further.

What Josh couldn't understand was why she had been so upset in the first place. If he had read the signals right, she was head-over-heels in love with him. And she was a woman who believed in commitment. So why had she gotten so riled up over the idea of being engaged to him, he wondered bleakly.

Josh moved restlessly away from the window. Maybe McCray was right. Maybe he wasn't very good at dealing with women. Maybe he lacked a sense of romance, or something.

Josh gave up that depressing line of thought in favor of something more practical. He would do another tour of the house. He had already checked all the locks on the windows and doors once tonight, but doing it a second time wouldn't hurt.

He let himself quietly out of the room and went down the stairs. His ankle no longer twinged very much when he walked and his ribs only protested when he rolled over in bed. It was a relief to feel almost normal again.

Josh went through each first-floor room and then double-checked the small basement windows. When he had stalled as long as he could, he went slowly back up the stairs to the second floor.

He came to a halt outside Maggie's room. Unable to resist, he cautiously tested the knob. To his surprise, the door opened easily.

"Maggie? Don't be afraid. It's me."

She sat up in bed. "I heard you walking around." She sounded wary but not frightened. "Checking locks?"

"Yeah." He closed the door and stood watching her in the shadows. "Everything's fine downstairs."

"Good."

"Maggie?"

"What is it, Josh?"

He tried to think of a way to introduce the topic of their relationship. Words failed him. But he couldn't bring himself to leave her bedroom just yet. He struggled with another approach, another reason to stay for a while.

She looked so inviting there in bed with her hair loose and soft around her shoulders. There was just enough pale moonlight filtering in through the window to enable Josh to see her. The sight made him ache with need. He wanted her so much it hurt.

"I, uh, I've made the plans for the trap I'm going to set," Josh finally said. He began wandering around the room, examining things in the shadows. He touched the perfume bottle on the dresser and ran his fingers along the spines of some books. *Mysteries, no doubt,* Josh thought, unable to read the titles in the darkened room. Maybe one day his book would be on her shelf. She liked what she had seen so far of it. It had been an enormous relief to hear that this afternoon.

"Tell me about your plans," Maggie urged softly.

He went over to the bed and stood looking down at her. "I'm going to need your cooperation."

"How?"

"I want to make it look as though the two of us have left town for a few days. I want people to think we've gone off together. Seattle or Portland. Anywhere. It's important that everyone thinks we're out of the area."

"I see." She sounded thoughtful and distant. "I suppose this is what you meant when you said a phony engagement would be a useful cover story?"

He forced himself not to react to that. "Let's not talk about the engagement. Just tell me if you'll help me make it look as though we've taken off for a few days."

"All right. I might as well. My reputation is in shreds, anyway. What does it matter if everyone in Peregrine Point thinks I'm off having a wild weekend. Heck, it may do wonders for my image around here. What happens after we take off for a passion-filled holiday?"

"I come back here at night and set up a stakeout."

"A *stakeout!*" Now she sounded genuinely interested. "A real stakeout? Just like in a mystery novel?"

"A real stakeout," he confirmed, amused by her enthusiasm.

"You think the intruder will strike when we're out of town?"

"I think it's a good possibility. I think the guy is getting desperate and frustrated. I think he'll make a move with a bit of encouragement from us."

"This is exciting," Maggie said. "I'll help you bait the trap, Josh, on one condition."

"What condition?"

"That you let me come with you on the stakeout."

He winced. "Stakeouts are not a lot of fun, Maggie. They're incredibly boring, for one thing. And I'll be doing it in a car. There are certain, uh, physical needs that have to be attended to from time to time. It's easier for a man to handle a stakeout like this, if you see what I mean."

"Nonsense! I used to go camping when I was a kid. I can use the bushes when I have to."

Josh sought for a stronger argument. "I'm hoping to catch the guy, Maggie. If he shows up, I'm going to try to grab him. At the very least, I plan to get close enough to ID him. Things could get rough."

"Then you'll need a partner along to cover your back," she declared. "You can't talk me out of this, Josh. I'm the client, remember? I'm giving the orders around here. If you're planning a stakeout, I insist on being allowed to help."

He eyed her narrowly. "You promise you'll follow orders?"

"I promise," she said eagerly.

"I mean it, Maggie. If you come with me, you'll do exactly as you're told and you won't take any risks. Understood?"

"Sure."

Josh swore softly. "All right, you can come along."

"Oh, Josh." Maggie leaped out of bed and threw her arms around him. "Thank you, thank you, thank you. I can't tell you how much this means to me." She hugged him fiercely. "A real stakeout."

The feel of her soft breasts pushing gently against his chest was enough to turn the smoldering need in Josh into a raging fire. After his first startled reaction to her hug, he recovered instantly and started to pull her closer.

But Maggie was already dancing out of reach. "You'd better get some sleep, Josh. Sounds like we might be up all night tomorrow. We'll both need plenty of rest. See you in the morning."

She was right. That was the hell of it. "Yeah. Sure. See you in the morning." It took an astounding amount of willpower to let himself back out the door and into the hallway.

It was better this way, Josh told himself as he stalked back to his own room. At least she was feeling enthusiastic and friendly again. If he was careful, he could recover the territory he seemed to have lost this morning with his brilliant notion of a phony engagement.

A thought struck him then that made him smile. Stakeouts were usually very long and extremely dull. A man and a woman trapped for hours together in the front seat of a car had to do something to pass the time.

Josh was feeling much more cheerful—even optimistic—when he finally undressed and got into bed. He fell asleep at once.

10

JOSH WAS WAITING a discreet distance down the hall from Odessa's bedroom door the next morning at five. He cleared his throat politely and glanced pointedly at his watch when the Colonel emerged in a bathrobe and slippers.

"Right on time, Colonel."

The Colonel looked up, alarmed. Then he scowled ferociously, his mustache twitching. "What the devil do you think you're doing, young man?" he demanded in a soft growl.

"I wanted to talk to you privately," Josh murmured. "I figured this would be the best time to catch you. Besides, I figure after that little stunt the three of you pulled on Maggie yesterday morning, a little rough justice was in order."

"Stunt?"

"The timing was a little too perfect to be sheer coincidence. All three of you emerged from your rooms simultaneously. It was a neat little ambush, Colonel, and you might as well admit it. I decided to set my own this morning."

The Colonel sighed. "Odessa and I have always been so discreet. How did you find out?"

"I'm an early riser. And I've got real good hearing." Josh grinned. "Hey, I know just how you feel. Come on downstairs. I've already got the coffee going. Heck, I'll even fry us a couple of eggs. Me, I've been sleeping the sleep of your typical chaste and gallant gentleman, but I'll bet you've worked up quite an appetite."

"No respect for your elders. That's what's wrong with your generation. If you'd served under me, I'd have straightened you out in that department." The Colonel tightened the tie on his bathrobe and followed Josh toward the stairs. "You won't, uh, mention this to Maggie, will you?"

"Why? You afraid she might demand that you do the right thing?" Josh shot the Colonel a dry look.

The older man had the grace to blush. "I suppose I did rather put you on the spot yesterday morning, didn't I?"

"You sure as hell did. And I don't mind telling you it was lousy timing, Colonel. Because of your little surprise foray, I damn near lost the war."

The Colonel eyed him sharply. "What do you mean by that?"

"I mean," Josh said, "that the business of playing the heavy-handed patriarch outside my bedroom door has made Maggie skittish. She's spent the past twenty-four hours thinking up reasons why she can't marry me. You'd be amazed at her creativity."

"Can't marry you?" The Colonel glared at him as they reached the bottom step and headed for the kitchen. "Why can't she marry you? See here, you haven't already got a wife and half a dozen kids stashed away somewhere, have you? Because if so, sir, I can personally assure you that I will not tolerate this behavior of yours."

"No wife and no kids." Josh went into the kitchen,

which was already smelling nicely of freshly brewed coffee. He grabbed the pot and filled two mugs. "But you rushed things yesterday morning. Maggie's nervous now. I've got a job ahead of me, undoing the damage you did."

"Nonsense." The Colonel accepted his mug and sat down at the small table. "She'll come around. You just see to it you do what's right and proper by her. She's a small-town girl at heart. Kind of old-fashioned in a lot of ways. And don't you forget it."

"My intentions are honorable," Josh drawled. He sipped his coffee and watched the Colonel carefully. "They have been from the start. Which is more than I can say about yours, isn't it?"

The Colonel's head came up proudly and his eyes flashed. "What the devil is that supposed to mean? Now see here, if you're talking about my intentions toward Odessa, you can apologize at once. My intentions toward her always have been and always will be honorable."

"They why haven't you married the lady?" Josh asked calmly.

The Colonel heaved a sigh. "It's that damn gold-mining stock of hers. I'm afraid she'll think I'm marrying her to get my hands on it. I've got my pride, sir."

"Have you considered going to a lawyer and getting a prenuptial contract that would protect her assets?"

"I raised the subject once. Delicately, you understand. But my Odessa is a romantic at heart. She doesn't care for the notion of prenuptial agreements."

Josh decided to take a chance. "How about if I told you that Odessa's stock isn't worth the paper it's printed on?"

The Colonel looked shocked. "Are you certain of that, sir?"

"I had someone research it back at the office. I wanted to check out Odessa's theory that her nephews were after the stock. The mining company she bought twenty years ago went bankrupt nineteen years ago. The mine was never worth a damn thing."

"I've always wondered about that stock. She never seemed to get any income from it as far as I could tell. But a man hesitates to inquire into a woman's finances. Extremely bad form, you know."

"Private investigators do it all the time," Josh explained wearily. "A lot of investigations boil down to money."

"An interesting thought." The Colonel brightened. "Are you saying this one is going to boil down to money, too?"

"That's my hunch. I've ruled out all the other motives. It's either money or a psycho case. Frankly, I'd prefer money. I like nice clean motives when I can get them. The nut cases make me nervous."

"Yes, I can understand that." The Colonel leaned back in his chair and peered at Josh. "So, what's the plan? You do have a plan, don't you? I assume that's why I found you waiting for me outside Odessa's door this morning?"

"Yes, sir, I've got a plan. But I could use some backup help here inside the house. I want someone to take care of Odessa and Shirley just in case things go wrong. It'll mean staying awake most of the night."

The Colonel looked pleased. "Be honored to assist you sir. I'm still capable of doing sentry duty. And I've still got my old service revolver upstairs, you know. Been a while since I used it, of course, but I reckon there are some things you don't forget."

"If everything goes as planned, you won't have to use it. But I'll feel better knowing you're awake and armed upstairs tonight."

"Certainly."

Josh folded his arms on the table. "Now, here's how it's going to go down, Colonel. Maggie and I are going to leave town on an overnight trip to Seattle. As soon as we're out of the house, I want you to call Dwight Wilcox and tell him you're worried about the furnace. Tell him it gave you some trouble again and you want him to double-check it. Make sure he knows that Maggie and I are out of town."

The Colonel narrowed his gaze. "You really think Wilcox is the one behind these incidents?"

"I think he's the one who's been staging them, yes."

"Don't suppose the oil companies are paying him, do you?"

"Uh, no. No, in all truth, I don't think anyone's after your research, sir."

The Colonel nodded. "Well, it was just a theory, of course. Hate to say it, but Odessa's right. That boy just doesn't seem bright enough to plan this kind of thing without getting caught."

Josh smiled grimly. "That's the whole point, Colonel. He is going to get caught. Tonight."

AT FIVE MINUTES TO eleven that night, Maggie got up on her knees in the front seat of the rental car Josh had chosen for the stakeout. He had told her his black Toyota was too well-known in the area. She reached into the back seat for another bag of potato chips.

"Only one more large bag left," she reported.

Josh wistfully eyed the sweet curve of her bottom, which was nicely outlined in a pair of snug-fitting jeans. "That's okay. We've still got the cheese crackers and the jalapeño dip. And we haven't even started on the chocolate bars."

"Do you always eat like this on a stakeout? I've never seen such a collection of junk food." Maggie turned around and dropped back onto the front seat.

"I told you surveillance is boring. I like to reward myself." Josh took a swallow from the can of cola in his hand. He leaned back into the corner of the seat and turned his gaze toward the manor.

The big house was visible through the stand of trees where he had parked the nondescript rental car two hours ago. The manor looked like a Gothic castle in the pale, watery moonlight. Its fanciful architectural embellishments made Josh think of pictures he had seen in old children's books.

From amid the trees, he could keep an eye on the kitchen door and the small ground-level windows of the basement. He could also watch the only approach to the old house, which was from the main road.

"You think he'll just drive right up to the manor, hop out and do his dirty work?" Maggie asked as she popped a potato chip into her mouth.

"Well, he sure as hell isn't going to make his approach from the other side of the house. The beach is too dangerous this evening because of the high tide and the storm that's on its way in. Even if he made it as far as the manor from that direction, he'd still have to find the cliff path at night and climb it. Too tricky. My hunch is that Wilcox will take the easy way."

Maggie slid him a sidelong glance. "I suppose you operate on hunches a lot in this business, don't you?"

"Uh-huh." Josh reached into the bag on her lap for a potato chip.

"Josh?"

"Yeah?" He munched on the chip.

"I was just wondering. Do you plan to stay in this business for the rest of your life?"

The question startled him. He turned his head to find her watching him intently in the shadows. "What?"

"I was just wondering if you would want to keep running Business Intelligence and Security, Inc. after you've sold your book."

"Selling the book is not a sure thing, Maggie."

"I think you will sell it."

Her confidence gave him a quiet thrill. Josh stretched his shoulders and resettled himself in the seat. He studied the approach to the manor while he thought about her question. "I don't know what I'll do if I sell the book."

"Do you still like your work?"

"What's liking it got to do with anything? It's a job. I'm good at it. It's a living. A fairly good one, to be perfectly honest."

"Yes, but does it give you any real satisfaction?" Maggie persisted gently.

Josh slanted her a curious glance. "What are you trying to say?"

She crunched another potato chip. "Nothing."

"Maggie, don't give me that. You're after something. What is it?"

She stirred uneasily. "It's just that I've had this feeling for several days now that you're kind of burned-out. I was wondering if maybe that's the real reason you came over here to the coast for a month."

Josh groaned. "You and McCray. A couple of amateur psychologists."

"It's true, isn't it? You're here because you burned out back in Seattle."

He exhaled slowly. "Yeah. It's true."

"What really happened in that 'accident' that had you on crutches when you first arrived?" she asked softly.

"A kidnapping case went sour. Things got a little rough when I went in after the jerk who had taken the girl. He was trying to use her as a shield."

Maggie looked suitably horrified. "What happened?"

"The girl is safe. The jerk's back in jail."

"My God, Josh, you could have been killed!" Maggie frowned. "You were playing hero again, weren't you?"

"I told you, it never pays. The kid I rescued was only seventeen. She didn't even thank me. In fact, she hated me for saving her. The guy who had her was her boyfriend, you see. She thought they were going to run off together and live happily ever after. She didn't believe me or her father when we told her she was in love with a two-bit ex-con who planned to take the ransom money and run. Last I heard, she now blames me for ruining her entire life."

"Little twit. I don't suppose it's any consolation to know that in a couple of years she'll be thanking you."

"I don't need her thanks. I was just doing her father a favor. Good public relations. He's head of a large corporation that uses BIS services. He came to me after he got the ransom note because he didn't want any publicity. I should never have agreed to help. Jobs like that are always messy."

"What's going to happen when you go back?"

"What do you think will happen? I'll go back to work."

"What about the book?"

"I'll work on it when I can."

"Josh, maybe you need more than a month off," Maggie said hesitantly. "You know, when you think about it, you really haven't even had the month off you had planned to take, anyway, have you? Here you are, back at work. This is just another job."

"Believe me," Josh growled, "this is not just another job."

"Well, you can hardly call it a vacation."

He thought about that. He had gotten a good start on his novel, he had found the woman with whom he wanted to spend the rest of his life and he was on a stakeout, waiting to catch Dwight Wilcox in the act of breaking and entering. "You're right. It hasn't exactly been a vacation. But it has been interesting."

She coughed delicately and stuffed another potato

chip into her mouth. "So maybe you should take an extra month or so here at the coast after you wrap up this case."

Josh went still as it finally dawned on him she was trying to say something very important. "Here? You think I should spend the extra month hanging around Peregrine Point?"

"You said yourself it would be a good place to write your book. And you fit in very well at the manor. You've been extremely helpful, to tell you the truth. If you're about to catch Dwight Wilcox in the act of staging some mischief tonight, then it strikes me that I'll be in the market for a new handyman tomorrow morning."

Josh nearly choked on his cola. He finally managed to swallow the laughter and the soft drink. "Maggie, are you by any chance offering me a two-month job as handyman here at the manor?"

"It wouldn't be much of a job because I can't afford to pay very much. Room and board is all it would amount to, I'm afraid. At least until I get the manor back on its feet financially."

"I see."

"Think of it as sort of a change of pace," she continued eagerly. "It might do wonders for your burned-out condition if you spent a couple of months doing something entirely different for a while. And you'd have plenty of opportunity to work on your book. Who knows? You might even get to like it out here. Look at me. I love it here."

Josh finished the cola and carefully set the can on the floor of the car. He said very softly, "So do I."

Maggie stopped munching potato chips. Her eyes widened in the shadows. "You do?"

"Your offer is tempting, Maggie."

"It is?" She watched him anxiously.

"Yeah. But there's only one way I can accept it."

"What's that?" she demanded instantly.

He turned his head finally to look at her. His stomach was clenched with anticipation. Josh was afraid that he was moving too fast again. But he reminded himself that she had been the one to start this crazy conversation. He also reminded himself that opportunity didn't always knock twice. All his instincts were clamoring for him to make the move; and he had always been inclined to follow his instincts.

"The only way I could accept your offer, Maggie, is if you agreed to let our engagement story stand while I'm living at the manor."

She looked stunned. "But, Josh—"

"I'm serious, Maggie. I'm too old to play games. If I stay, I'm going to be spending the nights in your bed. And I won't have the Colonel, Odessa, and Shirley—as well as everyone in Peregrine Point—think we're just having an affair. I've got my pride and so do you. This is a small town. People will talk."

"Oh, Josh, I understand." She threw herself against him, her arms curving tightly around his neck. Her eyes were wide and searching in the shadows. "You want to protect me from the gossip. It's the gallant side of your nature. It's really very sweet of you."

Josh grinned slowly. "I've got news for you, Maggie. I am not sweet. I've told you I want to give the engagement a chance. That's my price for staying on around here as your handyman."

Maggie was quiet for a long moment. He could tell she was torn between doubt and desire. Josh knew she wanted him but she was still trying to wade in the shadows of their relationship. She was wary of going deeper because she still didn't know him very well. She needed time. He understood that.

Maggie took a deep breath. "All right, Josh. All right, I'll do it. We'll give our engagement a chance while you're here."

Josh felt a wave of relief wash over him. He had two months to work on her now, he thought in triumph. In two months' time, surely she would get to know him well enough to feel secure about his intentions.

"You've just hired yourself a new handyman," Josh said. He lowered his head and began to kiss her slowly, letting her feel the depth of his need.

Her response was instantaneous. Maggie's desire for him was a heady thing; it set a match to his own passion.

Josh groaned and twisted slightly in the seat so that he could ease Maggie's slender, supple body between his thighs. She smiled at him in the moonlight and crowded close. Josh could feel the warmth and the softness of her against his hardening body, and the sensation sent shudders of desire through him.

"Maggie—" Josh froze as he glimpsed a shadowy movement from the corner of his eye.

"Josh?"

"Bingo."

Maggie tensed. "What's wrong?"

"It's Wilcox. He's here. Early, too. Must have decided that as long as you and I were gone, it would be safe. He's figuring that the Colonel and the others will be in bed by now."

Maggie sat up quickly, peering into the darkness. "Are you sure? I don't see anything."

"He didn't drive up to the manor. He walked. Must have parked his car farther down the road. I caught a glimpse of something under his arm. Tools, probably. Damn it to hell." Josh disentangled himself from Maggie and opened the car door. He had disconnected the interior lights of the vehicle earlier.

"Josh? Be careful. Please."

"I will. You stay put, understand?"

"Maybe I should follow you," Maggie suggested helpfully. "In the mysteries I've read, the hero always gets into trouble when he doesn't have backup."

Josh moved to squelch that idea at once. "No. You're not going to follow me. I don't want you anywhere near the house." He shut the door with a firm *thunk* and started through the trees toward the manor. He didn't look back. He was afraid Maggie might view that as an indication that he was having second thoughts about allowing her to accompany him.

He wanted her safe.

The shadowy figure of Wilcox moved steadily toward the manor. It was easy to keep track of him through the trees. Wilcox didn't once check behind to see if anyone was tracking him. He was intent on his goal; a man on a mission.

Josh edged closer, using the deep shadows of the

trees for concealment just in case Wilcox got smart at the last minute and took a good look around.

Wilcox walked along the side of the manor and went right up to the kitchen door. Josh shook his head in amazement at the man's boldness. He watched as Wilcox set down the parcel he was carrying and slipped a key into the kitchen-door lock.

It had undoubtedly been very easy for the handyman to get a key to the back door, Josh reflected. Much too easy. Josh decided he would institute some new security precautions around the place when this was all over.

It struck him quite forcibly that he was already thinking of Peregrine Manor as his home.

Josh waited until Wilcox had let himself into the darkened kitchen before he followed. He paused on the back-door step and listened as Wilcox clomped across the tile floor. When he was certain Wilcox was in the hall and heading for the basement, Josh silently let himself into the kitchen.

He moved out into the hall when he heard Wilcox's big boots on the stairs that led down to the basement. This was good enough, Josh decided. He had Wilcox neatly trapped. All that was necessary now was to close the basement door and lock it from this side and call the sheriff to report an intruder. While waiting for the sheriff to arrive, Josh would make certain Wilcox didn't wriggle out through one of the ground-level windows.

Piece of cake.

A snap.

Like shooting fish in a barrel.

No heroics required.

This was the way a job was supposed to go—simple and neat.

Josh caught the unmistakable whiff of kerosene just as he was about to shut the basement door.

And suddenly he realized what had been in the parcel under Wilcox's arm. Not tools for staging another act of mischief—*kerosene.*

Wilcox had gotten desperate, all right. He was planning to set fire to the manor. The fact that the odor of the highly flammable liquid was strong on the stairs meant the handyman was already going to work.

So much for simply locking the door and calling the sheriff. The kerosene would do untold damage to the Colonel's files, besides which the least little spark would start a blaze that could burn down the manor.

"Hold it right there, you bastard!" Josh flicked on the light switch as he leaped down the steps.

The lights came on, revealing Wilcox caught in the act of pouring a thin stream of kerosene across the concrete floor. He was working his way slowly and methodically toward the Colonel's filing cabinets.

Wilcox looked up, startled. At least Josh assumed the handyman was startled. His expression was barely altered. Maggie had been right. Wilcox had all the animation of a banana.

Dwight set the kerosene can down at his feet. "Stay back, January. It's too late." He dug into his hip pocket and came up with a cigarette lighter.

Josh swore but wasted no more breath trying to talk the fool out of what he obviously intended. He reached the bottom step and threw himself forward in a long, flat dive just as Wilcox flicked the lighter and touched the flame to the thin rivulet of kerosene.

The trajectory of his dive brought Josh down on Wilcox like a ton of bricks, carrying both men heavily to the floor. But even as he rolled on the concrete, struggling to pin the other man, Josh heard the terrifying whoosh of fire.

There was a shout from the top of the stairs.

"Josh!"

It was Maggie. Josh heard her racing down into the basement. He could smell the kerosene burning and he wanted to yell at her, order her to get out of the firetrap.

He forced himself to ignore everything but the job at hand. First things first. He could do nothing about the fire until he had Wilcox under control.

And Wilcox had somehow managed to produce a knife in his right fist. *The man was good with tools.*

Josh slammed a body blow into his opponent and started to roll to his feet. Wilcox lashed out with a series of blade thrusts. Already off balance, Josh threw himself out of the range of the blade, stumbled...and came down far too heavily on his weak left ankle. Pain tore through him. So did rage.

"You son of a bitch!" Josh kicked out with his left foot, ignoring the agony. He had no choice; he was going to have to use his right foot to anchor himself.

The bone-shattering blow connected with Wilcox's forearm. It sent the knife flying and it caused Wilcox to crumple. The last of the fight went out of him. He lay in a helpless heap on the floor.

An instant later, foam from a fire extinguisher cascaded over everything in sight.

Josh closed his eyes as the white stuff splattered across his face and covered his shirt. "Point it toward the fire, Maggie."

"I'm trying. It's heavy."

Josh wiped off the foam and opened his eyes. Maggie was, indeed, struggling with the big, unwieldy extinguisher. But she had managed to douse the flames.

She set the extinguisher down and looked at him triumphantly. "We did it. We saved the manor."

Josh looked at her and then looked at the can of kerosene that was sitting a short distance away. He felt a little sick as his imagination conjured up horrifying possibilities and might-have-been scenarios. He wanted to shake Maggie for the risk she had just taken.

"I told you to wait in the car. That thing could have gone up like a bomb," Josh said evenly, exerting an incredible amount of effort to control his temper.

"But it didn't," she replied cheerfully. "I got to the fire in time and you got Wilcox. We make a great team, don't we, January? What do think about ditching your friend McCray and taking on a new partner? Peregrine Point doesn't have an investigation agency."

Before Josh could think of a response to that there was another shout from the top of the stairs. The Colonel lumbered down the steps, a huge, old revolver in his fist. Odessa and Shirley were right behind him, clutching at their robes.

"Oho!" yelled the Colonel exultantly. "You got him. Always knew you were a martial-arts man. Said it the first time I saw you, if you remember, January."

Josh took a deep breath and got a grip on his temper. He turned toward Wilcox. It was time for some answers.

"All right, Wilcox. Who paid you to do this little job?"

There was a stunned silence behind him as everyone in the basement absorbed the implications of the question. Josh knew he needed to act swiftly if he was going to get to the bottom of the thing. If Wilcox had time to recover from the shock and the pain he was in right now, he might think twice about talking.

"He didn't pay me nothin'," Wilcox muttered. "Said he'd tell everyone in town I had a record if I didn't do what he said. I'd never have gotten any more work. Don't ya see? I had to do it. He forced me. It was blackmail, that's what it was. And he kept complainin' 'cause nothin' ever worked."

"Good grief," Maggie breathed.

Wilcox turned his head toward her and regarded her with something that might have been hurt reproach. "You was supposed to sell after the first couple of incidents. You was too stubborn. That was the problem. It weren't my fault. I told him that."

"Did you?" Maggie asked quietly. "What did he say?"

"He said I had to go back and try somethin' else." Wilcox cradled his broken wrist. "So I did. And look what happened."

"Yeah," said Josh. "Life's tough sometimes. But the way I see it, there's no need for you to take the rap for this all by yourself."

Wilcox peered intently up at him. "You can't touch

him. He'll have covered his tracks. He's real clever. Not dumb like me. It'll be my word against his."

"No." Josh shook his head. "I can nail him. All I need is a little information. I can nail anyone if I have the right information."

"I'd like to see that." Wilcox grimaced. "I'd like to see you nail him, all right. Made my life hell, he has."

"Tell me who set you up, Dwight," Josh urged gently. "And I'll set him up for you."

Wilcox stared at him with what might have been eagerness. "Yeah?"

"Yeah."

"Like to see that." Dwight nodded. "Yeah, I'd really like to see that. Bastard. He deserves it."

Maggie frowned. "Who deserves it, Dwight?"

"That fancy real-estate man. You know. The guy with the pinkie ring. O'Connor," said Dwight.

11

JOSH STOOD MOTIONLESS in the darkest shadows of the O'Connor Real Estate office. He had been there nearly three hours. It was two in the morning. Not a single car had moved down the main street of Peregrine Point for the past hour.

One of the hardest things about this kind of work, Josh reflected, was the waiting. Of course, now that he was changing jobs, he wouldn't be spending many more nights like this one. He planned to spend his evenings curled up in bed with his new boss.

He wondered when he should tell Maggie that he planned to stay at Peregrine Manor permanently—not just a month or two.

Josh reached down absently to massage his aching ankle. Maggie had wanted to put an ice pack on it but he had told her there was no time for first aid. He didn't know how long O'Connor would wait for Dwight Wilcox to report, but Josh figured it wouldn't be long. When Wilcox didn't show, O'Connor would get nervous. And when he got nervous, he would most likely want to destroy anything that could be used as evidence.

Josh had already amused himself going through the files with a tiny penlight. He could have done the search without the light if it had been necessary—there was enough of a neon glow filtering in through the windows to illuminate much of the office interior.

He had found what he was looking for inside a small, locked drawer. He had the file in his hand.

Josh heard the soft purr of the Mercedes engine from a block away. His body responded with the adrenaline rush that always went through him at times like this.

O'Connor parked the silver Mercedes outside the office and got out. Josh watched as Clay glanced quickly around and then dug his keys out of the pocket of his expensively styled trench coat. He was so nervous he dropped them on the sidewalk.

His head ducked deep into his upturned collar, Clay hurried to the front door of the office and shoved a key into the lock. He didn't bother to turn on the lights.

Josh watched from the shadows as Clay headed unerringly across the room to the small, locked drawer. He waited until he heard O'Connor's sharply indrawn breath.

"Looking for this?" Josh reached out and switched on the light. He idly slapped the file of papers he was holding against his leg.

"*January!*" Clay stared at the file, his mouth working. "What the hell are you doing here? You're trespassing. I'll have you arrested."

"Will you?" Josh strolled over to the desk and sat down behind it. He opened the file folder and glanced at the incriminating paperwork in front of him. "Not exactly a routine multiple listing, is it, O'Connor? But, then, Maggie had no intentions of selling in the first place. So you tried to convince her."

"What the hell are you talking about?" Clay's face was turning an ugly shade of red. He was sputtering. "That file is private property."

"This file," Josh said coldly, "is an agreement to sell Peregrine Manor quite cheaply to a New York development firm."

"There's nothing wrong with an offer like that. Real-estate people are always soliciting clients. It's the way we make our living."

"Yeah. Except that the manor isn't for sale. And you knew it." Josh flipped through the paperwork. "Hell of a commission for you in this, isn't there, O'Connor? Not the usual six percent."

"It's a finder's fee," O'Connor raged. "Perfectly legitimate."

"Only if the manor was actually for sale. And only if you had informed the seller of the true value of the property. Which you did not, did you?" Josh slanted O'Connor an interested look. "You didn't tell anyone, including Maggie, what the New York firm was really willing to pay for that stretch of land, did you? When did the New Yorkers first put out feelers?"

"They expressed an interest shortly after Agatha Gladstone died," Clay replied stiffly. "Nothing out of the ordinary about that."

"Except that you forget to mention their interest to Maggie. Instead, you decided to see if you could interest the New York crowd in a real steal of a deal. You'd get the land for them dirt cheap and in exchange they would pay you a fat finder's fee. Nice work if you can get it."

A speculative gleam appeared in O'Connor's eyes. Josh could read the look on the other man's face, even in the dim light. He had seen it often enough before on the faces of people who had been caught redhanded.

Their first assumption was that the person who had caught them might be interested in making a deal. The theory was that everyone else had the same kind of morals as they did. *Just good business.*

"They want to put in a world-class resort and spa here on the coast," Clay eagerly explained. "Big development companies like the ones behind this deal have to keep a low profile when they go into a new area to pick up land. If people know they're buying, the prices start shooting up in a hurry. Keeping quiet is just good business. That's all."

"Just good business." Josh closed the file, wondering how often he had heard that excuse over the years. "But in this case there wasn't going to be any business at all, was there? Because you couldn't talk Maggie into selling. And you sure as hell didn't want to tell her how much the manor was really worth. If you couldn't get it cheap, you couldn't do a deal with the New Yorkers."

"The manor is worthless to them. It's just an old house. What they want is the land."

"So you decided on a plan. You'd drive Maggie into selling by making it appear that the manor was falling apart around her. If you could convince her that it was too expensive to keep it going and that business was going to fall off, she'd have to let it go. But Maggie can be stubborn, can't she?"

"Damn stubborn. You don't know what I went

through trying to get her to sell. I had to pretend I was falling for her. I was willing to take her to bed, if necessary. What the hell. No big deal. It probably would have been mildly amusing. She's kind of cute—if you like the sweet, innocent type."

Josh jumped out of his chair in a flash. He barely noticed the pain in his ankle as he whipped around the corner of the desk and grabbed a startled O'Connor by the collar.

"What the hell...?" O'Connor's eyes flared wide with fear and anger.

"You got desperate tonight, didn't you?" Josh slammed O'Connor up against the wall. He leaned in close. "You decided to take drastic action. Any idea what the penalty is for arson in this state, O'Connor?"

"*Arson?* I don't know what you're talking about. I told Wilcox to stick to mechanical stuff."

"Yeah, well, he didn't. Apparently you pushed him a little too hard. Tonight he tried to torch the manor."

O'Connor looked genuinely astounded. Then he looked ill. "My God! What happened?"

"Nobody got hurt, if that's what you mean. You won't be facing murder charges."

"Murder." O'Connor looked more nauseated than ever. He started to crumple. He licked his lips. "Look, you said everybody's okay. Nobody got hurt. So why don't we cut our losses and make a deal? Huh? Where's the harm? I'll split the finder's fee with you if we can convince Maggie to sell. Come on, January. You're sleeping with her. Everybody in town knows it. Surely you can talk her into selling."

"Forget it," Josh said. "Your problem, O'Connor, is that once in a while when I'm real bored, I like to play good guys and bad guys. Guess who gets to be the good guy tonight?"

SHORTLY BEFORE DAWN Josh let himself into his room. The manor was silent. Everyone else had apparently retired while he was busy talking to the local sheriff.

He didn't bother to turn on the lights. Instead he stripped off his clothes in the darkness, yawned, and pulled back the quilt on the big, canopied bed.

"Hi," said Maggie in a soft, sleepy voice. "I was wondering when you'd get home. Lot of paperwork in your business, I guess."

Josh smiled slowly as he looked down at her. A sense of deep happiness and satisfaction welled up inside him. "I'd have finished the paperwork a lot faster if I'd known you were going to be here in my bed waiting for me."

"Where else would I be?" Maggie opened her arms and smiled. Love glowed in her eyes. "Welcome home, hero."

Home, thought Josh as he gathered her close. That was where he was now. Home.

He lost himself in Maggie's sweet warmth. Nothing had ever felt so right.

"I JUST CAN'T BELIEVE IT," Odessa declared for what must have been the hundredth time the next morning. "He seemed like such a nice young man."

"I never did like him," Shirley announced. "Always said O'Connor was soft around the edges."

"Dwight's the one I feel sorry for," Maggie said,

carrying a plate of crumpets and honey over to the kitchen table. "He was virtually blackmailed into doing what he did. I wonder how Clay found out about his past?"

"Wilcox let something slip once when he was doing a small job for O'Connor." Josh slathered honey on a crumpet. "O'Connor did a little research after he got in touch with the New Yorkers. He realized he could use someone like Wilcox to help him push Maggie into selling."

"Well, it's all over now," the Colonel added with satisfaction. "We can open the manor after the first of the year and it should be in good financial shape by early spring. We didn't lose much time, thanks to our man January, here. You did a fine job, sir. A fine job."

"Thank you," Josh acknowledged humbly. "I like to think I give an honest day's work for an honest day's pay."

Maggie's eyes sparkled with laughter as she bit into a crumpet. "You get what you pay for. That's what I always say."

"And sometimes a little more than you expected, hmm?" Josh took a large bite out of his own crumpet.

The Colonel cleared his throat portentously. "Speaking of the unexpected, Odessa and I would like to make an announcement. We are officially engaged as of this morning and we will be getting married as soon as possible."

Odessa blushed becomingly. "We're so excited."

Maggie put down her crumpet. "*Married?* You two? Why, that's wonderful. Congratulations. I'm thrilled for you. But why the sudden decision?"

"Yeah," Shirley said bluntly. "How come, after all this time?"

"I guess it's just in the air," Odessa answered brightly. "The Colonel surprised me by popping the question this morning and I said yes before he could change his mind. Apparently he's had some foolish notion that I would think he was marrying me to get control of my mining stock. But I told him I trust him completely. Always have. He's a perfect gentleman." She gave Josh an expectant look. "Have you two set the date yet?"

"No," Maggie replied quickly before Josh could answer. "But we do have some news. Josh is going to be staying on around here for a month or two. He's thinking about making a career change, you see, and he wants to test the waters. If everything works out, he may opt to stay in Peregrine Point permanently."

The Colonel frowned. "Sounds a bit unsettled, if you ask me. What's the matter with you, January? Can't you make up your mind?"

"*My* mind's made up," Josh told them. "I'm waiting for Maggie to make up hers."

"Why the delay, Maggie?" Shirley peered at her. "Take it from me, in this world a gal's gotta grab her opportunities."

Maggie felt herself turning a vivid pink. Everyone at the table, including Josh, was watching her. "There's no point trying to intimidate me. I refuse to be rushed. Josh needs time, in spite of what he says. I want him to be certain about what he's doing."

"I'm certain," Josh countered.

"No, you're not," Maggie shot back.

"You're the one who's still got questions." Josh

licked honey from his fingers and stood. "But I think the mail has arrived, so maybe we can get started on helping Maggie make up her mind."

Maggie glared at his broad back as Josh left the kitchen. She saw that he was limping again this morning. Her glare turned into a look of concern.

"Don't fret, Maggie." Shirley chuckled. "Josh is tough. He'll do just fine."

"I suppose. But I wish he hadn't reinjured that ankle."

"Give him a few days and he'll be as good as new," the Colonel said.

"Right," Josh agreed, limping back into the kitchen with a small stack of mail in his hand. "Good as new in a few days. No sweat." He shuffled briskly through the letters. "Ah, here we go." He selected a white manila envelope from the pile and tossed it onto Maggie's lap.

"What's this?" She picked up the envelope, frowning.

"Answers." Josh sat down and started applying honey to another crumpet.

Maggie tore open the envelope and dumped the contents on the table. For a moment she couldn't make sense of the assortment of official-looking forms, licenses, and records that lay in front of her.

Then she saw that every one of the formal-looking pieces of paper in front of her bore the name and description of one Joshua January. She jerked her head up to meet Josh's watchful gaze.

"This is a file on you, isn't it?"

He nodded. "Anything you want to know about me should be in there somewhere, Maggie."

"Is that so?" Anger shot through her. She flattened her hands on the table and pushed herself to her feet. "Will it tell me if you love me, Josh? Will it tell me that? Because that's the only question that you haven't answered for me. I already know everything else I need to know about you."

"Maggie…" Josh started to get to his feet, obviously taken aback by her reaction.

"I don't need *data* on you, Josh." Maggie picked up the pile of forms and papers and hurled them into the air. "I just need to know if you can love me as much as I love you, damn it! A real simple question, Josh."

"You love me?" Josh stared at her, a slow smile warming his cold eyes. "You love me, Maggie Gladstone?"

Maggie was battling tears now. She wiped them away with the back of her hand. "Of course I love you, you big idiot."

"I was sure you did, sweetheart, but you never said it. You kept saying you needed time."

"I said *you* needed time. Time to figure out that you loved me. You kept giving me all sorts of stupid reasons for letting our engagement stand. You said it was a good cover story. And then you said you thought maybe things would work between us, so we might as well give the engagement a chance. And then you agreed to stay on here for another month or two while you recuperated from burnout. But you never once said you loved me."

"Maybe that's because I've never said those words to anyone else in my life and I wasn't sure how to say them to you."

"Oh, Josh." She wiped her eyes again.

"I love you, Maggie." Josh shoved his chair back and moved around the table to take her into his arms. He folded her close, heedless of the smiles on the faces of the Colonel, Odessa and Shirley. "I fell in love with you that first night when you opened the door and told me I didn't look like what you'd ordered up in the way of a private investigator."

"*Josh.*"

"I'll be staying on for a lot longer than a month or two, sweetheart. I've decided I need more than a vacation. I need a career change."

"Oh, Josh." Maggie wrapped her arms tightly around his waist and squeezed.

Josh sucked in his breath. "Easy, honey. The ribs took a beating last night when I was rolling around on the basement floor."

"Oh, dear. I knew you should have stayed in bed today." Maggie stepped back and examined him from head to toe. "I really think we should take you to the Peregrine Point Clinic for a thorough check, Josh."

"No. I am not going to another doctor," he stated. "All I need is plenty of rest and relaxation. I came out here to recuperate—if you will recall. So far, I've had very little opportunity to do so, but I intend to start working on it immediately. I'd like to be in reasonably good shape for my wedding."

Maggie raised her head, smiling brilliantly. "When is that?"

"How about the end of the month?" Josh suggested.

"The end of the month?" Maggie was instantly

horrified. "I can't possibly get ready for a wedding by the end of the month."

"I think we can manage." Josh grinned at the faces of the three people who were still sitting at the table. "We'll have lots of help."

"Might as well make it a double wedding," the Colonel announced cheerfully. He beamed at Odessa. "No sense going to all the expense of two receptions in a short period of time."

"You're right," Josh agreed. "We're going to have to watch the budget around here until the manor is taking paying guests again."

"Spoken like a born innkeeper," Maggie said. "I think you'll go far in the business, Josh."

IN SPITE OF the short notice, most of Peregrine Point showed up for the double wedding celebration at the manor. The cars filled the small parking lot and stretched in a line all the way down the driveway to the road. The guests swarmed through the first floor of the big house, filling the beautiful rooms with laughter and chatter.

Midway through the reception, Josh finally found himself alone for a moment. He stepped out onto the front porch and glanced down at his watch. He frowned. McCray was rarely late.

Just as that thought flickered through his mind, Josh heard the sound of a car coming up the driveway. He grasped the porch railing and leaned forward to watch as a familiar blue Oldsmobile came to a halt in front of the manor. There were two men in the front seat. McCray got out first and came around the hood of the car.

"Well, hell, January. Don't you look spiffy." Mc-Cray cast a perusing eye over Josh's black-and-white formal attire. "Congratulations, pal. Are we in time for the party?"

"There's still plenty of champagne left." Josh glanced at McCray's passenger, who was just getting out of the car.

The man looked to be in his late sixties. Obviously still hale and hearty, he was built like a mountain. The gray trench coat he wore was stretched across shoulders that appeared to be a yard wide.

"That's him?" Josh asked quietly.

"That's him. Sorry we're late. Took me a while to find him. He was in the middle of one of his literacy classes. But when I told him who was waiting for him, he dropped everything and got into the car."

The big man lumbered up the steps and stuck out a hand. "You're January?"

"I'm January." Josh shook the beefy hand. "Thanks for showing up here today."

"I don't mind telling you, I'm a little nervous. After all these years…"

A high-pitched feminine shriek interrupted the big man's words.

"Ricky!"

Josh turned to see Shirley standing frozen in the doorway. She was resplendent tonight, having chosen to wear nearly every rhinestone in her extensive collection. Her eyes were filled with shock as she took in the sight of the huge man in front of her.

"Hello, Shirley." Ricky "The Wrecker" Ring stood uncertainly in the porch light. "Been a long time, honey. You're just as pretty as I remembered."

"Ricky, it *is* you. I ain't dreamin'?"

"I figure I'm the one who's dreamin'," Ricky said in a hoarse voice. "Thought you'd have found someone else a long time ago. Someone worthy of you, Shirley. I couldn't believe it when this here McCray showed up telling me you were living on the coast and had never married."

Shirley took a hesitant step forward. "I thought you hated me. I thought you believed I was the one that ratted on you all those years ago."

Ricky looked genuinely startled. "Hell, no, honey. You'd never turn rat. I knew that. You were always loyal and true-blue. It was the feds who nailed me. They used wires and tapes. All that new-fangled technology. I never stood a chance. I was always an old-fashioned kind of guy. I realized the day they put me away that when I got out, I was going to have to find a new line of work. I'm not cut out for carrying on the old business under modern conditions, if you know what I mean."

"Ricky, are you sayin' you've gone straight?" Shirley was obviously overjoyed.

"Straight as an arrow, honey. Record's clean from the day I got out of prison. I know I'm not what you deserve. I knew it back in the old days, too. I didn't contact you after they sent me up 'cause I didn't want to mess up your life again. Told myself you deserved a chance to start fresh. But these guys say that as long as I'm clean, you might be interested in takin' me back."

"In a hot minute, Ricky." Shirley hurled herself into his arms, her rhinestones flying. "Lord, I missed you, lover. You were the best there ever was. I never stopped thinkin' about you. Not once."

"I never stopped dreamin' about you, honey." Ricky's arms closed around her.

"I think we ought to leave these two alone," Josh murmured to McCray. He opened the front door of the manor.

"Yeah, kind of makes you misty-eyed, doesn't it?" McCray glanced inside at the crowd of people milling about. "So, what do you say you introduce me to your bride? I'd like to meet the lady who is about to make me sole owner of BIS."

Josh smiled as Maggie materialized from a throng of well-wishers. She came toward him, looking glorious in yards and yards of white lace and satin. He thought he had never seen anything half as beautiful in his entire life. She was everything he'd been searching for all his life. She was his future.

"There you are, Josh. I've been looking for you. It's time to cut the cake." She tilted her head to look at McCray. "Are you his ex-partner?"

"I'm McCray. And I just want to say, Miss Gladstone—"

"Mrs. January," Josh corrected dryly.

McCray chuckled. "I just want to say, Mrs. January, that I am very impressed with you. Never thought any woman would be able to take the chill out of this guy. All I can say is that you must be some kind of female."

"Heavens, Josh is not the least bit cold," Maggie said, laughing gently. "He just likes to hide his true nature behind that tough-guy image."

"Is that so?" McCray arched an ironic brow at Josh who smiled blandly back.

"Yes, indeed. You only have to get to know him to realize—" Maggie broke off as she caught sight of the couple out on the porch. "Who on earth is that with Shirley? She's kissing him."

"Ricky Ring," Josh explained. "I had McCray check him out. He's been clean for years. Turns out he never forgot Shirley. Just figured he wasn't good enough for her. That's why he hasn't contacted her."

Maggie's eyes widened in astonished delight. "So you arranged to bring him here to be reunited with Shirley? Josh, that was wonderful of you. You are so sweet. Isn't he sweet, McCray?"

"Sweet enough to give you cavities," McCray agreed. "Would somebody mind pointing me in the direction of the champagne?"

"Straight down the hall," Josh advised. "The other groom is pouring. You can't miss him. He's wearing the same kind of funny suit I've got on. You can call him Colonel."

"I'll find him." McCray slapped Josh on the shoulder and ambled off to find the Colonel.

Maggie turned to Josh. "Shirley looks so happy out there. It really was nice of you to go to the trouble of tracking down Ricky Ring. Do you suppose she'll be leaving us to go live in Portland, now?"

"Wouldn't surprise me. I think we'd better go cut that wedding cake. Odessa and the Colonel will be waiting." Josh took Maggie's arm, aware of a satisfying sense of possession. *She's Mrs. Joshua January now*, he reminded himself. She was his wife. Life couldn't get any better than this.

"You know, Josh, I've been thinking."

"About what?"

"About our partnership," Maggie said. "It's got so many possibilities."

"Yeah, I think the inn is going to do just fine." Josh already had a lot of plans for the place. McCray was buying him out of BIS, and Josh planned to invest some of the cash in Peregrine Manor.

Maggie looked up at him, her eyes bright. "I wasn't talking about the manor. I was talking about opening Peregrine Point's first private-investigation agency."

Josh came to an abrupt halt. "What the hell are you talking about?"

"Josh, I'm sure I've mentioned this before."

"No, I don't believe you did," Josh said grimly.

"Well, why not?" Maggie smiled enthusiastically. "We can give you an office right here in the manor. You can work on your Adam Carlisle mysteries when you aren't working on a case—which will be most of the time, because there won't be many cases to work on here in Peregrine Point."

"Try zero cases."

"Oh, I expect we'll get the odd job now and again. Human nature is the same in small towns as it is in big cities. And once in a while you're going to feel the urge to play hero. It's your nature."

"Maggie..."

"I was thinking we could call the agency January Investigations. When I'm not busy running the manor, I'll give you a hand on your cases."

"Gosh, thanks."

"I'm really looking forward to learning the ropes of the private-investigation business, Josh."

Josh couldn't help it. He started to laugh. He was still grinning a few minutes later when Maggie cut into the wedding cake and found the little box hidden inside.

The look on her face when she opened it and discovered Agatha Gladstone's emerald brooch was priceless.

"*Josh!*" Maggie's eyes were shining as she looked up at him. "You found it. You found Aunt Agatha's brooch. How on earth did you do it?"

"I keep telling you, I'm a trained investigator. I'm real good at spotting clues."

She threw her arms around his neck as the crowd of reception guests cheered. "You're a perfect hero," she whispered against his throat as she hugged him tightly.

"Yeah. Well, I've learned that once in a while it pays."

HARLEQUIN®

Temptation®

BEGUILED
Lori Foster

Lori Foster sold her first book to Harlequin Temptation in 1996, and her rise to stardom since then has been astronomical. Just three years and six books later, she is a bona fide bestselling author, from Waldenbooks to Amazon.com, and has garnered rave reviews from every possible source. Not bad for a wife and mother and "housewife extraordinaire" whose first novel

was written longhand and never saw the light of day. Still, Lori's priorities have not changed—family first, writing second. She lives in Ohio with her high-school-sweetheart husband, Allen, and three strapping sons, who inspire her to create exceptional heroes.

From the Editors...

Lori is so prolific and full of innovative ideas that it's hard to keep up with her. She has brought a sensitivity and sensibility to "erotic" romances that define the Temptation Blaze miniseries and that readers can't seem to get enough of. Which is a good thing, because there's no end to the projects that Lori is, as always, more than enthusiastic about pursuing. The New York Times bestseller list isn't far off for this star in the making.

"...fun, sexy, warm-hearted...just
what people want in a romance."
—Jayne Ann Krentz

Beguiled
Lori Foster

PROLOGUE

HARSH WIND THREW icy crystals of snow down the back of his neck, causing him to shiver. He raised his collar, then shoved his hands deep into the pockets of his coat, resisting the urge to touch the gravestone. The grave was all but covered in white, making everything look clean, but Dane Carter didn't buy it. Not for a minute.

He'd missed the burial by almost four months. His family was outraged, of course, but they'd never really forgiven him for past transgressions, so he figured one more didn't matter. Except to himself.

His face felt tight, more from restrained emotion than from the biting cold. The death of his twin was a harsh reality to accept, like losing the better part of himself even though he and Derek hadn't been in contact much lately. Dane had been away from the family, disconnected from the business, for quite a few years now. He deliberately took the cases from his P.I. firm that kept him out of town as much as possible. Though his office was only an hour away, he'd been out of reach when his brother had needed him most.

Though everyone seemed to accept Derek's death as an accident, concerned only with keeping the news out of the media to avoid a panic with the shareholders, Dane couldn't let it rest. He wouldn't let it rest. He had a nose for intrigue, and things had begun to smell really foul. It wasn't anything he could put his finger on, just a gut feeling, but his instincts had held him in good stead as a private detective for several years now—ever since he'd left the family business in his brother's capable hands.

He hunkered down suddenly and stuck one hand through the snow to the frozen ground. "What the hell happened, Derek? This was a lousy trick to play on me. I never wanted this, not the company, hell, not even the family most of the time. You left too damn many loose ends, brother."

The wind howled a hollow answer, and disgusted with himself, Dane drew his hand back and cupped it close to his face, warming his fingers with his breath. "And what about this Angel Morris woman? I got a letter from her, you know, only she assumed you'd get it. Seems she doesn't know you're gone and she wants to pick up where the two of you left off. I believe I'm going to oblige her."

His mind skittered about with ramifications of deceit, but he had to cover all the bases. According to the records he'd uncovered, Angel Morris had been seeing Derek on a regular basis until the takeover of her company. Derek had used information Angel gave him to make the takeover easier, and Angel had gotten fired because of it. She had plenty of reasons to despise Derek, and he certainly deserved her enmity. Yet now she wanted to see him again. After so long, he had to wonder if Angel had assumed Derek was dead, but with Dane's return, she felt she had unfinished business. After all, no pronouncements had been made.

As far as the outside world was concerned, Derek Carter was still running the business. Only a select few knew of his demise. The family had thought it best if

Dane filled in for a while. If he pretended to be Derek no one would start rumors about a company without a leader, or a family with a scandal. All in all, Dane wasn't sure which possibility worried his mother more. The company was her life, and the Carter name was sacred in her mind. She wouldn't want either one damaged. And if Derek had been murdered, if the accident wasn't an accident at all as Dane feared, it would certainly hit the news.

But that wasn't why Dane had agreed to come back, why he was filling in for his brother. No, he wanted the truth, no matter what. And he'd damn well get it.

If Angel knew anything, if she was involved with Derek's death in any way, even peripherally, Dane would find out. He may have disassociated himself from the family, but he could be every bit as ruthless as the best of them.

Dane shook his head. "I'll be seeing her first thing tomorrow, alone, away from the family as she insisted. I'll let you know how it goes." With that banal farewell, he turned and trod back through the snow to the road where his car sat idling, offering warmth, but no peace of mind.

What a laugh. Dane Carter hadn't had peace of mind since he'd walked out on his family, regardless of what he told them, what he insisted to himself. Maybe Angel, if she wasn't an enemy, could prove to be a nice distraction from his present worries. His brother had always had excellent taste in women.

CHAPTER ONE

ANGEL TRIED TO METER her breathing, to look calm, but her heart felt lodged in her throat and wouldn't budge. She hated doing this, had sworn she'd never so much as speak to the man again after his last, most devastating rejection. But she'd been left with little choice.

With her shoe box tucked beneath her arm and one hand on the wall, offering support, she made her way down the hall to Derek's office. She still felt awkward without her crutches, but she knew better than to show him any weaknesses at all. When she reached the open door, she straightened her shoulders, forced a smile, and tried to make her steps as smooth as possible.

Derek sat behind his desk, his chair half turned so that he could look out the window at the Saturday morning traffic. The rest of the building, except for the security guards, was empty, just as she'd planned.

He was still as gorgeous, as physically compelling as ever, only now he looked a little disheveled, a little rumpled. She liked this look better than the urbane businessman he usually portrayed. The only other time she'd seen him relaxed like this was right after he'd made love to her.

That thought licked a path of heat from her heart to her stomach and back again, and she had to clear her throat.

His chair jerked around and his gaze pierced her, freezing her on the spot. Even her heartbeat seemed to shudder and die. Only his eyes moved as he looked her over, slowly and in excruciating detail, as if he'd never seen her before and needed to commit her to memory, then their eyes met—and locked. For painstaking moments they stayed that way, and the heat, the intensity of his gaze, thawed her clear down to her toes. Her chest heaved as she tried to deal with the unexpected punch of reacting to him again. It shouldn't have happened; she didn't care anymore, wasn't awed by him now. Her infatuation had long since faded away, but seeing him with his straight brown hair hanging over his brow, his shirtsleeves rolled up, made him more human than ever. His gaze seemed brighter, golden like a fox, and she tightened her hold on the shoe box, using it to remind herself of her purpose.

She saw some indiscernible emotion cross his face, and then he stood. "Angel."

His voice was low and deep. As he rounded the desk his eyes never left hers, and she felt almost ensnared. She retreated a step, which effectively halted his approach. He lifted one dark eyebrow in a look of confusion.

Idiot. She didn't want to put him off, to show him her nervousness. That would gain her nothing. She tried a smile, but he didn't react to it. Moving more slowly now, he stepped closer, watching her, waiting.

"Can I take your coat?"

She closed her eyes, trying to dispel the fog of emotions that swamped her. When she opened them again, she found him even closer, studying her, scrutinizing her every feature. He lifted a hand and she held her breath, but his fingers only coasted, very gently, over her cheek.

"You're cold," he said softly. Then he stepped back. "Can I pour you a cup of coffee?"

Angel nodded, relieved at the mundane offer. "Thank you. Coffee sounds wonderful." Walking forward, she set her shoe box on the edge of the desk and slipped out of her coat, aware of his continued glances as he collected two mugs from a tray. She didn't mean to, but she said, "You seem different."

He paused, then deliberately went back to his task. "Oh? In what way?"

With one hand resting on the shoe box, she used the other to indicate his clothes. "I've never seen you dressed so casually before. And offering to pour me coffee. Usually you—"

He interrupted, handing her a steaming mug. "Usually I leave domestic tasks to women, I know." He shrugged, gifting her with that beautiful smile of his that could melt ice even on a day like today. "But you insisted no one else be here today, so I was left to my own devices. It was either make the coffee, or do without."

Angel fidgeted. "You know why I didn't want anyone else here. Your family would have asked questions if they'd seen us together."

He nodded slowly. "True." Then he asked in a low curious tone, "Why are you here, Angel?"

Flirting had never come easy to her, but especially not these days. She smiled. "I've missed you, of course. Didn't you miss me just a little?"

He stared a moment longer, then carefully set his mug aside. "Most definitely," he said. He took her coffee as well, placing it beside his, then cupped her face. Strangely enough, his fingers felt rough rather than smooth, and very hot. He searched her every feature, lingering on her mouth while his thumb wreaked havoc on her bottom lip, smoothing, stroking. "Show me how much you missed me, Angel."

Now this was the Derek she understood, the man who always put his own pleasures first, the man who had always physically wanted her. That hadn't changed. Without hesitation, surprised at how acceptable the prospect of kissing him seemed when all day she'd been dreading it, she leaned upward. He was much taller than her, and her leg was too weak for tiptoes, so she caught him around the neck and pulled him down.

When her mouth touched his, tentative and shy, she felt his smile. She kept her eyes tightly closed, mostly because she knew he was watching her and she felt exposed, as if he'd guess her game at any moment. It had been so long since she'd done this, since she'd kissed a man, and she was woefully out of practice and nervous to boot. If necessity hadn't driven her to it, she'd have gone many more months, maybe even years, without touching a man. Especially this man.

But now she was touching him, and shamefully, to her mind, it was rather enjoyable.

Tilting her head, she parted her lips just a bit and kissed him again, more enthusiastically this time, nibbling his bottom lip between her teeth. His humor fled and he drew a deep breath through his nose. "Angel?"

"Kiss me, Derek. It's been so long."

The errant truth of her words could be heard in the hunger of her tone, something she couldn't quite hide. His answering groan sounded of surprise, almost anger, but kiss her he did. *Wow.* Angel held on, stunned at

the reaction in her body to the dampness, the heat of
his mouth as he parted her lips more and thrust his
tongue inside. His body, hard and tall and strong,
pressed against hers. It had never felt this way, like a
storm on the senses. Her heart rapped against her
breastbone, her stomach heated, her nipples tightened,
and he seemed to be aware of it all, offering soft encouragement every time she made a sound, every time
she squirmed against him. She wasn't being kissed, she
was being devoured.

"Damn, Angel."

"I know," she said, because everything was different, somehow volatile. "I didn't plan on…this."

He paused, his lips touching her throat, then raised
his face to look at her. He said nothing, but his hand
lifted and closed over her breast, causing her to suck
in her breath on a soft, startled moan. Oh no. She was
so sensitive, and she hadn't realized. "Derek…"

He kissed her again, hard, cutting off her automatic
protest, then backed her to the desk. His groin pressed
against her, making her aware of his solid erection, of
the length and heat of it. Her plans fled; there was no
room in her brain for premeditated thought, not when
her body suddenly felt so alive again, reacting on pure
instinct. His hand smoothed over her bottom, pulling
her even closer, rocking her against him. Her leg protested, but she ignored it, an easy thing to do when his
scent, his strength, filled her.

"How long has it been, Angel?"

She clutched his shoulders, her head back, her eyes
closed, as he kneaded her breast with one hand, and
kept her pelvis close with the other. Surely he knew as
well as she did, so she merely said, "A long time."

"And you've missed me?" He nibbled her earlobe, then dipped his tongue inside. "Why didn't you call?"

Even in the sensual fog, she saw the trap. "After the way you acted last time?" She was astounded he would even ask such a thing!

He hesitated, then asked, "How exactly did you expect me to act?"

She stiffened as she pulled back. "Not like you couldn't have cared less! And after the way you'd betrayed my trust! You got me fired, you—"

"Shhh." He kissed her again, lingering, and his hand started a leisurely path down her body, measuring her waist, which thankfully was slim again, then roving over her hip. Her thoughts, her anger, turned to mush. She caught her breath with each inch he advanced. His fingers curled on her thigh, bunching her skirt, then moved upward again, this time underneath, touching against her leggings. He cupped her, startling her, shocking her actually. But she didn't move and neither did he. She tried to remind herself that this was what she'd hoped for, but it wasn't true. She'd stupidly hoped for so much more.

His fingers felt hot even through her clothes, but he was still, just holding her, watching her again. "Why now, Angel? Why this secret arrangement?"

She decided a partial truth would serve. "There's been no one but you."

"And you needed a man, so it had to be me?"

"*Yes.*" That was true, too. She didn't know who to trust, who to fear, so for what she needed, no one else would serve. But she hadn't planned on her own honest participation. Her body reacted independently of her mind; she felt shamed by her response to a man she should have loathed, but overriding that was some inescapable need, swamping her, causing her whole body to tremble. Maybe the pregnancy had altered her hormones or something, but she'd never in her life felt like this, and it was wonderful.

She pressed her lips together and squeezed her eyes shut. Her body felt tightly strung, waiting, anticipating. She dredged up thoughts of the past, of all the reasons she had to despise him, why his touch could never matter...

He seemed a bit stunned as she moaned softly and her fingers dug into his upper arms. He held her close, his own breathing harsh while his mouth moved gently on her temple. In all her imaginings, she had never envisioned this scenario, allowing him to touch her there, with her half-leaning on his damn desk, her face tucked into his throat. His heartbeat drummed madly against her own, and she grabbed his wrist to pull his hand away. "Derek, no."

Her voice shook with mortification, freezing him for an instant.

"Shhh." He dropped her skirt back into place and softly rocked her, soothing her. She bit her lip to keep her tears from falling, but even now she was painfully aware of his scent, his warmth. And the delicious, unexpected feelings didn't leave now that his touch was removed, they only quieted a bit.

She put one hand on his chest and lifted her face. He didn't smile, didn't ask questions. She couldn't quite look him in the eyes. "I'm sorry. I...I don't know what came over me."

"Am I complaining?"

She shook her head. No, he looked pleased, but not really smug. Not as she'd expected. "That's never happened before. I don't understand."

"What's never happened?"

"Between you and me. Usually everything was just so…controlled. And uncomfortable. I've never felt…"

His face darkened, and she hastened to explain. "I don't mean to insult you, but Derek, you know yourself that sex between us was…well, *you* seemed to like it okay, but I was a little disappointed. Not…not that it was all your fault. It's just that I didn't…it wasn't…"

He smoothed her hair, his jaw tight. He seemed undecided about something, and then suddenly he clasped her waist and lifted her off her feet. He sat her on the edge of the desk, roughly spreading her thighs and stepping between them in the same movement. Pain shot through her and she gasped, curling forward, her hand reaching for her leg, wanting to rub away the sharp pounding ache. Her breath had left her and her free hand curled into his biceps, gripping him painfully. Derek froze, then growled, "What the hell?"

Her teeth sank into her bottom lip, but God, it hurt, and with more gentleness than she knew he possessed, Derek lifted her into his arms and headed for the leather couch.

Nothing was going right. "Derek, put me down."

"You're as white as a sheet." He looked down on her as he lowered her to the sofa cushions, and she flinched at the anger in his eyes. "I noticed you were limping a little when you came in, but I didn't realize you were hurt."

"I'm not," she protested, the issue of her leg meant for another day. "Really, I'll just…"

"You'll just keep your butt put and tell me what's wrong. Is it your hip? Your leg?"

Before she could answer he reached beneath her long

skirt and caught at her leggings, hooking his fingers in the waistband and tugging downward. ''Derek!''

With his hands still under her skirt, his eyes locked on hers, he said, ''After what we just came close to doing, you're shocked?''

Flustered was more apt, and appalled and embarrassed and... ''Derek, please.'' But already he had her tights pulled down to her knees. She felt horribly exposed and vulnerable. He explored her thighs, being very thorough, and it was more than she could bear. ''It's my lower leg,'' she snapped. ''I broke it some time back and it's still a little sore on occasion. That's all.''

He stared at her, and she had the feeling he didn't believe a single word she'd said. ''Let me get your shoes off.''

She sat up and pushed at his hands. ''I don't want my shoes off, dammit!''

''At the moment, I don't care what you want.'' And her laced-up, ankle-high shoes came off in rapid order, then her tights. As he looked at her leg, at the angry scars still there, his jaw tightened. ''Damn.''

Angel bristled, her only defense at being so exposed. ''It's ugly, I know. If it bothers you, don't look at it.''

One large hand wrapped around her ankle, keeping her still, and the other carefully touched the vivid marks left behind by the break and the subsequent surgery. ''A compound fracture?''

''So you're a doctor now?''

He ignored her provocation. ''This is where the break was, and this is where they inserted a rod.'' His gaze swung back up to her face, accusing.

Disgruntled, but seeing no way out of her present predicament, she said, ''I'm fine, really. It's just that when you sat me on the desk, you jarred my leg and it...well, it hurt. It's still a little tender. I only recently got off crutches.''

His gaze was hot with anger. "And you're running around downtown in the ice and snow today?''

"I wasn't running around! I came to see you.''

"Because you needed a man,'' he sneered, and her temper shot off the scales.

"Damn you!'' Struggling upward, pulling herself away from his touch, she pointed to the shoe box still sitting on his desk. "I came to bring you that.'' Then she added, ''Whether you wanted it or not.''

He turned his head in the direction she indicated, but continued to kneel beside the couch. "What the hell is it?''

Angel came awkwardly to her feet and limped barefoot across the plush carpeted floor. She picked up the box, but then hesitated. She hadn't planned to raise hell with him, to anger him and alienate him. She had to move carefully or she'd blow everything. She closed her eyes as she gathered her thoughts and calmed herself. She hadn't heard him move, but suddenly Derek's hands were on her shoulders and he turned her toward him.

"What is it, Angel?''

He sounded suspicious, an edge of danger in his tone. She'd always known Derek could be formidable, his will like iron, his strength unquestionable. But she'd never sensed this edge of ruthlessness in him before. She shuddered.

"I don't mean to shock you, Derek. And I realize you weren't all that interested when I told you, but I was hoping you'd feel different now.''

His arms crossed over his chest and he narrowed his eyes. "Interested in what?"

She drew a deep breath, but it didn't help. "Our baby."

Not so much as an eyelash moved on his face. He even seemed to be holding his breath.

"Derek?"

"A baby?"

She nodded, curling her toes into the thick carpet and shivering slightly, waiting.

"How do you know it's mine?"

She reeled back, his words hitting her like a cold slap. After all she'd been through, everything that had happened, not once had she suspected he might deny the child. That was low, even for him. She had to struggle to draw a breath, and once she had it, she shouted, "You bastard!" She swung at him, but he caught her fist and the box fell to the floor, papers and pictures scattering.

"Miserable, rotten..." Her struggles seemed puny in comparison to his strength, but he had destroyed her last hope, delivered the ultimate blow. She wanted to hurt him as badly as she'd been hurt, but he was simply too strong for her and finally she quit. He hadn't said a word. Panting, shaking from the inside out, she whispered, "Let me go."

Immediately, he did. Keeping her head high, refusing to cry, to contemplate the hopelessness of the situation in the face of his doubt, she went to the couch and sat, snatching up her tights and trying to untangle them so she could get them on.

Even though she refused to look at him, she was aware of him still standing there in the middle of the floor, fixed and silent. When he squatted down to pick up the contents of the box, Angel glanced at him. His face was set, dark color high on his cheekbones. He lifted one small photo and stared at it.

All Angel wanted to do was get out. She jerked on her shoes, pulling the laces tight, fighting the tears that seemed to gather in her throat, choking her. She'd humiliated herself for no reason. She'd allowed him to touch her for no reason. He wasn't going to acknowledge the baby.

"I'm sorry."

She glanced up as she shrugged on her coat. Derek still crouched in the middle of the floor, a single photo in his hand, his head hanging forward.

Angel frowned. "What did you say?"

He slowly gathered up the rest of the things and came to his feet. "I said I'm sorry. The baby looks like me."

"Oh, I see. Otherwise, you wouldn't have believed me. In all the time you've known me, I've proven to be such an execrable liar, such an adept manipulator, it's of course natural that you would have doubts. Well, it's a good thing he doesn't have my coloring then, isn't it? You'd never know for sure."

"Angel..." He reached a hand out toward her, and there was something in the gesture, a raw vulnerability she'd never witnessed. In fact, too many things about him seemed different, some softer, many harder edged. Had something happened to him in the months since she'd last seen him?

She shook her head. She would never be drawn in by him again. "Those things are yours to keep. They're duplicates. Records, photos, a birth certificate, which if you notice, has the father's name blank."

"Why?"

He sounded tortured now and she frowned, tilting her head to study him. "You weren't interested, Derek, though I admit I was hoping you'd changed your mind by now."

"I'm interested," he growled.

She thought of the last time she'd called him, the hell he'd put her through. "When we spoke on the phone, you rudely informed me you didn't want any attachments to a baby. You told me I was completely on my own, not to bother you."

He actually flinched, then closed his eyes and remained silent. But she had no pity for him, not after all that had happened. "That's not why the name is blank, though. Remember what you told me about your family? Well, I love my son, and I won't lose him to anyone, not to you, not to your damn relatives."

He looked blank and her irritation grew. "Your mother is a damn dragon, determined that everyone live according to her rules. You said that's why your brother left, why he became so hard. Your family frightens me, if you want the truth. Especially your brother."

His golden eyes darkened to amber. "That's ridiculous."

"You said he was the only one strong enough, independent enough to leave the company without a backward glance, to go his own way and tell the rest to go to hell. You said he was the only one who could make your mother nervous or your sister cry. You said he could do anything he set his mind to."

"No one makes my mother nervous, and my sister is a younger replica of her. Nothing touches them."

Angel buttoned her coat. "You've changed your mind then, but I won't. I won't take a chance that they'll try to take him away from me. I don't want them to know about my baby."

"Our..." He stopped and she saw his Adam's apple bob as he swallowed. "Our baby."

This was a point too important to skimp on. She went to him, holding his gaze no matter that he tried to stare her down. She pointed at his chest and forced the words out through stiff lips. "I don't know what new paternal mode you're in, but don't try to take him from me, Derek. I swear I'll disappear so quick you'll never find me or him again. I can do it. I've made plans."

"No."

She was incredulous. "You can't dictate to me! Not anymore. Whatever power you held over me, you gave up months ago when you rejected my pregnancy."

He didn't shout, but his near whisper was more effective than any raised voice could be. "Is that right? Then why are you here?"

She had to leave, now, before she tripped herself up. She turned toward the door. "There's an address in with the papers and photos. A post office box." She slanted her gaze his way. "I'm sure you remember it. You can get in touch with me there."

"Give me your phone number."

"I don't think so. But I'll call you soon."

"You're playing some game, Angel, and I don't like it."

She had her hand on the doorknob and slowly turned. "It's not a game." As she stepped through the door, she said over her shoulder, "And I don't like it either. Think about the baby, Derek, what you'd like to do, and I'll call you tonight. We can talk then, after you've gotten used to the idea."

He took two quick steps toward her. "What I'd like to do?" He frowned. "You want me to marry you?"

"Ha!" That was almost too funny for words. As she pulled the door shut, she said, "I wouldn't marry you if you were the last man on earth."

And she knew he'd heard her ill-advised words, because his fist thudded against the door.

Well, that hadn't gone off quite as planned. Actually, nothing like she'd planned. She'd hoped to seduce him, to regain his interest. She needed his help, his protection, and that was the only way she could think to get it. Sex had been the only thing he'd been interested in before, so it was what she'd planned to offer him now.

Only it felt as if she was the one seduced. Damn, why did he have to have this effect on her? Her body was still warm and tingling in places she'd all but forgotten about, and all because of a man she thought she'd grown to hate.

A man who had never affected her so intensely before.

Damn fickle fate, and whatever magic had made Derek Carter into a man her body desired.

CHAPTER TWO

DANE HIT THE DOOR once more for good measure, vexed with himself and the turn of events. Dammit, he hadn't meant to touch her. He had intended to get close to her, but not that close. He'd wanted to learn about her, to discover any involvement on her part, whether or not she could provide a clue to his brother's death. But he'd also planned to keep his hands to himself.

She'd made that impossible.

He'd wanted her the minute he'd seen her. She was lush and feminine and seemed to exude both determination and vulnerability. He'd also been stunned because Angel Morris looked nothing like the usual polished, poised businesswoman his brother tended to gravitate toward.

And then she'd demanded he kiss her.

Without knowing the exact nature of her relationship with Derek, he couldn't take the chance of turning her away without raising suspicions. And at the moment, given everything that had just transpired, he needed to keep her close, not drive her away.

He'd suspected she was there for a purpose, but God, he'd never considered a child.

Stalking across the office, he picked up the phone and punched in a quick series of numbers. His hand shook as he did so, and he cursed again. He could still feel the tingling heat of her on his hand, still pick up the faint hint of her scent lingering in the office. Angel might have been sexually aroused—her first time with him, to hear her tell it—but he felt ready to burst, not only with lust, but with a tumultuous mix of emotions that nearly choked him.

If not for her injured leg, he had a feeling they'd have both found incredible satisfaction. He'd have taken her and she would have let him. He grunted to himself, disgusted. Making love in his brother's office, on a damn desk, with a woman he barely knew and whose motives were more than suspicious. His own motives didn't bear close scrutiny.

"Sharpe here."

"Be ready," Dane barked, frustrated beyond all measure. "She should be leaving the building any second now." After receiving Angel's note, Dane had gone through her file, learning what he could about her, which wasn't much. When he'd first decided on the tail, he'd been reacting on instinct, his life as a P.I. making decisions almost automatic. Now he was driven by sheer male curiosity, and the possessive need to keep what was his. She had his nephew, and that formed an iron link between them that he wouldn't allow to be severed.

"Description?"

All his agents were very good, but Alec Sharpe, a brooding, almost secretive man of very few words, was the best. Dane trusted him completely.

"Blond, petite, probably limping a little. Wearing a long wool skirt and a dark coat."

"Got it."

The line went dead and Dane sighed, putting the phone down. Alec would contact him again using the car phone once he was sure of his lead. He figured it would take Angel at least a few minutes to maneuver out of the building. If she was parked in the lot, that would take even more time. If she hailed a cab, no telling how long he'd be left waiting.

Alec knew he was still checking out the circumstances of his brother's death, but no one else did. So far he'd found only enough to raise his concerns, but not enough to form any conclusions.

His brother's home had been discreetly searched, his papers riffled through. And Derek had some unaccounted time logged in his otherwise very orderly date book that made Dane think he'd had meetings best left unnoted.

Dane settled himself back behind his brother's desk and began going through the papers and pictures Angel had given him. The first picture of the baby had shaken him and he stared at it again for long moments. It was a photo taken at the hospital of a tiny red-faced newborn that looked almost identical to the twin photos his mother still displayed on her desk. The shape of the head was the same, the soft thatch of dark hair, the nose. He traced the lines of the scrunched-up face and a tiny fist, then smiled, feeling a fullness in his chest.

The next picture was more recent, and the changes were amazing. As plump as a Thanksgiving turkey, the baby had round rosy cheeks, large dark blue eyes, and an intent expression of disgruntlement that reminded him of Derek. Dane wanted to hold the baby, to touch him, make sure he was real. He was a part of his brother, left behind, and Dane knew without a doubt he'd protect him with his life. He hadn't even met the baby yet, but already the little fellow had found a permanent place in his heart just by existing.

Dane turned the picture over and found the words,

Grayson Adam Morris, November 13, 1997. A very recent picture, only a week old. And the name, it was respectable, solid, except that it should have read *Carter,* not *Morris.* Dane intended to see to that problem as soon as possible.

There were also copies of the birth records, and the baby's footprints, not much bigger than Dane's nose. He made note of the hospital Angel had gone to, the name of the doctor who'd attended her, and considered his next move. He shook his head, then looked impatiently at the phone. As if he'd willed it, the phone rang and he jerked it up.

"Yeah?"

Without preamble, Alec said, "She's getting on a bus and she has a baby and some tall guy with her."

Dane went still, then shot to his feet. The baby had been here with her? "Are you sure it's a baby?"

"Bundled up in a blue blanket, cradled in the guy's arms. I don't think it's her groceries."

"Who's the guy? Are you certain he's with her?"

"Tall, dark hair, sunglasses. Wearing a leather bomber jacket and worn, ragged jeans. He's holding her arm, they're chatting like old friends. You want me to find out?"

"No." His hand clenched iron-hard on the phone, and Dane decided he'd figure that one out on his own. "Just concentrate on the woman. You can see if he goes home with her, but other than that, ignore him."

"I'm on it. I'll get in touch when we reach a destination."

Again Dane hung up the phone, only this time he used a little more force than necessary. Damn her, had she been lying all along? Why would she bring the baby and a boyfriend with her when she claimed to have missed him—*Derek?* Didn't she think that was a bit risky, considering he could have followed her out?

He seethed for almost a half hour before Alec called him back with an address. The guy with Angel had in fact gone into the same building, and the building was located in one of the less auspicious areas of town. Dane pulled on his coat and put everything back into the shoe box, tucking it beneath his arm. He couldn't risk leaving anything behind where his family might find it. He locked the office on his way out.

Angel Morris thought she knew how to deal with him, but she was judging her moves on how Derek would react. Dane wasn't a game player, never had been and never would be. His family had figured that out too late; the sooner Miss Morris figured it out, the quicker they could get things settled. He intended to explain it all to her this very day.

WITH THANKSGIVING not too far off, many of the houses had Christmas decorations already up. All the shops he passed had their front windows filled with displays. But as he neared the address given to him by Alec, the spirit of Christmas melted away. Bright lights were replaced with boarded-up windows. Graffiti rather than green wreaths decorated the doors. None of it made any sense. Dane knew Angel had lived in a very upscale apartment complex while working for the Aeric Corporation. He knew from her file that she'd lost her job there after Derek had taken information from her to assure the success of a hostile takeover. But surely she wasn't destitute. She'd made a good yearly wage.

Wary of the denizens in the area, Dane parked his car in a garage and walked the last block to Angel's home. The bitter November wind cut through his clothes and made him shiver, but filled with purpose, he easily ignored the cold. When he reached the brick three-family home that matched the address Alec had given him, he gave a sigh of relief. Calling the house nice would be too generous, but it was secure and well-tended, located on a quiet dead-end street of older homes. Angel and his nephew should be relatively safe here.

At least until he moved them.

The front door wasn't barred. He entered a foyer of sorts and looked at the mailboxes. There was no listing for an Angel Morris, and he frowned. Then he saw an A. Morton and his instincts buzzed. Going on a hunch, he figured that had to be Angel. Why would she hide behind an alias, unless she had a reason to hide? He recalled his purpose in first starting this ruse. Though it was obvious she knew nothing of Derek's death, he couldn't discount the possibility that she might have helped set him up for the fall, even innocently. She certainly had plenty of reason to hate him and want him out of her life, and she professed to fear his family, so why then had she approached him today? Because she was surprised he *wasn't* dead? Did she have contact with an insider who had informed her of his resurrection? Very few people were privy to the fact of his and Derek's relationship.

The apartment number listed was on ground level and he went to the door, then knocked, bracing himself for the sight of her again. She'd really thrown him for a loop with her sensual response to him. And he knew in his gut her reaction hadn't been feigned. Just remembering it made his every muscle tense.

"Come on in, Mick."

Dane tightened his jaw and his temper slipped. So

the guy who'd been with her, Mick, was welcome in any time? Did she respond as hotly with Mick as she did with him? Dane turned the doorknob and stepped inside.

Angel was lying on a sofa, her injured leg propped up on pillows. She wore only a flannel shirt and loose shorts cut down from a pair of old gray sweats. Thick socks covered her feet. She shoved herself half upright and stared at him in undiluted horror.

Dane looked at her from head to toe, and as a man he appreciated the earthy picture she presented. But he'd use caution from here on out. Angel seemed to vacillate between fear and awareness. Dane decided that either way he'd use her emotions against her to find out for sure what her purpose might be.

Her fair hair was tousled and spread out over the arm of the sofa. Her breasts beneath the worn flannel looked soft and full, without the casing of a bra. Her legs were very long and pale. He saw the vicious scars on her left leg, still angry and red, and his simmering temper jumped in a new direction.

He closed the door quietly and her incredible green eyes went wide and wary. "Derek."

He indicated her cushioned leg. "You're hurt worse than you let on."

Color washed over her face as she started to rise from the sofa. Dane was beside her in an instant. He caught her shoulders, pressing her back down, feeling the narrow bones beneath his hands, aware of her smallness, her softness. "Be still. It's obvious you overdid it today. You shouldn't have been up and around."

He perched on the sofa cushion next to her, feeling her apprehension while he examined her leg, trailing his fingers gently over her smooth skin. Just seeing the scars left behind made him wince in sympathy.

She seemed to gather herself all at once. "Just what are you doing here?"

"Checking up on you."

"How? How did you find me?"

"I had you followed." His gaze swung from her leg to her outraged face. "Why use an alias?"

Angel paled a little. "What are you talking about?"

"Your mailbox."

Rather than answer, she tried bluffing her way with anger. "That's none of your business. And why do you care anyway?"

He was good at lying when it suited him. "Because I have the feeling you'd never have let me get this close. But I second-guessed you, didn't I?" He waggled a finger in her face, bringing back her healthy surge of angry color. "I think I'll keep close tabs on you from now on."

She gasped and he added a not-too-subtle warning. "You can keep your secret, Angel—for now. But when I'm ready, I will know what's going on."

Her lips firmed and her look became obstinate. But beneath it all, he saw a measure of pain. "You're not completely mended yet, are you? Were you hurt anywhere else?"

She gave him another stubborn frown and his attention dropped to her body. Holding her gaze, he asked quietly, "Would you like me to find out for myself?"

She jerked and her arms crossed protectively over her breasts. "All right! I also had some bruised ribs and a few cuts and scrapes—all of which are now healed."

He continued to look at her, and she turned her head away. "My shoulder was dislocated, too."

"Good God. What the hell happened to you?"

Even before she spoke, he knew no truths would cross her beautiful lips. Amazing that he could read her so easily after only knowing her such a short time, but he could.

Her chin lifted and she said, "I fell."

"Down a mountainside?"

"Down a long flight of stairs, actually."

Keeping his hands to himself became impossible. He cupped her cheeks in both hands. Whatever had happened, it had been serious, and talking about it obviously agitated her. "You could have been killed."

She started, and her eyes met his. For the briefest moment she looked so lost, he wanted to fold her close and swear to protect her. *Idiot*. Then she shook her head and that stubbornness was back tenfold, forcing an emotional distance between them. "My leg is the only thing scarred. Nasty-looking, isn't it?"

Without missing a beat, he said, "You have beautiful legs. A little scarring won't change that." And it was true. Her legs were long, smooth, shapely. He imagined those long legs wrapped around him while he touched her again, only this time she would climax, holding him inside her so he could feel every small tremor, every straining muscle. He nearly groaned.

He let his hand rest lightly on her knee and moved his thoughts to safer ground. "You've no reason to be embarrassed, Angel. The scars will fade."

"You think a few scars matter to me?"

He did, but he wasn't dumb enough to tell her that, not when she was practically spitting with ire. She hadn't forgiven him yet for Derek's past sins, and for his own, in questioning the baby's parentage. But she would. He'd see to it.

He put his hand to her cheek and noticed again the way her pulse raced, how she held her breath. "I'm sorry you were hurt." Then he kissed her. As angry as he was, he needed a taste of her again. She may have decided her little sampling of lust in the office was enough, but he'd found only frustration. He'd barely touched her, barely begun to excite her, and she'd heated up like a grand fireworks display, perilously close to exploding. He was still semi-hard because of it and caught between wanting to bury himself inside her, to see her go all the way, climaxing with him, and wanting to shake her into telling him what her ridiculous game was.

At first she froze, but seconds later her body pressed into his. One small hand lifted to his neck and that simple touch made him shudder. He pulled back, not wanting to test himself. Angel stared at him, wide-eyed.

"Nice place," he said, hoping to distract her and himself. His gaze wandered around the sparse room, taking in the worn wallpaper and faded carpet. He didn't really mean to be facetious, but she took it that way.

"You don't have to like it, Derek, since you don't live here."

He dropped his gaze back to her flushed face. With one arm above her, his body beside her, he effectively caged her in. He could tell she didn't like it; he liked it a little too much. "I want to know why you're living here. What happened to your apartment?"

Her eyes narrowed. "I lost it."

"Why?"

"Because I hadn't paid the rent."

He sighed. This was like pulling teeth, but she obviously wasn't going to make it easy for him. "Okay, we'll play twenty questions. Why didn't you pay the rent?"

Angel stared at him, then put one arm over her eyes and laughed. "God, you're incredible. Everything is so simple for you."

Wrapping long fingers around her wrist, he carried her arm to her stomach and held it there. He felt her muscles clench. "Why didn't you pay your rent?"

In a burst of temper, she slapped his hand away and half raised herself to glare at him. "Because I had no money, you ass! I lost my job, thanks to you, and no one else would hire me for what I was good at. After you finished, I was considered a *bad risk*. I tried everywhere, and in the process, ran through a lot of my savings. For a short time, I had a job as a waitress, but then I had the accident and was laid up for a while. People won't hire women on crutches, you know. My savings weren't so deep that I could afford to stay in an expensive place, keep up my medical insurance, and pay additional medical bills besides, so I moved here. Satisfied?"

Her shout had awakened the baby, and Dane looked toward the sound of disgruntled infant rage. Angel groaned. "Now look what you've done. Well, don't just sit there, get out of my way."

Her mood shifts were almost amusing, and fascinating to watch—when she wasn't ripping his guts out with regret for the way his brother had treated her. She started to sit up, and again he pressed her back. "I'll get him."

"No!"

He caught her chin and turned her face up to his. "Now or later, Angel, what difference does it make? I want to meet him. I promise, I'll bring him to you."

She bit her lip and her eyes were dark with wariness, but she apparently realized there would be no contest if they tried to match strength or wills. At least, not at the moment. He had the feeling, on a better day, her strength would amaze him.

Dane stared a second more, wishing there was a simpler way to reassure her, then went to fetch the baby. He followed the sounds of the cries to where Grayson was making his discontent known. When Dane entered the room he was assailed by the scent of powder and baby lotion, soft soothing scents. Grayson's pudgy arms and legs churned ferociously, and with incredible care, Dane lifted him to his shoulder. The baby was soaking wet.

Cloth diapers and plastic pants were on top of a dresser, along with a few folded gowns. Dane scooped up what he thought he might need and went back to the main room and the worried mother. Angel immediately reached her arms out.

"No, he's soaked, which means I'm soaked. No reason for both of us to become soggy. I think if you talk me through it, I can get him changed."

Angel's mouth fell open and she stared at him as if he'd grown an extra nose. He smiled at her reaction.

She looked dumbfounded and utterly speechless.

"I know," he said, grinning, "changing diapers isn't part of my established repertoire, either. But I'm efficient at adapting."

In the short time he'd known her, she'd thrown him off balance more times than he cared to think about; it was only fair that he get a little retaliation when and where he could.

He didn't know a hell of a lot about babies, but he figured now was as good a time as any to learn. "Where should I put him to clean him up?"

Finally managing to close her mouth, Angel fretted, then pointed to a table. "There's a plastic changing pad there. You can put him on that and change him."

"Good enough." Dane shook out the padded plastic sheet with one hand, spread it out on the table, and carefully laid Grayson down. The baby wasn't pleased with delayed gratification, so Dane hurried. With Angel's instructions, he got the baby diapered and dried and redressed, all in under five minutes which he considered a major accomplishment. Grayson had stopped squalling, but he still fussed, one fist flailing the air, occasionally getting caught in his mouth for a slurpy suck or two.

This time when Angel held out her arms, Dane handed the baby to her. The entire right side of his shirt was wet and clinging to his chest.

She looked away, pressing her face against the baby. "He's hungry."

"Do you want me to get him a bottle?"

"No." Angel cleared her throat, then said, "He's… breastfed. I just…need a little privacy."

"Oh. *Oh.*" Dane looked at her breasts, imagined the process, and didn't want to take so much as a single step from the room. He also couldn't bear to hear the baby whimpering. "I'll, uh, just go in the kitchen and try to rinse out my shirt."

"You do that. And stay in there while it dries."

He leaned down and caught her chin. Her eyes opened wide on his and she drew in a deep startled

breath. "All right. But don't always expect me to follow orders, honey. You're going to have to get used to
me being here." Knowing he shouldn't, but unable to
stop himself, he leaned down and pressed a firm kiss
to her mouth. It felt damn good. He walked out while
she sputtered.

He wanted to kiss her again, as a starting point,
knowing where they'd finish. He wanted to show her
he was no sloth in bed, contrary to her damn miscon-
ception. He wanted to find out the truth about his
brother's death and her involvement with him, and he
wanted to protect her and take care of her and Grayson.
There were a lot of *wants* piling up on him too quickly
and contradicting each other.

Christ, what had his brother gotten into?

He pulled off his shirt and rinsed the damp spot under running water, then wrung it out and hung it over
a chair to dry. The apartment, thankfully, wasn't cold.
He scratched his bare chest and looked around.

Her tiny kitchen was all but empty. The cabinets
held the essentials, but not much else. With further inspection, he found the refrigerator was in similar shape.
Dane frowned, then began snooping. Hell, maybe he
should call her Mother Hubbard.

The conclusion he came to was not a happy one.
Damn the little idiot, she should have contacted him
sooner, before she got in such miserable shape. He immediately snatched that thought back because if she'd
tried, she would have encountered his family, and the
mere thought made him queasy. She was right to fear
them.

He had wondered what she was after, why she'd
come to him if indeed marriage wasn't her goal. Now
he assumed sheer desperation had been her motive. She

needed financial help, and as the baby's father, he could give it. She was proud, and she claimed to have already suffered several rejections from Derek, a possibility that made Dane so angry he wanted to howl. But pride was no replacement for desperation, especially with a baby to think about. But if that's all it had been, then why hadn't she simply said so? Why come on to him, pretend she still cared?

He sat in a kitchen chair, stewing, listening to her murmur to the baby, hearing the sweet huskiness of her voice. Goose bumps rose on the back of his neck. He called out, "Angel, why don't you use disposable diapers? Aren't they easier?"

There was a hesitation before she said, "I don't like them."

Which he translated to mean they cost too much. His fingertips tapped on the table top, followed by his fist. "Where did you take therapy for your leg?" He hoped it was someplace close, so she hadn't had to travel too far.

There was mumbling that he couldn't decipher, then she said, "I didn't take therapy. And what do you know about it anyway?"

He stiffened. No therapy? With a lot of effort, he curbed his temper. "I've seen similar breaks. I recognize the incisions on your ankle and knee where they inserted the titanium rod. It was a hell of a break, so I know damn well therapy was suggested."

Silence. He almost growled. He did stand to pace. "How long ago were you hurt, Angel, and don't you dare tell me it isn't any of my damn business!"

Another pause, and a very small voice. "A couple of months ago."

It took him a second, and then he was out of the

kitchen, stalking back to the couch to loom over her. She took one fascinated look at his naked chest, squeaked, and pulled her flannel shirt over her exposed breast as much as possible. Grayson's small fist pushed the shirt aside again. But Dane was keeping his gaze resolutely on Angel's face anyway. In a soft, menacing tone, he asked, "A couple of months ago, as in when the baby was born?"

She gave a small nod. "Grayson was early, by a little more than six weeks. The accident started my labor."

His insides twisted and he could barely force the words out. "Who took care of you?" He drew a breath and felt his nostrils flare. "Who helped you when you were in the hospital? When you first came home?"

Her gaze shifted away and she smoothed her hand over the baby's head, ruffling his few glossy curls. The sound of the baby's sucking was loud and voracious. "There was no one, Derek, you know that. No family, no close friends. Grayson and I helped each other."

Without meaning to, without even wanting to, he looked at the baby. Grayson's small mouth eagerly drew on her nipple while a tiny fist pressed to her pale breast. His eyes were closed, his small body cradled comfortably to Angel's. Dane felt a lump in his throat the size of a grapefruit and had to turn away.

So he'd seen her breast? So what. He'd seen plenty in his day, just never any with a baby attached. He didn't feel what he should have felt at the sight of her pale flesh, which was undiluted lust. Lust he understood, but this other thing, whatever the hell it was, he didn't like.

He snatched up his still-damp shirt and shrugged it on, then grabbed his coat. There were a lot of things

he had to do today. "I'll be back in a couple of hours."
He looked at her, his expression severe. "Make sure
you're here when I get back, Angel. Do you understand?"

She hugged the baby tighter, then waved a negligent
hand without looking at him. "Go on. Just go."

"I'll be back."

She nodded, more or less pretending he was already
gone. Dane didn't know what to say to her, what to
think or feel. He was reaching for the doorknob when
a soft knock sounded, and a second later it opened.

It was a toss-up who was more surprised, Dane, or
the young man standing in front of him, his arms laden
with a large pizza and a wide grin on his face.

That grin disappeared real quick, replaced by a ferocious look of menace. "Who the hell are you?"

Dane, at his most autocratic and not in the least
threatened by the rangy youth, lifted his eyebrow and
turned to Angel. "I think that may be my question."

CHAPTER THREE

"NO," ANGEL SAID, keeping her voice low and managing to cover herself as Grayson fell asleep and released her breast. He was such a good baby, so sweet. She loved him so much she'd gladly do anything necessary to protect him. "It's not your question because it's none of your business."

She quickly buttoned up her shirt. Mick automatically put the pizza on the coffee table and took the baby from her while Derek stood there, that damn imperious eyebrow raised high, and watched. Slowly, because her leg really was aching, she lifted herself into something closer to a sitting position, resting against the arm of the couch with her leg still outstretched.

"Well." Derek smiled, but it wasn't a particularly nice smile, more a baring of teeth which Mick responded to with a scowl. "I'm not leaving until I know who he is." He sat down and stretched out his own long, strong legs, at his leisure, and waited.

Angel sighed. God, she really didn't need this. First the trip downtown, which had tired her leg terribly. Then the kiss and his naked chest... Her mind was turning to mush.

Mick bristled. "Just who the hell do you think you are, coming in here and demanding answers?"

"The baby's father."

"Oh." Mick straightened, blinked, then glanced at

Angel. Derek had said that with so much relish, so much ridiculous pride, she was temporarily stunned herself. His complete acceptance was such a swift turn-around, she was having trouble accepting it.

It took her a moment before she nodded, giving Mick permission. She knew he wouldn't say another word without it and yet Derek wasn't likely to leave unless he got his answer. She knew how incredibly stubborn he could be. And even though he wasn't acting like himself, he could pull out his ruthlessness at any moment. She didn't want Mick caught in the cross fire.

"I'm Mick Dawson, a neighbor." Mick jutted his chin. "And a friend."

"A very good friend," Angel added, thinking of how much help Mick had been to her since she'd first moved here. She surveyed Derek, lounging at his leisure, his shirt tight across his broad shoulders and his hands laced over his flat stomach. She wanted to kick him for looking so damn good. "You asked who helped me. Well, once I moved here, Mick did. He picks up my groceries for me, gets my mail and paper." She waved at her leg. "Until recently I've been pretty much out of commission. Mick lives upstairs, his mother owns the building, and he's been an enormous help."

Mick started to hand her the baby back, still keeping one eye on Derek, and that seemed to galvanize Derek into action. "I can take him," he said, reaching for Grayson. "You should go ahead and eat."

Mick again looked at her for guidance. Derek's willingness to take part wasn't something she'd counted on. It was an awkward situation, but it shouldn't have been—not if he would just act like himself. But he didn't seem to be in an accommodating mood today, which she supposed was like him after all.

Exasperation made her tone extra sharp. "Really, Derek, weren't you just about to leave?"

He smiled. "I can stay a little longer. Besides, I like holding the baby." He pressed his cheek to the top of Grayson's head, and his expression caused a silly sick reaction in Angel's stomach. "He smells good."

Mick folded his arms and stared. "So you're just now showing up? You waltz in today and pretend to be the happy father? To my mind, you're about two months too late."

Oh no. Angel tensed her muscles in dread of Derek's response. "Mick…"

Derek nodded, cutting off Angel's warning. "I agree. Actually, I'm close to a year late by my calculations. But I'm going to be near at hand from now on." Then without missing a beat, he asked, "How old did you say you were?"

Mick grinned his sinister street-tough grin. "I didn't." Before Derek could react, he added, "But I'm sixteen. And before Miss Morris makes it sound like I've done her any big favors, she's helped me out a lot, too. Without her, I doubt I'd make it out of high school."

Angel couldn't stand it when Mick did that, put himself down, especially since he was such a remarkable young man. Unfortunately, he still didn't believe her about that. "That's not true, Mick, and you know it. You're very bright and you'd have figured out that math with or without my help." She turned to Derek, for some reason anxious for him to understand. "Mick works two jobs, plus school, plus he pretty much runs this place. His mother is often…sick."

Mick gave Derek a solemn, measuring look. "My mother is an alcoholic."

Angel closed her eyes on a wave of pain. Mick had such a chip on his shoulder with everyone but her. He asked for disdain, as if he felt it was his due, then would fight tooth and nail to prove a point. She still wasn't certain what that point might be, though.

With no visible sign of reaction, Derek looked at Mick. Angel knew Mick looked much older, much wiser than any sixteen-year-old boy should look. She also knew, deep down, he was still a kid, a little afraid at times, a lot needy given that his life had been nothing but empty turmoil. Her praise always embarrassed him, but he thrived on it. And she loved him like a little brother. If Derek said anything at all that would upset Mick, she'd manage to get her sorry butt off the couch and kick him out.

But he surprised her by cradling the baby in one arm and offering Mick his hand, which Mick warily accepted. "I appreciate what you've done for her. Did she move here when she was first hurt?"

"Yeah, not long after." Mick narrowed his eyes again, very nice dark brown eyes that she knew all the high school girls swooned over. But Mick didn't spare time for serious girlfriends. He was too busy surviving. "If I hadn't been here, I don't know if she'd have made it. She was pretty banged up, and Grayson was just a tiny squirt. Even getting herself something to eat was difficult, but she did it, because she had to stay healthy for Grayson. Truth is, I don't know how the hell she managed."

"Don't be so melodramatic, Mick." Angel didn't want them talking about her and she didn't want Derek to view her as a helpless, pitiful victim. He seemed to be hanging on Mick's every word, analyzing them and drawing his own conclusions. She didn't like the way his intense interest made her feel.

Later, after she figured out what he was up to, then she'd confide her biggest worry and hopefully he'd be able to take care of it. She cleared her throat. "Derek, you can put Grayson in his crib if you'd like. I don't want to hold you up."

He surprised her again by agreeing. After he settled Grayson, he came back in and walked over to her, giving her a gentle kiss on the forehead that made her skin tingle and her breath catch. She frowned at him, but held her tongue. When they were alone, safe from Mick's protective nature, she'd set him straight about his familiarity.

Derek looked at Mick. "Could you walk me out?"

The bottom dropped out of her stomach. "What for? I think you can find your way out the door. It's straight ahead."

Derek grinned at her. "Man talk, honey. Mick understands."

"It's all right," Mick said to her, then followed Derek out despite her protests.

For all of two minutes, she fretted, imagining every kind of hostile confrontation. But when Mick came back in he was shaking his head and almost laughing.

"What? What did he want?"

"A list."

She searched his face, stymied. "A list of what?"

"Everything you might need." Her mouth fell open. "He also wanted to know if there was anyplace safe around here for him to park his car since he plans to be hanging around a lot. I told him he could use the garage."

"But you don't let anyone use the garage!"

"Yeah, but he has a *really* nice car. I wouldn't want it to get stripped."

She could imagine what kind of car he had: expensive. What was it about males of all ages that made them car crazy?

Mick picked up a huge slice of pizza and took a healthy bite, then went into the kitchen for plates. "You want juice to drink?"

Absently, her thoughts on Derek, she said, "Please." She made it a habit to drink juice, since it was healthier for the baby. Real juice was her one small luxury.

They ate in near silence, and Angel was aware of the passing minutes. When she caught Mick watching her watch the clock, he grinned. "I'm not about to leave until he comes back. He raised hell with me because the door was unlocked when he got here."

Indignation rose, hot and fierce, crowding out her other, more conflicting emotions. "He yelled at you?"

"No, he just told me I should be more careful. I, um, gave him your key. He's having a couple made, so I can have one, and he can have one. That way, he said, you can keep your door locked, and you won't have to get up to let us in if you're resting your leg or feeding the baby or something."

"Didn't you tell him you already had a key and that he didn't need one?"

"It didn't seem like a smart thing to do."

He was still grinning at her. She shook her head. Never before had she seen Mick take to another person this easily. "Well, I'll tell him. If he actually does come back."

"Oh, he'll be back, all right." Mick tilted his head

at her. "Are you going to tell him what's been happening?"

"Not right away. I have to find out first if he's going to get involved with Grayson, if I can count on him to help without having to worry that he'll sue me for custody. I can't risk having Grayson around that family. It's my bet the threats start with them. His mother, according to him, is as far removed from the grandmotherly type as a woman can get, and the stories he shared about his brother don't even bear repeating they're so dreadful. And," she said, when Mick's mouth twitched, "before you start grinning again, I don't need his help with anything but protection and you know it."

He handed her another piece of pizza. "For a little bitty single lady you've done okay. But you know as well as I do that things are getting worse for you. First the job, then your old apartment, then the accident. That bit with your car still makes me sick when I think of it. You can't keep up. You never get enough rest and your leg hurts all the time from overdoing it. You need to let it heal. Hell, you need therapy."

Angel had long ago quit trying to curb Mick's colorful vocabulary. Now she just rolled her eyes. "I'm getting more papers to type up every day. Pretty soon, everything will even out."

He only shook his head. He didn't really approve of the late hours she spent transcribing papers for local businessmen and college students, but he helped her anyway by picking up the papers and dropping them off. Like her, Mick knew she had few options.

They both looked up when they heard the doorknob turn. It was locked as per Derek's instruction. He looked supremely satisfied as he used the key to get in. "Much better."

Angel glared at him. "You're not keeping a key to my apartment, Derek, so forget it."

He didn't look daunted. "Mick, you want to help me carry a few things in?"

"Sure." Mick was already on his feet, setting the half-eaten slice of pizza aside. He looked anxious, and Angel imagined he was every bit as curious as she was.

Then she remembered herself. "Now wait a minute! I don't want or need anything from you! I already told you that."

Derek went out the door whistling. Mick followed him, trying to hide his smile. Angel hadn't seen him grin this often in one day since she'd met him. They returned with several boxes and various brands of disposable diapers. Angel could have wept. Using cloth had been so tiring and so much added work, but the expense of disposables was out of the question.

As they carried them in, Derek explained. "The woman at the store told me some kids are allergic to some kinds. You can tell me which works best and I'll pick up more of them. But this ought to hold you for now."

He set the boxes in the living room, a huge wall of them, then tiptoed into Grayson's room where she couldn't see him. The apartment was tiny, only the two small bedrooms, a closet-sized bath, then the open area of the living room and kitchen, separated by half a wall which cornered the refrigerator. Angel seethed, even more so when he came back out carrying the almost filled diaper pail. "Where are you taking that?"

"To the dumpster." He made a face, turning his

nose away. ''I left the clean ones in there in case you wanted to use them for dust rags or something.''

She started to get up, but he was already out the door again and she slumped back in frustration.

By the time he and Mick finished carrying things in, she had full cupboards, a stuffed refrigerator and freezer, a bathroom that practically overflowed with feminine products, and a sore throat from all her complaining, which Derek blithely ignored.

Not only did she now have the basics, but she had luxuries she hadn't recently been able to afford. Had Mick told Derek that she missed conditioning her hair and giving herself facials? That she missed creamy lotions and scented bath oils? Or had he figured it out on his own? She wouldn't ask. He'd simply have to take it all back; she wouldn't be bought. Material things weren't what she wanted or needed from him.

Mick dropped the last large sack behind the couch and straightened. "I've got to get going. I have to be at work in fifteen minutes."

Derek came in and handed him a newly purchased ice-cold soda, holding his own in his other hand. Another luxury she'd avoided. She had milk, water, tea and for health reasons, juice. The soda looked so good, her mouth watered.

Derek propped his hip on the back of the couch, close to her head, and Angel forgot about the soda to scoot away. Derek winked at her, knowing damn good and well she didn't want him that close, before turning to Mick. "Where do you work?"

"Part of the week at the garage on the corner. The weekends at the Fancy Lady. It's a neighborhood bar. I wash dishes there."

Mick had his chin jutted out, his obstinate expression

that dared Derek to make a wisecrack. Instead, Derek appeared thoughtful. "Aren't you too young to work in a place like that?"

"I look old enough. No one ever questions it."

"I suppose not." Again, he stuck out his hand. "I appreciate your help today, Mick."

"No problem."

"You know, if you ever wanted to work just one job, for decent pay, I have a friend who's looking for someone."

Mick narrowed his eyes, skeptical. Few things had ever been given to him, and when something good came along, he generally doubted it, and with good reason. "Doing what?"

"Various things. Cleanup, phone duty, running errands. The hours are flexible, but the pay's good."

Silence dragged out while Mick considered the suggestion. Finally he shrugged. "I'll think about it."

"Take your time. The job's not going anywhere." Derek locked the door behind Mick after he left, then turned to Angel. He stared at her until her pulse picked up and her blood raced. "Now."

Startled, she stiffened her shoulders and frowned. "Now what, you...you...? How dare you come barging in here rearranging my life?" She'd been so enthralled, listening to the male bonding taking place before her eyes, and then he'd looked at her with such warmth in his gaze she'd practically jumped when he spoke. Now all her grievances came swamping back. "You can take all this right back out to your car, and you can hand me back my key." She thrust her hand, palm up, toward him. "Right now."

Derek leaned against the door, studying her for a

moment, seemingly gathering his thoughts. After a moment, he said, "I like Mick. He's a good kid."

That threw her off guard. Again. Slowly, her hand fell back to the couch. "Yes, he is. I don't know what you were up to with that job offer, but if it isn't legitimate, I'll...."

He grinned. "You'll what? No, don't answer that. The possibilities are too frightening to contemplate." He walked to her and sat down beside her on the couch, then took her hand before she could try to get up. "It's a real job, certainly a better one than what he'll find around here. I thought you'd like to know he was working someplace safer. Hell, I could even get my friend to throw in a car with the job, to make sure he's protected when driving."

Angel was struck speechless. Between his touch and his words, she couldn't seem to draw enough breath. Such generosity had never been a part of Derek, at least not a part she'd seen. "I don't understand you."

His thumb rubbed over her knuckles. She tried to tug her hand away, but he held firm. "I know you don't, and I'm sorry about that. Sorry about a lot of things." He gave her a sideways look, then sighed, the sound tinged with real regret. "I hesitate to make you angry, but—"

"Then don't."

"Here's how it's going to be, honey." His tone was stern, his expression determined. "You're going to keep everything I've just given you. And you're going to use it, too. And enjoy it, I hope, but I suppose that's up to you. I know you don't like me or trust me right now, and that's okay. I understand it. But I'm not just going to disappear or come visit once a month for fifteen minutes. And I'm not going to sit back and ignore you when I know you need things. I can help you, and you're going to accept my help. God knows, you should have had it all along."

Angel shook her hand free, then kept it held protectively away from him. A glint of amusement brightened his eyes. She felt swamped in confusion, uncertain what to do or say next. She'd never dealt with Derek in this mood, firm but concerned and caring. It was sort of...sweet. *No, whoa on that thought.* She would not be suckered in by him. Never again.

Glaring at him, she said, "Why don't you just tell me now what you're up to and save us both some time?"

"What I'm up to? Well, all right. Let's see. I want to help you. I want you to trust me again—"

"Ha!"

"—and I want to be with you." He said that last part with a small smile, and his fingertips grazed her chin. She ducked her face away. "I want to be a part of Grayson's life and be a father to him. I want to show you that I can be responsible and honorable and that I'm not a total jerk. I want...a lot of things."

She stared at him hard, unnerved. "You're an alien, right? Derek was zapped into space and you were sent to replace him? That's the only thing I'll believe."

He laughed, but his eyes looked sad. "Would you like that, if the real Derek was gone for good?"

None of this, most especially his somber tone, made any sense. Angel dropped her head against the back of the couch and sighed. "I never wished you any harm, Derek. Not even when I thought I hated you, when you suggested we'd both be better off without the baby. I just didn't want to ever see you again."

"But you invited me back into your life. I may be

trying to take up more of that life than you're comfortable with, but I won't hurt you again. I promise.''

Without lifting her head from the couch, she turned her face toward him. In a soft whisper, she said, ''Do you actually believe I'd ever trust you again?''

''Yes.'' He said it without hesitation. His eyes were dark and sincere and intense, probing into her mind, trying to read her thoughts. ''I can get you to trust me again.''

The mere possibility scared her half to death. She could never leave herself that vulnerable again; her baby's well-being depended on her strength. ''And then what? You'll steal my baby away from me?'' Her chest squeezed tight with the thought and she knew her voice shook. She couldn't help it. She'd known the risks involved when she contacted him, but Mick was right. She couldn't handle things on her own anymore. The threat was there and it was real and she was afraid, not so much for herself, but for Grayson. He relied on her, and she had to protect him. That's what mattered most.

If it was Derek's family behind the awful threats, as she suspected, he might well be the only person who could protect her.

Derek stood, giving her his back. His fists rested on his hips and he looked angry and frustrated and somehow heartsick. ''I would never take him from you,'' he said, the words low and raspy. ''I'd swear it to you, but I realize my promises mean nothing—yet. All I want to do is help.''

''But you never wanted to help me before. You made it clear you wanted no part of me or the baby.''

She heard him swallow, then he turned to face her. He looked angry, and almost confused, a bit desperate.

"I was an ass. An idiot and a bastard. *I'm here now, Angel.* Don't shut me out."

She really had little choice in the matter. It was difficult to say the words, but he seemed so different, not at all like the man she'd known. Her reactions, her feelings toward him, were different, too. He touched something inside her that the old Derek hadn't gotten close to. She supposed anyone could change, and she knew how Grayson had affected her life, the impact he'd made on her.

As if reading her mind, he whispered, "Grayson hit me like a punch in the heart. A tiny little person, part of my blood." His eyes narrowed. "You said it yourself. How holding him made you feel."

"But I carried him and went through all the changes the pregnancy caused. I got sick in the mornings, stayed awake at night as he kicked, stayed tired *all* the time. I felt him grow and I saw him born. I saw him take his first breath, give his first cry."

"You think I don't regret missing all that?"

He sounded so sincere, but she just didn't know. Unless he planned to take the baby from her, she could see no reason for an emotional deception. She searched his face, but it was a futile effort; whatever he felt was well hidden. Damn, she had so few choices in this. "All right."

He let out a gust of air, ran a hand through his hair, rubbed his chin, then smiled. "Okay. Shew, I'm glad that's settled." He looked much relieved, his shoulders no longer so tense, his eyes no longer worried. "Okay. On to the next battle. I want to move you someplace else."

Angel could only stare at him in disbelief. "You're

nuts. I give ground on one little thing and you want to take over!''

"Come on, honey, you can't *like* living here."

She wanted to shove his condescension back into his face until he choked on it. "I most certainly do like it," she lied, knowing Mick to be the only redeeming factor of her present residence. "I'm close to the downtown businesses and I do transcription at home for a lot of the offices and the students. I make enough money to keep the rent paid and my health insurance active. It's convenient and I enjoy the people and I'm not moving."

He pursed his mouth and studied her, then must have decided not to push his luck. "I'll let that go for now."

"You'll let it go forever!"

"Now, about therapy." Angel rolled her eyes, which didn't even slow him down. "I've known people with compound fractures. It can take months to heal with proper treatment, and you've not had that."

"I have a very good doctor."

"Who no doubt told you that you needed therapy."

That was true, but it had been out of the question. Not only did she not have anyone to watch Grayson, but she had no way of getting back and forth each day to the therapist and her insurance would have only covered a small percentage of the bill. She shook her head at Derek, hopeless. "It's been almost two months. It's too late for therapy."

"Nonsense. I know the perfect person. I'll have her come here. What would be convenient for you?"

Angel rubbed her eyes. He was coming too fast and too hard, and suddenly she was tired. He'd invaded her life, her emotions. She'd had such a simple plan, and she'd thought for a while it might work. Then he'd held

Grayson, and he'd kissed her and taken off his shirt and bought her disposable diapers and lotion and she just couldn't take it all in. She didn't have it in her to continue fighting him, at least, not right now. "Derek, please. Let off a little. You're here. You've met your son. My apartment is stuffed with new purchases. Isn't that enough for now?"

"I have a lot to make up for."

She certainly wouldn't argue that point with him. "Well, let's save it for another time, okay? Right now, I'm exhausted. I worked really late last night finishing up some papers that were due this morning and Grayson still wakes up during the night to be fed. If you'll take yourself out of here, I'd like a nap."

"What papers?"

With barely veiled impatience, she explained once again. "I transcribe files or notes for the local offices when one of the secretaries is ill, and I do term papers and such for students at the college. I'm sure you remember I have top-of-the-line office equipment, even if my computer *is* getting a little dated."

"You don't have to continue working. I can give you money."

Just like that, he expected her to become totally dependent on him. She wanted to get up and smack him, and she wanted to cry. Neither would have brought about the results she needed. "I'll pretend you didn't say that."

He stood there, obviously undecided, and she waited. But he only smiled, his look rueful. "Come on, I'll help you into bed."

Panic edged into her weariness. She didn't want him touching her again, getting so close. He'd kissed her, and that brief touch had unnerved her, had made her belly tingle. When he'd taken off his shirt, she'd almost groaned. He'd been her first lover, her only lover. And she'd never found fault with his physique. Though their single night together hadn't been great, she knew a lot of the blame was due to her own uncertainty. And now, she missed so much the closeness of being with a man, not necessarily sexually, but with gentleness and concern, a special friendship between two people who know they're destined to be lovers. Or who have been lovers in the past. The intimacy was there for her, whether she despised him or not.

But despising him was no longer an issue. He was too damn different.

"No thank you," she muttered, shaken by her own revelations, afraid of her own weaknesses. But true to form, he wasn't listening and had her pulled up close to his side before she could move away. With one hard muscled arm around her waist, the other holding her elbow, he practically carried her into her room. She could feel his heat, his strength, and it felt too good to be coddled, to have some of the burden lifted, even if in a superficial way.

Closing her eyes didn't help, only made her more aware of the shifting of muscle, the hardness of his body, his incredible heat and enticing scent. The man even *smelled* different, more welcoming, more comforting. More exciting.

Her bedroom door had been shut until now and when Derek stepped inside he paused to look around. She pulled away from him, her hands shaking, and he took her elbow to assist her to the bed. Her hobbling gait embarrassed her.

"Really, Derek. How do you think I ever managed when you weren't around?"

Her sarcasm was wasted, judging by his frown. "I've been wondering about that myself." He lifted her legs onto the bed and pulled the sheet and blankets over her. "Are you comfortable?"

With him looming over her while she rested in a bed? His shoulders looked hard, his chest broad. When she'd glimpsed him with his shirt off earlier, she'd noticed the remains of a tan. He'd been in warm weather recently, sunning himself.

His hair hung over his forehead, soft and silky dark and a tracing of beard shadow was showing on his face. No, she was far from comfortable. "I'm fine."

"This is a pretty room. It...suits you."

The things he said seemed so strange, as if another man had taken over his body. Derek had never before commented on furniture or even noticed it as far as she could tell. Her belongings were nice, but they weren't picked by an interior decorator as his had been.

Still, they were hers, and she loved them. She'd hated to spend so much of her dwindled savings on movers when she'd left her old place, but she'd been unable to do the work herself, had no friends to call on, and she refused to live on someone else's furniture.

Besides, the familiar objects gave her comfort, as if her entire life hadn't been reorganized by the vengeful hand of fate.

Unable to help herself, she said, "The bed is new."

"Oh?" He looked it over, but she could tell he hadn't realized it.

"I thought about burning the other one, sort of as an exorcism given the hideous memories attached to it, but that seemed wasteful in my financial predicament, regardless of the sentiments attached." She propped a pillow behind her head and smiled at him, enjoying his scowl and the two spots of hot color high on his lean cheekbones. "I sold it instead. Cheap."

Like an animal of prey moving in, Derek slowly approached the bed and leaned over her, his eyes never leaving hers. He braced an arm on either side of her head and lowered his face until only inches separated them. Angel pressed back into her pillow and held her breath.

His voice was low and rough, compelling. "You keep pushing me, honey, practically daring me with those big green eyes of yours."

He looked away from her eyes to her mouth, and she bit her lip. "Derek..."

"Shh." His lips brushed hers, light, teasing. "I told you I'd never hurt you again. You can believe it. Besides, it's too soon for much, but not for this."

That was all the warning she got before his mouth settled warmly over her own, devouring. Angel gasped, clasping the soft blanket next to her hips, tightening her fists to keep from kissing him back. But it was impossible. Nothing like this had ever happened to her. Surely it hadn't been like this before or she'd have remembered.

Heat exploded, radiating out to her arms and legs in tingling waves; behind her closed eyes, tiny sparks ignited. She squirmed—then felt his tongue at the same time he groaned, giving her the sound, letting her feel it deep inside herself. Wet, warm, he shifted for a better angle and she leaned up to him, anxious for more.

It seemed an eternity before the kiss ended, before Derek was slowly pulling away, taking small, nibbling, apologetic kisses along the way. He breathed hard, but when he lifted his head, there was a gentle smile on his mouth.

Angel didn't trust herself to speak.

"Don't look like that," he chided.

"Like...like what?"

"Like you're afraid, and sorry." His thumb rubbed the corner of her mouth. "One way or another, everything really is going to be okay."

Reality intruded. "Derek, swear to me you won't tell anyone about Grayson."

"You'll believe me?"

Tears filled her eyes. "Do I have a choice? I don't want to run again. I don't—"

"Again?"

He had her rattled, that was the only reason she'd made such a slipup. Shaking her head, she said, "If you tell your family about Grayson, I'll go."

His large warm hand cupped her cheek. "I won't let them bother you, and I won't let you go."

She was afraid they were already bothering her, because she couldn't think of another single enemy she could have. Why they would want to hurt her, she couldn't guess. Unless they knew of Grayson and were afraid she'd come to Derek for marriage. She just didn't know what lengths they might go to in order to protect their son from a woman they'd consider beneath him.

Her hands shook, as did her voice. "How could you stop them if they knew? Especially your brother." She shivered, knowing her fear of the brother was out of proportion, based on Derek's dramatized bragging and her own wild imagination. But in her mind, he'd become her nightmare, and she was very afraid. "Out of all of them, I fear him the most."

He leaned back, watching her carefully. "Angel..."

"No! They can't know. Ever. If that seems selfish

of me, I don't care." Her hands trembled, despite her tight grip, because she knew if he decided to take her baby away, he could. And she was already proving how weak she was against him. "I'm a good mother, Derek, I swear it."

He sighed. "I never doubted it, honey." He shoved himself reluctantly from the bed and pulled a pen from his pocket. Using a notepad on the bedside table, he scribbled down some numbers. "I'm going to give you my number."

"I already have it."

He stalled, looking harassed for a moment, then shook his head. "It's hard to reach me at home these days. Here are the numbers to my cellular and my pager. You can always reach me with them. If you ever need me, for anything, call either one of these numbers."

Angel nodded, feeling foolish for her outburst. She was just so weary, so tired of being afraid. He cupped her cheek again.

"I'll be back tomorrow." His gaze probed hers, demanding. "You'll be here?"

"Yes."

"Good." He leaned down and kissed her once more, a light kiss that still made her shiver. "Pretty soon, you'll stop looking so afraid, Angel. And you'll start to trust me. I promise."

As he walked out of the room, Angel looked at the paper with his numbers. Somehow, just having someone to call made her feel safer.

She heard the front door close, the lock turn, and she dropped her head back on the pillow, closing her eyes. As she drifted off to sleep, the paper was still in her hand.

CHAPTER FOUR

"I WAS TAILED last night," Dane said the minute Alec had taken his seat. He looked at his closest friend, waiting for his reaction.

"From the woman's place?"

"No, thank God. Later, from my house. It was dark, and I have no idea who it was, but I don't like it. I want you to set up a watch at her apartment. Something is definitely going on and I don't want her hurt."

"The man who was with her yesterday?"

Dane shook his head, again remembering how protective Mick had been. "No, he's a kid and a blessing as far as I can tell. If it hadn't been for him, she'd probably never have made it."

Alec said nothing. It was one of the things Dane liked most about him. He didn't pry. In fact, he was one of the most closemouthed bastards he'd ever met.

"Something about her just doesn't add up. It's like she wants Derek around, but she's forced to it." Then he shook his head again. "No, that's not entirely true. There's something there—but it sure as hell isn't trust or friendship. She initiated things, but now that I'm, or rather Derek's, interested, she's trying to back off. I think she got more than she bargained for."

"You want me to check into her background, the time she spent with your brother?" Alec's eyes were almost black, the same as his hair, and piercingly direct. Dane knew he could find out anything he wanted. *How* he found things out sometimes left him curious.

"No." He didn't want anyone snooping into Angel's past but himself. He had no idea what clues he might uncover, but they were his business and no one else's. He didn't question his protective attitude. He'd find out what happened to his brother, but he'd find it out his way, and isolate Angel's involvement as much as possible. After all, she was his nephew's mother; for now, that was all the excuse he needed. "I'll take care of it. In fact, I have Raymond coming in today."

Alec snorted, shifting his big body uneasily in the chair. He was in his usual jeans and a flannel shirt, his hair pulled back in a ponytail. He looked like a mugger, or the typical bad guy. Dane grinned.

"You don't like him either? Why?"

Alec shrugged, indifferent. "I don't really know him."

"Dammit Alec…"

"Something about him just doesn't sit right. You know it yourself."

"Yes. I know you're also suspicious of just about everyone." Dane assumed his own dislike of Raymond was personal. He was engaged to Dane's sister, Celia, and Raymond reminded him too much of his own family, ruthless, business-oriented. He probably suited Celia to a tee.

"I do have some info for you."

Dane straightened, his thoughts once again in perspective. "Let's have it."

"Where your brother's car went off the road, there's an extra set of skid marks. Two cars were going fast that day, and two cars braked. Unfortunately, your brother's was the one that went off the berm." Alec handed him a file folder. "I checked with the police on duty that day. They say that's a dangerous curve and people are always squealing their tires there, that the extra marks don't mean anything and could have been from long ago. I don't think so."

Dane took the folder, his temper heating as he pondered his brother trying to escape another car. He would find out what had happened.

"There's another thing."

Dane looked up.

"Your brother had been in a local bar, not the classiest of joints, which is what drew my attention, and he'd been drinking it up right before the accident. The bartender said he'd met someone there, but that nothing seemed unusual about it. He didn't have a description, only that it was a male."

"Dammit!" Dane exploded from his seat and paced around his desk. Playing the role of his brother was wearing on his nerves. Using Derek's office, his name, made him edgy. He'd left this life behind long ago and though he hadn't moved far away, he'd still managed to keep an emotional distance from it all; now he was back under the worst possible circumstances. "Why are the cops blowing this off?"

"You know as well as I do, everyone claims your brother was acting goofy for a month. They just summed this up to stress."

"Bullshit. My brother could run two companies and not be stressed. He was primed for it, raised to do it. And he thrived on it." Unlike Dane, who hated every minute of the corporate business agenda. He wondered why his mother didn't know any of this, why she hadn't pursued the truth.

"I'm not arguing with you."

Pressing a fist against his forehead, Dane muttered, "So what does Angel have to do with all this? I don't believe she was directly connected to Derek's death, but it is possible she helped pave the way for the killer, maybe unknowingly. She could be our only lead to what really happened since she was the last person to be close with him. But why would Derek have treated her so poorly?"

Alec shrugged, not forthcoming with a verbal response.

A knock on the door had both men swinging their heads around. "Come in."

Raymond Stern sauntered in, his three-piece suit immaculate, his hair styled. Dane winced at the sight of him. The man, though pleasant enough, represented everything Dane disliked about the corporate world and his family. "Thank you for stopping by, Raymond."

Raymond looked at Alec, a suspicious frown in place. "No problem. You said you wanted to talk?"

Dane nodded and reseated himself behind his desk. Alec stood. "I'll be going now, unless you need something else?"

Dane shoved the file folder into a drawer before answering. "No. I'll be in touch with you later."

As Alec left, his eyes briefly skimming over everything and everyone in the room, Raymond asked, "A crony of yours?"

"One of my top men."

A look of disbelief, or maybe scorn, passed over Raymond's features. "Is he working on something right now?" Before Dane could answer, Raymond continued. "I think this P.I. business is fascinating, regardless of how your sister feels about it."

"Oh?" Dane cocked one eyebrow, wishing he could

plant a fist in Raymond's face. "And how does Celia feel?"

He chuckled. "That you'll outgrow it. She seems to think now that you're enmeshed back in the office, you'll want to stay."

There was an unasked question in his tone. Dane started to reassure the man that once he married Celia, the business would be his, with Dane's blessing. In truth Dane wanted no part of it. He was already bored with the endless paperwork and the tedium of board meetings. But he decided against it. Let Raymond stew. Let him wonder if the company was part of the marriage bargain.

"Celia has never liked it that I stepped out of the family's affairs."

"I think it's incredible that you've always been located so close, yet I never met you."

"My own offices aren't that far away, true, but I've traveled a lot, especially in recent years. Some cases require constant surveillance, and that means you follow all leads, regardless of where they take you." He didn't add that he deliberately hadn't kept in touch with his family, hadn't clued them in to where he would be or for how long.

And now his brother was dead and he hadn't even made it to the funeral.

Quickly closing that particular subject in his mind, Dane went on to another. "I asked you here because I know you transferred over from the Aeric Corporation."

Raymond straightened with pride. "That's right. Derek was there often once his intent was known, and he and I met. I agreed it was a natural acquisition, combining your family's interests in health products manufacturing with Aeric's research capabilities. When Derek finalized everything, he asked me to join him here.''

"You were at the funeral?"

Shaking his head, his eyes downcast in a regretful way, Raymond said, "No, unfortunately I missed it, also." He looked back up, his expression resigned. "I hadn't realized what happened until I reported here a week later. Derek had given me time to tie up my own loose ends and I spent two final weeks at Aeric, then took a break to sell my house and move closer. When I reported to work here is when I was told. That's also the day I really got to know your sister." A small smile now curved his mouth.

"I see."

"When I asked to see Derek, I was referred to Celia. Things were still in an uproar, your mother most upset and Celia constantly on the verge of tears. They couldn't locate you and they needed everything to be kept quiet, contained. Derek's death hit them all very hard…" Raymond stuttered to a halt. "I'm sorry. I wasn't making accusations. I realize it was very difficult for you as well."

"Yes." Dane knew that Raymond had shown up when the company needed him most, his past experience and lack of emotional involvement, along with Derek's written blessing, making him the ideal man to take temporary control. Every effort was made to keep the stockholders from panicking. If nothing else, he owed Raymond his gratitude for that.

But Dane deliberately kept his own dialogue brief in the hopes Raymond would say more. Trying to get information from his sister or mother had proved most provoking. Anytime he mentioned Derek's name, they would turn solemn, overwhelmed with the loss. The entire episode of the takeover of Aeric seemed very hush-hush.

"Anyway, I guess you could say your sister and I hit it right off. I care deeply for her."

And deeply for the Company, but Dane kept those thoughts to himself. His sister was old enough, and certainly wise enough, to choose her own husband.

"Did Derek associate on a regular basis with anyone else at Aeric?"

Raymond shrugged. "Most everyone on the board, the managers, the—"

"No, I mean in a social way."

"Well, there was the woman, secretary to the R&D department."

Research and Development. Dane already knew what Angel's position had been. Somehow, Derek had gotten information from her that had enabled him to take over the company.

And then he'd dropped Angel cold.

"Were they close?"

Raymond shrugged, looking thoughtful. "Everyone thought so. She'd never dated much, and then suddenly she had a steady date. At that time, no one realized Derek was after the company. But I suppose it should have been more obvious that he was using her. She was a mousy sort of person, not real talkative, withdrawn, but apparently good at her job. Good enough that the head of R&D often sent her top-secret information through a P.O. box to work on at home."

"A post office box? That's unusual." Derek remembered the address Angel had given him, not a home address, but the anonymity of a post office.

Raymond shrugged. "Her supervisor was from the

old school and didn't trust the company computers, swearing too many secrets had been stolen. But he trusted the wrong person. Angel got the last of the information, a huge breakthrough worth top dollar that would have offset the takeover attempt, and she gave it to Derek. Of course, we found all this out after Derek dropped her." He laughed. "She got fired real quick. Most everyone else was able to keep their jobs."

"I see."

"Why do you ask?" Raymond straightened. "She's not here asking for a job, is she?"

Raymond looked appalled by the possibility. "No, of course not. I just wondered if I could get in touch with her, to talk to her about Derek."

"Why?" Raymond's eyes narrowed and he shifted forward. "What's going on?"

Keeping his tone smooth and nearly bored, Dane said, "Not a thing. It's just that I hadn't seen my brother for some time. I'd like to talk to the people who knew him." Raymond relaxed and Dane asked, "What happened to her, do you know?"

Dane had to keep his hands beneath the desk. His fingers had curled into fists as Raymond spoke and he imagined Angel's humiliation, her hurt. He didn't like feeling so much anger toward a dead man, especially when that man was his twin. The conflicting emotions ate away at his control.

"I have no idea. I haven't seen her since I left Aeric. And Derek broke things off with her during a board meeting, for everyone to see. He asked her to sit in on the meeting, then deliberately told everyone where he'd gotten his information. That pretty much proved she couldn't be trusted in the company."

"Good God." Sick dread churned in the bottom of his stomach.

Raymond laughed. "Yeah, she was stunned to say the least. But maybe it taught her a lesson about keeping business dealings private. As I'm sure you already know, even though you haven't been involved in some time, there's no room for deceit in the corporate world. You absolutely have to be able to trust your employees. Especially when they're in the position she was in."

Dane could barely see, he was so angry. The rage ran through him, red-hot, and he wanted only to get to Angel, to apologize, to... He stood abruptly, coming around his desk with stalking steps. He went to the coat tree and grabbed up his coat. Raymond quickly stood to face him.

It took two deep breaths before Dane could trust himself to speak without breaking Raymond's nose. This was exactly why he hated the business, why he had to separate himself from his family. Ruthless barracudas, all of them, with no thought for humanity or dignity. It sickened him.

Raymond looked at him warily. "Is that all you wanted?"

"Yes, thank you." He couldn't bear to shake the man's hand. He turned toward the door instead and opened it. "I appreciate your help, Raymond. Unfortunately, I have an appointment at my own offices shortly, so I'll need to ask you to go."

"Yes, of course." He hesitated. "You know, Derek and I were somewhat better than associates before he died. If you'd ever like to talk about him, to know about him, I'd be glad to tell you what I can."

Dane's smile actually hurt, but he managed it. "Thank you. I'll keep it in mind."

"Will you be at dinner tonight?"

Damn, he'd forgotten his mother planned a family gathering. He had hoped to eat with Angel, to get to know her better. "Probably," he conceded, knowing his mother would demand a valid reason for missing the meal. It was to be a formal dinner in preparation for his sister's marriage, where the duties of the company would be discussed.

"I know it's difficult for you, stepping in here and keeping your own business afloat. If I can help in any way…"

"I'll keep that in mind. Thank you."

Raymond finally left with a lagging step, looking as if he had more to say but was reluctant to press. Dane knew he sensed where the present power lay, but that was just a fabrication of his mother's fancy. He didn't want the damn company. In fact, he would only stay in charge as long as was necessary to find out what had happened to Derek, to uncover the truth.

And to get things settled with Angel.

ANGEL SLOWLY HUNG UP the phone, her fingers tight on the receiver to keep her hand from shaking. Why wouldn't it stop? She'd never hurt anyone, she held no power. There was absolutely no reason for someone to harass her.

For one insane moment, she wanted to call Derek, but she quickly quelled that absurd thought. She wouldn't rely on him, ever again. For all she knew, he could be behind all this. That thought made her stomach queasy.

Moving slowly, she made her way to the bathroom and splashed water on her hot face, then leaned against the counter and took deep breaths.

When the knock sounded on her front door only seconds later, she jumped, her hand going to her throat. The apartment was quiet, Grayson sleeping soundly in his crib. It couldn't be Mick because he had left for school hours before after dropping off more papers to be typed, and no one ever called on her other than him. Derek would surely be at work and—

The knock sounded again, this time a little harder and she feared Grayson would wake. She hurried to the door, hesitated just a moment, then called out, "Who is it?"

"Ah," she heard in deep, satisfied tones, "much better than just letting anyone in. I see you're learning."

"Derek?" She turned the dead bolt and unlocked the door, swinging it open. "I always lock my door, except when I'm expecting Mick." She looked him over, the casual way he leaned against the doorjamb, his open-neck shirt, so unusual for him. "What are you doing here this time of day?"

His gaze went over her from head to toe. She wore a long caftan of muted gray-and-blue plaid. It was old and worn and the material draped her body softly. It unzipped down the front, making it easy for her to feed Grayson. Right now, the zipper was just low enough to show her cleavage and assure Derek that her breasts were unrestrained by a bra. Typically of late, her feet were bare; since injuring her leg, she seldom bothered with shoes at home.

A long low whistle filled the air between them and Angel felt herself blushing. Self-consciously, she tried to smooth her hair which hung loose, but when she realized what she was doing she dropped her hand and scowled. "Aren't you supposed to be at work?"

"Yeah, but I missed you so I'm here instead."

Before she could move, or even guess what he would do, he leaned forward and kissed her. The touch of his mouth was warm and soft and fleeting, leaving her stunned. Then Derek pushed in past her, taking his welcome for granted. The door closed with a snap.

"Don't do things like that."

"Why not? You like it, and I can guarantee I love it."

She felt her temper rise and he quickly held up both hands. "Okay, okay. You don't like it. You're entirely repulsed."

"Derek..."

"What?" He smiled at her, a beautiful smile and she looked away. "I really do enjoy it, sweetheart. And I honestly did miss you." He stepped closer to her once again, his gaze bright and probing. "You didn't mind yesterday in my office. You asked me to kiss you then."

Angel drew a blank. He was right, she had pushed the issue. But that was when she'd thought he might not be interested, when she'd thought he'd need motivation.

For a single moment she wondered if he was toying with her, but his expression was enigmatic, impossible to read. "This is a bad time," she said, suspicious and determined to resist his classic charm. "I have tons of things to do."

"I can help."

"Derek..."

He came close to laughing, but swallowed it down. "Okay, I'm sorry. I'm pushing again. But damn, I have so much to make up for and I'm anxious to get started."

Nonplussed, she moved past him, removed a large

basket of laundry still needing to be folded, and sat on the couch. "The past is the past, Derek. You can't erase it, and since you haven't contacted me in all this time, I have to assume it didn't matter much to you until now."

"You're surprised at my easy acceptance of things?"

More than surprised. She was amazed.

His hands were deep in his trouser pockets, his coat pushed back, and he rocked on his heels as if in thought. Finally, his head down, he sat beside her. Silence hung heavy in the air. He turned to her. "I'm sorry." He shrugged his wide shoulders, his expression earnest. "I have no excuse, nothing, to explain why I was such a bastard. I wish I did, I wish I could pull up some believable tale to help smooth things over, to take away some of the hurt. But what I did to you was unforgivable. I know that. Still, I want you to forgive me." Dumbfounded by this outpouring of emotion, she allowed him to take her hand, holding it when she would have pulled away. "Do you think you can?"

When she merely frowned, he added, "For Grayson's sake?"

Angel stared at him, so many things he'd said clogging in her brain. He wanted forgiveness, even though he admitted there was no excuse for his behavior? And to use the baby's welfare against her...but that was her biggest concern, her reason for contacting him in the first place.

Only he didn't act the way she'd expected, as she'd planned for. She'd expected grudging help in calling off his family—if indeed they were behind the threats. She didn't even want to contemplate the possibility of another enemy.

She wanted only to live in peace, to be able to take care of herself and her son without fear of danger.

His hand was large and warm and again she noticed the roughness, which had never been there before. To buy herself some time, she said, "What have you been doing?" She turned his palm over and looked at it. "You have callouses."

He blinked at her, then looked down at his hand. With a twisted grin, he said, "Chopping wood, if you can believe that."

"It might be difficult."

"I know. I'm not normally the physical type."

She shook her head. "No, you're in shape, always have been. But from a gym, not from physical labor."

She continued to look at his hand and he raised it to her cheek, curling his fingers around her jaw and lifting so that her gaze met his. His eyes were bright, intent. "I'm glad you noticed, but it doesn't matter. Will you try to forgive me?"

His voice had been so soft, so cajoling. She hated herself for wanting to believe in him again, for wanting so many ridiculous things. But she'd been so alone for so long now. Her mind scurried for some response, some way of making him back off.

"We could start over," he said. "I'm different now, everything will be different. If I start to backslide and I disappoint you or Grayson, then you can toss me out."

At her skeptical look, he made a cross on his chest. "I promise. The decision is yours. You're right about my family, they wouldn't make good relatives at this point for Grayson and they'd likely make your life a living hell."

If Angel was right, they were already making her

life hell—and determined that it get much worse. But she kept the words unsaid for now.

Derek smiled. "And since I plan to be involved, that means they'd make me miserable as well. They don't need to know anything about Grayson, or about you for that matter. At least, not until you're ready."

As she opened her mouth, he interjected, "*If* you're ever ready."

She had no defense against his optimism, his good humor. It was beyond her to remain disgruntled when he was being all she'd ever hoped for—for Grayson's sake. "All right."

His grin was wide and sexy and suggestive. "Thank you. Damn, but you know how to keep a man on pins and needles. I hope this is the last time you test me, because my heart can't take it."

She snorted, not ready to believe his heart was involved. Then to her disbelieving eyes, he set the laundry basket between them and began folding baby blankets. Angel stared.

"Shocked you, have I? Well, good. God knows you've done me in enough times lately." He lifted a small gown, struggled with it for a moment, then handed it to her. "I think I'll leave the more complicated garments to you, and stick to the blankets and—" His voice trailed off as he lifted a pair of panties from the basket. They were pink and satiny and her blush was so hot, she knew her face had to be bright red. She snatched them from his hand.

"Not a single word out of you or you can go."

"I'm mum." He continued to fold, now in silence, but she could see his devilish smile.

He was so very different, so unlike the Derek she knew, the man she couldn't forgive or ever care about, not with the way he'd turned on her. This Derek was considerate and warm and somehow, more of a man because of it. In the past, she'd been drawn to his confidence, his good looks and his sophistication. She'd been overwhelmed by his attention, so flattered she hadn't been able to think straight. Then he'd abruptly discredited her in every way possible.

They worked in near silence, other than Derek humming, until all the laundry was done and put away. After Angel had placed her unmentionables in her dresser, leaving Derek to put up the baby's things, she found him standing over Grayson's crib, just watching the baby sleep. When she crept in to stand beside him, it somehow felt right to be there together, sharing the sheer joy of seeing the baby, hearing his soft breathing. When Grayson made a grumbling squeak in his sleep, Derek smiled, a small, proud smile that touched Angel's heart and made her feel too warm and full inside. She turned around and walked out.

She'd barely reached the kitchen before she felt Derek's hand heavy on her shoulder. Her pulse raced, her breathing quickened. Slowly he turned her, and he whispered, "Angel," his tone low and husky and affected by some emotion she couldn't name but understood. Even before she met his gaze, she knew he was going to kiss her. She tried to tell herself it was necessary, that she had to keep him interested to have his help, but she knew she was lying. She wanted his kiss.

And he didn't disappoint her. This was no casual peck as he'd given her when he first arrived. No, this time his mouth devoured hers, without hesitation, hot and hungry, his tongue immediately sliding inside while his hands held her face and kept her close.

Just that, nothing more. He didn't touch her anywhere else, didn't put his arms around her or pull her body into full contact with his. She could feel his heat, crossing the inches that separated them, and she wanted to be closer. But lovemaking was new to her and she wasn't sure how to initiate anything, or if she even wanted to.

Derek slanted his head, his breathing harsh in her ear, and a low groan came from deep in his throat. In the next instant, he pulled his mouth away and pushed her head to his shoulder. "This is crazy. I can't believe how you affect me."

Angel didn't know what to say to that. Crazy? It surely felt odd, but in a wonderful, miraculous way. Her hands were caught between them and she could feel his heartbeat, fierce and fast. "Why is it different this time?" she asked aloud, and all the confusion she felt could be heard in her tone.

Derek laughed, then groaned and squeezed her tight, finally pulling their bodies close together. "Because it just is, because I'm different."

He pushed her back so he could see her face and smiled at her. "I'd like to take you to lunch."

The topic had changed so suddenly Angel was caught off guard. "I...I can't go anywhere. Grayson..."

"We'll take him with us."

She shook her head, not even considering the possibility of them being seen in public together with the baby. "No, I already ate." She pondered all that had happened, all he'd done so far, then suggested, "Why don't you come here for dinner instead." She felt ridiculous, making such an offer, extending the verbal olive branch. But they did need to get reacquainted; she needed to decide if and how much she could trust him. She drew a deep breath and plunged onward. "I can cook us something."

He searched her face, and his continued silence made her wish she could withdraw her offer. Then he shook his head. "Damn, I'd like that. I swear I would. I can't imagine a better way to spend my evening."

"But?"

He released her and turned away. "My mother has this damn dinner planned." He waved a hand, essaying his feelings on the affair. "My sister is getting married soon and it's a sort of celebration dinner. All family is expected to attend."

"I see."

He ran a distracted hand over his face, then laughed. "I doubt you do. But at any rate, I appreciate the offer. Will you give me a rain check?"

"Yes, of course."

He looked at her, *into* her, and she shivered. His hand came up to cup her cheek. "Aw, Angel, you do know how to drive a man crazy."

She didn't know what he meant by that, so she ignored it. "If you're hungry now, I could make you a sandwich."

Like a starving man, he grabbed up her offer. "Thank you. Anything is fine. And while I eat, will you tell me more about Grayson, about yourself?"

That seemed like an odd request. As she pulled lunch meat out of the refrigerator, she glanced at him curiously and said, "You know everything there is to know about me."

"Not true. Tell me about the pregnancy, when you found out—"

Slowly, feeling as if she'd been doused in ice water, Angel turned back to him. She dropped a package of cheese onto the table with a thunk. It was cheese he had bought, so she knew he must like it. "About the pregnancy. Now why would you want details on that?"

Wary now, he shrugged and said, "I'm just curious."

"I see. Are you trying to verify that Grayson really is yours? Is that why you were so awful when I first called to tell you I was pregnant? You thought I was lying about you being the father?"

"Of course not!"

"You doubted me in your office. You had the nerve to ask me if I was certain."

His face tightened, his mouth grim. "It was a legitimate question, Angel." He faltered, looking tormented. "I just wasn't expecting you to..."

"Legitimate? When you were the only man I'd ever been with?"

There was a heartbeat of silence. "Ever?" His eyebrows rose in incredulous disbelief.

She slapped down a knife on the table. "So you thought once you humiliated me, once you'd *used* me, I would just willingly jump in bed with another man? You thought I found my one experience with sex so titillating I had to race out for more, and since you weren't available, I'd take any man who was?"

As she spoke, her voice rose almost to a shout, but it all came back on her, all the pain and mortification. She laughed, but it wasn't a happy sound. Derek sat staring at her, his expression almost comically blank.

Well, he wasn't used to hearing her yell. She'd always been meek and agreeable with him, so much so she'd made his objective pathetically easy. He'd overwhelmed her with his bigger-than-life persona, but not anymore. Now she'd changed, thanks to the way he'd screwed up her life. And he had changed as well.

"Believe me, Derek, you were the only one. And once with you was more than enough."

It was her sneering tone, meant to show him her loathing, only it didn't work.

She'd started to tremble and Derek was suddenly there, his arms around her, his lips against her temple. "Shh, baby, I'm sorry. So sorry."

"Just go back to work, Derek. Leave me alone."

"I can't do that." He leaned back, keeping her pelvis pressed to his, but putting space between their upper bodies. "You don't want me to do that. For whatever reason, Angel, you contacted me."

She opened her mouth, but she couldn't think of a single thing to say.

"Shh. It's all right. You don't have to tell me now. I'll wait until you're ready."

That he suspected her of having ulterior motives should have alarmed her, but she was just too tired to fight with him. And since she desperately needed his concession, she nodded, relief making her slump against him.

"I was an idiot in the office yesterday. Of course I know you haven't been with anyone else. Sometimes men just say…stupid things." He seemed to be floundering for the right words as his hands coasted up and down her back, soothing. "We won't mention that again, okay?"

Reluctantly, she nodded.

"Good." He stepped back, but rather than sit at the table again, he began compiling his own sandwich. "I do want to hear everything—no matter how insignificant—that's happened to you since we've been apart."

He gave her a sharp, assessing glance. "I have a lot of catching up to do. All right?"

"Yes." The distraction of simple conversation would help her regain her balance. She didn't want to confide in him yet, not until she knew she could trust him with Grayson's safety. "Yes, I'll tell you... everything."

He stayed longer than she would have guessed, and he asked more questions than she could answer. When Grayson awoke, Derek changed the baby, cuddled him for long moments, and when Grayson demanded to be fed, he finally took his leave. But he promised to come back the next day.

And though she was annoyed with herself, Angel already looked forward to his next visit.

CHAPTER FIVE

DINNER SEEMED TO LAST forever. All Dane wanted to do was go home and ponder Angel's revelation. *She'd been a virgin.* God, he still felt stunned. And entirely too aroused.

From what she'd told him, she'd only been with Derek once, and that had been a disappointment.

Possessive heat filled him. She hadn't really belonged to Derek, not the way a woman should, not the way she would belong to him. Guilt plagued him as he considered making her his own while knowing Derek had been her first and only. But with every minute that passed, he felt more determined to tie himself to her. There were numerous reasons, none of them overly honest, but still, they served his purpose.

He adored Grayson, already loving him as if he were his own. Dane had never thought to fit the bill of *father*—his chance had been lost to him so long ago. But it was precisely because his chance had been lost, and why, that he wanted to protect Grayson. Angel was right to fear his family; they would take over without giving her a single chance if he let them. But her fear also seemed exaggerated and somewhat pointless. Sooner or later they'd find out about the baby. It was inevitable.

He planned to be there when they did, to soothe her fears.

Angel also deserved his protection, and the luxury the Carter name could supply. Whatever else Derek had become, he'd still been a wealthy man. Grayson had a birthright that would pave much of his way in the world. Derek should have seen that Grayson received his due; for reasons of his own, he hadn't, and Dane was determined to correct the oversight.

He also still believed Angel to be the most likely link in discovering what had happened to his brother. So far, nothing seemed to fit. Derek was capable of some pretty ruthless behavior, but the way he'd treated Angel seemed out of character even for him. Much of the cruelty had been deliberate and unnecessary. Why had Derek done it? And what was the real reason Angel had contacted him again, despite the damn past they shared? There were secrets there, things he had to discover, and that too, was a good reason to stay in touch with Miss Angel Morris.

The biggest reason of all, of course, was the chemistry between them. When he touched Angel, all his senses exploded like never before. And not even the memory of her and Derek's past experiences could dampen her responses; it was driving him insane.

Damn his brother for complicating things so, for hurting her. And most of all for letting himself get killed. What had Derek been up to?

"Dane?"

Startled out of his ruminations, Dane looked up to see his mother frowning fiercely across the table at him. She did it well, he thought as he speared a bite of asparagus and chewed slowly. Her look was so forbidding that most people immediately apologized even before they knew what they'd done wrong. At sixty, she was still a slim, attractive woman with her light-brown hair stylishly twisted behind her head, and her brown eyes sharp with intelligence. She kept herself in top physical shape; her pride would tolerate no less.

Dane stifled a bored yawn. He'd quit playing his mother's games long ago. "Did you want something, Mother?"

She pinched her mouth together at his lack of manners and deference due her. "Where in the world is your attention? You haven't been following the conversation at all."

Celia smiled toward him. "Do you have a big investigation that's got you stumped, brother?"

He sent her a chiding glance. Celia had been teasing him about being a P.I. since he'd walked in the door. She'd had the gall to ask him if he carried a spy kit. His sister seemed different than he remembered, more lighthearted, more playful. He liked the changes.

To his surprise, Raymond blurted, "You aren't still wondering about the Morris woman, are you?"

His mother straightened to attention, jumping on the topic like a dog on a meaty bone. She had plans for Dane, he knew. She'd sat him at the head of the table— a major concession for her, and an indication of what she expected from him in the future. She wouldn't want any threats to her plans, and his interest in anyone or anything other than the company would certainly be considered a threat.

He hadn't yet told her of his intentions, or rather lack thereof, toward the family and the company. He wanted everything settled first before he dropped his news on her.

"What's this, Dane?" Her face was alarmingly pale, her eyes flashing. "What's Raymond talking about?"

"Nothing of any import, Mother. I merely asked

Raymond a few questions about Angel Morris. I was curious since Derek had been seeing the woman for a while."

Celia turned quiet and gave her attention to her food. His mother wasn't so reserved. Her hands fisted on the table, yet she managed to keep her tone calm. "He wasn't *seeing* her, for heaven's sake. He merely associated with her to ease the effort of the takeover. She was a secretary of sorts, no one important. Certainly no one important to Derek."

Forcefully keeping his emotions in check, feigning a certain lack of interest, Dane asked, "Do you know what happened to her?"

His mother carefully laid aside her fork, then looked down her nose at him. She sat to his right, Celia and Raymond to his left.

"After she was terminated, you mean? Why would I care?" She made a rude sound of condescension. "You certainly didn't expect us to employ the woman, did you, not after she gave away company secrets."

Celia spoke up for the first time, her voice clipped, her expression stern. "I already told you, Mother, Derek stole that information from her."

Dane felt as though he'd taken a punch on the chin. His mother made an outraged sound and Raymond sat watching them both, his expression somewhat satisfied. He stared at his sister and saw that two spots of bright color had bloomed on her cheeks. "What did you say?"

Celia gave her mother a lingering frown, then turned to face Dane. "Mother persists in making this woman out as a villain, even though I've told her repeatedly that it isn't so. If anything, she was a victim, and we certainly should have employed her in an effort to make amends. Derek explained to me himself that Angel hadn't volunteered the information to him. He rifled through her personal belongings until he found what he wanted."

Raymond held his fork aloft, using it to emphasize his point. "Ah. But she should have seen to it that the material was well secured. That was her responsibility. The heads at Aeric trusted her, and she let them down."

"I suppose part of the blame is hers," Celia agreed, her tone snide, "in trusting Derek too much, in thinking him honorable toward her—"

Dane's mother gasped, coming to her feet in furious indignation. Her hands slapped down on the cloth-covered tabletop while her voice rose to a near shriek. "How dare you suggest otherwise, Celia Carter? He was your brother!"

Looking belligerent and stubborn, Celia forced a shrug and met her mother's gaze. "Mother, he *stole* that information from her. He led her on, made her believe he cared for her, and then took shameful advantage. Would you rather I call that honorable?"

Raymond patted Celia's hand. "Sweetheart, he only did what was best for the company. That was always his first priority." His eyes slid over to Dane. "As is true of any CEO."

Dane waited, watching while his mother visibly struggled to regain her control. Such an outburst from her surprised him and piqued his curiosity. When she had grudgingly reseated herself, pretending to be appeased by Raymond's words, and Raymond had taken a healthy bite of his braised pork, Dane asked, "Are you saying, Raymond, that you wouldn't have a problem with using a woman that way?"

Raymond promptly choked, covering his mouth with his napkin.

"Really, Dane, enough of this nonsense!" his mother protested. "Raymond has been an enormous help to us and deserves better from you."

Celia looked at Dane, a wicked smile of appreciation curving her lips, then proceeded to pound her fiancé on the back until he'd managed to catch his breath. Dane leaned back in his chair, enjoying the dinner for the first time that evening.

Damn, so much to think about. So Angel was innocent all the way around. That fact twisted his guts, making him feel guilty as hell, as if he were the one who'd betrayed her. He determined to make it up to her somehow. Whether she wanted him to or not.

An hour later as they all gathered in the salon for drinks and conversation, Dane cornered his sister. Raymond was busy schmoozing their mother, and Celia was blessedly alone, staring out a window at the dark night. As he approached, she looked down at his hand and the drink he held.

"I thought you abstained."

He lifted the glass in a salute. "Pure cola and ice. Nothing more."

"It irritates Mother, you know. That you won't have a social drink."

Dane thought of Mick, so defiant as he explained his mother was an alcoholic. "In my line of work, I see too many drink-related cases. Men and women who abandon their families in favor of a bottle. They all started out as social drinkers." Shaking off his sudden tension, he smiled at Celia. "Besides, I enjoy irritating Mother."

To his surprise, his teasing wasn't returned. Celia

turned fully to face him. "How do you do it, Dane? How do you just turn your back on everything, on all of us?"

A frontal attack. He hadn't expected it of his sister, but he relished a moment to clear the air. He'd missed her in the time he'd been away. Though she was a lot like his mother, her strength and determination not to be underestimated, she was also a woman who thought for herself, who didn't blindly accept his mother's dictates. He'd found that out tonight. In the years he'd stayed away, his sister had evidently come into her own.

Too long, too damn long. "There's nothing for me to stay here for, Celia. You know that. Mother made certain she drove me away—"

"She's sorry for that, Dane." Celia touched his arm. Her eyes, the same hazel shade as his, were dark with concern. "She realizes now that you really did love Anna, that she shouldn't have interfered."

He snorted. "Is that what you call it, interference? She deliberately destroyed my life, accused my fiancée of all kinds of reprehensible things, and just because she didn't approve of Anna's family."

Celia bit her lip, then forged on. "You were both so young. Besides, she did take the money, Dane. Mother didn't force it on her."

"She made Anna feel as if that were the only option, as if she couldn't possibly be my wife. Mother made sure she knew she'd never fit in." Even as he said the words, he accepted that he wasn't being a hundred percent truthful with her or himself. "Anna was pregnant, you know. After she ran off, she lost the baby. My baby."

Celia covered her mouth with a hand. "Oh no, I didn't know. I'm so sorry."

"I told Mother. I was angry and hurt and I wanted her to understand exactly what her manipulation had cost me. Do you know what she said?"

Numbly, Celia shook her head.

"She said it was for the best."

Celia lowered her forehead to Dane's shoulder and her voice was quiet, almost a whisper. "Mother's set in her ways, Dane. She means well, and she really does love you. It's just that sometimes she doesn't think."

He had nothing to say to that. It amazed him that his sister would always try to defend their mother, no matter what she did.

"Will you stay on at the company this time? We need you here."

Lifting a hand to his sister's fair hair, giving one silky lock a teasing tug, he said, "You already know the answer to that."

She sighed. "I suppose I do. But I was hopeful."

"It's not for me, sis. I don't feel comfortable there and besides, I love playing detective too much to give it up."

She smiled at his teasing, then turned to face the window again. "I miss him so much."

"Me, too. Even though we hadn't been in contact much lately, I always knew he was here. There were only miles separating us, and I knew we could get in touch if we chose to." Dane wanted to tell her that he suspected Derek had been murdered, but he held back. His sister had enough on her plate for the moment. "I'm proud of how you stood up to Mother."

She made a disgusted sound. "She's hurting. And it angers her if anyone even suggests Derek might not have been perfect. But I can't sit by and watch her persecute an innocent woman.''

Dane thought his sister was pretty damn special at that moment, and more than ever, he regretted the amount of time he'd let pass without seeing his family.

''How long are you willing to help out?''

Until I see things settled, he thought, but he only shrugged. ''I don't know. We'll see. Right now, I have every agent in my own business maxed out, working on two or more cases at a time. And running between offices isn't getting any easier.'' Especially while trying to uncover a murderer.

He looked up at that moment to see Raymond watching him while his mother chatted in Raymond's ear, no doubt regaling him with stories of old acquaintances, money and power. It was all his mother knew, all she cared about, and Raymond, with his desire to ingratiate himself, provided the perfect audience. Dane nodded then looked away. ''Do you love him?''

Celia laughed. ''You say that as if such a thing is unimaginable.''

''I just want you to be happy.''

''I'd be happy if you stayed on.'' She quickly raised her hands. ''But I understand why you can't. Dane, why were you asking questions about Angel Morris?''

She effectively sidetracked him and he rubbed his chin, wondering what to tell her. Finally he said, ''I suppose it just surprises me what Derek did. I don't like to think him capable of such things. Can you even begin to imagine what Angel Morris must have felt like?''

Celia leaned into him, their shoulders touching. ''If it's any consolation, I think he regretted it. He was very distracted those last few weeks. And unhappy. He told me once that Angel would never forgive him, and that he didn't blame her. It was almost like he'd *had* to hurt her, though I never understood why. I planned to ask him, to understand, but then he died.''

Dane didn't understand either, but he felt better for having talked with his sister. His mother he simply hoped to avoid so she couldn't try to nail him down on his intentions. He didn't want anyone to know his plans until he'd figured everything out. At this point, he wasn't certain who to trust, so he trusted no one.

Not even Angel. The more he learned, the more reason he had to wonder why she'd ever contacted Derek again in the first place. She had to hate him for all he'd done to her. But, his thinking continued, Derek had also given her Grayson, and the baby appeared to be the most important thing in her life. Maybe for that reason alone, she'd been able to give up on some of her anger and resentment. Maybe she'd come to the very reasonable conclusion that Grayson deserved a father and all that Derek could provide. It could be only misplaced pride that still made her insist she wanted nothing from him. Heaven knew, he'd had a hard enough time making her accept the essentials, food and diapers and damn shampoo. She also had plenty of reason to hang on to that pride, given the way she'd been treated.

As Raymond and Mrs. Carter joined them, Raymond smoothly slipped his arm around Celia and gave her an affectionate peck on the cheek. Watching them, Dane pondered the idea of starting over. Ever since Anna had abandoned him, allowing his mother to buy her off, he'd avoided relationships. He hadn't met a woman he'd wanted to see more than twice.

Anna hadn't trusted him, had believed his mother's

tales over the truths he'd given her. He'd never admit it to anyone, but Anna's actions had proved his mother right; she wasn't the woman for him. He expected, needed, a woman to give him everything, not merely her trust, but her unwavering loyalty. Her soul. Anna hadn't been able to do that, and while he still regretted the loss, it was more the manipulation that he resented. He'd long since gotten over his first love. It had been a lesson to be learned, and he'd learned it well.

This time, he could think more clearly. He'd make certain the same didn't happen with Angel. He'd reason with his brains, not his heart, and sooner or later, he'd win her over. His ruthlessness was an inherent part of his nature. After all, much as he might dislike it on occasion, he was still a Carter.

Angel didn't stand a chance.

"I DON'T LIKE IT. I think you should tell Derek."

Angel was so sick of hearing Mick's refrain. He and Derek got along wonderfully, but then who wouldn't get along with him? Derek was generous and thoughtful and attentive and protective. He'd shown up every day for the past week, helping with everything from bathing the baby to shopping and housework. Twice he had brought over dinner, then cleaned up the mess so Angel could get caught up on her typing. He'd tried to give her money, but after she'd told him exactly what she thought of that idea, he hadn't mentioned it again.

Instead, he asked questions, hundreds and hundreds of questions. Sometimes it made her nervous, though she couldn't say why. He just seemed so…different.

"The job he got me is awesome."

She smiled at Mick's enthusiasm. He'd been with

her since six o'clock while they went over his home-
work. Now it was nine and he'd done little else but
talk about Derek in between lessons in calculus and
conjugating Spanish verbs. "So you like it?"

"Are you kidding? What's not to like? It's a private
investigations office and the people there are so laid
back and friendly. It's like a big family."

Angel's heart twisted. Mick had never had much
family to brag about. His mother was more absent than
not, and even when she was around, she didn't demonstrate any maternal instincts. Mick had pretty much
raised himself, and Angel knew what a lonely existence
that could be.

"They've been telling me some of the cases they've
dealt with. Incredible stuff, like shoot-outs and drug
busts and all kinds of stuff. This one guy, Alec Sharpe,
he's actually sort of scary, but don't tell Derek I said
so."

Angel smiled in amazement. If the man spooked
Mick, who wasn't afraid of anyone as far as she could
tell, he must be one frightening character. She pretended to lock her lips with an imaginary key. "Not a
word, I promise."

"The guy has the darkest eyes and he's real quiet
and when he talks, even if it's just to ask for coffee,
everyone around him shuts up and listens. I think he's
sort of a boss or something."

Angel gathered up pencils and pens and put the cal-
culator away. "What do you do there?"

Mick made a face. "All kinds of stuff, from cleaning
and running out for doughnuts to making coffee and
putting files away. But they're all real nice about it.
They don't act like I'm getting paid, but more like I'm
doing them a huge favor and they really appreciate it.

And Alec gave me this really cool car to drive. It has the best stereo.''

Angel knew Mick would be paid more working there than he had made doing both jobs before. And it had been agreed he wouldn't work past six o'clock on school days, and only until the afternoon on the weekends. She was so incredibly grateful to Derek, seeing the change in Mick. He was more like the average kid now, happy and proud. And he adored Derek.

Of course, Mick didn't know everything that had happened between Angel and Derek in the past. And she'd never tell. Derek was doing his best to prove the past really was over; not for the world would she take away Mick's present happiness.

"Why do you still dislike him so much, Angel?"

"Mick…"

"He could help," Mick said, anxious to convince her. "The phone calls were bad enough, but now the letter—"

She rubbed her head. "I know. The letter proves whoever it is knows where to find me. I've been thinking about this a lot." She hesitated, almost afraid to voice her suspicions out loud. "It's possible Derek is the one behind all this."

He stared at her hard, then got to his feet and paced away. "You don't really believe that."

She didn't want to believe it. But the letter proved her alias hadn't worked—an alias Derek had noticed his first time to her apartment. She didn't want to think he could be so vindictive, but he might have slipped up and told his family, and they were using the information to drive her away. That she could believe only too well.

"I don't know what all's going on between you two,

but I do know you're in trouble. You're being stalked, and whoever's been making the calls could have gotten your number from anywhere, maybe even from the ads you ran for typing. But now he knows where you live. The letter proves that. If you keep putting off telling Derek, you could end up hurt."

"Well, I can't do anything about it tonight. Derek had business and couldn't come over. And it isn't something to discuss on the phone."

Mick nodded slowly as he slipped his jacket on. "I'll try to watch out for you, Angel. I wouldn't let anyone hurt you if I could help it, but I can't always be here."

Her blood ran cold with his words. "Mick, if you ever, *ever* hear anything suspicious, or see anyone around the mailboxes, you call the police. Don't you dare try confronting anyone on your own."

He didn't reply to that, merely made his way to the door. "I'll lock this behind me."

"Mick?"

"Call him, Angel. Tell him what's going on. He cares about you and Grayson. I know he does."

It would have been nice if Mick didn't act like the typical domineering, overprotective male. Why were men, of all ages, so blasted stubborn? She sighed. "I'll think about it."

Mick looked at her a moment longer, then nodded. "All right. I'll see you tomorrow?"

She smiled at him. She was very lucky she'd met him when she had. Knowing him, having his friendship, had made her life much easier. "Yes. Get some sleep so you're well rested for that test."

"Yes, ma'am."

After checking that the door was securely locked, Angel peeked in on Grayson. He was sleeping soundly, which would give her a chance to take a quick shower. With all of Derek's help of late, her leg had more time to rest. It didn't hurt as often anymore, but tonight it was sore. She'd sat too long typing at her desk earlier and the muscles felt cramped. A hot shower usually helped.

Leaving the bathroom door open so she could hear Grayson if he cried, she stripped off her clothes and reached into the tub to adjust the temperature of the water. Once the steam started billowing out, she slipped in under the spray.

It felt wonderful to once again wash her hair with scented shampoo, to use all the toiletries she'd given up on due to lack of funds. At first she'd tried returning the things to Derek, but he'd been so sincere in wanting her to keep them, so anxious to *relieve the guilt of his past sins*—his words for his execrable behavior of the past—that she couldn't deny him.

She lingered for a long time, relaxing in the hypnotic warmth of the steam and stinging spray, until she became sleepy and knew she needed to put herself to bed. Grayson still woke during the night for a feeding, and he was usually up with the birds in the morning.

She was just stepping over the side of the tub when the phone rang.

Her first thought was that it might be Derek, and ridiculously enough, her heart leaped. He'd taken to calling her several times a day, whereas before her phone had seldom rung at all. Many times now he'd called to tell her good morning, or good-night, even if he'd spent hours at her apartment.

Wrapping a thick white towel around herself, she hurried out of the bathroom and into the kitchen to snatch up the phone. She was smiling as she said, "Hello?"

A rough, rasping breath answered her, then turned into a growl. Her smile died a quick death.

Shaken, Angel started to slam the phone back down, and then she heard, "Bitch. Give me what I want."

The rasping tones didn't sound human and her blood rushed from her head, leaving her dizzy. "I don't know what you want," she said, her voice shaking despite her efforts to sound unaffected.

"Yes, you do." There was a laugh, taunting and high-pitched. "You're not as innocent as you like to pretend, Angel *Morton*. But your time is up. Do you hear me?"

"I'm hanging up now," she said, determined not to let the caller get the upper hand.

"Did you get my letter? I know where you are now. You better watch your back…"

Angel slammed the phone into the cradle. Her heart was beating so hard, it rocked her body and she quickly wrapped her arms around herself. She was only marginally aware of the water dripping from her hair down her back, leaving a puddle on the floor. Goose bumps rose on her skin, but she was frozen, unable to move.

When the knock sounded on the door, she let out a startled, short scream, jumping back two steps and bumping into the kitchen table. A chair tipped over and crashed to the floor. Grayson woke, his disgruntled wail piercing in the otherwise leaden silence.

She heard Derek call out, "Angel!" at the same time a key sounded in the lock. The door immediately swung open. She couldn't help herself, she gaped at him. How had he known to show up just when she needed him most?

In the next instant, doubt surfaced, and she had to wonder if it was a coincidence, or part of a plan. Was it possible he was working with his family to drive her away? Had she inadvertently stepped into the lion's den?

Derek stormed in like an avenging angel, took one look at her standing there with nothing more than the towel covering her, then crossed the room with long, angry strides. He grabbed her shoulders. "What's the matter? What's happened?"

Angel managed to shake herself out of her stupor. She clutched at her towel with a fist. "What are you doing here?"

He looked nonplussed by her calm question and tightened his hands on her. "I wanted to see you." His head turned in the direction of Grayson's wails and a fierce frown formed. "You're both okay?"

"Yes, of course."

"But you screamed." He turned back to her, raised one hand when she started to speak, then shook his head. "First things first. Go get dried off. I'll get the baby."

She was shaking all over, but he thankfully didn't comment on it. "Thank you. I think the phone disturbed him, and then your knock..."

Derek started her toward her bedroom with a gentle push. "I understand, babe. Go. We'll talk about it in a minute."

Regardless of what he'd said, Angel followed Derek into the baby's room and made certain everything was all right. She never let Grayson cry, and even now, when she was so rattled, she couldn't stand to hear him upset. Derek cradled him close to his chest, rocking him, murmuring to him, and Grayson immediately began to quiet, his yells turning into hiccups as he recognized his father's scent and voice. Derek held his face close to the baby's, nuzzling, kissing his tiny ear, his cheek, smoothing his large hand up and down Grayson's back. Angel's throat felt tight and her chest restricted.

He turned suddenly when he realized Angel had followed him. Slowly, his gaze ran the length of her, lingering, she knew, on the still harsh scars of her left leg. His attention returned to the baby. "Go get something on, Angel, before you catch cold."

She wondered if her leg repulsed him; his voice had sounded unusually gruff and low. It really was ugly and overall she looked like a drowned rat at the moment. "All right. I'll...I'll be right back."

In the bathroom again, she quickly dried off, dragged a comb through her tangled hair, then shrugged into her housecoat. It was long and thick and covered her from head to toe. She hurried back in to Grayson. The baby now had his entire fist stuffed in his mouth, sucking loudly. She knew from experience that would only suffice for so long.

"Let me have him. After I nurse him, he should fall back to sleep."

Derek gave her a long look before nodding. "Let me change him first."

He disappeared into the other room and Angel paced. The letter this afternoon, then the phone call.... It was the first time she'd heard a voice. Usually the calls consisted of heavy breathing and ominous silences. Again, chills ran up her arms and she ducked her head, her brain working furiously. Mick was right; she had to trust Derek, had to tell him of her suspicions. But she wouldn't tell him everything. She'd only confide about the most recent events. After she saw how he reacted to that, then she'd consider telling him the rest.

When he touched her shoulder, she again jumped, whirling about to face him, her hand pressed to her throat. His expression was dark, his eyes narrowed, and she tried a nervous laugh.

"I'm sorry. You startled me."

"Obviously. But we'll talk about that in a minute."

She took the baby, quickly settled herself on the couch and then looked at Derek. He always left the room when she nursed Grayson, giving her the privacy she needed, but this time he stared right back. Slowly, his gaze never leaving her face, he took the chair opposite her. Heat bloomed inside her. "Derek…"

"No more secrets, Angel."

Grayson rooted against her, anxious for his meal, and she knew, judging by Derek's expression, arguing would gain her nothing. She pulled her gaze away from him, deliberately ignoring his very attentive audience, and went about feeding her baby. She felt stiff, unable to relax, so many things racing through her mind.

After a moment, Derek rose from his chair and reseated himself beside her. The soft, worn cushions of the couch slumped with his weight and her hip rolled next to his, bumping into him. He felt warm and hard, his presence overwhelming. Angel was acutely aware of his undivided concentration on her breast. She kept her visual attention firmly placed on Grayson.

Casually, Derek slipped his arm around her shoulders. She had trouble breathing. She moved Grayson to her other breast, closer to Derek, and as he nursed he began to fall back to sleep. He looked precious, and she couldn't hold back a smile.

"He's beautiful, Angel." Derek's warm breath

fanned her temple and she shivered. "You're beautiful."

His voice sounded with awe, and as he scooted even closer, seeming to surround her with his heat and scent and power, she felt herself relaxing. This felt right. Derek was doing nothing untoward, only taking part in what was rightfully his. His left arm moved across her abdomen in an embrace, just below the baby, circling both mother and son. He kissed her temple, a light, loving kiss. Slowly, Grayson released her nipple and a drop of milk slid down his chin. With his fingertip, Derek wiped it away

They neither one moved. She knew Derek was looking at her, studying her, but there was nothing lurid about his scrutiny. He dipped his head and kissed Grayson on his silky crown. In a low, husky whisper, he asked, "Would you like me to burp him and put him back to bed?"

Angel nodded.

As he was lifted, Grayson stretched and groaned and gave a loud belch, making any further efforts unnecessary. Derek grinned as he hefted the small weight to his shoulder and got to his feet. He looked down at Angel. "I'll be right back," he whispered. "Don't move."

Other than covering her breast and nervously shifting, she obeyed.

It was late, now close to eleven o'clock, but she was far from sleepy. So many emotions were pulling at her, fear and anxiety and anticipation, but also a deep contentment. Derek was everything a father should be, and she couldn't quite work up the energy to distrust him anymore. It took all she had as she fought herself to keep from falling in love with him. Despising him was out of the question.

Derek stepped out of the baby's room, softly closing the door behind him. For long moments, he merely stared at Angel across the room. The time of reckoning, she thought.

For the life of her, she couldn't seem to move. Her heart began racing, her palms grew damp. She saw Derek lock his jaw, saw his shoulders tighten and flex, and she knew, without him saying a single word, he was caught in the same inexplicable flow of emotions as she.

What would happen next, she couldn't guess, but she was anxious to find out.

And then the phone rang.

Angel gasped. Both wary and disgusted by the interruption, she stared toward the kitchen where the phone was located.

Derek frowned at her. "Do you want me to get that for you?"

"No, I'll..." She shook her head, wiped her palms across her thighs. And still she sat there, staring at the phone.

Sparing her a curious glance, Derek stalked to the phone and snatched it up on the fifth ring. "Hello?" He kept his gaze on Angel as he spoke and she tried to clear her expression, but she could see he'd already read too much there.

"Hello?" he said a little more forcefully. He looked at the receiver, then gently placed it in the cradle. As he walked back to loom over Angel, she could see the questions in his eyes. "What's going on, honey?" His tone was soft, menacing.

She shook her head. "I don't know."

He waited, not moving away, not saying another word. She recognized his stubborn expression, only now there was more of a threat there, more determination than ever.

"Sometimes I get strange calls."

She hadn't meant to make such a bald confession, but it just slipped out. After a deep breath while he raised one eyebrow, encouraging her, she continued. "Sometimes, eight or ten times now, someone has called and just…breathed in the phone. Today I finally heard a voice. He…said things to me." She lifted her gaze and got caught in his. "He called right before you got here."

Derek's eyes darkened, his eyebrows lowered, and suddenly he was crouching there in front of her, his hands holding hers, hard but not really hurting her. It did give her the feeling she couldn't get away, even if she tried.

His gaze was so intense, so probing, she squirmed. "You thought it might be me," he accused.

He didn't sound angry precisely, though she couldn't pinpoint the dominant emotion in his tone. She straightened her shoulders and frowned right back. "I wondered. I have no enemies that I know of, no reason for threats. You're the only person who ever seemed to despise me, and I've never really understood why."

There, let him deal with that, she thought and jerked away to walk carefully into the kitchen. She needed something to drink, some warm tea. And she needed to escape his close scrutiny.

Out of the corner of her eye, she watched Derek stand, then pace around her tiny living room. He had his hands back in his pockets and his head down in deep thought. She was familiar with that look now, that show of serious introspection. She'd seen it a lot lately, though in the past she couldn't recall Derek ever doubting himself, ever giving so much thought to anything pertaining to her.

She put water on to boil, then asked, "Would you like some tea?"

"Thank you."

After righting the fallen chair, she sat at her small kitchen table, waiting for the water to get hot. Moments later she felt Derek's hands on her shoulders, heavy and warm.

"The problem is," he whispered, "I'm not making the calls. And I don't despise you." His hands slipped up to her throat, caressing, then smoothing her damp hair back behind her ears. "On the contrary, Angel, I want to take care of you."

Anger caused her eyes to narrow. She wanted to believe him, to understand and accept his help. She twisted to face him. "Why? Why now, when you made it plain months ago how you felt? You deliberately humiliated me in front of my supervisors. You didn't just break things off, you tried to break me. *Why?*"

His eyes closed and he turned his head away. "You're right, of course. I can't undo the past. I can only have regrets, which don't amount to a hill of beans. But I'm here now and I'd like to help."

Since that was what she'd wanted all along, what her entire plan had been, she should have been relieved. But somehow everything was different than she'd expected. He wasn't the same man, easy to be detached from now. The Derek who'd first hurt her had been more of an illusion to her, an image of strength and power that had seduced her by sheer impression. She hadn't really known the man, other than in the most superficial ways; she'd merely been attracted to his image. But now she genuinely liked and respected him. When she could set the past aside, he was fun, and when he held Grayson, the affection in his eyes filled her with an insidious warmth that expanded her heart. More often than not, she didn't understand what she was feeling.

Only one thing was certain; Grayson could be at risk if she didn't find some sort of protection.

She got up to serve the tea, collecting her thoughts. After she sat his cup near him on the table, she said, "I've gotten several anonymous calls lately, more than ever before. Usually, it's just breathing and such. They started before I'd moved, when I lived in my old apartment. After I moved here, they stopped for a while and I thought I'd lost whoever it was. But just recently they started up again. It's possible my phone number was taken from one of the posted ads around the colleges. The ads are generic, offering typing, but since I've been transcribing for colleges ever since the accident, it could be my number was relocated that way."

Derek nodded. "Very possible, I suppose. But the person making the calls would have to be damn determined."

Angel shivered. "He spoke for the first time today. He said, very clearly, that I couldn't hide. He called me a few…choice names and told me to give him what he wanted."

She saw Derek's jaw go hard and knew he was clenching his teeth. He stared at her and she shrugged helplessly. "I don't know what he wants. I wish I did."

"Go on."

"I also got a letter in my mailbox."

"Where is it?"

She pulled an envelope from the basket on top of her refrigerator and handed it to Derek. The letter was now wrinkled from her many hours of examining it, but Derek had no trouble making out the typed message. *"I've found you,"* he read aloud. He was silent for a long time, his face dark, his expression tight. He threw the letter on the table and turned on her.

"You thought I was behind this?" he asked, his teeth clenched, color high on his face. "You thought I would resort to sneaking around and stuffing threatening letters in a woman's mailbox, in *your* mailbox?"

His reaction was genuine and for the first time she felt absolutely positive that he played no part in the harassment.

A little truth now certainly wouldn't hurt. Problem was, as she tried to give it, tears gathered in her eyes, and she couldn't quite work up the nerve to accuse his family, the most likely of suspects. Not yet.

She shook her head. "No," she said, trying to sound sure of herself. "I don't really think you're behind it. But the letter came after I contacted you. Before that, all I'd gotten was phone calls. And you noticed the fake name on my mailbox that day. Now tonight, you showed up right after the call, and it was the first time he'd ever spoken to me. That's a lot of coincidences." She searched his face, hoping he'd understand. "I had to consider you, Derek. I couldn't take any chances with Grayson's safety."

Seconds ticked by, then he reluctantly nodded.

She drew a deep breath of relief. "The whole reason I contacted you again, the only reason I introduced Grayson to you is because deep down, for some incredibly insane reason, I guess I still trust you. Even after everything that happened, I thought... I thought you would help. I *hoped* you would help.''

She swallowed, the sound audible, almost choked. ''Derek...I've been so scared, and I don't have anyone else to go to.''

A stunned moment of silence fell between them. She could feel the waves of emotion emanating from him, anger and regret and need. Then she was in his arms and it felt so good, so right, she curled closer and snuggled tighter, trying to fit herself completely against his long, hard length. His arms wrapped around her, urgently, almost violently, while his mouth nuzzled down her face, giving her small anxious biting kisses until finally he reached her lips and then he was devouring her and she was glad, so very, very glad.

CHAPTER SIX

DANE KNEW HE SHOULD pull back, that he was making a terrible tactical error. He wasn't completely in control, and he should be. But he couldn't put so much as an inch between them. He wanted, needed her, right now. Even two seconds more would be too long to wait. And Angel was so soft and anxious against him, her breasts pressed to his chest, her pelvis cradling his own. She wanted him, too, and that was all that mattered. The deceptions, the worries, could be taken care of in the morning. He'd make it all okay, one way or another, but for now, tonight, he wouldn't say a single thing that would put a halt to her greed.

Growling low, he slid his hands down to her backside and cuddled her even closer. She felt so damn good.

"Angel."

She pressed her face into his throat and shuddered. "I don't understand this, Derek," she said on a near wail. "I've never felt like this before."

How could he possibly explain it to her, when he didn't understand it himself? He knew she would compare him to Derek, and as much as he'd loved his brother, as dedicated as he was to finding out the truth, right now claiming her took precedence over everything else.

He shushed her with more kisses. "I've never felt

this way either, honey. Don't worry about it now. Just
let me love you.''

She opened her mouth against him and took a soft,
greedy love bite of his throat. Gasping, he quickly
picked her up, mindful of her injured leg, and hurried
to her bedroom, nudging the door shut behind them
until it closed with a secure click. He didn't want to
take the chance of waking Grayson. He wanted no interruptions at all.

He didn't put her on the bed, choosing to stand her
beside it instead. He wanted her naked, and he wanted
to look his fill. It felt as if he'd been waiting forever.

As he grasped the cloth belt to her robe, ready to
pull it free, she caught his wrists. His gaze darted to
her face and he was amazed to see how heavy and
sensual her eyes had become, her thick lashes lowered,
the green eyes bright and hot. Her high cheekbones
were colored, but with need, not embarrassment. She
took soft, panting breaths as she looked up at him.

She licked her lips, and even that innocently seduc-
tive sight had him trembling.

"I don't want to disappoint you, Derek."

He'd never before minded being mistaken for his
twin. Through his entire life people had often done it,
sometimes even his parents. Before their father had
died, he and Derek had often played tricks on him,
deliberately confusing him.

But now, he hated it. He had to struggle for breath.
He gave her a hard quick kiss, which turned tender and
hungry and lingered sweetly. When he pulled away, it
seemed to take a great effort on her part for her to get
her eyes open. He smiled. "There's no way you could
disappoint me, honey."

"My body's changed. The baby..."

Still holding her gaze he tugged the knot out of the belt and pushed the robe off her shoulders. She dropped her arms and the robe fell free all the way to the floor. Angel lowered her head and turned slightly away.

For nearly a minute he was speechless. She was more beautiful than any woman had a right to be, and there was absolutely nothing motherly about her heavy, firm breasts, the stiff dark nipples. Her rib cage expanded and fluttered with her uneven breaths and her belly looked soft and slightly rounded, very pale. He spread one large, hot palm over her stomach and heard her small gasp.

"Derek…?"

"Shhh. I've never wanted a woman the way I want you, Angel. Trust me when I tell you there's not a single thing about you that could disappoint me." Her legs were long and so sexy, even with the harsh scars on her left shin. He immediately pictured those long legs wrapped around him, her heels digging into the small of his back, urging him on, and he groaned as his erection pulsed, demanding release.

Slowly, so he wouldn't startle her, he slid his palm downward until he was cupping her, his fingers tangling in the dark blond curls over her mound. They felt damp and soft under his fingertips, her flesh swollen, and he breathed deeply through his nose, trying to ease the constriction in his lungs. He held still, just holding her like that, letting her feel the heat of his palm, letting the anticipation build.

Angel moaned and stepped up against him. Her hands gripped his biceps, her forehead pressed to his shoulder.

Dane swallowed and smiled grimly. "Do you remember when I touched you in my office?" he asked against her temple.

She nodded her head.

He licked her ear and gently nipped the lobe. "You were so close then, Angel, and I'd barely done anything to you. Little more than kissing." He nearly groaned with the memory.

Her hips jerked, encouraging him. Anticipating her response, he inched his fingers lower, gliding over her warm flesh, opening her soft, plump folds, learning her, exploring. She was already so hot, so silky wet, and it amazed him the way she reacted to his touch. It also made him nearly crazy with a frenzied mix of lust and overwhelming tenderness.

Her body felt frozen against his, very still, waiting. Even her breathing became suspended, as if she was afraid to move for fear of missing something. Determination swelled within him. He had no intention of leaving her with complaints; her views on the joys of sex were about to be altered.

"Open your legs a little more for me, Angel." He could tell that she responded to his words, and he wasn't about to disappoint her. "Let me feel you. All of you."

With a shudder, her face well hidden against his chest, she carefully widened her stance. Immediately he pressed one finger deep inside her, at the same time he braced his free arm around her waist.

She needed his support.

Her body went alternately stiff and completely yielding. Holding her against him, acutely aware of her broken breaths, her soft moans, the way her fingers dug into his chest, he stroked her. He could feel her tightening, feel the small shudders moving up and down her body. He eased her a little away from him and she allowed the small separation, her head falling back on her shoulders, her still-damp hair trailing down to tickle against his arm. He saw her breasts heaving and dipped his head down to take one plump nipple into his mouth.

"Ohhh…"

He lapped with his tongue, nibbled with his teeth, drew deeply on her. Her hands raised from his chest to his head and her fingers tangled in his hair, tugging, trying to draw him even closer.

"I have to sit down," she moaned.

"No." He blew on her damp nipple, watching it go painfully tight. The pregnancy had no doubt made her breasts extra sensitive, and he intended to take advantage of that fact. "Right here, Angel. We'll get to the bed in a minute."

He switched to her other breast and heard her give a soft sob of compliance. Voluntarily, she parted her legs even more and then thrust against him. He slid his finger all the way out, teasing, then worked it heavily back into her again. "You're so wet for me, honey," he said on a groan, amazed and thrilled and so hot himself he wanted to die.

Forcefully, making him wince, she brought his mouth back up to her own and this time she kissed him, awkwardly but with so much hunger he thought he might burst. He rubbed his heavy erection against her soft hip while he carefully forced a second finger inside her. He found a rhythm that pleased her and went about seeing to her satisfaction. He was playing it safe, not about to remove his clothes or lie with her on the bed, knowing his control was thin at the moment and any little thing could send him over the edge. He wouldn't risk taking his own completion before he'd seen to hers.

Within minutes she was crying, her body tight and trembling, her hands frenzied on his back and shoulders. Slowly, he eased her down to the side of the bed so that her legs hung over the edge, then knelt between them. She dropped back, her hands fisting in the bedclothes, her hips twisting. Dane lifted her legs to his shoulders and before she could object—if indeed she would have given how close she was—he cupped her hips in his hands and brought her to his mouth.

She tasted sweet and incredibly hot and he was beyond teasing her, so close to exploding himself. His heart thundered and her scent filled him as he nuzzled into her, driving himself ever closer. As his tongue stroked over her sensitive flesh, as he found the small engorged bud and drew on it, teasing with his tongue, tormenting with his teeth, she gave a stifled scream and climaxed.

Quickly, wanting to feel every bit of her, he pushed his fingers back inside her. Her feminine muscles gripped him, the spasms strong as she pressed herself even higher, moving against his open mouth and continuing to cry and moan and excite him unbearably. It went on and on and he almost lost control. He was shaking all over when she finally quieted, her eyes closed, her lashes damp on her cheeks, her mouth slightly open as she gulped air.

She never so much as blinked when he lifted her legs gently to the bed and stood to look down at her. Slowly, drinking in the sight of her limp, sated body, he pulled his shirt free from his pants and began unbuttoning it. He forced himself to go slow, to savor the moment of his claiming. Even to his own mind, his thoughts, his responses, seemed primitive, maybe even ruthless. But he wanted her to be his and his alone—a feeling he'd never encountered before, not even with Anna. He wanted to take her so thoroughly, possess her so completely, she'd be willing to forgive him anything, willing to trust him in all matters.

She gave a shuddering sigh, lifted one languid hand to her forehead and pushed her hair away from her face. Dane watched her, so suffused with heat the edges of his vision blurred.

While he tugged his belt loose from the clasp with one hand, he dropped his other lightly to her soft thigh. Her skin felt like warm silk to him, and tempted him more than it should have.

Her lashes fluttered as his fingers trailed higher, and finally her eyes opened. She looked dazed and relaxed, on the verge of sleep. He smiled and carefully worked his zipper down past his throbbing erection. "You scream very well, Angel. I liked it."

"Oh." Her cheeks filled with color and she swallowed. When her gaze dropped to the open vee in his slacks, her eyes opened wide. *"Oh."*

Dane sat on the bed beside her, his hand still on her thigh. "No, don't get up. I like seeing you sprawled there." She relaxed back again and he used the toes of his left foot to work off his right shoe, while at the same time surveying her body. He traced a nipple with his fingertip, around and around until she made a protesting sound. Then he dragged his fingers over her ribs and to her belly. She shifted abruptly.

"Ticklish?"

"Derek..."

Leaning over, he pressed a lingering kiss to her navel. "I love the way you taste, honey."

She made a groaning sound of renewed interest, then tried to turn away from him. He caught her hips, stopping her.

"Derek, you can't expect me to…"

"Yes I do." Once again his fingers slid between her legs, anchoring her in place while he kissed his way up her abdomen to her breasts. "I expect you to let me pleasure you, and I expect you to continue enjoying my efforts."

He raised his head for just a moment, pinning her with a look. "You came, Angel. A nice long, hard climax. And if I didn't miss my guess, it was your first. So don't try to deny it."

She gasped. "I wasn't going to!"

"Good." When he drew her nipple into the heat of his mouth she writhed against him, then fisted her hands in his hair.

"No, Derek."

He jerked upward and pinned her hands next to her head. "Yes."

She said quickly, before he could kiss her, "I want you to take your shirt off. I want to see you, too. It's not fair for me to lie here…exposed, while you're completely dressed."

His grin was slow and wicked. He knew it, but didn't care. She wasn't denying him at all as he'd first thought. She only insisted on her fair share. "All right."

He pushed himself off the bed. "Don't move, Angel. You inspire me, lying there like that."

He shrugged his shirt off and grabbed the waistband of his pants. He stepped between her legs as he pushed them down, removing his Skivvies at the same time. When he straightened, he was naked.

Angel's gaze roamed over him and her face heated again. He stifled a laugh, delighted with her. Her particular brand of innocence and hot sexuality was driving him crazy. He loved it. He loved... No, his thoughts refused to budge any further in that direction. He firmed his resolve.

Using a knee, he spread her legs even more and lowered himself over her. Propped on his elbows, he smiled down at her. "Hi."

Rather than smiling back, she traced his face, over his eyebrows, the bridge of his nose, the dip in his chin. "You took me by surprise, Derek. Everything is so different..."

"So you keep saying." He didn't want to talk about that right now. Thinking of his brother with her like this was enough to make him howl at the moon.

"What happened was...unexpected."

"But nice?" He again caught her hands and trapped them over her head, leaving her submissive to his desires.

She looked thoughtful as she continued her study of his face. "Very nice. Incredible really. But ever since I saw you again, it's been that way. You look at me, and I get all hot inside. You touch me and I can't think straight. I try to despise you; I have good reason to despise you, but I can't. It doesn't make any sense. Unless having the baby changed me somehow."

"Angel." She was killing him with her words, but he didn't know how to tell her that.

"After everything that happened between us, I thought I'd always hate you."

He groaned. "Don't, babe." He kissed her, hard and long, his tongue thrusting deep, stroking in a parody of the sex act. He rubbed his hairy chest against her sensitive nipples and felt her legs bend, coming up to hug his hips. The open juncture of her legs was a sweet torture, her damp heat against his belly, her soft thighs cradling him. He rubbed against her, his muscles bound so tight he felt ready to break.

She shifted, and then his erection was smoothly pushing against her wet sex. Angel began moving with him, their mouths still fused together, both of them breathing rapidly, roughly.

She jerked and pulled her mouth away, crying out.

Dane was stunned as she quickly climaxed again, shuddering beneath him, her head arched back, her heels digging into his thighs.

His control snapped. Shaking, he grabbed up his slacks and fumbled like a drunk for his wallet. He found a condom and viciously ripped the packet open with his teeth. Angel was still gasping breathlessly and when he turned, catching her legs in the crook of his elbows, spreading her wide and driving into her with one hard thrust, she cried out again.

He couldn't think. His brain throbbed and his vision went blank and all he could do was feel and smell and taste her. She'd invaded his heart, his soul. He was the one who felt possessed and he rebelled against it even as he felt himself spiraling away. He squeezed his eyes shut and growled and pumped and when he heard Angel groan he knew she was with him yet again. It was too much. It felt like he exploded, his entire body gripped in painful pleasure, but it was so damn wonderful he never wanted it to end.

It took him a long time to come back to reality, to hear Angel's soft sniffling, to feel the shudders in her body. Slowly, feeling drugged, he struggled up to his elbows again. Tears dampened her eyelashes and her lips looked swollen. His heart twisted.

Damn, her leg. His arms were still tangled with her legs and he knew she had to be in pain. He'd taken her roughly, almost brutally. That he'd hurt her made him wince in self-loathing. Carefully, he straightened, letting her legs down easy. She groaned and pressed her face to the side, away from him.

He cupped her chin and turned her back. "Angel, honey, I'm sorry."

She shook her head.

"Babe, look at me."

Her eyelashes lifted and she stared up at him. The tears in her eyes twisted his guts. He pressed his forehead to hers and kissed her gently. "I'm so sorry, sweetheart. I didn't mean to hurt you."

She frowned.

"I got a little carried away." He tried a smile but it felt more like a grimace. "You moaned, and all rational thought fled my mind. I'm sorry." He sounded like a parrot, apologizing over and over again.

"Derek…"

Goddammit, he hated having her call him that. "Shh. It's all right." Her hair, dry now and tangled impossibly, lay wild around her head. He tried to smooth it. "Can I get you anything? Some aspirin or something?" He felt like an idiot, having sex with a woman then offering her medicine for the pain.

She shook her head again and her voice, when she spoke, was tentative and as soft as a whisper. "I'm fine, just a little…stunned. Is it always like that?"

Now he felt confused. Buying himself some time, he sat up and carefully moved to the side of her. Her body had been damp and warm from their exertions and combined heat, and she shivered in the cool evening air. He pulled the corner of the spread up to cover her, but left her leg bare. Gently, he massaged her calf and saw her wince.

"Dammit, I'm an unthinking bastard. I—"

She laughed, catching his hand and twining her fingers with his. "No, you're not. I'm fine, Derek."

He forcefully ignored the continued use of his brother's name. "Then why were you crying?"

She sat up and put her arms around him, burrowing close. "Because it was so wonderful."

His heart pounding, Dane hugged her back. "I didn't hurt you?"

She laughed. "Maybe a little, but I didn't notice...until after."

He pressed her back down on the bed and stood. "I'll be right back." With those words, and one last glance at her naked body, he left the bedroom. He wanted to make sure the apartment was secure for the night. There were three windows, one in the kitchen over the sink, but it was too small for an intruder, and one in the living room on that same wall. He checked to make sure it was locked, then realized the window was so old and warped, opening it would be a true effort. He'd be in the bedroom, so he wasn't worried about that window. He'd already locked the front door when he'd first come in. He glanced at the phone, scowled, but put that particular worry from his mind. Right now, he wanted to concentrate on Angel.

He peeked in on Grayson to see the baby sleeping soundly. He'd been afraid their commotion might have disturbed the infant, but Grayson was snuggled warm and comfy in his crib. He lay on his side, and one chubby cheek was smooshed, his rosebud mouth slightly open.

Damn, Dane felt good. He hadn't felt this good in… He'd never felt this good. Angel was the perfect bed partner, wild and abandoned and responsive. She burned him up. She was also sweet and caring and strong.

And she had Grayson, his nephew, the strongest bond he had left to his brother. In his heart, Grayson was his own.

As soon as he set things right with Angel, they'd be able to work together to find out what had happened to Derek. Likely, the threats to her and Derek's death were related. He hated the unknown, hated how ineffectual he felt when dealing with the whole problem. Somehow he had to uncover a mystery and protect Angel at the same time. Thank God the threats to her were so far only abstract, not physical. Long before they got too serious, he intended to have everything resolved. From here on out, he'd double his efforts.

Dane returned to the bedroom moments later with a damp washcloth. He'd disposed of the used condom, and set two more on the nightstand. The night was still young, and he was still hungry.

Angel looked almost asleep and the fact she hadn't been concerned with him roaming her apartment assured him that she was starting to trust him, at least a little. It also proved, to some degree, that she had nothing at all to hide.

She opened her eyes and blinked sleepily up at him when he sat on the edge of the mattress. "What are you doing?"

"I was just going to make you more comfortable." So saying, he swiped the warm, damp cloth over her

face, her neck, then down her body. She smiled and
arched into his hand with a sigh of pleasure.

"You wore a...a..."

Dane cocked one eyebrow. "A what?"

Pointing down to his lap, she said, "You know. Before you made love to me."

"A rubber? I didn't want to take any chances. Much
as I adore Grayson, the last thing you need right now
is another pregnancy, what with your leg and—"

"And my financial situation and the threats."

Dane leaned down and kissed her. "I'll take care of
the threats. Don't worry about that. And as far as I'm
concerned, you don't have any financial worries. I can
take care of everything." As quickly as he said it, he
raised a placating hand. "I didn't mean that quite the
way it sounded."

But Angel was already scowling fiercely. "I've told
you enough times now, Derek, I don't need anything
from you."

Dane eyed her heaving breasts, her flushed cheeks,
and tossed the washcloth away. "I wouldn't say that's
precisely true." In the next instant they were sprawled
on the bed again. Angel moaned his brother's name.

As he shoved the spread out of his way so nothing
would be between their bodies, he whispered, "I'm
spending the night, honey, and in the morning we'll
figure everything out. But for now, I want you again."

"Derek."

He'd have to settle things soon. Being called another
man's name while making love to a woman who was
quickly obsessing his mind couldn't be borne.

In the morning, he thought. He'd clear it all up in

the morning. Then Angel could begin accepting things. She could begin dealing with Dane Carter. And he'd be sure to remind her how much more she liked him than Derek.

CHAPTER SEVEN

ANGEL WOKE WITH A GROAN. She felt sore in places she'd never thought about before, her muscles protesting as she stretched, her mind foggy from too little sleep.

She and Derek had made love several times during the night. The man seemed insatiable, yet she wouldn't complain. Everything he'd done to her had been wonderful, if a bit shocking. She smiled as she looked toward the window and saw that the sun was coming up in a blaze of orange light. She loved dawn in the winter, the promise of sunshine when the weather was so bleak and cold.

Turning back to the center of the bed, she reached for Derek, only he wasn't there. Angel frowned, and then her gaze fell on the clock on the nightstand. Eight-thirty. Good grief, she hadn't lain abed so late in ages. She wondered if Derek was in another part of the apartment, but it was then she noticed the note on his pillow. She straightened in the bed and unfolded the slip of paper.

Sorry I had to run off, but I had to be at the office early today. I didn't want to disturb you—any more than I already had through the night.

Angel smiled. She could almost hear the boasting tone of his voice in the teasing words.

A lot to do. I'll call you later. Stay in the apartment and don't worry. I'll take care of things.

D.

Don't worry, indeed. How did he presume to magically "take care of things"? she wondered. She dropped the note as she yawned and stretched once more. Time to get up and check on Grayson. At least Derek had had the foresight to leave the bedroom door open. He'd closed it during the night, against her protests, but true to his word, he'd heard Grayson when the baby awoke, and had even fetched him to her so she hadn't been forced to leave the warmth of the bed. After she'd nursed him, Derek had taken him back to his crib, then since they were both awake, he'd made love to her once more. Even that last time it had turned fast and furious and she'd bitten his shoulder to keep from screaming like a wild woman.

Her face heated with the memory of Derek's satisfied smile. He'd looked at the small teeth marks on his shoulder and grinned with pride.

Unaccountable man. Angel smiled.

It was as she was slipping on her housecoat that the crash sounded. Breaking glass and a loud thunking sound, followed by a low hissing. Her heart leaped into her throat and it took her a moment to unglue her feet, to get herself in motion. She raced out of the bedroom, and was immediately assailed by the smell of smoke. Billows of it poured out of the kitchen into the rest of the tiny apartment.

"Oh my God." Angel stared, then ran for Grayson.

The baby had just been jarred awake, and his face was blank for only a second before he began to squall. She jerked him up into her arms, wrapped a blanket tightly around him and then raced to the front door. It took her too much time to manipulate the lock and she was cursing as she finally got the door to open. Once in the hallway she froze, wondering what to do, if maybe the fire had been deliberately set for just that reason, to get her out of the apartment, vulnerable. Shaking, her heart beating too fast, she tried to soothe Grayson even as she ran the length of the hall to Mick's apartment.

She pounded on the door, trying to look around herself, to be aware of any danger. The door opened and Mick's mother stood there, her face ravaged from a long night, her clothes rumpled as if she'd slept in them. She looked unsteady and very put out. Before Angel could say anything, Mick came around his mother.

"What's happened?" He jerked Angel into the apartment and looked her over. She knew her housecoat was only hastily closed and she tried to adjust Grayson to better cover herself.

"A fire. In my apartment. Someone broke a window I think."

Mick stared at her, then started to thrust her aside, determined, she knew, to investigate. Angel grabbed his arm. "No! Just call the fire department, for God's sake."

He shook her off and spared a glance for his mother. "Make the call. I'll be right back."

Mrs. Dawson made no effort to stop her son, frustrating Angel beyond measure. She watched the woman pick up the phone and try to make a coherent call, but it was obvious she was hungover.

Gently, Angel took the receiver from her and gave the details as best she could. The man on the other end told them all to vacate the building and that someone would be there right away. Angel prayed Mick would hurry back. She'd never felt so afraid in her life.

Mick stormed back just as Angel was trying to bundle Grayson up. "It's okay. It was only a small fire and it's out now, but to be safe, let's wait for the firemen outside." He went into his own room and fetched two blankets to bundle Angel in, and then slipped on his own coat.

His mother made grumbling noises and held her head. "I think I'll just go over to Jerry's. You can handle this, can't you, Mick?"

Mick gave a quick, abrupt nod. "Yes." Mrs. Dawson picked up her coat and walked out, one hand holding her head. Mick's face looked set in stone.

He took Angel's arm and started her outside. Already they could hear the sirens. He put his arms around Angel and the baby, trying to lend his warmth and comfort.

Angel wished with all her heart that he was her son. "Thank you, Mick."

He ignored that. "First thing once the place is declared safe, you're calling Derek."

She swallowed. "All right."

"You have to tell him everything now, Angel. No more playing around."

"I know."

She could feel how tense he was, his anger tangible. "Damn, I wish I'd seen whoever it was."

Angel was eternally grateful he hadn't.

It only took the firemen minutes to confirm what Mick had told her. Someone had broken her small kitchen window with a rock, then tossed in a bundle of gas-soaked rags. The result had been more smoke than anything else. Mick had smothered the flickering flames with a blanket, much to the firemen's disturbance. They lectured him on safety matters, on the importance of walking away from a fire rather than trying to handle it himself. Mick, she could tell, only half-heartedly listened to their speeches.

Endless questions followed, but finally it was all put down to a prank. It was obvious to the firemen that while the fire could have become serious, that hadn't been the intent. More of a lark, they said, their tones edged with anger. Angel didn't tell them about the other threats, the phone calls and the letter. She wanted to talk to Derek first. She had a feeling he'd want to be with her when she spoke to the police.

Mick skipped school that day, opting to stay with Angel instead. He'd already missed his morning classes arguing with his mother, who'd come home drunk once again. Angel felt for him, even as she gladly accepted his company.

The apartment was a mess, the smell of smoke lingering on everything. All of her clothes stank. She could do nothing about her jeans, but Mick loaned her a fresh sweatshirt to wear. They were in the apartment for mere moments, only long enough for her to gather the necessities for Grayson and a few of her own things. She didn't have apartment insurance, and the thought of the expense of replacing several things overwhelmed her. The firemen had suggested she call a professional cleaner to tackle the smoke damage and the singed areas of her kitchen, but she knew she couldn't afford it. She would have to do the cleaning herself.

Mick hovered over her as she settled herself on the couch in his mother's apartment. He handed her the phone. "Call Derek now. You've put it off long enough."

She sighed, knowing he was right, but not sure how to tell him. He was going to be angry, no doubt about that. And her thoughts still felt so jumbled.

Buying herself a little time, she thumbed through the personal phone book she'd retrieved from her desk. Her eyes closed as she thought of all the papers still to be typed, all of them gray with ash dust. How such a small fire had done so much damage she couldn't imagine. Her world was quickly unraveling around her, her choices falling away one by one until now she had no choices at all—she needed Derek. The idea didn't panic her nearly so much as it had only a week ago.

Deciding not to dawdle anymore, she found Derek's work number and punched it in. A secretary answered.

Angel cleared her throat. "I'd like to talk to Derek Carter please."

A very polite voice regretfully turned down her request. "I'm sorry, ma'am. Mr. Carter can't take your call right now."

Angel drew a calming breath and tried to pull herself together. Yelling at a secretary wouldn't gain her a thing. "You don't understand. I *have* to speak with him. It's an…an emergency."

There was a slight hesitation before the secretary said, "Just a minute please."

But it wasn't Derek who came on the line. Angel didn't recognize the impatient male voice, but at his inquiry, she repeated her request.

Suspicion crept into his tone when he asked, "Who is this?"

Because she was rattled, Angel answered without thinking. "Angel Morris."

Stunned silence followed, then a rough laugh that was quickly squelched. "Well, well. I'm sorry to be the one to break it to you, sweetheart. But Derek Carter is dead." There was another moment of silence where Angel could hear her own heartbeat, and then he added, "Maybe I can help you. What do you need?"

Angel dropped the phone as her heart kicked violently in panic. She couldn't draw a deep enough breath. Mick frowned at her and picked up the receiver. "Angel?"

She shook her head, slowly coming to her feet. She knew her face was white, her breathing too fast. It couldn't be true; it was likely part of the threat, some vicious game to taunt her, confuse her.

A cleansing rush of anger ran through her. First the damage to her apartment, and now this contemptible prank. She absolutely refused to believe it was any more than that.

Mick started to speak into the receiver but Angel snatched it away from him and slammed it down in the cradle. "No. Don't say anything else to him."

"Him? What's going on, Angel?"

She paced in front of Mick, her stride stiff and angry. "He said Derek's dead, but I know it can't be true! It can't be."

Mick frowned. His face turned pale with confusion and concern. "Of course it's not." He looked undecided for only a second, then determination replaced every other emotion on his face. "Come on." He hauled Angel along behind him with a firm grip on her arm.

"Where are we going?"

"To his company. You'll see for yourself that Derek is just fine, and then you're going to tell him everything. This is starting to get too damn weird."

"Yes." Angel nodded, not at all concerned with her mismatched clothing, her tangled hair, or her ash-smudged face. She only cared about seeing Derek, alive and well.

Her reaction was telling, she thought, but she refused to dwell on it. He was okay. She was certain he was okay. Her hands shook with anger and her heart ached as she bundled Grayson into a blanket and followed Mick out the door. Once she knew for certain it was all part of the threats, that Derek was indeed fine, she intended to tell him everything.

She'd never doubt him again.

DANE STARED AROUND at the solemn faces watching him. He knew his mother wanted to protest this little meeting he'd called, but so far she'd held herself silent. That alone confused him, because his mother had never been one for circumspection. She had a tendency to go after what she wanted with the force of a battering ram.

Which made her acceptance of Derek's *accident* all the more suspect. He pushed that aside for the moment.

The meeting wasn't officially with the board; it was a family matter and Dane intended to treat it as such. His two uncles, both older and naturally calm, held positions on the board, but it was their positions as heads of differing departments, as well as the fact they were family, that had guaranteed their presence here now. His mother was again seated to his right. His cousin, an amicable sort in charge of the sales department, was at the end of the table. They were waiting for Raymond and his sister, who had each been attending to previous meetings of their own.

His sister walked in first, looking chic in a stylish business suit, her fair hair loose, her face pale. She knows, Dane thought. His sister was well aware of how he felt about playing corporate head; it wouldn't take much deduction on her part to realize he was ready to make his exodus from the company. He hoped his mother would consider giving the position to Celia instead of Raymond. It would be his recommendation, with the promise he'd visit more often if his wishes were met. It was blackmail of a sort, something his mother could understand and appreciate.

Raymond hurried in right behind Celia, straightening his tie and tucking his shirt in more firmly. His hair was mussed, his face flushed. Very unusual for Raymond, who made a great effort to always look immaculate and composed. Dane had the disquieting thought that the two of them had been together, possibly playing around rather than attending to business. What in the world his sister saw in the man, he didn't know. Dane watched Celia give Raymond an inquiring glance, saw him quickly smile and pull out her seat, then take his own beside her. Maybe they hadn't been together, he thought, seeing his sister's dark frown, but at that moment his mother cleared her throat, impatient.

Dane stood. He wanted to get this over with quickly. He'd been at the office for hours now, anxious to get back to Angel. He pictured her lying soft and warm and exhausted in her bed and his groin tightened. He should have been well sated, but he was beginning to believe no amount of time with her would be enough.

He had to tell her everything, to remove all secrets between them. In truth, he should have done so before making love to her, but he hadn't wanted to risk being turned away. Now, he needed her help, both to find the truth behind Derek's death, and the source of the threats against her. In his gut, he knew the two were undeniably tied together, and they needed to share information in order to get to the truth.

Dane now had two agendas, avenging his brother and protecting Angel. He couldn't do either one while playing the role of his twin, with Angel or at the office.

He glanced around the table at the curious expressions of his family. "I have a few announcements to make, then you can all get back to your plans."

His mother stared ahead stonily, her mouth pinched, her eyes hard. For the first time, Dane noticed the signs of her age, the tiredness, the brittleness that suddenly seemed a part of her. He turned to his sister and saw that she was staring down at her hands.

Only Raymond seemed attentive, almost anxious, and Dane wished there was some way to exclude the bastard, to kick him out on his ear. But as Celia's fiancé and his mother's first pick, the man had a right to sit in on any and all business.

"To say I was pleased to step in for my brother would be a lie. You all know I have my own business to run and cases are piling up with me absent so much."

His mother shifted, crossing and recrossing her legs.

"I never wanted to be a part of this company, at least, not for many years now. Everything is now in order. I think it's past time I—"

A wild commotion in the outer office drew everyone's attention. Dane frowned, staring at the closed door and the raised voices coming through it. His mother came to her feet. "What in the world?"

Raymond also stood, his eyebrows lowered, his eyes flickering back and forth. "Would you like me to see what's going on?"

The uncles gave a disinterested glance over their shoulders, and everyone started murmuring at once.

The door was thrown open and Angel, looking ragged and harassed and determined, pushed her way in, despite Dane's secretary's hold on her arm. Dane felt his mouth fall open, his heart lurch. Behind Angel, Mick hovered, Grayson in his arms.

Angel ignored everyone but him, her gaze zeroing in on him, and then her face crumbled and she cried out. She'd obviously strained her leg again, given the awkward way she rushed toward him.

Dane skirted the end of the table and met her halfway, gathering her up in his arms, filled with confusion. "Angel?" He stared over her head toward Mick, who looked too grim by half.

She pushed back in his arms, her fingers clutching at his dress shirt. "They said you were dead!" She yelled the words at him, and now she seemed more angry than anything else. Her face was smudged, her hair wild, and she began to babble. "I wanted to talk to you because of the fire, but I was told you were busy and then they came right out and told me you were dead! I had to see for myself. I had to know you were all right. When I got here, they told me Mr. Carter was in a meeting and couldn't be disturbed, but don't you see, I had to have proof." Her hands went busily over his face, reassuring herself, confirming his safety.

Dane glanced around at the stunned faces watching them, aware of the mounting tension, the delicacy of the situation. Everyone was now standing, expectant. Angel's babbling barely made sense and he hesitated to upset her further. Few people knew Derek was dead, so who the hell had told her? But first things first. "What fire?" he demanded, concentrating on the one thing that wasn't guaranteed to get him in any deeper.

Angel drew a shuddering breath. "Oh, Derek. Someone threw a mess of burning rags through my kitchen window! Everything in the apartment stinks of smoke."

His mother gasped and went two shades paler, grabbing the conference table for support. "Dane, what's going on here? Who is this person?"

The muscles in his face felt like iron. "Give me a minute, Mother."

"Oh my God! It's Angel Morris, isn't it?" Celia stepped forward, trying to get a better look at Angel. "What in the world happened to her, and why is she calling you Derek?"

Dane closed his eyes. He heard the conference room door slam and looked up to see Mick standing against it, Grayson held in his arms, his expression so hard he looked more like a man than ever.

Raymond barked out, "I'm calling security!" and reached for the phone. His movements were jerky and frantic.

"No." Dane stopped him with a word, and everyone seemed to turn to stone, frozen and shocked and confused.

"This is insane," Raymond argued. "She's upsetting the women!" And again he reached for the receiver.

Dane released Angel as she slowly backed away from him. "No, Raymond, everything is fine."

"Fine?" Raymond argued, filled with outraged indignation. "The woman is mad, coming in here calling you by your dead brother's name. For God's sake, man, your mother and sister have been through too much already.''

His mother did look shaken, pale and drawn and confused, but Celia looked titillated. Her eyes were bright and wide and didn't budge from Angel's face. ''You are Angel Morris, aren't you?''

Angel looked around the room at all the avid expressions and she swayed. Dane grabbed her, but she jerked back from him and her expression was so dark, so accusing, he felt it like a blow. Her bloodless lips moved twice before the words finally whispered out. ''You're not Derek?''

Again Dane reached for her, firmly taking hold of her shoulders while she tried to shake him off. ''Dammit, Angel, sit down before you fall down.'' Then he looked around the room and ordered, ''*Everyone out.*''

His mother started to protest and he said, ''*Now.*''

Grayson chose that inauspicious moment to give one short, protesting cry. Dane thought it might have been Mick's tight hold on the baby that prompted the objection.

Again, everyone froze.

Drawing on lost reserve, Dane again tried to take control of the situation. ''Mick, I want you to stay. Please sit down so everyone else can leave.''

Obligingly, looking as if he wouldn't have left anyway, Mick went to the leather couch and sat. He whispered nonsense words to Grayson and glared at anyone who tried to get closer to the baby.

Dane took Angel to the same couch, trying to support her weight when he saw how badly she was limping, but she sidled away from his touch as if she found him repulsive. Once she was seated, Dane strode over to the door and held it open. "All of you, wait outside. I'll explain everything in a minute."

One of his uncles shook his head. "Can't wait to hear it."

The other agreed. "Always did say that boy knew how to shake things up." They left together. His cousin gave him an uncertain, wide-eyed look and hurried out.

Raymond stopped, holding Mrs. Carter's arm. "Are you sure you don't require security?" he asked. "I could get them up here, just in case. Or I could stay with you, as a precaution. You can't be too careful with crazy people."

Dane ground his teeth together, sparing only a very brief glance at his mother's angry, drawn face. "Out, Raymond."

Mrs. Carter stared up at her son. "Don't trust anything that woman tells you about Derek."

"Mother..."

"I'm giving you the benefit of the doubt, son. Do what's right, for us and yourself." With that caustic warning, she walked out, Raymond hanging on her arm.

Celia paused in front of Dane. Her lips were trembling, her eyes wet with unshed tears. But she brazenly tried to act in control, unwilling to contribute to the chaos. "I hope you know I'm not budging from this outer office until you give me a full report."

Dane nodded, appreciating her reserve.

Celia licked her lips nervously, then ventured, "I could hold the baby while you two talk."

"No!" Angel sat forward on her seat, but Dane ignored her, his attention on his sister.

"Thanks, sweetheart, but Mick can handle things and the baby's already used to him." Celia looked so crushed, Dane touched her cheek and added softly, "Get Mother something to drink. She looks ready to faint. And be patient, please."

Celia nodded at him, offering up a shaky smile. "Good luck."

As he closed the door, Dane muttered, "I'm going to need more than luck now." He drew a long, calming breath before turning to Angel. His mother's warning rang in his ears. Would Derek have seen his actions as a betrayal? Had he felt justified in his treatment of Angel? Things had seemed so simple when he'd first started this. Now he felt mired in conflicting emotions. But one thing was certain, he couldn't lie to her anymore.

Angel's entire posture showed how wounded she felt, both physically and emotionally. She stared at Dane, her expression fixed, her arms crossed belligerently over her chest. As she'd been doing since Grayson's birth, she held herself together by sheer force of will.

Something inside Dane felt like it was breaking apart. Despite his mother's warning, despite his loyalty to his twin, Dane knew he couldn't ever hurt her again. And that meant he had to give her the full truth. "Derek's dead. He died months ago."

For about ten seconds she looked shocked, then she jerked to her feet. Comprehension dawned in her face and her eyes widened on him, appalled. "Oh my God."

Dane nodded slowly. "Yes, I'm the dreaded evil twin, of course." He took a measured step toward her. "I can explain everything, honey."

Her eyes went wild. "Don't you come near me. I don't want to hear anything you have to say."

"Well, you're going to hear it," he said, tightening himself against her disdain. He was well aware of how she felt about him, and the damn reputation Derek had amplified. But it still hurt as he felt her emotional withdrawal, the separation between them growing. He bit off a curse, knowing if he didn't push now, he'd lose her for good, along with the opportunity to discover what had really happened to Derek.

"Angel…"

All signs of fear were replaced by anger. Her face was flushed, her body practically vibrating with her temper, her scorn. "You miserable lying bastard."

Dane closed his eyes and tipped his head back. He heard Angel's furious whispering, heard Mick grumble a reply, and quickly faced her again. "You're not going anywhere, babe."

"The hell I'm not!" She tried to take the baby from Mick, but he resisted her efforts. She turned her cannon on Dane again. "You can't dictate to me, and I'm certainly not going to listen to any more of your lies. There is absolutely no excuse for what you've done!"

Mick glared at Dane, but spoke to Angel. "Nothing's changed. There's still someone trying to hurt you, and your apartment is still a mess. Think of Grayson. At least hear…" He looked at Dane, then shrugged in his direction. "At least hear him out. Whoever the hell he is."

Dane tightened his jaw. "Dane Carter." The formality of an introduction was ludicrous.

Angel sneered. "Derek told me all about you. You're the worst of the lot!"

"I was going to explain everything to you today, Angel. In fact, I was just telling my family that I won't work for the company—"

"I don't care what you were telling them."

"Angel." He felt hollow inside. "Honey, you have to hear me out. The only reason I came back to the company in the first place is because I think Derek was murdered."

He shouldn't have blurted it out like that, but he knew he had to make her listen. Angel wrapped her arms around her middle and sank back onto the couch, slowly rocking. "No, no, this can't be happening."

Dane knelt down in front of her. "I'm so sorry, honey. At first, when you contacted me, I was suspicious of you, thinking you had more reason than most to hate Derek, to want him dead. I thought you might have had something to do with setting him up and then when I came home, you thought you hadn't succeeded. There's been no official announcement of Derek's death and my family has done everything they could to keep the news quiet." He spoke quickly, hoping to get his explanations out while she was still listening.

She laughed, a harsh, broken sound and rocked that much harder.

"It took me only a short time of knowing you to realize how ridiculous that theory was."

"No, not at all," she said, her grin twisted and mean. Provoking. "I did despise him. Almost as much as I despise you."

"Angel," he chided. "You don't mean that. Not after last night."

He caught her right fist just inches from his face and stared at her in incredulous disbelief. "Dammit, Angel, that wouldn't have been a little ladylike tap! Are you trying to—"

A split second later, her left fist connected with his temple, almost knocking him off balance and making his brain ring. "Goddammit!" Dane caught both her hands and pulled her to her feet, struggling to subdue her. "If you can refrain from inflicting your vicious temper on my head, I think we can get this all straightened out!"

Angel tugged her hands, obviously accepted that he had no intention of releasing her, and went still. "Let me go."

"Not on your life. We have a hell of a lot of talking to do and I think we'll accomplish it more easily if my brain is left intact." He lowered his voice to a mild scold, somewhat amused by her despite his still ringing ears. "I had no idea you were such a fury. Why don't you just settle down and behave yourself."

She growled, anger flushing her face crimson. "Behave myself? *Behave myself!* Do you mean I should try conniving and manipulating and lying!" She jerked against him again, but he held tight. "You and your brother are two of a kind."

Dane grew somber. "No, actually we're not." He let her go and paced two steps away, out of harm's reach. "Angel, this is the first I've seen my family in years. We hadn't been on the best of terms, precisely because I'm not like them. I don't approve of what Derek did to you—"

"What you did was worse," she growled, then grudgingly dropped back into her seat.

She looked defeated and he hated it. "I suppose it was, regardless of what my excuses are. But I want to make things right. That's what I've been trying to do this morning. I want to take care of you and Grayson, and don't shake your beautiful head at me! The threat to you is very real, dammit. Derek is dead, and somehow you're tied to it!"

She gave him a look of contempt. "You think I don't know how serious it is? Someone tried to run me off the road. That's the accident, you know, that started my labor and injured my leg. I almost died. Obviously whoever did that isn't very happy that I survived."

Every muscle in his body jerked at the ramification of her words. His heart pounded, his knees locked. *She could have been killed.* And he'd been thinking the threats against her weren't physical? "Goddammit, why didn't you tell me this sooner?"

Her brow lifted. "Trust goes both ways."

He let loose with a string of curses that had Mick chuckling and Angel frowning.

"At first I thought the accident was just that—an accident. I was disoriented for a long time and in a lot of pain after the wreck, not to mention I had a brand-new baby to take care of. There wasn't a lot of room in my thoughts for suspicions. But then, the phone calls started and I got spooked. Then I had to wonder."

"And finally," he said, his voice low and barely controlled, "you realized you had to have some help. That's when you came back to Derek. Not because you wanted to, but because you truly had nowhere else to turn."

She nodded. "I thought if nothing else, he might be willing to check into things for me."

They stared at each other, and Dane read her thoughts. She'd been willing to try seducing Derek to gain the help she needed, to get protection for her baby.

She had truly despised Derek, and now she felt the same about him. Angel was still very pale, but more collected. Her eyes glinted with raw determination and he knew it was only her concern for Grayson that was keeping her in the same room with him. He had his work cut out for him. "Derek was run off the road. Unlike you, luck wasn't on his side that day."

Angel closed her eyes on a sigh. "You should probably know, someone followed us here today. From the time we rushed out of the apartment until we pulled in the lot, we were followed."

Dane hesitated only a second, then stalked to his desk phone and quickly punched out a series of numbers. He waited, but then the office door opened and Alec strolled in, holding up his blinking cell phone. "No need to call me. I'm right here." Raymond tried to follow him in, but Alec slammed the door in his face.

Angel sank back against her seat with his entrance, but Mick perked up. "It's Alec!"

The dark visage merely nodded in their direction. "I got there too late to find out what was going on until they'd already left the building." His look was reproachful when he added to Dane, "You left earlier than I thought you would."

Again Angel surged to her feet. "What is he talking about, Der...Dane?"

Satisfaction settled into his bones. Finally, finally she was calling him by his rightful name. "Alec works for me, honey. I'm the one who hired Mick, not a friend. And I've had Alec watching you for several reasons. At first, because I thought you might take off before I could figure out what's going on, whether or not you could give any insight into Derek's death. But then for your safety when I couldn't be there."

Her eyes narrowed. "So you told him you were spending the night with me last night?"

Mick made a choking sound and got up to stroll to

the other end of the room, pretending to keep all his attention on Grayson.

Feeling as if a trap were closing around him, Dane tried for a show of bravado. "I didn't have to tell him. Alec's good at what he does or I wouldn't have him working with me. He knew I had gone in your apartment, and he was able to figure things out quickly enough, given I didn't leave right away."

Alec nodded. "That's about it. Only I didn't figure on you rushing off so early today or I'd have been there to cover her."

"That's my fault. I made up my mind on what I wanted to do and saw no reason to wait. I should have contacted you."

Angel threw up her hands. "*Someone* should have contacted me!"

The conference room door crept open and Celia tried peeking in. Her eyes were huge and went immediately to Alec. "Why is he allowed in and I'm not?"

Dane groaned. The last thing he needed added to the mix was his sister's curiosity. Alec merely turned away and headed for the door, while Celia quickly started backing out. "Dane?" she called, but Alec kept going until they were both on the other side of the closed door. Dane could hear his sister's loud and nervous protests.

"I can always count on Alec to know what needs to be done." Dane's smile had no seeming effect on Angel. She glared at him.

"Honey, there's a lot we have to settle." He sat close to her on the couch and pretended not to notice her efforts to move away. "First off, I want you to know that last night was genuine."

"Spare me your diatribe on last night, Der—Dane. I won't believe anything you have to say about that."

Dane had to trust she'd eventually change her mind, but now wasn't a good time to push her. Instead, he concentrated on what had to be done. "Tell me about the fire."

She did, in totally detached tones that made Dane want to shake her. Didn't she care about last night? Hadn't it affected her at all? The way she was behaving now, last night might as well have not happened. The timing was unfortunate, but he'd been counting on it to soften her some when presented with his truths.

Mick filled in some of the details on the fire, apparently more concerned with it than Angel was at the moment.

Dane decided he'd make a quick trip by there to check out the apartment himself. Maybe there was a clue that the others had missed. "I'll pay for the damages and the cleaning, Mick, so that the apartment will be as good as new."

"You don't need to do that. It's my mother's building. We'll handle it."

Dane's respect for the youth doubled. "It's the least I can do, given all you've done to keep her safe." Seeing that Mick's pride would force him to argue further, he added, "Angel, you and Grayson can come to stay with me."

She snorted. "Not on your life."

Inconspicuously drawing a fortifying breath, Dane took his last shot, and prayed she wouldn't fight him too hard. He knew things were happening too fast, for him as well as her. Without hesitation, he'd gladly taken over his brother's life, his role in the company. He'd consoled himself with the fact he was trying to find his brother's killer. Even as he'd walked through his brother's office and gone through his desk and personal notes, he'd been empowered by the fact that he had a mission, a purpose. But now he was taking Derek's woman and son, too, for no other reason than he wanted them. Despite all the very real motives he had justifying his actions, he knew the truth, and it was tough to swallow.

Regret that he hadn't taken the time to make his peace with Derek squeezed his heart. Still, he had to think Derek would approve of what he was about to do. Regardless of how he'd treated Angel, Dane refused to believe he'd want Angel terrorized, or his son abandoned. Grayson deserved the family name, and the power and protection that came with it.

With renewed resolution, Dane said, "It seems like the best solution, honey."

"How do you figure that?"

"Because as soon as I can manage it, we'll be married."

CHAPTER EIGHT

ANGEL STARED AT DEREK...no, *Dane*. She had to remember that. This man—a man she'd slept with—was a total stranger. He'd betrayed her, used her, and as far as she could tell, despite all his assurances to the contrary, he was no different from his family. *But everything about him had seemed different.*

No, she didn't trust him, and she'd been right to fear him all along.

"We could make it a Thanksgiving wedding," he said, sounding absurdly enthusiastic. "Not very romantic, I know, but there you have it. I really do think the sooner the better."

Angel could only shake her head. "I'm not marrying you."

"Have you forgotten my family, honey?"

What a joke. As if she could ever forget such a thing. "It's not likely, not when I've suspected them most from the start."

"Suspected them?" Dane sounded confused, his eyebrows slowly drawing down.

"They, more than anyone, have reason to want me gone. After all, I know firsthand just how unscrupulous Derek could be, when they're bound and determined to make him out a saint. If I chose to go to the papers..."

"Being snide isn't going to help anything."

"It's making me feel a damn sight better!"

"Angel, my family wouldn't try to physically harm you."

"Ha!"

He sighed. "Okay, look at it this way. It's obvious whoever tried to run you off the road, succeeded with Derek. Now surely you're not going to suggest my family could be responsible for that? The two incidents are too closely related to not be done by the same person or people."

He was right, and that made the peril even worse. When she'd thought she knew who was after her, it was bad enough. But not knowing...

"I just found out about Derek today. Before now, my reasoning seemed sound."

"Possibly. I had my own suspicions about why my mother has been so accepting of Derek's death. Normally, she'd be looking for a person to blame, and you could have been a target. But I think you may have hit the nail on the head. She knew he was unscrupulous, knew the way he'd treated you lacked any sense of professional honor. Could be she just didn't want any reporters getting wind of the story and embellishing on it."

Angel's brain felt stuffed to overflowing with problems, and she needed to get away from him so she could think. She looked toward Mick, but Dane quickly regained her attention.

"You still need my protection from the family, honey, just not in the way you thought. Look at yourself. You haven't made the best first impression on any of them, and believe me, they'll use your little show today to their advantage. They'll call you a crazy woman running in here all mussed and smelling of

smoke. Just the fact of the danger involved is enough
to give them an edge. They'll gladly use anything they
can to cow you. My mother would love to claim you
unfit, taking into consideration your financial predicament, your insecure life, compared to everything their
money and influence can provide—''

''All right!'' Angel stood and began pacing. It
seemed her options were sorely limited, and by her
own design, she'd put herself in his family's righteous
path. She couldn't, wouldn't lose Grayson, not to anyone, not for any reason.

Dane slipped up behind her, not touching her, but
his warmth did and her stomach gave an excited little
flip. *Fool,* she thought, disgusted with herself and her
feminine responses to him.

Well, she'd wondered many times why things were
different now, why she would be more attracted to Derek now after the way he'd used her. She had her answer
of sorts, the mere fact that it wasn't Derek, but his
brother instead. Again, she shuddered with the humiliation of it. Everything Derek had told her of Dane had
scared her spitless. He'd been like a dark, silent enemy,
someone she'd wanted to avoid at all costs. But now,
she didn't really fear him at all. On the contrary, she
was madder than hell.

''As my wife, they couldn't touch you, Angel. Grayson would be safe, and you would be safe, from them
and the threats.''

''Why?'' Angel whirled around to face him, his motivations very suspect given everything she now knew.
It had seemed strange enough that Derek would be interested in her, but then she'd found out he only wanted
to use her. What could possibly be driving Dane?
''Why would you want to marry me, damn you?''

Dane's eyes lifted briefly to where Mick hovered in the corner. Then he leaned down until their foreheads nearly touched. He didn't look at her face, choosing instead to stare at her mouth. "Grayson is my nephew, but I care about him as if he were my own. I'd gladly kill, or die, for him. And we're good together, babe. Last night proved that." His fingers touched gently on her cheek, then dropped away. "I think we could make a go of things. It's the only logical solution."

Weary defeat dragged her down and she rubbed her forehead. He hadn't said anything about caring for her. His reasoning was so far from love as to be laughable. But then, she didn't love him either. *She didn't.* How could she possibly love a man she didn't even really know? She felt boxed in and almost desperate, as much by the circumstances as her own emotional needs. "I'd want a marriage of convenience."

Dane straightened with a short, curt laugh. "Hell no."

"Dane—"

"I love how you say that, Angel. You have no idea how damn difficult it was being called by another man's name."

He was impossible and she couldn't deal with him. She felt caught between a good cry and a hysterical laugh.

Dane took her shoulders and gently shook her. "Let me take you home. To my house. You look exhausted and we need to talk without the threat of my family bursting in any minute. You need to tell me everything this time; no more secrets. And Grayson needs to get settled down. We have a lot to take care of today."

Since she didn't know what else to do, she finally nodded. Dane let out a long breath of relief and smiled at her. "Don't look so glum. Marrying me won't be nearly the hardship you're imagining. I promise."

Her look of intense dislike was rudely ignored.

The outer door opened then and Dane's sister marched in, looking militant for all of three steps— until Alec's long arm appeared, grabbed her by the shoulder, and tugged her back out again. The door closed quietly on her outraged complaints.

Dane chuckled. "I think my sister is anxious to meet the baby."

It was almost impossible to beat down her panic. "Dane..."

"Shh. I won't let anything happen to him, honey. You're going to have to trust me on this."

Before she could tell him she had no intention of trusting him ever again, he continued. "Let me do the talking, okay? I don't want my family to know everything yet. My mother might want to start her own campaign to find Derek's killer, and that could put you at risk."

"Then what will you tell them?"

He shrugged. "As little as possible."

He went to the door and opened it. Angel could see Dane's sister standing on her tiptoes, one manicured finger poking at Alec. Angel marveled at how the woman stood up to him, as scary as he appeared, so cold and hard. But Alec seemed to ignore her, arms crossed over his chest, his black gaze pinning Raymond across the room. Dane's mother sat quietly beside Raymond, her hands clasped in her lap.

"Celia, would you like to meet your nephew?"

Halting in midcomplaint, Celia squealed, loudly, which caused Alec to wince. "Then he really is Derek's son? I wasn't wrong in that?"

She looked so anxious, so excited, Angel felt her heart twist. Dane laughed. "Yes, he really is."

Casting only a quick triumphant glare at Alec, Celia rushed in. Alec shook his head and chuckled behind her.

As Celia cooed over the baby, Mick willingly gave him up to her. Seeing her baby in Celia's arms made Angel begin to shake. This was exactly what she hadn't wanted to happen, what she had always feared the most.

There was more chaos as Dane's family started their interrogation. He gave an edited version of how they'd met and when. He managed to make it sound romantic while excluding any suggestion of suspicions, and explained about Grayson in the process. He told them of the fire and why Angel had appeared looking so harried. They waited to hear why she'd called him Derek, but Dane ignored that and Angel realized he had no intention of explaining. It seemed he didn't care what his family thought, and given his closed expression, they were just as reluctant to question him.

"How do you know the baby is Derek's?"

Silence fell as every face turned to Mrs. Carter. Feeling stiff from the roots of her hair all the way to her toes, Angel met the older woman's glare and refused to look away or give any sign of defense. Mrs. Carter could think whatever she wanted; Angel had no reason to be ashamed.

But Dane laughed. "Excellent, Mother. If you don't believe the baby is his, then I don't have to concern myself with your interference."

Raymond looked at Grayson over Celia's shoulder. "I don't remember Ms. Morris ever dating anyone else. In fact, it caused a buzz in the company that she was dating at all, especially that Derek had shown an interest. But the baby is…what? A couple months old? That's cutting it close.''

Dane narrowed his eyes, and he suddenly looked near violence. ''He was born six weeks early.''

''Ah. Then the timing fits, doesn't it?''

Celia beamed. ''Of course it does. He looks just like Derek and Dane. Mother, I don't have a single doubt.''

Angel had always heard what a formidable dragon lady Mrs. Carter was, but now, she looked so vulnerable it pained even Angel. As she approached the baby, she breathed hard, her nostrils quivering as she tried, and failed, to find some measure of control. Her hand came up to touch the baby's head. ''He does have a family resemblance.''

Celia smiled and rocked the baby.

Dane's tone was very gentle, but firm, and only Angel seemed to notice the way he watched his mother. ''I don't mean to rush off, but we have a lot to do today and we'd better get to it.''

Stepping forward, Raymond looked at each family member in turn. He wasn't a scary-looking man, like Alec, but he did appear rather cold and calculating.

''I'd be glad to help you out around here, Dane. It does seem you have your hands full at the moment, and as you'd been saying before the…ah, interruption, you have your own business to run.''

Angel wanted to deny her familiarity to Dane, but the truth was, she could already read him, and what she saw in his complacent gaze was a sort of evil anticipation. He didn't smile, but she could see the satisfaction in his gaze as he faced the other man. ''Thank you, Raymond, but I was going to suggest Celia take over. The board will, of course, have to approve her, but with my mother's backing—'' He glanced toward his mother, who gave an imperial nod of her head, but withheld any verbal comment "—and of course my own, I don't think it should be a problem. Anyone who wants to fight it, would have to fight me. And I assure you that's not a pleasant prospect.''

Angel noticed that Dane had just made his sister a very happy woman. Like her mother, she kept still, but as she kissed the baby again, Angel could see a small exuberant smile on her face.

With that apparently settled to his satisfaction, Dane glanced at his watch. "We have to get going. I need to get Angel and Grayson settled down in my house.''

"In your house?''

"Yes, Mother. I've asked Angel to marry me as soon as I can arrange it, and she's agreed.''

Dane's announcement started a new flurry of comments and Angel wished there was some way to remove herself and Grayson. They all deserved to fight among themselves; she just didn't want to take part in it. Mick sidled up beside her, and she had the feeling he was as disoriented by the Carter family as she.

"I can keep the baby while you go on a honeymoon.''

Angel's heart skipped a beat at Celia's anxious offer, but Dane easily covered her reaction. His arm slipped around her shoulders and gently squeezed, offering her reassurance, she knew. But with him so close, she felt far from comforted.

"Thanks, but we're not going to even think about anything like that for a while. And Grayson is too young to be left. If you want to visit him, you can come to the house and sit with Angel sometime.'' His arm squeezed again, and he added, "Call first, though, and clear it with Angel. I know you wouldn't want to wake Grayson from a nap or interrupt his feeding."

Celia looked at Angel, and there didn't appear to be any animosity in her expression. "You'll join us for Thanksgiving? Please? I realize it's short notice, but then all of this is, and we're very anxious to get to know the baby better." Tears welled in her eyes and she snuggled Grayson closer. "He's all that's left to us of Derek, now."

Angel licked her lips, feeling cornered. Celia's sincerity smote her, made her feel petty and mean. But she was still afraid, and she refused to trust any of them. "I... Dane and I will discuss it."

Dane gave her an admiring glance for her tact. "Yes, we'll let you know, sis. It may be we'll have our wedding by then, if I can get a wedding together in two days. I really have no idea how these things are done."

"I can help."

"No thanks. Angel and I can handle it, I'm sure, once we have a chance to sit down and put our heads together."

Regaining her aplomb, Mrs. Carter said, "This is absurd! I've just discovered my grandson, but you're refusing us any rights. You can't simply cut us out this way. I won't have it."

Dane smiled at his mother. "Watch me."

"You've always been deliberately difficult, but this time I insist you be reasonable! We're talking about Derek's son, his heir, and you want to whisk him away?"

"No one is stopping you from visiting, Mother, as long as you check with Angel first."

Her face flushed darkly. It was apparent to Angel that Mrs. Carter wasn't used to asking permission for anything. "Check with her? Don't be outrageous! We have as much right as anyone to be with the child. In fact, more." Her eyes narrowed. "And frankly, I think it's unconscionable that she's dared to keep this a secret."

Dane stared at his mother, his eyes narrowed. "I'm sure you can understand her reasons."

"Dammit, he's my grandson!"

Having heard enough, Angel stepped forward, away from Dane's side. She lifted her chin and spoke firmly. "But I'm his mother."

The two women stared at each other, and Angel had the feeling they were coming to an understanding. It wasn't easy to face the older woman down, but she couldn't allow Dane to continue shielding her. Now that they knew about Grayson, they were bound to have regular contact.

Mrs. Carter looked undecided on how to react, but Celia interceded and smoothed the waters. "The important thing is that you're going to be family, Angel. I hope you'll let me know if there's anything I can do to help you get settled."

Angel didn't want to be a part of this family; the very thought appalled her. But Celia was so sincere, Angel didn't have the heart or the energy to tell her that. "Thank you."

Raymond took Mrs. Carter's arm and consoled her, as if she'd been horribly victimized. Dane rolled his eyes, then began making plans.

"Alec, could you take Mick with you to the apartment and pick up whatever Angel or Grayson might need?"

Alec nodded and Angel noticed a look passing between them. She started to question Dane, but Mick looked thrilled for the excuse to be with Alec and Angel couldn't disappoint him by countermanding Dane's order.

Then Dane handed Alec a credit card. "And stop at the store to buy whatever needs to be replaced."

Angel glared at him. It was time she stood up to Dane, too. She went on tiptoe to look him in the eye, then whispered low, "Don't press your luck."

He grinned, but quickly removed the sign of humor. "Uh, did you have a better suggestion to make?"

"No. But you've been steamrolling me and I don't like it. Stop treating me like I can't make my own decisions."

"Is that what I've been doing?" His words were soft, intimate. He totally ignored the rapt faces of his family.

"Yes, and I don't like it." She tried to sound firm, rather than affected by the tender way he watched her.

"I'll try to reform." His sincerity seemed doubtful, but then, right in front of his whole family, he kissed her. "It won't be easy though, honey. I like taking care of you."

Bemused, Angel wondered if this was part of his plan to convince his family they were marrying by choice, rather than need. Before she could completely sort her thoughts, Dane took control, settling things to his satisfaction.

WITHIN AN HOUR they were ensconced in his house, a spacious ranch out in the middle of nowhere with a wraparound porch and too many windows to count. It sat about a quarter of a mile from the road and was surrounded by gently rolling hills and huge, mature trees.

Angel had shivered at the isolation of it; her life would be irrevocably changed now, but then, that had been true of so many recent events: meeting Derek, being dismissed from her job, the car accident. Grayson's birth. Because of the baby, she couldn't truly regret her ill-fated relationship with Derek.

And if she hadn't met Derek, she'd never have met Dane.

That thought shook her, and made her face her own feelings. Lately, she'd been so busy surviving, getting through one day at a time, she'd almost underestimated how precious life could be. Not once had she ever considered that Derek might be gone. What if it had been Dane? What if the murderer had finally reached her?

Life was too short to carry grudges or pass up chances. The awful fact of Derek's death was just starting to sink in, making her tremble all over again. If she put her emotional hurt aside, she could understand Dane's behavior toward her. It hadn't been unconscionable as Derek's had been, but rather motivated by the strong need to find a killer.

Angel intended to help him in his efforts.

She glanced around the house without much interest. It was open and airy, the colors bright and clean. It had been professionally decorated and seemed impersonal to Angel, not at all suited to Dane.

She fed Grayson while Dane grilled her on a dozen questions and she did her best to answer them to his satisfaction. Dane was antsy, pacing around her as he tried to find out exactly when her accident had occurred, when the phone calls had begun. Angel had contacted Derek for the last time when she was five and a half months pregnant. He'd turned her away. Shortly after that, he'd died. Two months later, her own car was run off the road, starting her labor. The timing made Dane even more agitated.

Angel put Grayson down for his nap in an empty guest room. Dane lit a fire in the family room then called Alec at her apartment. Unfortunately, though Alec was very thorough, there were no additional clues to be found there.

Angel was tired, but she had no idea what the sleeping arrangements would be. She assumed they would share a certain amount of intimacy. Dane had certainly been insistent, and with her new revelations, she wasn't averse to the idea. She wanted him; in the middle of all the crisis they'd managed to find something very special. Dane made her feel things she'd never felt before, things she hadn't even known existed. She had no idea how much time they might have together so she didn't intend to waste any of it.

Which meant she needed to clear the air first. "Dane?"

He had just hung up the phone and now he lifted his head to stare at her.

"I never wished Derek any physical harm. I'm so sorry for what happened to him."

Just that quick, the distance between them was narrowed. Dane strode to her, stopping a mere inch in front of her. "I don't know if it means anything honey, but Derek regretted what happened." His gaze was searching, warm and direct. "Celia claimed he was almost sick with remorse, and that he knew you'd never forgive him. She said he seemed preoccupied by it all in the time before his death."

Angel nodded, thinking that was at least something, though she wasn't certain she believed it.

Dane laid his large warm hands on her shoulders and

gently squeezed. "When I think of all the time we could have saved if either of us would have simply been honest, it sickens me." He drew a deep breath and let it out slowly. "You've been at risk all this time, and I didn't know it. If anything had happened to you—"

Angel gently laid her fingers against his mouth. He was trying his best, even willing to sacrifice himself to marriage to keep her safe. The least she could do was be totally honest with him. He was right about that.

She tipped her face up to him and had to catch her breath at the tender look in his eyes. Somehow, despite the fact he was the mirror image of Derek, her heart had always known he was different. She still didn't appreciate the underhanded way he had manipulated her, but knowing she hadn't been taken in by the same man twice was a balm to her pride.

He lifted one finger to caress her cheek, unnerving her, sending her thoughts in scattering directions. She smiled. "Dane, if you'd admitted who you were when I first contacted you, I'd have taken off."

He frowned at that possibility.

"I was so afraid of you," she explained, "of all the Carter family, but especially you." His eyes darkened to golden amber, and her stomach muscles constricted in reaction. She had to force herself back on track.

"Derek had told me so many horrible stories of how ruthless and unforgiving you could be."

He pulled her close, pressing her head to his shoulder and rocking her. She had the feeling he was comforting himself as much as her. "Derek and I had major disagreements on the family, and on the company. He felt challenged by all the games, while I was sickened by them. I suppose he didn't like it much that I walked away." He hesitated, then whispered, "And now he's gone."

Needing to reassure him, Angel pushed back and smiled up at him. "He always spoke of you with admiration, making you out to be bigger than life, and twice as frightening. I didn't trust anyone in your family, and there was only a marginal amount of trust for Derek. But deep down, despite everything, I thought he'd do the right thing for his son."

Dane pulled her close again. "So you're saying it's actually a good thing I didn't introduce myself up front?" He kissed her chin, featherlight, then her temple. "If I had, you'd have taken off and who knows what might have happened to you?"

He shuddered roughly with the thought, and then he kissed her. All her turbulent emotions of the day seemed to swell and heat into one overwhelming need. She wasn't used to the sexual demands of her body and didn't know how to temper them. All that they'd done the night before, all the ways he'd touched her and pleasured her, came swamping back. Heat pounded beneath her skin and her legs suddenly felt weak and shaky. She wanted to lie down beneath him, she wanted him inside her again, making her shudder with nearly painful pleasure. She wanted him to help her forget— at least for a little while.

"Let me make love to you, Angel."

The quiet plea was whispered into her ear, his warm breath a caress on its own. She wanted him, and that single focus drowned out everything else.

He'd asked her to marry him so he could protect Grayson. He was noble enough to go to any lengths to make sure the baby was taken care of. And now he needed her, if only in a physical way.

It was such a huge risk, letting her heart get involved when he'd made his motivations crystal clear. But she found she had no choice. She'd used up all her energy for the day, and for now, nothing seemed more right than making love with Dane. "Yes."

DANE WANTED TO SHOUT like a conqueror when Angel went soft and willing against him. God knew, after the turmoil of the day, he needed a distraction and he couldn't think of a nicer one than sinking himself into her warm body.

He did nearly shout when her small hand suddenly snaked down his chest and cupped over his fly. He choked and got an erection at the same time.

"Angel?" Her name was a harsh groan, but he couldn't help that. Too many emotions were slamming into him. He'd planned on wearing her down slowly, using the advantages he had: her love of Grayson and her need for protection, combined with their compatibility in bed. Loving Grayson wouldn't be a hardship; the baby was adorable and had owned Dane's heart from the first moment he'd met him. And even before he'd known Angel had no part in Derek's death, he'd felt compelled to protect her. He'd die before he let her suffer the same fate as his brother.

No woman had ever affected him so strongly.

He didn't understand her sudden submission to his lust, not when she'd been outraged only an hour or so before, but he wasn't fool enough to question her on it. He covered her small, soft hand with his own and pressed hard, catching his breath at the exquisite feel of her holding him. He watched her bright green eyes widen, saw her lips part on a deeply indrawn breath, and he kissed her again. He wasn't gentle. He possessed her mouth with his own, giving her his tongue and groaning when she sucked on it. Her fingers curled around his erection, stroking, proving what a deft learner she could be.

His revelations of the day, the fear he felt for her, his frustration in being unable to solve the mystery of his brother's death, all clamored inside him. He needed her, her comfort. Being with her overrode everything else.

He lifted his fingers to her breast and teased. Already her nipples were peaked, thrusting against the worn material of the sweatshirt she wore. Dane moved his mouth down to her throat, over the sensitive, ultrasoft skin beneath her chin, then to her ear. When he took a breath, he noticed the smoke smell still clinging to her and wanted to pull her into himself, to make her a part of him and forever keep her safe. She and Mick had claimed the fire to be a mere threat, without the intent of burning her out, but he wasn't so sure and the idea that someone could have gotten to her so easily filled him with an ice-cold rage. He *would* protect her.

Ruthlessly, hoping to banish the disturbing thoughts, he backstepped her up to the brick wall beside the fireplace and pinned her there with his hips. His hands jerked up her sweatshirt and he covered both plump, tender breasts with his rough palms. "You're mine now, Angel."

She moved against him, inciting him, encouraging him, and he reacted to her on a primitive level. He jerked back, lowered his head and carefully closed his teeth over one erect nipple. Angel cried out. He knew her breasts were sensitive; he'd found that out last night, taking extra care with her then. But now, he wanted to dominate her, to make her beg, to make her admit that she needed him, and not just for convenience and the safety he afforded. It was disquieting to feel such depth of emotion with this one particular woman. He hadn't wanted to ever again care so much, not like this. But now he had to admit, especially to himself, that what he felt for Angel had no comparison. It was crazy, given the short amount of time he'd known her, but he couldn't fight it—didn't even want to try. He wouldn't feel guilty about it, either. Derek had thrown away his chance to have her. Dane felt guilty for a lot of things, but not for this.

"Dane," she cried, digging her fingers into his back, and he relished the small pain for bringing him a measure of control.

"Say my name again," he told her as he began unfastening her jeans.

"I want you, Dane."

"Now, Angel, right here."

Her eyes widened, but he tugged her jeans down to her knees and turned her. "Brace your hands on the wall."

"Dane?" Eyes wide with confusion, she looked at him over her shoulder.

"Do it, honey." Not waiting for her to comply, he took her wrists in his hands and flattened her palms on the wall, wide on either side of her head. "Now don't move."

He could hear her frantic breaths, her small whimpers, a mixture of excitement and uncertain anxiety. Grimly he smiled as he released himself from his slacks. He was rock hard and throbbing and more than ready to explode. When his arms came around her to ply her breasts, his fingertips plucking at her nipples, his erection just naturally nestled in the cleft of her rounded bottom. Angel gasped, pressing her head back, and at the same time, pushing her hips more closely to him.

He moved his pelvis, stroking her, teasing. He felt blind with lust, but also determined to accomplish his goals. "I want to get married tomorrow, no later than Wednesday."

"Yes."

A startled squeak escaped her when his arms squeezed her tight, but his relief was a living thing and there was no way to get close enough. He hating rushing her into marriage after everything else she'd been through. She deserved a proper courtship, with moonlight dates and flowers and gentle promises, all the things she hadn't had, all the things women wanted. But he had to do what he thought was best for both of them, and right now, tying her to him was his first priority.

Slowly, making himself as crazy as she, he dragged his palm down her ribs to her belly, and when she held her breath he bit her shoulder, a soft, wet love bite—then cupped her fully, taking her by surprise, loving the sound of her startled pleasure as she jerked and moaned.

His fingers gently pressed and found her ready for him, her feminine flesh swollen, the soft petals slick and hot. His middle finger glided over her, barely touching until her hips began moving in a counterpoint. He kept the pressure light and easy, teasing. She tried to hurry him, to encourage him to give her what she now needed, what she desperately wanted, but he resisted. Once, she started to drop her hands but he quickly repositioned her as he wanted her, vulnerable to him, submissive. Judging by the sounds of her panting breaths and raw moans, she loved it as much as he did.

"Dane, please..."

Just as he'd plucked at her nipples, he used his fingertips now to torment her again, but this flesh was so much more sensitive, the feelings so acute, she cried out and almost jerked away from him. His free arm locked around her, holding her in place for his sensual torment.

"You're mine, Angel. Mine." His words were harsh, commanding, breathed against her temple as he thrust against her, his fingers unrelenting.

To his satisfaction and deep pleasure, she came.

Her arms stiffened, her head dropped forward and her body jerked and bucked as her hips pressed hard against him. Dane groaned with her, encouraging her, continuing the gentle abrasion of her most sensitive flesh. As she quieted, he praised her, telling her how crazy she made him, how special she was. He had no idea if she heard him, and she gave no reply other than her gratified groans.

He'd never before resented the use of protection, but now, as he fumbled in a rush to get the condom in place, he cursed the use of them.

Angel was barely staying upright, her body now slumped fully against the wall, her arms no longer stiff and straight. Her cheek pressed to the warm brick and he feared the abrasion against her soft skin, so he pulled her away and lowered her to the carpet, entering her at the same time.

Her tight jeans restricted his movements, but it didn't matter. He simply needed to be inside her, like he needed his next breath and the occasional sunshine and a few hours' sleep. *He needed her.*

Riding her hard, pushing errant thoughts of the danger from his brain, he concentrated on the pleasure. Angel didn't join him again, but chose to watch him instead, her eyes soft in the firelight, her body pliant to his urgent thrusts. One hand lifted and she smoothed his shoulder, smiling gently.

Knowing she watched his every move, that she witnessed every emotion to pass over his face, knowing she could see his explosive pleasure as he came, made it all that much more powerful. He didn't disappoint her, and let himself go completely. He ground his teeth together to keep from shouting and strained against her, knowing she had just taken his heart. His body went rigid and he took his own orgasm with a low, endless growl of blinding pleasure.

He loved Angel Morris, he thought as he slumped against her. He loved her more than he'd ever thought to love anyone or anything. He loved her enough to give his life for her, to do anything to keep her bound to him.

Well damn, he thought, the effort almost painful to his muddled brain. That sure shot a hole in his altruistic plans of merely offering protection. It was also enough to scare ten years off his life.

CHAPTER NINE

"WELL, THAT DIDN'T go quite as I had planned it."

The words, so softly spoken, drifted around Dane, but it took considerable effort on his part to lift his head. He felt not only physically appeased, but emotionally full, and he didn't want to move, not yet, maybe not ever. He didn't want to lose the feeling, the closeness, and he didn't want reality, with all the present problems, to intrude. But he finally managed to struggle up onto his elbows.

Angel, tender and warm and womanly beneath him, looked at him with gentle, shining eyes, a tiny satisfied smile on her mouth.

God, he loved her. The profound acknowledgment shook him. He'd been careless with her, and just as he'd lost his brother, he could have lost her, too.

He tenderly tucked a pale curl behind her ear. "What didn't go as you planned? Did I disappoint you, sweetheart?" He asked the outrageous question to give his brain a chance for mental recovery. Looking at her now, with the realization of how easily she could crush him, was going to take some getting used to. He wasn't accustomed to feeling fear, but what he felt for Angel scared him down deep in his bones, clear to his masculine core. It also made him feel near to bursting and kept his male flesh, still buried tight inside her, semi-hard. Nothing would ever be enough with her.

Feeling the way he did, realizing just how special she was, made him doubt what he knew about Derek. His brother couldn't have used Angel as vindictively as everyone thought. No man could possibly spend time with her and not appreciate how special, how unique she was.

Her smooth brow puckered as she frowned at him. He had to laugh, and luckily that lightened the moment for him, at least to the point he could talk coherently without fear of professing undying love. Angel had been badly misused by his family, and he hadn't done much better by her, though that would quickly change. He fully intended to rush her headlong into marriage. Burdening her now with his excess of emotion before she'd had a chance to get used to the rest would be grossly unfair.

And besides all that, he was suddenly a horrible coward. He simply didn't want to lay his heart on the line, not when the odds were she'd disdain his love. She wanted him on a physical level, there was no denying that, not with the heated scent of their lovemaking still thick in the air. And they had the mutual love of Grayson, a binding responsibility for them both. He'd have to build on those things, and hope it would suffice.

Touching his fingertips over one tightly drawn eyebrow, he grinned. "How can you look so embarrassed after what we just did? Your pants are around your knees, I can feel your nipples hard against my chest, and you're still holding me inside you." He leaned down and brushed his mouth over hers. "So tight, Angel, like you never want to let me go."

"Dane." Unconsciously, she lifted her hips into his and he groaned.

"What didn't go as you planned?"

She looked shyly away, charming him anew. That she could be so wild one minute, and yet timid the next, kept his lust on a keen edge, and sharpened the emotional needs he felt to tie her to him, to keep her safe.

"I wanted this time to be different."

He laughed again. She never ceased to surprise him. "More different than making love against a brick wall with your—"

"Dane, hush!" She pressed her hand against his mouth and he kissed her palm, silently laughing.

"I'm sorry," he said, the words muffled until she drew her hand away. "You're too easy to tease."

"This time, I wanted to do stuff…to you. It doesn't seem fair the way you always give so much and I just take."

Those overwhelming emotions washed over him again in a wave of heat, stealing his thoughts and turning his body iron hard. He crushed her against him, burying his face against her throat. He was reminded of the near-fire at her apartment by her smoky scent, and the fact that someone was trying to hurt her, and had likely killed his brother. The events that had brought them together were never far from his mind. Because those same events could tear them apart.

Gently pulling away from her, he sat up. Angel started to do the same, looking at him uncertainly, but he stopped her by lifting one of her feet to his lap and removing her shoe. "You need a shower and some sleep. And Alec and Mick should be here soon." He caught her pants and stripped them the rest of the way off.

"I don't need sleep. I need to see the rest of your house."

"And you will." *Later, after she was rested up.* She may be doing a good job of holding herself together, but he was still running on adrenaline, and a compelling need to ensure her safety. Their lovemaking had only served to blunt the edges of his urgency a bit.

Once he had her naked from the waist down he caught her under the arms and lifted her with him as he stood. He pulled the sweatshirt free, surveyed her naked body with a deep satisfaction, then cupped her face in his hands. "You listen to me, Angel Morris." His thumb coasted over her bottom lip and she nodded.

"We have plenty of time to play sexually. The rest of our lives in fact because I intend to keep you. For better or worse, for richer or poorer. Eventually, we'll both get to do some exploring. But don't ever think you've disappointed me. For one thing, it's not possible, not when you go so wild when we're together. Not when I know that wildness is only for me. That's more of a gift than most women ever give, and most men ever deserve. We're being forced into this marriage, but the perks, to my way of thinking, are damn enticing."

His gaze traveled from her mouth to her breasts, then down, lingering on the damp curls over her mound. His tone dropped, rough with renewed arousal. "As far as I'm concerned, I don't have a single complaint. As your husband, I'll have you on hand day and night, and the way I see it, that's a hell of a bargain. All right?"

She nodded, but her eyes had gone dark and soft again and he knew what he'd said had turned her on, that his words of explanation had put visual images in her mind. Seeing her reaction put them in his mind as well. He hadn't been this horny or insatiable since high school, and he had to wonder just how much of it was based on a desperate need to reaffirm what they had, before it was taken away. "Come on. While you're showering I'll keep an eye on Grayson and get us something to eat." He eyed her pale naked body as he led her into the hall bathroom, unable to keep his hands from patting her rounded behind, smoothing over her waist and belly. He drew a deep breath and chastened himself to behave. "I'll also find you a robe to wear until your other stuff gets here."

"It feels strange, Dane. Being naked with a man, not being the only one to keep an ear trained for Grayson." She drew a breath, watching him closely. "Not having to be so afraid."

He hoped that meant she felt a measure of trust for him. "I'm not going to let anything happen to you, babe. You can rest a little easier now."

She turned to face him as he pulled two thick towels out of the cabinet and set them close to hand.

"It feels strangest of all to be in your house. That's going to really take some getting used to."

"It's our house," he said firmly, wanting her to feel comfortable, determined to get her fully enmeshed in his life, so much so she wouldn't be able to help but love him back. "When I took over Derek's office, my mother wanted me to move into his house as well. But I drew the line at that. The memories there are too sharp, too suffocating. I feel enough like an interloper as it is, usurping his office, his files...his woman."

Angel shook her head. "I was never that, not really. Derek and I had a brief fling, but it ended long before he got possessive. I'm not sure if he intended to use me all along, or if he just jumped on the opportunity when it presented itself. But almost from the first, I felt more for you than I ever did for him." She looked around, then smiled. "I'm glad this is your house, not his."

He, too, looked around. "I paid to have it decorated because I was clueless and didn't have the time to worry about it anyway, not traveling as often as I did. It's a home base of sorts, but it's always felt kind of...cold to me. So if you get in the mood and want to change things, go right ahead. Just don't ever let anyone in unless I'm here with you."

"I'm not an idiot."

He nodded agreement. "Far from it. But right now, I'm not willing to trust a single soul with your safety. The house is secure, but only if you use the security system correctly. There's an intercom for the front and back door. Don't take any chances, okay?"

She gave a grave nod. He didn't want to frighten her again, but they both knew just how much danger she was in. Hopefully living with him would keep her out of harm's way while he continued his investigation of Derek's death. He would probably bring the police into it shortly, once he'd had a chance to go over things with Alec.

The future stretched out before him, and for the first time that he could remember in too many years to count, he saw more than an endless, empty void. He wanted a future with Angel, with Grayson.

And he wouldn't let anything stand in his way. Not even a murderer.

MOTHER NATURE conspired against them.

Looking out the kitchen window, Angel sipped her coffee and then sighed. Finally the sun was shining again, though she knew the weather wouldn't clear for a while. Record-breaking lows were predicted for the rest of the week.

She also knew Dane was frustrated, that if it had been up to him, they would have been married already. But the most horrendous snowfall of the season, a good twelve inches, had all but canceled Thanksgiving and confined everyone indoors, making a wedding impossible. It had also stalled his investigation, putting personal queries on hold.

Dane had improvised Thanksgiving, forgetting the plan to meet with his family—to Angel's relief and Celia's disappointment. For lack of a turkey, he made a superb pork roast and surprised Angel with his culinary talents.

It had felt right somehow to spend an evening in the kitchen with Dane, bumping hips and sharing chores, working together. Grayson sat in his pumpkin seat watching them, and the setting would have been picture perfect if it hadn't been for the fact that someone evil was still out there, still a threat, keeping them both edgy despite their efforts to the contrary.

The weather provided the ideal excuse for them to linger in bed, forcing away the dark cloud of menace with an overload of sensuality. Just a few hours ago Dane had awakened her from a sound sleep with warm hands and a warmer mouth, gently encouraging her higher and higher until she'd had to muffle her shouts with a pillow. It amazed her that every time with him seemed better, more intense. She wasn't certain how much more she could take, but was anxious to find out.

He'd left her limp and exhausted in the bed. He had kissed the tip of her nose, told her he'd be home in a few hours, and then lovingly cupped a breast before turning away and hurrying out. Dane often hurried away from her, as if he were afraid if he lingered, he wouldn't go at all.

Angel had never felt so pampered, or so loved. Only he'd never said anything about love.

It worried her, how easily she had adjusted to being with Dane. He was the perfect father to Grayson, the perfect companion to her, even if he was overly autocratic on occasion.

She understood his worry because she shared it. No matter how many times they went over it, they couldn't come up with a single reason for someone to kill Derek and try to kill her. The idea of never knowing, of always having to be on guard, made her angry.

She had just come up from the basement with a large load of laundry when the phone rang. Expecting it to be Celia, who'd made a habit of calling daily, she balanced the laundry basket on one hip and used her shoulder to hold the phone to her ear. "Hello."

There was no reply, and within a heartbeat the fine hairs on the back of her neck stood up and gooseflesh rose on her arms. *No.* She forced a calm tone and said again, this time more firmly, "Hello?" but still received no answer and she quickly hung up the phone.

Frozen, she stood there, trying to convince herself that it was an accident, a coincidence. Not once since she'd moved in with Dane had there been a threatening call. There was no reason to think this was one of them. She drew a deep breath and tried to convince herself she was right.

At that moment Dane came in. Snowflakes glistened in his hair and his mellow golden eyes were warm with welcome.

When he saw her just standing there, he hurried to

take the basket from her. "Angel, are you all right? Have you hurt your leg again?"

She swallowed hard and automatically repeated the words that had become a litany. The man was too over-protective by half. "Quit pampering me, Dane. It's getting annoying."

"I have a cleaning woman for this—"

"Who hired on to do your laundry, not mine and Grayson's. Besides, I'm perfectly capable of taking care of myself. I don't want a stranger muddling through my things. And," she added when she could see he was contriving more arguments, "the maid hasn't been able to come here in this weather. Grayson has laundry that needs to be done every day."

"Oh." He looked distracted for just a moment, then suddenly drew her into his arms and swung her in a wide circle. "All right, I'll let that go for now, but only because I have a few surprises for you and I don't think you'll be properly appreciative if you're angry."

"You've found out something?" she asked, her entire body tensing in hope.

Dane lightly kissed the bridge of her nose in apology. "No, I'm sorry, babe. There's nothing yet, but we're working on it. I contacted a few personal friends in the police department and they're doing some checking for me, looking things over again. Something will turn up soon, I promise."

Angel bit her lip as disappointment swelled inside her. She didn't think she could take much more waiting. And she knew it was even harder on Dane. He felt compelled to avenge his brother, and to protect her and Grayson. He'd taken on a lot for her sake, and she worried constantly about him. If he got hurt because of her...

"Hey, no long faces now, honey." He kissed her again, this time more lingering. "I want to see you smiling, not frowning."

She considered telling him about the phone call, but at the moment, his expression so expectant and happy... There would be plenty of time to talk about that later—if it was even important, which she was starting to doubt. The last phone call she'd received had been verbal, and this one had been silent. Likely there was no connection at all, just a wrong number.

"Where did you rush off to this morning?" she asked, shaking off her eerie mood.

Backstepping to a kitchen chair, he sat and pulled her into his lap. His heavy coat was damp in places and he struggled out of it, then laid it on the table next to the laundry basket. One rough fingertip touched her cheek. "My sister is dying to get back out here and see Grayson. And you. She's overflowing with questions and curiosity."

Celia called at least once a day, and she was always cordial and inquisitive, but cautiously so, as if she were taking pains not to be pushy. Angel couldn't help but like her. The rest of his family had been ominously silent.

"How would you feel about having her and Raymond to dinner? The roads are much better today, and with no more snow predicted, by Tuesday they should be fine."

Angel wondered at his reasons for the sudden invitation, but said only, "She's your sister, Dane. If you want to have her over, that's fine." She hesitated, then added, "Maybe you should invite your mother, too. It might help to smooth things over with her."

"Not yet." He said it easily, but Angel was aware of his sudden strain.

"Dane, what ever happened between the two of you? I know Derek told me once that you just didn't see eye to eye, but—"

His laugh, a sound bordering on sarcasm, interrupted her. "A difference of opinion, huh? Well, Derek was right about that. But it's past history honey, and I don't want to bore you."

"Shouldn't I know what's going on, since the past probably plays a part in the tension now? What if your mother says something? I don't like to be kept in the dark."

"It doesn't concern you."

And that, she thought, was the crux of the problem. She wanted everything about him to concern her. "I'm sorry." She tried to get off his lap, but he made a rough sound at her movement and hugged her close.

"Dammit, I didn't mean that quite the way it sounded." He gave her a frustrated look, then shrugged. "All right, you want me to bare my soul, I suppose I can live through it."

He was in such a strange mood, teasing one minute, then solemn, then teasing again. "I don't mean to push you."

"Ha! All right, I'm sorry." He tightened his hold on her. "Don't rush off."

Angel gave him an impatient look.

"All right, dammit, but as soon as I finish this stupid tale of woe, we're moving on to your surprise, okay?" After a brief hesitation, he said, "I was engaged to be married once." His hands looped around her and he looked off to the side, staring at nothing in particular, merely avoiding her gaze.

"Mother didn't approve, of course, but then I'd already started bucking her on almost everything. Derek went to the college of *her* choice, I went to a state college. Looking back, I realize how infantile I acted, opposing her just for the sake of opposition, but she was so damn controlling about everything, it just naturally rubbed me the wrong way."

Angel couldn't begin to imagine anyone attempting to control Dane. The very idea was ludicrous.

"Both Derek and I had gotten our business degree in the same year my father died. He and Mother had always planned for us to take over, but not that soon. His heart attack took everyone by surprise. Mother, never one to grieve for long, wanted us to jump into the company together. I wanted to get my MBA. Derek was born to run a corporation, was anxious to get started, but I resisted her. I was glad to let Derek handle things, and despite all her carping and complaining, I went back to school."

A heavy silence fell and Angel felt him shift slightly, as if he were uncomfortable.

"I met a woman while I was in school, and I wanted to get married. Since that didn't meet with Mother's plans, she did everything she could, including disowning me so I couldn't touch my inheritance money, as a way to discourage me. But the more she did, the more determined I became. When I told her I fully intended to go through with the wedding, she...she bought Anna off."

Angel had no idea what to say to that. She waited, hoping he'd elaborate. And finally he did.

"I don't like to think it was the money that enticed Anna. She wasn't from the same background as me, and my mother intimidated the hell out of her. She

spelled out this grandiose life Anna would be expected
to live up to and it spooked her. When Mother offered
her the money, she took it and walked away.''

What a fool, Angel thought. She knew Dane had
money, but he didn't flaunt it. His house was very nice,
but it wasn't ostentatious. Everything about him was
casual and comfortable and understated. Anna must not
have known him at all to believe such idiocy. Or maybe
it just hadn't mattered to her. "I'm sorry."

Dane shook his head impatiently. "The worst part
was, she was pregnant with my baby."

Angel stiffened, seized by a mingling of jealousy and
confusion. Where was the child now?

As if he'd read her thoughts, Dane gave her a
squeeze. "By the time I'd caught up with Anna, she
told me she'd lost the baby."

He looked so troubled, Angel curled down against
his chest and hugged herself close to him. She'd never
before seen Dane like this, and she didn't like it. Derek's death had filled him with calculating determination, with a purpose. His mother's disdain had only
seemed to amuse him. But now he sounded hurt deep
inside. She preferred his arrogance any day. And at that
moment she'd have given a lot to ease his pain.

His large hand settled against the back of her head
and he idly tangled his fingers in her hair. "I've never
admitted this to anyone, but to this day, I'm not sure
Anna didn't have an abortion. I blamed my mother
because it was a hell of a lot easier to blame her than
to accept that I might have been wrong about Anna,
that I might have made a colossal mistake marrying a
woman who didn't care enough about me to believe in
me. She told me, rather tearfully in fact, that she'd been

afraid and taking my mother's bribe seemed her only choice.''

Angel could feel his pounding heartbeat, a little faster now, and she slipped her hand inside his shirt, smoothing her fingers over his warm, hair-rough skin. Dane went still even as his breathing changed, grew a little rougher and quicker. Angel pulled his shirt from his pants and pushed it upward, kissing his chest, his small tight nipples. Dane groaned and quickly yanked the shirt over his head.

Whispering against his chest, Angel said, "She could have come to you, and that's what bothers you most?"

Dane tilted his head back against the chair. "She didn't trust me."

"I trust you. I've been trusting you with not only my life, but Grayson's." He started to speak and she straightened, cupping his jaw with her palms, holding his head still as she attacked his mouth. Dane groaned again and Angel used that as her cue. With their lips still touching she breathed, "I'm not like her, Dane. Your mother can't send me away. Only you could do that now."

Rather than answer, he kissed her again, and there was hunger in the way he held her, the way his mouth moved heavily over hers. He might not love her, but he needed her, and from that, love could grow.

He pulled himself away from her with a harsh sound of impatience. "Damn woman, you distract me."

"I'm glad."

Laughing, he avoided her mouth as she tried to capture his again. "Your surprise, remember?"

"We could do that later?"

"Insatiable wench. Stop that!" He caught her hands

and pulled them away from his belt. When she pretended to pout, he grinned. "Show just a modicum of patience, okay? Now, first off, Mick got your apartment rented, so you can stop worrying about that."

That wasn't at all what she'd been expecting. Dane had insisted, against her and Mick's protests, on keeping up the rent until Mick found a new tenant. Angel knew Mick and his mother needed the money, and she'd felt bad leaving as she had, without notice, but Dane wouldn't hear of her paying the rent herself, and Mick hadn't wanted either of them to pay. He was such a proud young man.

"Who is it?" Angel still worried about Mick. She talked with him often, but she missed their daily school lessons together. As soon as the weather permitted, she intended to start them back up again. Dane was all for the idea.

"You'd never guess so I might as well tell you." He took a moment to build the suspense, but when she gave an impatient growl, he grinned and said, "Alec."

At her look of surprise, he nodded. "Yep, I showed him the apartment myself. It's not too far from the office, and Mick is a fantastic manager, especially for a kid."

"And you wanted Alec there to keep an eye on him, to make certain he was okay?"

"Not at all. I knew you would worry, and I figured this would put your mind at ease for the most part. But Alec really was looking for a new place, and he likes it there."

Angel smiled at him. "It's a wonderful surprise. Thank you."

"That's only part of the surprise. Now don't get angry before you hear me out, okay?"

Like a red flag waved before her face, his words had the effect of putting her instantly on guard. She stiffened. "What have you done?"

"We've agreed that it's best to get married, and that means I want to do what I can to ensure you and Grayson are taken care of. I know how you feel about money, but it's silly. Thanks to my inheritance—"

"I thought your mother took that!"

He shrugged. "She gave it back, sort of another bribe to bring me back into the fold. It's been sitting in a bank gathering interest because I had no use for it until now."

"I don't want you going against your principles for me, Dane Carter!"

He laughed. "It wasn't a principle. It was plain stubbornness and the fact that I like to prick my mother's temper whenever possible. But since we'll be married Tuesday morning—"

"Whoa!" Angel held out her hands, astounded by having so much information thrown at her at one time. She needed a few minutes to assimilate it all. "What do you mean we're getting married Tuesday morning? Since when was this decided?"

He had the grace to look sheepish. "Ah... Actually just today. That was another part of your surprise. I talked with my doctor and the lab will do the blood tests tomorrow. As soon as we do that, we'll head downtown and pick up the license. A pastor from my sister's church has agreed to do the deed on Tuesday."

There was a brief struggle as Angel tried to remove herself from his lap and he was just as determined to keep her in place.

Dane won.

"You agreed to marry me, honey." He held her securely, his eyes never leaving hers. There was a look of challenge on his face, and something else, something not so easily defined. "We've made the deal, you and I. Grayson needs me, and I'm not about to turn my back on him, not now, not ever. If you're thinking about changing your mind, it's too late."

Realization hit, knocking the breath from her. He wanted things confirmed, he wanted a guarantee, and he was afraid to leave it up to her because he thought she might back out. Knowing he felt such an obligation for Grayson, and that he was afraid of losing the baby, was a revelation. But she couldn't merely condone his autocratic behavior. He'd become a tyrant in no time if she let him.

She scowled darkly, and grumbled, "Next time, check with me first before you set things up."

His eyes widened and the arrogance was immediately back in his gaze, along with a healthy dose of relief. "There won't be a next time, honey. I told you, regardless of why we're getting married, it's still forever."

As he said it, he leaned forward, then kissed her long and slow and deep. When he pulled away, he whispered, "I suppose I should get the rest of it over with."

"There's more?"

"I'm afraid so." He drew a deep breath, then blurted, "I paid off your and Grayson's medical bills."

She should have expected it. But with all that had happened the last few days, her accumulated bills had been the last thing on her mind. In a way, it was almost a relief to be rid of that particular burden, except that she didn't want their relationship to be about what material things he could give her. She wanted more than that.

When she only narrowed her eyes at him, he continued, evidently encouraged by her silence. "I also opened an account in your name. You can add your own money to it if you like, but there's a hefty sum already deposited. Only your name is on the account, so you can do whatever you want with it. Understand, Angel, this isn't for household stuff. If you want to redecorate the house—which by the way, I was thinking Grayson's room could really use some color..."

"Dane."

"Come on, honey, don't get all prickly on me." He ran a hand over his head and his frustration was almost palpable, forcing her to hide a grin. "As far as I'm concerned, what I have is already yours, only you're being too pigheaded about it to let me take care of you."

"Pigheaded? Gee, you smooth-tongued dog, you. You sure do know how to win a gal over."

"Dammit, Angel, I am not my damn brother! You don't have to worry about any hidden motivations on my part."

"And I'm not Anna," she said, just as firmly. "I won't be bought off. You're trying to make sure I have money so if or when your mother offers it, I won't be tempted."

He looked away, his entire body drawn tight, his shoulders rigid, which to Angel was as good as an admission of guilt. When he turned to face her again his eyes were diamond hard and probing. "Would you be tempted?"

"No!" Trying to calm herself, and at the same time, sort through the words that needed to be said, she took a deep breath, and then another. It didn't help. "Dane,

we need to talk. There's something I really need to tell you.''

He stiffened, as if bracing himself. "I'm listening," he said, but his expression remained fierce.

Grayson chose that unfavorable moment to give his patented, *I'm awake and I expect some attention* yell, effectively diverting them both. Angel gave Dane one long last look before hurrying out of the kitchen. She heard his soft curse behind her.

It was almost a relief to get sidetracked. She loved him, and he deserved to know that. But he already had so much on his mind, it might be easier for him to not be burdened with her love. He wasn't marrying her for that reason, so he might not even welcome her affections.

She needed to give it more thought before she made any grand declarations. After the threats were resolved would have been ideal, but with him pushing for marriage so soon, that was no longer an option.

She changed Grayson's diaper as the baby cooed at her, impatiently waiting to be fed, then pulled up the rocking chair in his room. She had just settled the baby against her breast when Dane spoke.

"He's such a little glutton."

Dane stood propped in the doorway, more handsome and appealing than any man had a right to be, especially now, with that boyish look of wonder on his face as he watched the baby greedily suckle. He'd put his shirt back on and had it all buttoned up, the sleeves rolled to his elbows.

At her silence, he walked the rest of the way into the room and knelt on the floor beside her chair. "I feel so much guilt, Angel, when I think about what Derek will miss.''

Angel silently watched him as he smoothed one finger over Grayson's cheek. "Aside from the way he treated you, which I really don't understand, he was a good man, and he was a damn good brother. He never gave up on me, never sided with the family against me. Most of the time when we were growing up, we were inseparable, best friends as well as brothers. I loved him a lot, but I can't help but be damn glad that I'm the one here with you and Grayson now."

"Oh, Dane." Angel felt tears gather in her throat. She could just imagine the hell he was putting himself through, and there was no way for her to help him.

He squeezed his eyes shut, his jaw tight. "I have to find out what happened to him. It's the very least I owe him, for having my life when his is gone, for taking over where he left off."

"Derek chose his own paths, Dane. You can't blame yourself."

He looked away, his face grim. "If I'd have come back instead of being so stubborn, I might have been able to help him. He might still be alive."

And we wouldn't have found each other. Angel shivered with the thought, then felt her own measure of gripping guilt.

The baby, recognizing Dane's voice, released Angel's nipple to turn his head. He stared at Dane, his blue eyes alert. Dane smiled, though his expression was still sad. "I love him, you know."

Angel nodded, a lump of emotion gathering in her throat.

Dane came to his feet and dug into his pocket. "I bought you this today. At least this time you can grant me the traditional rights of the groom to spend my money." He handed her a small black box, then gave his attention back to Grayson. The baby stared at him a moment longer before going back to his feeding. Some things were simply more important than others.

Awkwardly, Angel managed to open the small box. Her hands shook and it was difficult maneuvering with the baby in her lap. Inside the box, nestled in cream velvet, was the most beautiful diamond engagement ring she'd ever seen. It was large, but not *too* large, an oval diamond surrounded by rubies. Breathlessly, she whispered, "It's incredible."

"Then you like it?"

"Dane..." She reached for him with her free arm and somehow he managed to embrace them both, making Grayson squirm in protest.

"Why don't you finish what you were going to tell me before I have to go out again."

Surprised, she asked, "Where are you going now?"

Dane took the ring from her and slipped it on her finger. He seemed pleased by the snug fit. "I'm going to close out your post office box. It's too far from here to do you any good and besides—" his gaze met hers in a challenge "—with the threats against you, I want anything and everything that concerns you to come by me now, at least until things are resolved."

Angel curled her fist tight around the ring. "That's fine. I haven't used that box in ages anyway, not since I left Aeric. Take the key from my key ring. It's hanging by the phone in the kitchen."

Dane couldn't quite hide his satisfaction. She saw no reason to fight him on this, not when she didn't use the post office box anyway. "Now what were you going to tell me?"

She needed more time, she thought. Tonight, over dinner, without interruptions or the distractions of wedding dates or suffocating guilt, she'd tell him she loved him. But not now, not when they both felt confused and he was ready to head back out the door.

"Angel?"

"I don't want Grayson to be an only child."

Dane blinked at her, his gaze sharpening. "What did you say?"

Heat rushed into her cheeks, but at least she was giving him a truth. "I never had any brothers or sisters and it was awful. I...I know we'll be married for practical reasons, but I want another child. I thought you deserved to know that before we marry. Just so you're...prepared."

Dane searched her face in silence for several moments, looking more shocked than dismayed. Slowly, a smile broke over his face. He looked at Grayson and chuckled as the baby made grunting, squeaking noises while he nursed. "Nothing would make me happier, honey. As long as we wait a while so you're not over-burdened. I want your leg to heal completely and I don't want Grayson to be cheated out of being a baby. Just as you had no siblings, I had one that got half of all my parents' attention. I'm not complaining, but I think there must be a happy medium. And keep in mind, you run the risk of having twins with me. Three in diapers would be a bit much for even the most determined parent."

He hadn't refuted their reasons for marrying, but she wasn't discouraged. The practical reasons did exist, but there was also the love she felt. And tonight, she'd tell him so.

CHAPTER TEN

DANE STOOD BENEATH the post office overhang while the freezing wind whistled around him, blowing open his coat, pelting his face with a dusting of snowflakes caught in the frigid gusts. Nothing could penetrate the heat of his rage.

With deliberate movements he uncurled his fist and stared again at the name on the large manila envelope. His brother had sent Angel one final message.

The overwhelming urge to tear the envelope open was difficult to resist, but Dane knew in his heart he had to bring the letter to Angel. Not only was it a violation of her privacy to look inside, but she might take it as a measure of distrust as well. It could be a love letter—or it could be the information, the missing link to the threats, that they'd been looking for.

He didn't want her hurt.

He didn't want anything his brother might have put in the letter to cause Angel more heartache. And he didn't want to suffer the sweltering jealousy he now felt that was enough to ward off even the worst winter had to offer. *Damn it*. He didn't want his brother eulogized in Angel's heart with a final farewell.

Conflicting feelings of grief, guilt and possessiveness jumbled his thoughts.

The postmaster had watched with a jaundiced eye as Dane tossed out the majority of the mail unceremoniously stuffed into the large mailbox. Dane had only briefly glimpsed the numerous sale ads and magazines and offers before Derek's letter caught his notice. Now, with stiff steps and an anxious stride, he headed for his car. He couldn't understand his own urgency; he just knew he wanted to be with Angel and Grayson. He needed to know they were okay.

It took him all of five minutes to realize he was being followed. Using his cell phone, he impatiently dialed Alec's number.

"Sharpe."

"I'm being trailed," Dane said, no other explanations needed.

"I'm on it."

Over the past few days Dane had been aware of being followed. He couldn't get close enough to figure out who it was, so he'd alerted Alec to watch his back. Dane had told Angel he didn't want her out in the cold, but in truth, he wasn't willing to take the risk that whoever it was might be able to get to her. He preferred keeping her at home, safely behind locked doors and away from any threats.

This morning, he'd specifically opened the account in her name so she'd be protected financially if something happened to him. She'd accused him of not trusting her, but that was no longer true. He simply wasn't willing to leave her future to chance. Though he'd told her the sum in the account was hefty, he knew she couldn't begin to guess the amount. And he wanted it that way. Angel had a prideful tendency to fight him on every little thing he tried to give her. When she saw the bank records, she'd hit the roof. He smiled in anticipation. In some perverse way, he enjoyed arguing with her as much as he enjoyed loving her. Things would never be sedate between them, that was a certainty.

Alec shouldn't be very far behind, and now with Dane's signal, he'd close the gap and they would trap the driver between them.

"Dammit!" Dane muttered the curse into the open phone line as he saw the car swerve away.

"That him taking the entrance ramp to the highway?"

Dane watched his suspect speed away and knew, whoever the man was, he'd been on to them. "Yeah, that was him. How did he figure us?"

There was a shrug in Alec's tone. "Maybe he didn't. Maybe he was going that way all along."

"Nope. He was following me, I know it."

"Want me to go after him?"

Dane considered it, then shook his head to himself. "No, there's no point. I'm heading home to Angel and staying there. Though I doubt it'll do us any good, run a quick check on the plates, just in case we can get lucky for a change." Dane didn't for a minute doubt Alec had the plates memorized. Not much ever got by him.

"I'll get right back to you."

Less than three minutes later, Alec had his news. Both he and Dane had cultivated contacts in every facet of the police force. The information they received, and how they received it, wasn't always on the up and up. But it was generally beneficial to all, so the cops tended to work with them. "The license plate shows a newly rented car."

"*Dammit.*" Dane thumped his fist against the steering wheel, his frustration level high. "That means the name it's registered under is likely false."

"Yeah, 'fraid so. You want me to go check into the rental agency where the car came from?"

"There's no point. Whoever it is, he's covering his ass. I doubt he'll make any mistakes this late into the game." With an irritated sigh, Dane suggested, "You might as well take the rest of the day off. I'll let you know if anything comes up."

"All right. I do have a few personal things to take care of."

The line went dead before Dane could question that cryptic comment. It was the first time in the history of their acquaintance that Alec had ever alluded to a personal life. Though Dane was certain he must have one, he'd never mentioned it before.

It only took Dane another fifteen minutes before he pulled into the garage. As per his instructions, Angel kept the alarm on, and all the doors and windows locked. It was a hell of a way to live, constantly being on guard, but maybe with the help of Derek's letter they would be able to put the past, and the threats, to rest.

After turning off the car he used his remote to close the garage door. As he came in through the kitchen by the door that attached to the garage, he heard Angel laughing. Following the sound, the manila envelope still clutched in his hand, he found her sprawled on the family room carpet before the fireplace. Grayson was held over her head, and each time the baby gurgled, she laughed and lowered him for a tickling nip of his pudgy belly.

Without intruding, Dane watched their antics, a small smile on his face. Damn, but he loved her. The feeling was starting to settle in, not so scary now, more like a necessary part of him was finally working as it should. He pictured Angel with a baby girl, as well, his daughter, a child that would look like her mother, have her bright green eyes. He'd missed being a part of her pregnancy with Grayson, but this time, he'd be here. *I'm sorry, Derek. But she'll be my wife.*

"When did you come in?"

Dane hadn't even realized she'd turned to him, he'd been so caught up in the comforting images of baby and home and hearth, images he'd long ago given up on. "Just a minute ago." He strode over and sat cross-legged beside the two of them, reaching out to take Grayson into his own lap.

"What do you have there?"

Angel looked at the envelope, her expression inquiring. "It's for you, honey." He let her know by his tone the seriousness of the envelope. "Derek evidently sent it to you. It's postmarked some time ago, from before his death. Haven't you checked your box at all?"

Angel stared at the envelope like it was poison. "There was no reason. I only used it for the information my supervisor wanted me to work on at home. Files he wanted me to prepare before he made a presentation. He didn't trust very many people, or the regular mail. He figured a locked post office box was the most secure way to go. No one knew the number except the two of us."

"And Derek."

She nodded. "I usually kept those files locked up. But I was...anxious to see Derek one day, so I just stuck them in a desk drawer when he called to say he was coming over. I never considered that he might go through my personal things. He must have taken the box number off the envelope."

Dane hated hearing about her and Derek together. He didn't regret loving Angel, he couldn't, but he sometimes felt as if he'd stolen everything good from Derek. Forging his place in the family had never mattered to him, but it had been everything to Derek. Now Dane had taken Derek's place in the family, and in the office.

He'd gladly give up both those dubious perks, but he'd never give up Angel or Grayson.

He knew the night Derek stole the information from Angel was the same night he'd taken her to bed. For that reason, more than any other, Dane had hesitated to discuss it with her. The thought of Derek with her, how he'd hurt her, was almost too difficult to contemplate.

"I was asleep when Derek went through my desk," she said, her tone flat. "We were never…intimate after that, and a month later, he dropped me."

Several silent moments passed, then Dane tried to hand her the envelope. "Go ahead and open it."

With a shudder, Angel pulled back. "No thanks. I'd rather you did it."

"Are you sure?" Even as he asked it, Dane was laying Grayson aside on the blanket. The baby turned his head and directed an intent gaze at the bright flames in the fireplace. Dane slid a finger under the flap of the envelope and pulled it open.

There were several printouts inside, and Dane scanned them quickly. "These are details outlining industrial espionage at Aeric." His blood surged with the ramifications. He lifted one paper after another, finally coming to a personal note addressed to Angel.

"What?" Angel scooted around to peer over Dane's

shoulder. She picked up the discarded printouts and studied them.

Dane laid the last paper aside and stared at Angel. When she felt his gaze, she looked up.

"I'm sorry, honey."

"What is it, Dane?"

He touched her cheek. "Derek was trying to protect you." Dane lifted the sheaf of papers, holding them out to her. "He sent you these as an explanation of why he'd gone to so much trouble to alienate you, why he specifically did it so publicly. He wanted everyone to think your relationship was over, that you meant nothing to him. He suspected some level of danger after he'd discovered several discrepancies in various Aeric research files, shortly after stealing that information from you. He wasn't certain what was happening, but when he investigated further, small accidents started to happen to him. He was afraid you'd be in danger too, by association." Dane touched her cheek, then forced the words out despite the tightness in his throat. "Derek had no problem doing what needed to be done for the takeover, he saw that only as good business, part of the corporate game. But he hadn't deliberately planned to hurt you in the bargain. He cared for you, honey."

Angel squeezed her eyes shut and swallowed hard, clutching at Dane's hand. Dane knew, without asking, the regret she felt because he felt it, too.

The sound of a gun cocking seemed obscenely loud in the silence of the room. Both Angel and Dane jerked up their gazes, and there stood Raymond. The forty-five in his hand made an incongruous sight with his three-piece suit and immaculate presence. "Well, I commend your investigative skills, Dane. Of course, your damn brother pretty much spelled it out for you, didn't he? I knew he was too thorough not to have something written down. And Ms. Morris was the likely person to have the info."

Dane quickly tried to cover his shock, to act calm and in control. He was very aware of Angel sitting frozen beside him. "So that's the reason you've been harassing her?"

Raymond shrugged. "I lost her for a while there, you know, after she moved. It was tedious finding her phone number again, but I had no idea where she'd gone. Unlike you, I don't have connections in these matters. It was rather frustrating, never knowing when she might resurface, if she'd try to discredit me with that damn information your brother put together.

"I tried to hedge my bets a bit by telling your mother, regretfully of course, what a bitch Angel was, how she'd used Derek, how she was likely to come sniffing around with blackmail in mind. I had half hoped she'd find Angel for me, but your mother is getting old and has no taste for revenge. She only hoped to avoid a scandal. Luckily for me, you're not nearly so derelict in your familial duty." Raymond grinned. "You led me right to her."

"*Bastard.*" Dane came smoothly to his feet and deliberately stepped in front of Angel and Grayson, shielding them both with his body. "You killed Derek."

"Now that," he said with a shrug, "was an honest accident. I knew he'd been playing detective—funny that the two of you were even more alike than you knew. But he proved to be rather proficient at it. I tried a few minor scare tactics, and for a while there I thought they'd worked. But the bastard was just biding his time, letting months go by, waiting for me to make another move. He was careful not to call in the authorities, not wanting to scare me off.'' Raymond held up two fingers, a millimeter apart. "He came that close to nailing my name to his damn discoveries after I thought the coast was clear again.''

"My brother was no idiot. And he would have taken any theft from a company he owned as a personal insult.''

Raymond laughed. "He was a wily bastard, I'll give him that.''

It almost sounded as though Raymond had respected Derek, had maybe liked him. Dane felt sick with disgust.

"Needless to say I had to up the pressure to get him to back off, but the fool didn't drive quite as well as Ms. Morris.''

Dane had to fight the urge to lunge at Raymond. Only the fact that doing so would put Angel in more danger kept him still, but he didn't like it. Every muscle in his body twitched with the almost unbearable need to do physical harm. "How did you get in here?''

"I beat you home. Yes, that was me following you. Of course, as soon as I realized you had sicked your watchdog on me, I veered off. Mr. Sharpe really is a nasty-looking fellow. He gives me the creeps.''

"Alec's good at what he does.''

"It doesn't matter now, does it?'' Raymond smiled his perfect artificial smile. "As I was saying. It was easy enough to swing around and with a heavy foot on the gas pedal, I was able to get here before you. I hid in the bushes. Not very dignified, but then, you gave me little choice. When you started to close the garage door, I slipped a small wedge underneath it, and rather than closing tight, it reopened on its own. I waited just long enough to see if you'd double-check it. But you were in too big a hurry to see your ladylove. Such a hurry in fact, that I believe the two of you will elope.'' He grinned, his expression taunting.

Dane tried to calm his racing heart and his anger. He needed a cool head to deal with Raymond. He only wished he'd trusted in his instincts earlier and not given Raymond the benefit of the doubt. He should have beat the details out of him when he had the chance.

Determined to keep Raymond talking, he asked, ''Was that you in the bar with Derek the night he died?''

Raymond looked briefly surprised. ''You are good. And yes, that was me. I offered to take Derek out slumming, just because he'd become so maudlin with all his investigations and his regret over Ms. Morris. That's how I knew it wasn't over between the two of them. Women threw themselves at your brother, and he turned them all down.''

Angel made a small sound of distress, but Dane ignored her. He didn't want Raymond's attention to waver to her.

''I had hoped he'd confide in me, but he was keeping his secrets to himself that night, no matter how much booze I poured down him.''

Dane suppressed a growl. ''Alec was the one who discovered Derek had been to a bar that night. He also dislikes you on instinct. If I disappear, he'll be all over you.''

Raymond looked briefly alarmed by the prospect, then he visually shored up his confidence again. ''Once I'm married to Celia, he won't dare touch me.''

Dane narrowed his gaze, trying to figure ahead. "My sister isn't an idiot. She'll never marry you."

Raymond laughed. "She's anxious to be married." His gaze flicked to Angel and quickly back again. "And your mother, now that you've defected to the enemy camp, is anxious to turn the company over into my capable hands. In fact, I believe your mother would give me control whether Celia married me or not. But I've decided I want Celia. It seems like nice insurance if anyone should ever discover you didn't elope."

"I'll kill you."

Raymond merely laughed at the threat. "Not that your mother will question it, will she, Dane? After all, this won't be the first time you've walked away from your family without a backward glance—both times over a woman. You know, your mother has been trying valiantly to keep her mouth shut, to avoid just such a situation, hoping to make amends. Ah, you didn't know that did you? But I've become something of a confidant for her, and she's told me all about how she regrets the past. Too bad you won't have a chance to forgive her, to put her poor old mind to rest. She'll have to spend the rest of her days with regrets."

Angel staggered to her feet beside Dane and when he would have pushed her behind him again, she forced her way forward. "You've set yourself up a small problem, Raymond."

"What's that?" he asked with a touch of amusement. Obviously he believed he had everything well in control.

"I'd already suspected you. And I told people. The police have it on record that I thought someone was trying to kill me."

"They didn't believe you though, did they?" Raymond's smile was smug. "You didn't have enough proof. And I was careful, even with the smoke-fire, to keep the threats from being too serious, gaining too much attention." He laughed at Angel's comprehension. "Yes, that was a nice touch, wasn't it? Running you out of your apartment and then intercepting your phone call at the office. You reacted just as I planned, showing up at the company like a wild woman, demanding answers. I had hoped once you knew the truth, that Dane was only using you, you'd have enough pride to walk away from him. That would have made you more vulnerable. But no, you decide to marry the bastard."

He looked briefly beyond anger, almost enraged. Dane braced himself, but Raymond shook off his anger, his smirk once again in place. "I have everything planned. And unfortunately for you, both Celia and Mrs. Carter will back up the theory that you ran off together. Thanks to the information I sold at Aeric, and your sister's cut in the family coffers, I should be able to live rather comfortably from here on out."

Dane took a small step forward. "You're an idiot, Raymond. Will anyone believe I abandoned my company? Think about it. I walked away from my family, but I never shirked my own responsibilities."

Raymond shrugged again, totally unconcerned. "So now you're in love. Who's to say what you'd do?"

Grayson made a cooing sound and for the briefest moment drew Raymond's attention. Dane started to move, but the gun was quickly leveled at his head. "Ah, ah. I really don't want the mess of it here in the family room."

Angel shifted beside him and Dane grabbed her arm.

"You're not going to hurt my baby," she said, her voice low and fierce as she pulled away from Dane.

"I really hesitate to. After all, I'm not a monster. And the child seems to have softened Mrs. Carter quite a bit. But I see no way around it."

Angel stiffened. When she spoke, her tone was so mean even Dane blinked. "You can't kill us both at the same time," she taunted. "Try it, and one of us will be on you before you can take a second aim." She slipped further away from Dane, spreading out, making it more difficult for Raymond to maintain control.

Pushed past his composure by her goading, Raymond lifted his arm, taking point-blank aim. His eyes narrowed and his mouth drew tight. Dane felt Angel tensing beside him and realized in horror what she intended. She would attack Raymond, giving Dane the upper hand. The little idiot would sacrifice herself. Panicked, Dane prepared to beat her to it, ready to leap on Raymond full force. He could only hope Angel would use the moment to grab the baby and run.

In the next instant, a shrill screech filled the air, loud and outraged. Dane instinctively leaped toward Angel, pushing her behind him as he stiffened for the additional threat. But they weren't in danger.

Raymond, wide-eyed and frantic, tried to turn. He wasn't fast enough.

Celia lunged around the corner from the kitchen to the family room, still screaming and viciously swinging a heavy crowbar. Raymond ducked, but the length of iron connected with his elbow with satisfying force. There was a sickening crunch as bone gave way, and the gun fell to the carpet. Raymond screamed in agony, his arm hanging at a grotesque angle by his side.

"You miserable worm!" Celia yelled, the perfect

epitome of a woman scorned. She hit Raymond again as he tried to roll away, this time thumping the bar against his thigh and eliciting more screams. Dane had no doubt the man's arm was broken, and he couldn't be all too sure of his leg. Celia would have delivered a final blow to his head, ignoring Dane's curses as he reached for the gun, but Alec came storming in and grabbed her from behind. She struggled, and Alec had a time of it subduing her, but finally she calmed.

Alec still held on, his arms circling her, making soft hushing noises in her ear until the tire iron fell to the carpet by their feet. Celia turned in his arms, weeping.

Dane looked at Angel. He was breathing hard, the adrenaline still rushing. "Are you okay?"

She had Grayson squeezed tight in her arms, gently rocking him, kissing him. Tears rolled down her pale cheeks. The baby and Raymond seemed to be vying for the loudest cries, Raymond out of pain, Grayson out of upset. Angel's watery gaze met Dane's and she nodded. He could see her body shake as she drew in jerky, uneven breaths. "Yes. We're fine."

Dane pulled her close and tried to comfort her as best he could, but he himself was shaking with residual fear. Never in his life had anything ever terrorized him like knowing Angel could be shot and even killed. He kissed her full on her trembling lips, verifying her safety, her vitality and warmth. Then he turned to his friend, Angel still tucked safely to his side. He didn't know if he'd ever let her go again.

"Damn, but I'm glad to see you, Alec." It didn't matter that his voice shook, that his eyes felt glazed and moist. All that mattered was the feel of Angel beside him, safe and sound.

Alec smoothed his big hands up and down Celia's

back. "I followed her. I don't know how she knew what was going on, but I could tell she was upset."

Celia pushed back from him. "You followed me?"

Alec looked down at her, pushed her head back to his shoulder, and said, "Yeah."

Dane grinned. In the midst of all the chaos, he found Alec's actions incredibly humorous. "Well, I'll be."

"I already called the cops," Alec said, ignoring Dane's laughter. "They should be here any minute. Dammit, will you shut up?" he said to Raymond, while maintaining his tight hold on Celia. "You're lucky I didn't let her kill you."

Again Celia pushed back. "Why didn't you? He deserves it."

"It would have complicated things, especially for you."

"Oh."

Angel stepped away from Dane, then cautiously around Raymond, who was obediently silent. When she reached Celia, she touched the woman's shoulder. "Thank you. You saved our lives."

Celia sniffed and pulled away from Alec's masculine embrace while still standing very close to him. She wiped away her tears and then frowned at Alec, as if some of the drama was his fault. With an obvious effort she returned her attention to Angel. "I caught Raymond making a phone call today, but he hung up real quick when I came in."

Angel gave a quick peek at Dane and he frowned. Had she gotten a call and not told him? "Angel?"

She shrugged, but he could tell the careless effort cost her. "He didn't say anything, Dane, so I thought it was just a wrong number. I was going to tell you, but we got...distracted."

Dane would have had more to say about that, but Celia sniffed again. "Several times now Raymond's not been in his office when he should be. He was acting funny the last few days. I thought he was cheating on me. I knew he was up to something, but I thought it was just another woman, not...not this!" She indicated the entire mess with a wave of her hand.

Alec grunted. "Why the hell would he be after another woman?"

"How should I know?" she snapped. "He was sneaking around, showing up late. But then I had his letter of recommendation from Derek checked and found out it was forged."

Alec looked livid. "So you just decided to follow him and could have gotten yourself killed as well!" He bent down so he could stand nose to nose with Celia. "What the hell did you ever see in him in the first place?"

Angel grinned at Dane while the other two continued to argue. Dane shook his head and pulled Angel close again. He was almost afraid to stop touching her, reassuring himself she was truly okay. "If this isn't the most bizarre thing that's ever happened, I don't know what is."

As Dane spoke to her, Angel turned her gaze on Raymond. He wouldn't be walking any time soon. Angel shivered, and that made Dane furious all over again.

"I'd like to kill him with my bare hands."

Angel touched his mouth. "Shh. Don't say that, Dane. It's been awful, and you've lost so much, but I want it to end now. For all our sakes."

Grayson gave a last shuddering sob and snuggled close.

Dane pressed his lips to the baby's forehead. "Me, too. God, I was afraid for you and Grayson."

Angel sighed. "Oh, Dane. I feel awful. Your brother wasn't the villain after all. He was trying to protect me."

He smoothed her hair back from her face. "That'll be a comfort to my mother, I think."

"Your mother!" Angel blinked up at him. "Raymond said she was sorry, that she wasn't ignoring us because she was mad, just being careful not to say anything that might drive you away again. You need to talk to her, Dane. When I think of her suffering..."

Police sirens sounded in the distance. "I'll settle things with my mother, honey, just as soon as we get things taken care of here. And then," he added, cupping her face and holding her close, "you and I are going to talk. I have a few things to say to you, Angel Morris, and no matter how angry you get, you're going to listen."

ANGEL WATCHED DANE pace around the bedroom as Grayson began to doze in his strong arms. Dane wore only his slacks, and those were undone. His bare feet left impressions in the thick carpet and the flexed muscles of his forearms left an impression on her.

Love swelled, making her warm and shivery at the same time.

It had been a long day, filled with police interviews and questions and confrontations. Grayson had a difficult time settling down, too many strangers invading his small world at one time. But he charmed the detectives who'd run the investigation, as well as Dane's mother once she showed up. Angel smiled again. She was actually beginning to like Mrs. Carter. How could she not when the woman obviously adored her son and grandson as much as Angel did? Oh, she tried to hide it, but tonight her defenses had cracked just a bit, and Angel had seen the woman beneath the iron.

"Do you think it's okay to put him in his crib now?" Dane whispered, not halting in his even strides around the room. Grayson nestled close against the warmth of Dane's broad, naked chest, one small fist clutching his chest hair.

Angel smiled and laid her brush aside. She was freshly showered and in her nightgown, exhausted, but at the same time elated. Everything was over, all the fear and bad feelings and hurt put to rest. Her confession had been on the tip of her tongue when Grayson had begun fussing. "Do you want me to take him?"

"No, I can do it." Dane gave her a long, sizzling look. "Why don't you get under the covers? I'll be right back."

Her heartbeat picked up its pace and she slid into bed. When Dane returned, he removed his slacks, laid them over the back of a chair, then faced her with his hands on his naked hips.

Angel smiled. "If you ran a board meeting like that, you'd be sure to have everyone's attention."

He looked chagrined for just a moment, then dropped his arms and started toward her. "Right now, I only want your attention."

Angel eyed his naked body. "You have it."

"*Angel…*" He growled her name as he climbed into bed beside her.

"Your mother is a proud woman, Dane. It hurt me to see her so upset."

He stilled his hands, which had been in the process of removing her nightgown. "I know what you mean.

It nearly broke my heart to hear her admit to so much guilt. She said it was so hard losing Derek, and the only solace she could find was that maybe I'd finally forgiven her."

Angel stroked his head, knowing what his mother's confession had done to him. "I'm proud of you for how you handled it."

"I wish I'd known how she felt long ago. Maybe it wouldn't have gone on for so long."

"You're both too proud for your own good. But your mother is making the attempt to accept me."

"Ha!" Dane pulled down the right strap of her nightgown and cuddled her bare breast in his rough palm. "My mother adores you. She hides it well, but that's just how she is. I think she sees you as a link, a way to soften our reassociation even though I told her all was forgiven. And there were tears in her eyes when she finally got to hold Grayson." He kissed the slope of her breast, his mouth warm and gentle. "That's the first I've ever seen her cry. You know, she's going to spoil him rotten."

"Thank you for refusing her and Celia's offer to keep Grayson. I'm not ready to be separated from him yet. Not after being afraid for him for so long."

"Me, either. Maybe when I'm old and gray I'll be ready to let him out of my sight. But for now, they can visit him here, and we'll make a point of visiting them often."

They were both silent for a moment, Dane busy in his minute study of Angel's skin, caressing her, kissing her, Angel trying to formulate the words she knew she needed to say.

"My sister is holding up well."

Diverted, Angel asked, "Did you get a chance to talk alone with her?"

"Yeah. I don't think she ever would have gone through with the marriage to Raymond. She was as suspicious of him as I was." Angel felt him tighten and knew he was reliving the horror of the afternoon. He pulled her close and buried his face in her breasts. "You could have been hurt. I don't think I've ever been so frightened in my life."

Angel kissed his temple. "Thank God for your sister."

"Alec wants her." He lifted his head and there was another grin on his face. "Damn, but I can't get over it. Alec and Celia. Somehow it just doesn't fit."

"You know, Celia does have some say about it. Right now, she told me she's in no hurry to get involved with any man again. Raymond really hurt her."

"Mostly her pride. But she's tough. She'll get over it."

"And Alec wasn't speaking to her when he left."

Dane shrugged. "He's always quiet. It's just his way."

She wasn't convinced. "Don't get your hopes up, Dane. I can tell you'd like to see the two of them together, but all things considered, a romance between them would be difficult."

"That's what I thought about us. But look how much I love you."

Angel would have fallen off the bed if Dane hadn't been sprawled on top of her, anchoring her in place. "What did you say?"

"Don't look so shocked." He tugged the other strap of her nightgown down, baring her to the waist. "I know I deceived you from the start, that I was pretty ruthless at times to get what I wanted."

"When were you ruthless?" Angel felt both numb and cautiously elated. She couldn't quite believe what he was saying.

"I convinced you we needed to marry because you needed protection. But I could protect you without marriage. I lied to get you where I wanted you."

"You did?" Angel shook her head, trying to clear it. "I mean, you said you wanted to marry me so Grayson would have a solid home."

"I have enough money to insure Grayson would be happy and well cared for without marrying you. That just seemed a convenient way to trap you."

Her heart rapped against her ribs, threatening to break something. "I don't feel trapped."

His eyes darkened, turned warm and probing. "Good, because I still want you to marry me, but with no more secrets between us. I love you."

Angel licked her suddenly dry lips. "You know, you beat me to the punch. I was going to tell you the same thing tonight."

Very slowly, a slight, pleased smile tilted his mouth and Dane leaned down and kissed her. "Is that right?"

"Yes." Her breathing accelerated with the touch of his warm breath. "I knew ages ago that I loved you."

"You didn't know me ages ago, honey. Hell, our entire courtship has taken only a heartbeat."

"Well," Angel said, wrapping her arms around him and hugging him tight, "it was long enough to make me irrevocably and madly in love with you."

Dane grinned as he began tugging up the hem of her nightgown, groaning at the feel of her soft naked belly against his abdomen. "It's a damn good thing, because I have no intention of letting you go."

"Your mother did mention to me what an intelligent businessman you are."

His hand slid over her ribs, then lower, his fingers probing, and he closed his eyes when he found her warm and ready. "I know a good deal when I find it. You, Angel Morris—soon to be Carter—are a very good find."

EPILOGUE

"MICK, MICK!" Grayson came barreling around the corner of the house, chubby arms pumping the air, and threw himself around Mick's long legs. Mick was always greeted with the same amount of verve when he came over after school. He was one of Grayson's favorite people, a surrogate big brother.

Mick swung the seventeen-month-old toddler up into his arms. "Hey, buddy."

"Mick, Mick!"

Angel came in on the heels of her son and dropped onto the couch. "Thank God you're here. He's been screeching your name all day. I can't tell you how glad I am that school's almost over."

Mick, devastatingly gorgeous at eighteen, topping a few inches over six feet, grinned his killer grin at Angel while he tossed Grayson into the air, encouraging the screeches of berserk joy. "You look exhausted, Angel. Is this little monkey wearing you out?"

With a serene smile, Angel said, "I think it's his little brother or sister that's actually doing the trick."

Dazed by her news, Mick tucked Grayson under one leanly muscled arm and staggered into a chair. "You're pregnant?"

She smiled happily, pleased with his reaction. Now to get Dane's reaction. She heard the front door opening and leaned toward Mick. "I was hoping to have a few minutes alone with Dane, if you—"

"I'll take short-breeches here out to the swing."

"Mick, Mick!"

But as Dane stepped into the house and called out, "I'm home," Grayson launched himself from Mick's arms. Angel gasped, but Mick, quick on the draw, managed to juggle the toddler until he could get both feet on solid ground. And like a shot, Grayson was off again.

"Daddy! Daddy!"

Mick laughed. "To think, he used to be such a peaceful baby."

Dane entered with Grayson perched on his shoulders. He went directly to Angel, who dutifully lifted her face for a kiss. "My mother said you had something to tell me."

Angel glared. "She promised!"

"Promised what?"

Mick lifted Grayson from Dane's shoulders. "The squirt and I are going out to the swing."

"Wait a minute, Mick. I have something for you." Dane reached into his pocket and pulled out an envelope.

"What is it?"

As usual, Mick was still hesitant at the sign of a gift. But Dane, who delighted in trying to spoil Mick as much as he did Angel, only laughed. "I know the academic scholarship you got doesn't pay for everything, so this will help pick up some of the tab."

Mick merely frowned until Dane gave an exaggerated sigh of impatience and opened the envelope. He waved the paper under Mick's nose. "It's from the company. We have our own set of tax deductible donations, and this year, my mother decided to expand into scholarships. The two combined ought to take care of most of your schooling expenses. And let me warn you, if you even think of refusing it, you'll have to deal with Mother. Since Celia left the company and Mother's taken over again, she's more autocratic than ever. I believe she actually missed it. And she's taken to singing your praises, so don't even think to fight her on this.''

Mick looked ready to faint and with a numb expression, took the paper from Dane and read it. Silently, Angel relieved her son, who promptly planted a sloppy kiss on her check, then laid his head on her shoulder. With everyone else he was a dynamo of constant motion. With Angel, he loved to cuddle.

Very slowly, a grin settled over Mick's face. Then with a loud whoop, he jumped up and slapped the ceiling. Angel felt like crying every time he acted like the young man he was, rather than the old man he'd been forced to be. Since his mother's death, he spent more time than ever with her and Dane, and they were as close as a family could be.

After a gentle hug to Angel, and a bruising bear hug to Dane, Mick swung Grayson up and headed out the door.

''He's something else, isn't he?''

Angel smiled at Dane. ''You've been a good influence on him.''

He grunted. ''If only I could say the same for my sister.''

''Oh no, what did she do now?'' About six months ago Celia had decided she'd had enough of the corporate world, and following in Dane's footsteps, she was determined to become a P.I. Dane was horrified,

but didn't know how to stop her. In an effort to keep
an eye on her, he gave her a job at his office, which
rankled Alec no end. Just as Angel had predicted, nothing had come of a romance between them, and instead,
their constant bickering kept Dane on the brink of in-
sanity.

Dane gave Angel a telling look. "She almost got
shot, that's what she did. She was supposed to *locate*
that little chump who jumped bail, not try to bring him
in. I don't remember the last time I've seen Alec that
mad."

"Why was Alec mad?"

"Because he *did* get shot." Dane quickly grabbed
her when she paled. "Now, Angel, he's all right, just
a flesh wound. The bullet grazed his thigh. But he's
been raising high hell for the past two hours, and Celia,
that witch, has steered clear, which means I've had to
listen to it all."

It was too much, and Angel fell into a fit of giggles.
She'd been so worried about Celia, who'd become re-
clusive after her emotional hurt with Raymond. But
now Celia was determined to experience everything life
had to offer, and there was no one who could stop her,
not even Alec. And heaven knew, he tried hard enough.
Grown men might walk a wide path around him, but
Celia continually tried to go through him.

"I'm glad you think it's so funny. Between Mother
constantly working to reel me back into the company,
and Celia's antics, I'm ready to go hide under my
covers." He grinned at Angel. "Want to come with
me?"

"Maybe. But first I need to talk to you."

Dane groaned. "Tell me this won't be bad news,
babe. I can't take any more bad news."

Angel drew a deep breath. "I told your mother I'd need a leave of absence in about six months." Angel had agreed to fill in for vacationing secretaries, which she thought would be a week's worth of work a month, and instead it was turning out to be more like three weeks' every month. Something always seemed to come up so that she was required. Luckily her mother-in-law didn't mind when she did most of that work at home, so she could be with Grayson. On the days she had to be in the office, Dane adjusted his schedule. Or sometimes Mick, or Celia, or even Alec...

"Is my mother wearing on your nerves? I thought the two of you were getting along pretty good?"

"It's not that. Dane, do you remember when we first talked of getting married?"

He sat down and pulled her onto his lap. "If you're thinking of backing out now, it's too late. You signed the marriage certificate ages ago."

Angel playfully punched his shoulder. "I'm pregnant."

He froze for a heartbeat, then a gorgeous smile spread over his face. "Pregnant?"

She nodded. "Almost two months now. I waited to go to the doctor so I could be sure."

His large hand opened over her abdomen, and as usual, she quickened in response. "It's not twins?" he asked, looking at her body.

"The doctor doesn't think so, so you can relax."

He did, then he grinned some more. His hand on her belly turned caressing and he kissed her throat. "This time will be different, babe. I'll take care of you."

"Dane, I don't regret anything about my pregnancy with Grayson. If things hadn't happened as they did, I might never have had Grayson, and I might never have met you.''

''Angel.'' He kissed her, his hand still resting where his baby grew. ''I love you, sweetheart.''

Angel spoke past a wobbly, heart-filled smile. ''The only thing missing the first time around was you.''

Dane kissed her again. ''And this time you have me.''

''Yes. This time I have everything.''

next month...

Come back to temptation

for Lori Foster's...

WANTON

Alec Sharpe wanted to keep Celia
Carter safe, while he wanted to be in
the thick of an unsavory investigation.
The compromise? Alec would help
her, but for as long as he was
assisting her, she had to give in to the
craving they both felt.

Temptation #732 available in October.

Here's a preview!

CELIA BIT HER LIP. She felt naked in the tight, flesh-toned dress, too made up with the cosmetics that had spent more time in her drawer lately than on her face. She was very aware of her bare thighs, of her exposed arms and cleavage. Though the air conditioning hummed, she felt warm with embarrassment.

Heads turned appropriately as she sauntered through the dim interior and took a direct path to the bar. She didn't want to look too closely, but she was sure Mr. Jacobs, the slime, was here. She had his description and knew this was his prime hunting ground. This was where he chose the women. Hopefully, he'd choose her as well.

Sipping at the drink she didn't want, she glanced down the length of the bar to the small, round table located there, situated in the far shadows. The man occupying the table, blond and very good looking, perfectly matched the description she had been given. It was easy to recognize Jacobs; he had the same classic, refined, golden-boy appearance of her ex-fiancé, a look she now recognized as slick and phoney.

It took all her control to keep from reacting as he surveyed her through narrow, contemplative eyes. His gaze skimmed over her from her tousled hair down to her two-inch heeled sandals. Not wanting to be too obvious, to look too anxious, she turned her head away and flipped her hair over her mostly bare shoulder.

Seconds later her pulse jumped, then raced wildly as she sensed the approach of a man. She didn't turn to look, but she could feel the tingling awareness of him, could detect his male scent, not in the least subtle. *Yes!* He was going to take the bait. Her palms began to sweat in nervousness, but she ignored it. She felt him brush against her while taking his own stool, and that brief touch felt electric, making her jump in surprise. She struggled to moderate her accelerated breathing. He was looking at her; she felt the burning heat of his gaze as strongly as a firm stroke of flesh on flesh.

Mentally rehearsing the speech she'd prepared, she turned to face him, her smile planted as she leaned slightly forward to display as much cleavage as possible, given her small size. Her gaze slowly lifted, met his, and she froze in horror. "Oh no."

"Hello, Celia." The low, barely audible words were said in a familiar growl through clenched, white teeth.

"Oh no."

His smile wasn't a nice thing and sent gooseflesh racing up and down her spine. His eyes locked onto hers, refusing to let her look away and his lips barely moved when he spoke. "Close your mouth, honey, or you're going to blow your own cover. And I don't feel like fighting my way out of here tonight. But then again, seeing you in that dress, a fight might be just what I need."

She snapped her mouth shut, but it wasn't easy. The eyes looking at her weren't blue, weren't admiring, and didn't belong to the man she was investigating, the man still sitting a good distance away, now watching curiously. These eyes were too familiar, a cold, hard black, and at that moment they reflected undiluted masculine fury.

Her heart raced even faster, urged on by new emotions, new sensations. She felt nearly faint, and collected her thoughts with an effort.

Forcing a shaky smile that actually hurt, Celia whispered, "What are you doing here, Alec?"

"Don't miss this, it's a keeper!"
—**Muriel Jensen**

"Entertaining, exciting and
utterly enticing!"
—**Susan Mallery**

"Engaging, sexy…a fun-filled romp."
—**Vicki Lewis Thompson**

See what all your favorite authors
are talking about.

Coming October 1999 to a retail store near you.

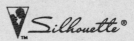